The Other Woman

Other works edited by Susan Koppelman

IMAGES OF WOMEN IN FICTION: Feminist Perspectives

OLD MAIDS: Short Stories by Nineteenth Century
U.S. Women Writers

BETWEEN MOTHERS AND DAUGHTERS:
Stories Across a Generation

The Other Woman

STORIES OF TWO WOMEN AND A MAN

Edited and with an Introduction
by Susan Koppelman

 FEMINIST
PRESS

Old Westbury,
New York

1984

Library of Congress Cataloging in Publication Data
Main entry under title:
The Other woman.

1. Short stories, American—Women authors.   2. Adultery—
Fiction.   3. Women—Fiction.   4. Love—Fiction.   5. Marriage—
Fiction.   I. Koppelman, Susan.
PS648.A35085   1984   813'.01'089287   84-10099
ISBN 0-935312-25-0 (pbk.)

Permission acknowledgments begin on page 345.

Cover design by Lea Smith
Cover art *Double Date Delayed* by Isabel Bishop. Reproduced courtesy of
the Munson-Williams-Proctor Institute, Utica, New York.
Text design by Lea Smith
Typeset by Monotype Composition Co., Inc., Baltimore, MD
Manufactured by Arcata Graphics Co., Fairfield, PA

This publication is made possible, in part, by public funds from
the New York State Council on the Arts.

You are to consider you live in a time which hath rendered some kind of frailties so habitual, that they lay claim to large grains of allowance. The world in this is somewhat unequal, and our sex seemeth to play the tyrant . . . by making that in the utmost degree criminal in the woman, which in a man passeth under a much gentler censure. The root and excuse of this injustice is the preservation of families from any mixture which may bring a blemish to them; and whilst the point of honor continues to be so place'd, it seems unavoidable to give your sex a greater share of the penalty. . . . Remember, that next to the danger of committing the fault yourself, the greatest is that of seeing it in your husband. Do not seem to look or hear that way: if he is a man of sense, he will reclaim himself . . . if he is not so, he will be provok'd, but not reformed. . . . Such an undecent complaint makes a wife much more ridiculous than the injury that provoketh her to it.

The first Marquis of Halifax, to his daughter, 1700

Now, why is it that man can hold woman to this high code of morals, like Caesar's wife—not only pure but above suspicion—and so surely and severely punish her for every departure, while she is so helpless, so powerless to check him in his license, or to extricate herself from his presence and control? His power grows out of his right over her subsistence. Her lack of power grows out of her dependence on him for her food, her clothes, her shelter.

Susan B. Anthony, 1875

Confusion of progeny constitutes the essence of the crime (adultery); and therefore a woman who breaks her marriage vows is much more criminal than a man who does it. A man, to be sure, is criminal in the sight of God; but he does not do his wife a very material injury if he does not insult her; if, for instance, from mere wantonness of appetite, he steals privately to her chambermaid. Sir, a wife ought not greatly to resent this. I would not receive home a daughter who had run away from her husband on that account.

Boswell's Life of Johnson, 1791

Masculine ethics, colored by masculine instincts, always dominated by sex, has at once recognized the value of chastity in woman, which is right; punished its absence unfairly, which is wrong; and then reversed the whole matter when applied to men, which is ridiculous.

Charlotte Perkins Gilman, 1911

Contents

Preface

This book is the product of ten years of research on short stories written by women in the continental United States or territories that later became states. Late in 1972 I became a member of the English department committee at Bowling Green State University whose purpose it was to decide whether all sophomore introduction-to-literature courses should use the same textbooks and, if so, which ones. Publishers' representatives eagerly supplied us with many books for our consideration, both multigeneric and single genre, both thematically organized and historical, both national and international. I was responsible for examining, analyzing, and reporting on all the short story anthologies.

I received some half dozen short story collections to consider. Amazingly enough, they were almost interchangeable. They had almost all the same authors, the same stories. Even the same typefaces and page sizes: all unending sameness. It seemed as if the editors of short story anthologies did all their research in other anthologies instead of in the pages of the periodicals that publish short stories and in the collected stories of various writers already anthologized.

Whatever was wrong with one anthology was wrong with all of them. It has always seemed to me that anthologies should reflect the conflicting, idiosyncratic, individualized, although educated and informed, vision of its editor or editors. Compiling a collection of stories is personal work; it reflects the strengths and weaknesses, the preferences for different orders of excellence, the unique funny bone, the limitations, advantages, and special interests of the editor. But it was clear that there was only one product in only slightly different packages on the market. Editors of collections blamed it on the publishers. Booksellers blamed it on the teachers. Teachers believed themselves powerless.

An analysis of the tables of contents revealed all the statistical dimensions of the collections: The first noticeable fact was that there were about seven male writers included for every one woman writer. Only the same few women writers were included in the collections that included women. This created the impression that there were far fewer women writing than men. Next I looked for writers of color. There wasn't a single woman of color except Diane Oliver, already tragically dead at an early age. She was included in only one collection, and that was the oldest. Three black men were included once each in three different anthologies. James Baldwin was the only homosexual writer included in any of the volumes.

I began to compare the original publication dates of the stories with each other and with the publication dates of the anthologies themselves. Almost all the stories by women had been published within ten years of the publication date of the anthology. Here and there was a story by Edith Wharton, Katherine Mansfield, or Willa Cather, and in collections that began with stories from the early nineteenth century, there was usually a story by Sarah Orne Jewett or Mary E. Wilkins Freeman—but never both. These "old" stories by women appeared in anthologies that contained more than twenty-two stories and were compiled to be historically representative.

Not only were women and writers of color underrepresented, they were misrepresented as well. They were misrepresented thematically, chronologically, and numerically. Women began writing much earlier both in time and in terms of the development of the short story genre than selections suggest: more women have written more stories than we yet know. Many, if not most, of the stories written by women in the nineteenth century were published in periodicals directed toward female audiences. Those periodicals have still not yet been indexed or searched thoroughly for lost literature. Additionally, the themes that women have most typically and frequently addressed in their writing have not been represented in anthologies.

Curious about whether this pattern also appeared in the short story collections I had read in high school and college, or that I had found in used bookstores for personal reading, I examined next the books on my own bookshelves. I reread stories by Mary McCarthy, Jean Stafford, Dorothy Canfield Fisher, Hortense Calisher, and Shirley Jackson. They were as good as the writers in the contemporary anthologies: Joyce Carol Oates, Flannery O'Connor, Eudora

Welty, Katherine Anne Porter. The earlier writers had not diminished in their power to move and impress me; they had merely
disappeared from the anthologies. They were old women, discarded
with the same cavalier carelessness with which old women, old
workers, are discarded by our society.

Next I looked into the books that had belonged to my mother
and her five sisters, all avid readers, in the 1920s and 1930s. When
my aunts moved from Cleveland, all their books were stored in our
basement. There I found Dorothy Parker, Katharine Brush, Zona
Gale, Fannie Hurst, Edna Ferber, Thyra Samter Winslow—still as
powerful as they had been when I had first encountered them as a
young girl.

Further research in anthologies published as far back as the 1880s
revealed the patterns that still prevail: women, ethnic and racial
minority, working-class, and explicit homosexual writers have been
underrepresented, misrepresented, and replaced rather than supplemented by current writers. When these writers have been included
at all, they have been presented as an occasional Sylvia Plath or
"local colorist." Only the very earliest collections of stories from
the *Atlantic Monthly* and *Lippincott's Magazine* in the late 1860s
included equal numbers of male and female authors, all of whom,
however, were white.

Yet a careful study of the history of the short story genre clearly
reveals that women writers predominated in the early years of its
development, not only creating the majority of stories written
between 1830 and 1880, but also editing many of the periodicals in
which they appeared. And, of course, the majority of those reading
these stories written by women and published in periodicals and
annuals edited by women were women and girls.

However, because each decade's women writers were replaced
rather than supplemented by the women writers of the next decade,
readers have been denied a historical perspective on women's fiction
and, by extension, on United States fiction.

I began to look for women writers whose work had never been
collected in anthologies, using specialized bibliographies and literary
histories to track them down. Reading general histories of minority
communities, I discovered the names of writers considered by their
own historians to be part of their particular literary history. The
research was an act of faith growing from a belief that all kinds of

women had told their stories and that with time, hard work, and the help of sister scholars, they would be found. I committed myself to compiling an anthology of short stories that would recapture women's multi-racial, multi-ethnic, multi-regional stories—our literary history—the other half of the history of the development of the short story genre in the United States. I was excited to find how many other women had been writing: women of color; immigrant women; women whose politics were radical, whose religious ideas were unconventional; and women who weren't enough interested in men to make male characters central to the lives of the women in their stories. And once again I was struck by the fact that the stories included in standard anthologies did not deal with the themes and issues and types of characters most typical of women's stories.

One meets in the work of women writers certain themes that are explored again and again, embellished, analyzed, debated, celebrated, agonized over, viewed in general and in the abstract, and particularized in minute detail, focused on through one eye and then through the other. Some of these themes explore the dynamics of relationships between and among women: the sometimes supportive, sometimes insensitive, sometimes competitive, often intimate ones between sisters; the intense and often transforming ones between friends; the role-modeling by, and loving respect for, aging women; the free, usually precarious, often idiosyncratic lives of women who never marry; the emotionally laden, social-burden-bearing relationships between mothers and daughters; and the theme explored in this collection—the painful, ethically challenging, conventional and unconventional, often explosive, socially revealing relationships between women who are involved, either simultaneously or sequentially, with the same man.

Acknowledgments

I asked a number of people to read these stories and talk about them with me and sometimes each other, helping me to understand what was happening in them and which ones they thought most interesting or important to share with a larger audience. These women include my teachers Barbara Lehocky, Head, Reference Services Division, The Thomas Jefferson Library, University of Missouri, St. Louis; Susan Hartmann, Department of History, University of Missouri, St. Louis; and Joyce Trebilcot, Department of Philosophy and Director, Women's Studies Program, Washington University. Naomi Kane and Dorothy Ann Chase, wise-cracking women who are truly wise, also read many or all of the stories and offered their advice, as did Marilyn Probe and Claire Tomlinson.

Joanna Russ read the stories and spent long hours over the years conferring with me about them, sharing her wisdom and her literary judgment. She also read many drafts of the introduction, helping think through the ideas and perspectives on the issue, as did a number of others, who did not read the stories, but instead read the introductory material in various drafts to see if it made sense and rang true without reference to the stories. Among these are Emily Toth, whose help on this work and others extends from the smallest to the largest aspects of a project such as this, and whose wit and moral clarity are unfailing; Kossia Orloff, a scrupulous, diligent, and loving friend; Rebecca Kisky, a new and nurturant friend; Judy Stover, whose reading aloud of the introduction made the final editing lots of fun; and David Elliott, whose practical help will always be remembered. Still others talked with me about the issues involved in these stories without reference to either the stories or the introductory materials, but with an understanding of the nature of my project. They are Alix Kates Shulman, Shirley Frank, Florence Howe, Elaine Reuben, Shirley LeFlore, Jacqueline Zita, Gail Robbins, and Annette Kolodny. None of those mentioned is responsible for any of my conclusions or failures to reach conclusions, and a number of those in this extended and informal study group will probably disagree with at least some of what I say. I am enormously grateful to all of them and I hope that they, too, will write what they think and know and believe about this situation and these issues.

The following sister-scholars have shared with me their work, formally and informally, on the writers whose stories are included in this collection: Susan Allen Toth of Macalester College and Helen Eisen of St. Louis for Alice Brown and Mary E. Wilkins Freeman; Joanna Russ of The University of Washington, for James Tiptree, Jr.; Beverly Seaton, The Ohio State University, Newark Campus, for Helen R. Martin; Linda Wagner of Michigan State University and Lois Marchino of The University of Texas, El Paso, for Ellen Glasgow; Vivian Pollack of Cheyney State College, for Harriet Prescott Spofford; Nancy Walker of Stephens College, Emily Toth of The Pennsylvania State University, and Josephine Donovan for Mary E. Wilkins Freeman; Carol Farley Kessler of The Pennsylvania State University, Delaware County Campus, for Elizabeth Stuart Phelps; Joyce Brown of Gardner Webb College for Marjorie Kinnan Rawlings; Patricia G. Holland of the University of Massachusetts, Amherst and Katherine Kleitz of Tufts University for Lydia Maria Child; Susan Sniader Lanser of Georgetown University for Mary Austin; Seraphia D. Leyda of the University of New Orleans, Lake Front, for Helen Hunt Jackson; Mary Helen Washington of The University of Massachusetts, Boston, for Alice Walker.

Those who helped locate the little bit of information available about Martha Wolfenstein were many: Jacob Rader Marcus and Jonathan D. Sarna of the Hebrew Union College–Jewish Institute of Religion; Bernard I. Levinson of the Jewish Publication Society of America; my dear cousin Miriam Klein, alumna and historian of the Cleveland Jewish Orphan Asylum (now Bellefaire); Jack Girick of New York, oldest surviving alumnus of the institution who remembers Dr. Samuel Wolfenstein; Judah Rubenstein of the Cleveland Jewish Community Federation; Lorraine Miller, librarian at the St. Louis Jewish Community Federation; Nancy Gardner, librarian at the Cleveland *Plain Dealer*; Susie Hanson and Catherine A. Wells of the Case Western Reserve University Library; and Emily Toth of The Pennsylvania State University.

I want to thank Allison King for her friendship and support; Drs. David Alpers, Ray Clouse, and Alice Trotter for medical care; and Kaye Norton for careful, competent, and speedy manuscript preparation. My gratitude to Jo Baird of The Feminist Press is great for her dedicated work on this manuscript.

Additionally, I want to thank any others whose names I may have inadvertently omitted or who have requested that their names be omitted or who were strangers willing to share their experiences and ideas about this subject, but not their names.

Finally, I want to thank my husband, Dennis Mills, not only for reading every single new version of each sentence with patience and kindness, but for suffering with love and understanding through the drastic mood changes that constant engagement with this material and these issues wrought in me. And I want to thank my son, Edward Nathan Koppelman Cornillon, who made this remark in July 1983: "You can't bargain with barbarians." I keep thinking about it.

Introduction

*The material for feminist ethics at this point in its history,
is not primarily a body of concepts or a philosophy, but the
experiences and stories about and by women. Biography,
autobiography—including the ethicist's—fiction, poetry, and
oral history are the data of feminist ethics.*
"What is feminist ethics? A Proposal for Continuing
Discussion," Eleanor Humes Haney

All the stories in this collection are about women—both wives
and other women—who love adulterous men. These eighteen stories,
written by women who lived and worked in the United States
between 1842 and 1981, and chosen from a larger compilation of
sixty-nine stories, address one of the most frequently explored
themes in women's fiction. The writers examine the impact of men's
adulteries on the lives of women, the relationships between two
women who find themselves part of each other's lives because they
love the same man, and the larger community in which the events
in these stories occur.

Many of us come to these stories of loss and betrayal from similar
pain in our own lives. But there is no sense that we are experiencing
something new and strange. We "know how to do it," know many
of the different roles that are available to us in this situation, because
of the great chorus of rage and grief, sorrow and shame, bewilderment
and indignation that whirls around us, in all the forms of our
culture—popular music and grand opera, confession magazines and
great novels, movies, soap operas, the advice columns of Dear
Abby, and the stories we tell each other in laundromats, on coffee
breaks, after aerobics classes, and as we walk with our children in
the parks.

*It is because the history is a familiar one . . . that I
undertake to tell it.*   "No News," Elizabeth Stuart Phelps

This story is familiar as well from many traditional sources. There are the Biblical chapters about Sarah and Hagar and Abraham (*Genesis* 16–25) and about Jacob and his two wives, the sisters Leah and Rachel (*Genesis* 29–49). In recent years, the classical Greek tragedy *Medea* has twice been made into a film. And for generations, blues artists have sung about "Frankie and Johnnie": "He was her man, but he done her wrong."

Both men and women have written stories in which women play out ritualized roles when confronted with knowledge of betrayal by the men they love. Women are portrayed as sacrificial or forgiving, as patient, long-suffering, and understanding; or as envenomed, jealous, and outraged; as schemers and self-destroyers; as out to get all they can in a divorce settlement and as too possessive to let go for any amount of money; as without shame in their grieving and as ashamed of their grief. Both women and men have told such stories. But the women telling the stories in this volume offer other perspectives.

In these stories we learn not only what the women feel about the men in their lives, but what they feel for each other. We also often learn about the response of the community to the events. Central in these stories is the woman's response to the situation rather than the man's motivation for betraying her. These writers portray women in roles other than the traditional pitiable, ridiculous, or detestable betrayed wife consumed with jealousy and the devious, desperate, or dumb other woman ruthlessly pursuing another woman's man.

In addition to the sense of betrayal, the pain, bewilderment, and grief of individual women, the stories reflect the history of women coming to consciousness about the ways in which women have been conditioned to need, love, and find excuses for men who oppress women in this way. Additionally, these stories trace the history of women's struggle to define and honor the ethical boundaries of relationships between and among women.

A pattern emerges from these stories that highlights the vulnerability of women within the patriarchal institution of marriage.

Women who have remained outside marriage have traditionally been penalized by a society that has refused to recognize the worth of an unmarried woman. But married women have also been penalized by a legal system that stripped wives of all human rights. When a woman and a man married, they became one—and that one was he. Until the passage of the Married Woman's Property Law in 1848, a married woman had no right to inherit or own property including her own earned income (which was her husband's property). A married woman had no right to custody or guardianship of her children even after her husband's death (he could "will" them to the custody of another man). Husbands in many states, until the 1920s, had the legal right to beat their wives, so long as the stick used was no thicker than the judge's thumb. And until recent years, at their discretion and convenience, husbands could and often did commit their wives to insane asylums. There were no "sanity hearings." A woman's incarceration, often life-long, occurred at the will and whim of her husband, should he find her disobedient, uncooperative, or simply in his way if, for instance, he wanted to make room for another woman.

Dependence

The conditioned dependence of women on men is an important motif throughout these stories. From time to time, and among members of all social classes, the factors that combine to create that dependence shift. For some women, in fiction as well as in life, their dependence on a particular man, a husband or lover, is predominantly emotional.

> *"I saw God only through him; it was he that waked me up to worship. . . . I had a little print of the Lord appearing to Mary with the lily of annunciation in his hand, and I thought—I dare not tell you what I thought. I made an idol of my piece of clay."* "Her Story," Harriet Prescott Spofford

But for most women, the elements of dependence that bind them to their marriages and make them so vulnerable to their husbands' betrayals are emotional, social, and financial factors.

> *"There is so much more in marriage than either love or indifference. . . . There is, for instance, comfort. . . . when George ceases to be desirable for sentimental reasons, he will still have his value as a good provider."*
>   "The Difference," Ellen Glasgow

Reading these stories with an understanding that female dependence is a combination of these three factors leads to insights about how a woman may respond to her husband's faithlessness and how she perceives the other woman. As the balance among those elements changes from one story to the next, so does the response of the wife change both to her husband's infidelity and to the other woman.

Marriage confers two kinds of status on a woman: the married woman's "Mrs." signifies the achievement of adult female legitimacy; and, as a married woman, a wife shares her husband's socioeconomic status, which is usually either higher than the one she was born to or similar to the one her father conferred on the household she grew up in. The wife who manages her husband's household and maintains it to his liking and for his comfort, as does Margaret Fleming in "The Difference," is likely to be living on a higher socioeconomic scale than she could achieve by her own efforts as an employed single woman. Since the wife's greater prestige, status, privilege, and social authority are derivative, she experiences the other woman as enormously threatening; it is not only "love" that a wife might lose, but her livelihood. In stories where a wife is completely dependent on her husband, the other woman may be portrayed as a menacing figure, as in Harriet Spofford's "Her Story." The same other woman, however, may be seen by that husband as a waif, underprivileged and in a precarious situation. He may tend to confuse what he has to offer—social legitimacy and economic support—with ennobling love, and so he may romanticize their relationship.

On the other hand, from the perspective of the writer or the female characters in the stories in this volume, neither the wife nor the other woman is romanticized. Women know that no woman is irresistibly beautiful or seductive. To say that a woman is irresistible is to imply that her physical attributes or her appearance is responsible for what happens. There is the further implication that she is responsible for her appearance and therefore the ultimate "cause" of whatever ensues. An unrealistic assessment of a person's appearance, or the effect of one persons's appearance on another, is one step on the road to blaming the victim, as we know from such songs as "Devil Woman" and such social phenomena as rape defenses built on the victim's provocative dress.

The Wife and the Other Woman

> *For an instant, such is the perversity of fate, it seemed to the wife that she and this strange girl were united by some secret bond George could not share.*
> "The Difference," Ellen Glasgow

The most significant characteristic in these women's stories of the other woman is a wished-for, implied, or sometimes actually achieved bonding between the two women that occurs near the story's end and provides a moment of transcendence, in which the women triumph over the damage to their lives and self-esteem. That moment may express hope for reconciliation between the women, an affirmation of sisterhood, or simply a recognition of the commonality of their plight as women. Just as the reader cannot fail to see both women as subjectively innocent, so must the betrayed woman come to understand the humanity of the other woman and their underlying alliance of interests if she is to survive emotionally and spiritually.

> *A flash of anger stirred [Mattie], like a spurt of flame. . . . The shadow of the man, passing away, left clear the picture of [Elly]. . . . "I'd orter hided him for taking sich a young 'un along his low-down way."*
> "Gal Young Un," Marjorie Kinnan Rawlings

The reader gets a sense of each of the two women from the perspectives of the women themselves. Even if one of the two appears only briefly, she is portrayed either as a person living in accordance with values she honors, as is Rose Morrison in "The

Difference," rather than as a mysterious evil symbol, or as an innocent who is simply another victim of the husband's deceptiveness, as in "The Quadroons," "Chayah," "Turned," and "Gal Young Un."

As social and political changes in progressive years allowed greater numbers of women to earn their own living, as more women gained access to meaningful and fulfilling work, and as the stigma of remaining unmarried diminished, the figure of the other woman in the women's fiction represented here has become increasingly transformed into a nonthreatening figure. Sympathy for her is reinforced by practical realities that make her less menacing and more amenable to dispassionate examination. In "Chayah," "Turned," "A Captain Out of Etruria," "Gal Young Un," and "The Last Rite," the other woman is truly an innocent. In "A Poet Though Married" she is, in fact, an ally.

Whether the woman betrayed is the wife, as in most of the stories, or the other woman, as in "Chayah," or both women, as in "The Difference" and "Gal Young Un," she bears neither blame nor shame for the motivation, the method, or the acts of the man who betrays. There is no smug blaming of the victim. Harrie of "No News," for example, has, despite her best intentions, committed the cardinal sin of the abandoned wife—she has "let herself go." But that sin is examined in the light of *her* experience as well as, and in contrast to, *his* experience.

The Man

What hopeless lack of real moral strength, enduring
purpose, or principle in such a nature as John Gray's!
"How One Woman Kept Her Husband,"
Helen Hunt Jackson

The man is held responsible for his behavior in these stories. His infidelity may be seen as only one more flawed facet in a badly flawed character. Even if the other woman can be seen as intentionally alluring, as in "Her Story," the man is shown as responsible for succumbing. He is privileged by his maleness with the power of choice and these women writers view him as responsible for exercising that choice.

Because these are women's stories, it is women's values, women's communities, and the judgments of women that matter. There are no snickering back-slapping congratulations for back street affairs. There are no attributions of prowess to a man who is unfaithful. The writers represent a community of women judging men's adulterous behavior as a significant aspect of men's ethical character. The fabric of these men's characters is tightly woven: if he is immoral and dissipated in one way, he will be so in others. If he defaults on one commitment, he cannot be trusted in any way.

Community

The Papagos observed, and, not having visited Susie when
she was happy with her man, they went now in numbers,
and by this Susie understood that it was in their hearts that
she might have need of them. "Papago Wedding," Mary Austin

The twin issues of community membership and community values are addressed in a number of ways in these stories. Where there is a narrator, that person represents the community's values, as do the Old Maid narrators of "No News," "How One Woman Kept Her Husband," and the Old Woman in "Chayah." Direct portrayal of community intervention occurs on behalf of the deceived wife in "Gal Young Un" and the betrayed woman in "Papago Wedding." A total absence of community in "The Girl Who Was Plugged in" makes possible the unquestioned disappearance and unnoticed transformation of P. Burke; her recruiter is careful to determine that she belongs nowhere, with no one. And the dramatic tension of "The Last Rite" derives from the conflict between the values of the inherited community on the one hand and the chosen, intentional community on the other.

In this collection of other woman stories, the loss of community over the last century and a half is the most significant element of social change. Sociologists and historians have suggested many reasons for this. Increased mobility—both geographic and economic—has removed people from the communities in which they grew up. The assimilation of the children of immigrants repeatedly separates the generations. Vast technological changes in the means, modes, and locations of production, transportation, and communication have led to further alienation between and among people. But the story is even more complicated. While people urgently in need of work have left the farm for the factory, the mountains for the auto plants, the villages for the cities, others have taken advantage of the greater freedom to roam in search of communities more compatible with their interests and preferences than those among which they were born. For all these reasons, there has been a loss of community.

A study of women's history reveals that despite often unwelcome restrictions, women have been more protected, have had access to more support, and have been less vulnerable to deception when they have lived amid traditional monolithic communities among women who understood and shared their specific condition within the patriarchy.

The writers represented here also show how oppressed communities are rendered powerless to protect their own women when those women become the prey of men who belong to the communities that control the society, as in "The Quadroons" and "Chayah."

Besides the contrast between powerless, oppressed communities and majority communities whose men feel entitled to exploit the bodies and lives of female members of the oppressed communities, we see as well the gradual dying of community and the loss of its protections in the dominant culture. There are examples of the absence of community in the lives of women who belong to the dominant culture but are, for various reasons, alienated from it— as in "No News," in which Harrie has been taken far from home immediately after her marriage, and in "A Captain Out of Etruria," in which Lucy Anderson is incomprehensible to her "social set" because of her artistic vocation.

In "Turned," "Gal Young Un," and "A Perfectly Nice Man" we can see a pattern that develops when these stories are considered as a group: the creation of nurturant communities of women who are no longer vulnerable to men and whatever uses men might make of women as replaceable wife-things.

Romantic Love and Grief

". . . love is greater than all else," and then she wept softly
to herself.   "Chayah," Martha Wolfenstein

Besides economic dependence and legal subservience, women
have been encouraged from childhood to believe in the myth of
romantic love as the *sine qua non* of happiness, and to develop for
marriage and husbands a psychological dependence, a kind of force-
fed emotional addiction that deforms naturally healthy egos.

In the stories of this volume, we see the myth of romantic love
demolished again and again. These stories examine what happens
in so many marriages, instead of "and they lived happily ever after."
There is no type of woman who is immune to betrayal and there
is nothing that a woman can do or avoid doing to protect herself
and the marriage to which she is only one of the partners.

The betrayed woman learns that she must make an independent
life, assuming the responsibility for herself insofar as law and
practical possibility permit, whether or not she resumes her relationship with the man who has cheated on her.

These stories are also exquisite anatomies of grief, capturing, long
before Dr. Elizabeth Kubler-Ross abstracted for us from her studies
of dying people, the stages and process of responding to loss. The
betrayed women experience the various stages of grief, rather than
suffering the conventional and simple jealousy. Instead, jealousy
weaves itself, along with guilt and shame, through the grieving
process. Paralleling Kubler-Ross's five stages of grief—denial, anger,
bargaining, depression, and acceptance—are five stages of response
to the knowledge of a husband's adultery. They are denial, shame
and/or guilt, making excuses for him and trying to re-engage him,
depression, and, finally, transcendence.

What is consistent in all of these stories is that each one
acknowledges pain. Each one starts emotionally with pain, which
gathers intensity at different rates and disables more or less. But
the women in these stories pass through and transcend the pain, to
leave readers with the knowledge that there is another side to that
pain, an independence, self-possession, and self-esteem beyond pain.

The Cautionary Tale

*Only one episode of their life . . . I shall try to reproduce
. . . because I believe that its lesson is of priceless worth to
women.*   "How One Woman Kept Her Husband,"
                                                      Helen Hunt Jackson

One of the oldest forms of literature is the cautionary tale. These
are stories that tell us "what would happen if " and "what happened
when." *Charlotte Temple*, the 1794 novel by Susannah Rowson, the
first best-seller in the United States and unsurpassed in popularity
until the 1852 publication of Harriet Beecher Stowe's *Uncle Tom's
Cabin*, is a cautionary tale. It tells the story of a young woman,
naive, trusting, loving, who succumbs to her sweetheart's seductions,
becomes pregnant, is abandoned, suffers, and dies.

Many of the great nineteenth-century novels are cautionary tales
about what can happen if a woman is adulterous or lives a sexually
promiscuous life. Leo Tolstoy's Anna Karenina, an adulterous wife,
throws herself under the wheels of a train; Gustave Flaubert's
Madame Bovary, another adulterous wife, becomes so unhappy that
she takes poison and dies; Thomas Hardy's Tess D'Urberville is
executed by a self-righteous citizenry; and the successful prostitute-
actress written about by Emile Zola, Nana, dies of a hideously
disfiguring disease.

The other woman stories in this collection are also cautionary
tales. In the cautionary tale about the faithless husband, the
victimized wife is not responsible for adultery and betrayal. The
stories do not focus on prevention. Rather, they concentrate on how
the betrayed woman responds to her husband, the situation, and
the other woman, once he has precipitated the crisis. The only
totally disastrous course for the betrayed woman is passivity. Thus,
these cautionary tales about betrayed wives and other women
describe what would happen if a woman behaved in one way rather
than another when she is forced by her husband's philandering into
choosing a role, an attitude, a strategy for responding to those
circumstances.

The husband—it's "No News"—betrays his wife. What if she
lets him off without a fight? Rosalie, in "The Quadroons," does

this, and she dies. But because she is an enslaved woman, she is seen by the white woman writing her story as having no other choice. However, when the wife asserts her rights to her husband, when she holds on because she is confident of the justice of her claim to priority in his life, she can generally "keep" him, as does Ellen Gray in "How One Woman Kept Her Husband," Susie in "Papago Wedding," and as Margaret Fleming might in "The Difference." It is generally the presence of children in the marriage that makes the wife feel most confident of her rights.

When the wife has allowed herself to become completely vulnerable and totally dependent on her husband, leaving her emotionally subject to his whim, she loses her "soul" when she loses her man. Madness is the most persistent metaphor for the fate of the woman who has given over responsibility for her inner self to a man who proves a deceiver. Chayah and the nameless inmate of "Her Story" lose their minds.

Among writers who belong to oppressed groups, stories on the other woman theme are rare. When such stories do appear, the trio is defined in such a way that highlights political analogies. "Chayah" represents this pattern, serving as a warning to those members of oppressed groups who believe in the possibility of personal treaties between oppressor and oppressed.

It is the tradition of much literature for women *not* to survive such betrayals. Women are traditionally portrayed as dying of broken hearts. The heart-breaking husband is often brought to his knees, repentant, at his wife's deathbed. But his "I'm sorry" is brought at too dear a price when the price is her life. These women writers mock the tradition of killing off betrayed wives. This is particularly true in "No News." Alice Brown's story, "Natalie Blayne," also plays with the traditional pattern.

"A Captain Out of Etruria" is an example of the stories about women whose lives center around a strong sense of vocation, for whom the episode in their lives during which they are betrayed by a man to whom they have made an emotional commitment is portrayed as nothing more than that—an episode. These women are centered elsewhere than in biological roles and the myth of romantic love. Although their pain and grief are strong and genuine, so is their self-esteem; they recover and go on with their work.

New Directions

New directions taken with the other woman theme in recent years are represented by Lee Yu-Hwa's "The Last Rite," Louise Meriwether's "A Happening in Barbados," James Tiptree, Jr.'s "The Girl Who Was Plugged In," Alice Walker's "Coming Apart," and Jane Rule's "A Perfectly Nice Man." In each case, the other woman syndrome is used to examine large political issues.

The conflicts between the demands and privileges of traditional and revolutionary lifestyles, between the duties families define for individuals and those young adults would choose to assume, between inherited and intentional community, between political theory and practice, are explored in Yu-Hwa's story. Meriwether probes the juncture between racism and sexism, in which the central character is torn between the necessary refusal by black women to continue in the role of white women's nurturers and her understanding of the need for all women to nurture each other. The alienation from the self induced in women by the conditioning to and rewards for accepting patriarchal standards for judging female beauty is part of Tiptree's theme, as well as the absence of human connections in a world where community has degenerated into simple conglomeration. Walker examines the use of pornography to reinforce men's conditioning to perceive women as manipulable and bestial, as instruments rather than as persons. From the perspective of two women living together a joyfully reconstructed life, Jane Rule tells one of the most common other woman stories—that of the betrayed and abandoned pregnant wife. The characters refer to the humiliation and desperation of feeling devalued and deserted. However, because that pain is in their past and because the women have discovered "such an obvious solution," her story has comfortingly comic overtones.

All the women in these five stories have been or can be used against their own and each other's best interests, as tools, rather than as beings in and for themselves, with value *as* themselves. In each story we see women being reduced to functions—sexual, reproductive, commercial, domestic—separated into parts, only some of which men find desirable or useful. The women are separated from themselves as they are separated from each other. Participating in the partitioning of themselves, they are unable to imagine wholeness or to engage in alliances unless and until they start redefining the rules of the game. However, as the last two stories testify, women can assume the right to rethink the social order, to imagine a world in which they are not disadvantaged either by acceptance of hurts they cannot argue against with a logic oppressors are willing to accept or by acceptance of the heterosexual imperative in a patriarchy, all of whose institutions are designed to support men's power and privilege.

The wife in "Coming Apart" learns to imagine wholeness when she turns to the literature that has grown out of the black feminist movement. She creates her own consciousness-raising group by reading and garnering strength from her sisters to begin the struggle with oppression in her life. Her husband also begins to struggle, to face his own shame, and his shameful and shaming behavior. The wife can rescue herself. It is his willingness to try to rescue himself, his attempt to thrash through the issues of power, privilege, and racial and sexual exploitation that makes this the only story in the collection to project an optimistic future in which reconciliation between women and men is envisioned. It is significant that the story deals with minority characters. They are able to imagine, finally, coming together because he is able to think about his oppression of her in a context of their shared oppression.

Unanswered Questions and Consciousness Raising

Relationships, and particularly issues of dependency, are experienced differently by women and men. . . . Since masculinity is defined through separation while femininity is defined through attachment, male gender identity is threatened by intimacy while female gender identity is threatened by separation.
    "Woman's Place in Man's Life Cycle," Carol Gilligan

In addition to all of the economic, legal, political, and social factors that act to erode and destroy long-term, committed heterosexual relationships, there is a growing body of theory being

articulated by developmental psychologists that examines the meaning, the value and values, the rewards and costs of these relationships
to the women and men involved in them. It is often at the point
when the woman is most relaxed about the relationship, most
confident about the continuing solidity of the life partnership—
during pregnancy or when the children have finally grown and left
home, when graduation or publication or tenure is finally achieved
or the family business is finally solidly in the black, when major
shared goals finally seem assured of success—that the man seems
to become most vulnerable to drawing out and making something
more of those momentary interactions with strangers that reinforce
cherished and perhaps fading images of himself. Because for so
much of their lives women are reduced to contemplation of themselves as merely attractive objects, most women are neither fooled
by the promises nor tempted by the illusions of the results—when
they are successful—of that shared human impulse to test one's
continued desirability.

In the late 1960s and early 1970s, the theory-building cell of the
Women's Liberation movement was the consciousness-raising group.
Eight to fourteen women would gather together regularly. They
would choose a topic, define an aspect of life, or raise a question—
"What was it like when you first . . . ?" or "What happened when
. . . ?" or "How did you (learn to) deal with . . . ?" Each in turn
would tell about her personal experience as it related to the issue
or questions. Women listened to each other. It was a disciplined
listening. After each had told her story, comparisons were made
about what the stories had in common, how they differed, and what
these differences and similarities disclosed. Women generalized and
built theories. The truth we shared was our belief that women are
oppressed and that together women could build a social order in
which there would be no oppressed.

> "What was I, after all, but just another woman."
> "A Perfectly Nice Man," Jane Rule

We understood that where anyone is oppressed, women will be
oppressed; where the earth is polluted and ravaged, women will be
raped; where there is any form of censorship, women's voices will
be silenced; where work is alienating and labor is alienated, women

will be washing dishes alone. We believed that what we told each other about our lives would help us figure out what was wrong, how the wrong "worked," what changes needed to be made, and how we would make them. We are still telling our stories.

We must ask and find answers to questions about power in relationships between women and men; about dependence, inter-dependence, and autonomy; about freedom and responsibility; about honor and honesty and self-esteem. For these are the real issues, not monogamy and non-monogramy. And certainly, not yet, love.

Reading the stories in this collection is like the first part of a consciousness-raising meeting. Women have been telling stories like this, about this issue, for a long, long time, and in this book stories are collected from more than one hundred forty years of that long time. However, now we need the second part of the consciousness-raising meeting. We must talk together, analyze, and compare in order to understand this phenomenon of pain in our lives. And through these stories, we must try, as the heroine of "Coming Apart" tries, to understand by using our sisters' literary voices, to understand not only the problem they portray, but how, from the perspective of this problem, the oppression and dividing of women works, and how to change it.

> *"I felt I'd betrayed her . . . though I didn't know*
> *anything about it."*   "A Perfectly Nice Man," Jane Rule

In the 1960s, as the current wave of the women's movement began to gather impetus, feminists noted the competition between and among women for the attention of, approval of, and sexual and financial bonding with men. That competition fostered divisiveness among women across class and race lines as well as within families and between friends, much as the cultivated hatred between poor whites and poor blacks reinforces the system that exploits them both. Simultaneously, as women became more consciously feminist, women began to capture the attention of other women in social settings. Suddenly women noticed that women had the most interesting stories to tell, the most provocative questions to ask, and the most sensitive, sympathetic, and understanding ears for each other.

Once feminists agreed that competition for men was self-destructive, we believed we would go on to better relationships between women *and* between women and men. This new code of honor would work to the advantage of us all. To act with honor in this matter would reinforce our solidarity. Women would no longer be willing to be "other women." Men would be on their own.

> *"He's a perfectly nice man. It's just that I sometimes think that isn't good enough, not now when there are other options."*   "A Perfectly Nice Man," Jane Rule

Men would no longer accrue the benefits of being rare and precious; they would no longer be able to use their desirability to other women to behave irresponsibly toward the women with whom they had made commitments. It was to be a version of *Lysistrata*.

However, certain realities were not considered in formulating that new code that would lead to trust and solidarity, not to mention a shift in the balance of power and a revolution in the social order. One of those unconsidered facts is the relative scarcity of men. In each decade of our living, the ratio of men to women falls; there are fewer and fewer to choose among. We have evolved no method of sharing those who are available. Thus far in history, it is the men themselves who have taken it upon themselves to be shared. In addition, the constantly fed and fanned flames of homophobia by counterrevolutionary forces, including, among others, many in-name-only feminists, have continued to limit women's sense of their options. Men still hold economic, social, political and legal power and many women still believe that their salvation, their continued survival, lies in finding and holding on to the right man.

So other women still exist. And the realities, the pains, the outrages, the malice, the grief, the clumsiness, and even the humor of this set of relationships between women and women and men continues to be the focus of much women's literature.

Lydia Maria Child

The Quadroons
1842

Lydia Maria Francis Child (1802–1880), a New Englander, was a writer, editor, and conversationalist who did significant work in the abolition movement during the middle fifty years of the nineteenth century.

Her mother died in 1914 and after that Child's life was perapatetic. She lived sometimes with a married sister, sometimes with her brother, a respected Unitarian minister and professor at Harvard Divinity School. By the age of nineteen, Child was a self-supporting school teacher. Her first novel, Hobomok, *self-published in 1824, dealt with marriage between a white woman and an Indian, and was considered scandalous for its treatment of miscegenation. However, it was one of the earliest attempts by a United States author to create a native literature rooted in American issues, customs, and landscape. Her work was influenced by the writing of Catharine Maria Sedgwick, who was, at that time, this country's most successful author. In 1826 Child founded the first children's periodical in this country, filled with what has become the traditional mix of educational articles, poems, and stories, many of which she wrote herself.* The Juvenile Miscellany, *popular and financially successful, was the first secular reading material for many women writers younger than she, including Helen Hunt Jackson. Simultaneously, she was publishing short fiction in the elegant literary annuals and gift books that were beginning to dominate the publishing world.*

Two years later, she married David Lee Child, attorney and fellow abolitionist. Her meeting with William Lloyd Garrison in the early 1830s, however, affected her more profoundly than any other event in her life, catalyzing a conversion-like experience. She remained devoted to the cause of abolition throughout her life.

She wrote "The Quadroons" as a contribution to the first abolitionist literary

annual, The Liberty Bell, *compiled by "The Friends of Freedom," and published by the Massachusetts Anti-Slavery Fair of 1842. The fair was an annual fund-raising event for which this literary gift book had been compiled each year since 1839. "The Quadroons" is the second appearance in United States literature of a female mulatto. The first was Cora in James Fenimore Cooper's* The Last of the Mohicans. *Unlike Cooper's character, Child's creation was an exemplary figure, virtuous in all the ways prescribed for the Victorian woman, as described by historian Barbara Welter in her 1966 essay, "The Cult of True Womanhood: 1800–1860" as piety, purity, submissiveness, and domesticity. Rosalie, like Charlotte Temple (see Introduction) is seduced, impregnated, and abandoned. Not until Nathaniel Hawthorne's Hester Prynne in* The Scarlet Letter *(1850) was such a woman permitted to survive in fiction.*

Rosalie's life, death, and racial mixture provided a model for much United States literature, from the 1853 novel Clotelle *by William Wells Brown (the first Afro-American novelist in our history) to* Our Nig; or, Sketches from the Life of a Free Black *(1859) by Harriet E. Wilson, to Nella Larsen's 1929 novel* Passing, *to Gayl Jones's 1977 collection of stories titled* White Rat. *White writers have also adopted the character type that has come to be identified as "the tragic mulatto."*

It is equally important to see this story and this character as a continuation of a woman's literary tradition. Child was the first white writer to grant black and racially mixed women the right to be "ladies." Child portrays the enslaved woman as partaking with grace and virtue in the life typically reserved for the mistress.

Although this story has not been reprinted since the 1847 second edition of her short story collection Fact and Fiction, *the story had a wide readership and a great impact. It should be read as both a continuation of a sentimental tradition of seduction and abandonment and as a radical violation of racist barriers.*

> "I promised thee a sister tale
> Of man's perfidious cruelty;
> Come then and hear what cruel wrong
> Befell the dark Ladie."—*Coleridge.*

Not far from Augusta, Georgia, there is a pleasant place called Sand-Hills, appropriated almost exclusively to summer residences for the wealthy inhabitants of the neighboring city. Among the beautiful cottages that adorn it was one far retired from the public roads, and almost hidden among the trees. It was a perfect model of rural beauty. The piazzas that surrounded it were covered with Clematis and Passion flower. The Pride of China mixed its oriental-looking foliage with the majestic magnolia, and the air was redolent with the fragrance of flowers, peeping out from every nook, and nodding upon you in bye places with a most unexpected welcome. The tasteful hand of Art had not learned to *imitate* the lavish beauty and harmonious disorder of Nature, but they lived together in loving unity, and spoke in according tones. The gateway rose in a Gothic arch, with graceful tracery in iron-work, surmounted by a Cross, around which fluttered and played the Mountain Fringe, that lightest and most fragile of vines.

The inhabitants of this cottage remained in it all the year round; and perhaps enjoyed most the season that left them without neighbors. To one of the parties, indeed, the fashionable summer residents, that came and went with the butterflies, were merely neighbors-in-law. The edicts of society had built up a wall of separation between her and them; for she was a quadroon; the daughter of a wealthy merchant of New Orleans, highly cultivated in mind and manners, graceful as an antelope, and beautiful as the evening star. She had early attracted the attention of a handsome and wealthy young Georgian; and as their acquaintance increased, the purity and bright intelligence of her mind, inspired him with a far deeper sentiment than belongs merely to excited passion. It was in fact Love in its best sense—that most perfect landscape of our complex nature, where earth everywhere kisses the sky, but the heavens embrace all; and the lowliest dew-drop reflects the image of the highest star.

The tenderness of Rosalie's conscience required an outward form of marriage; though she well knew that a union with her proscribed race was unrecognised by law, and therefore the ceremony gave her no legal hold on Edward's constancy. But her high, poetic nature regarded the reality rather than the semblance of things; and when he playfully asked how she could keep him if he wished to run away, she replied, "Let the church that my mother loved sanction our union, and my own soul will be satisfied, without the protection of the state. If your affections fall from me, I would not, if I could, hold you by a legal fetter."

It was a marriage sanctioned by Heaven, though unrecognised on earth. The picturesque cottage at Sand-Hills was built for the young bride under her own directions; and there they passed ten as happy years as ever blessed the heart of mortals. It was Edward's fancy to name their eldest child Xarifa; in commemoration of a Spanish song, which had first conveyed to his ears the sweet tones of her mother's voice. Her flexile form and nimble motions were in harmony with the breezy sound of the name; and its Moorish origin was most appropriate to one so emphatically "a child of the sun." Her complexion, of a still lighter brown than Rosalie's, was rich and glowing as an autumnal leaf. The iris of her large, dark eye had the melting, mezzotinto outline, which remains the last vestige of African ancestry, and gives that plaintive expression, so often observed, and so appropriate to that docile and injured race.

Xarifa learned no lessons of humility or shame, within her own happy home; for she grew up in the warm atmosphere of father's and mother's love, like a flower open to the sunshine, and sheltered from the winds. But in summer walks with her beautiful mother, her young cheek often mantled at the rude gaze of the young men, and her dark eye flashed fire, when some contemptuous epithet met her ear, as white ladies passed them by, in scornful pride and ill-concealed envy.

Happy as Rosalie was in Edward's love, and surrounded by an outward environment of beauty, so well adapted to her poetic spirit, she felt these incidents with inexpressible pain. For herself, she cared but little; for she had found a sheltered home in Edward's heart, which the world might ridicule, but had no power to profane. But when she looked at her beloved Xarifa, and reflected upon the unavoidable and dangerous position which the tyranny of society had awarded her, her soul was filled with anguish. The rare loveliness of the child increased daily, and was evidently ripening into most marvellous beauty. The father rejoiced in it with unmingled pride; but in the deep tenderness of the mother's eye there was an indwelling sadness, that spoke of anxious thoughts and fearful foreboding.

When Xarifa entered her ninth year, these uneasy feelings found utterance in earnest solicitations that Edward would remove to France, or England. This request excited but little opposition, and was so attractive to his imagination, that he might have overcome all intervening obstacles, had not "a change come o'er the spirit of his dream." He still loved Rosalie; but he was now twenty-eight years old, and, unconsciously to himself, ambition had for some time been slowly gaining an ascendency over his other feelings. The contagion of example had led him into the arena where so much

American strength is wasted; he had thrown himself into political excitement, with all the honest fervor of youthful feeling. His motives had been unmixed with selfishness, nor could he ever define to himself when or how sincere patriotism took the form of personal ambition. But so it was, that at twenty-eight years old, he found himself an ambitious man, involved in movements which his frank nature would have once abhorred, and watching the doubtful game of mutual cunning with all the fierce excitement of a gambler.

Among those on whom his political success most depended was a very popular and wealthy man, who had an only daughter. His visits to the house were at first of a purely political nature; but the young lady was pleasing, and he fancied he discovered in her a sort of timid preference for himself. This excited his vanity, and awakened thoughts of the great worldly advantages connected with a union. Reminiscences of his first love kept these vague ideas in check for several months; but Rosalie's image at last became an unwelcome intruder; for with it was associated the idea of restraint. Moreover Charlotte, though inferior in beauty, was yet a pretty contrast to her rival. Her light hair fell in silken profusion, her blue eyes were gentle, though inexpressive, and her healthy cheeks were like opening rose-buds.

He had already become accustomed to the dangerous experiment of resisting his own inward convictions; and this new impulse to ambition, combined with the strong temptation of variety in love, met the ardent young man weakened in moral principle, and unfettered by laws of the land. The change wrought upon him was soon noticed by Rosalie.

> "In many ways does the full heart reveal
> The presence of the love it would conceal;
> But in far more the estranged heart lets know
> The absence of the love, which yet it fain would show."

At length the news of his approaching marriage met her ear. Her head grew dizzy, and her heart fainted within her; but, with a strong effort at composure, she inquired all the particulars; and her pure mind at once took its resolution. Edward came that evening, and though she would have fain met him as usual, her heart was too full not to throw a deep sadness over her looks and tones. She had never complained of his decreasing tenderness, or of her own lonely hours; but he felt that the mute appeal of her heart-broken looks was more terrible than words. He kissed the hand she offered, and with a countenance almost as sad as her own, led her to a window in the recess shadowed by a luxuriant Passion Flower. It was the same seat where they had spent the first evening in this beautiful cottage, consecrated to their youthful loves. The same calm, clear moonlight looked in through the trellis. The vine then planted had now a luxuriant growth; and many a time had Edward fondly twined its sacred blossoms with the glossy ringlets of her raven hair. The rush of memory almost overpowered poor Rosalie; and Edward felt too much oppressed and ashamed to break the long, deep silence. At length, in words scarcely audible, Rosalie said, "Tell me, dear Edward, are you to be married next week?" He dropped her hand, as if a rifle-ball had struck him; and it was not until after long hesitation, that he began to make some reply about the necessity of circumstances. Mildly, but earnestly, the poor girl begged him to spare apologies. It was enough that he no longer loved her, and that they must bid farewell. Trusting to the yielding tenderness of her character, he ventured, in the most soothing accents, to suggest that as he still loved her better than all the world, she would ever be his real wife, and they might see each other frequently. He was not prepared for the storm of indignant emotion his words excited. Hers was a passion too absorbing to admit of partnership; and her spirit was too pure to form a selfish league with crime.

At length this painful interview came to an end. They stood together by the Gothic gate, where they had so often met and parted in the moonlight. Old remembrances melted their souls. "Farewell, dearest Edward," said Rosalie. "Give me a parting kiss." Her voice was choked for utterance, and the tears flowed freely, as she bent her lips toward him. He folded her convulsively in his arms, and imprinted a long, impassioned kiss on that mouth, which had never spoken to him but in love and blessing.

With effort like a death-pang, she at length raised her head from his heaving bosom and turning from him with bitter sobs, she said, "It is our *last*. To meet thus is henceforth crime. God bless you. I would not have you so misrable as I am. Farewell. A *last* farewell." "The *last!*" exclaimed he, with a wild shriek. "Oh God, Rosalie, do not say that!" and covering his face with his hands, he wept like a child.

Recovering from his emotion, he found himself alone. The moon looked down upon him mild, but very sorrowful; as the Madonna seems to gaze on her worshipping children, bowed down with consciousness of sin. At that moment he would have given worlds to have disengaged himself from Charlotte; but he had gone so far, that blame, disgrace, and duels with angry relatives, would now attend any effort to obtain his freedom. Oh, how the moonlight oppressed him with its friendly sadness! It was like the plaintive eye of his forsaken one,—like the music of sorrow echoed from an unseen world.

Long and earnestly he gazed at that dwelling, where he had so long known earth's purest foretaste of heavenly bliss. Slowly he walked away; then turned again to look on that charmed spot, the nestling-place of his young affections. He caught a glimpse of Rosalie, weeping beside a magnolia, which commanded a long view of the path leading to the public road. He would have sprung toward her, but she darted from him, and entered the cottage. That graceful figure, weeping in the moonlight, haunted him for years. It stood before his closing eyes, and greeted him with the morning dawn.

Poor Charlotte! had she known all, what a dreary lot would hers have been; but fortunately, she could not miss the impassioned tenderness she had never experienced; and Edward was the more careful in his kindness, because he was deficient in love. Once or twice she heard him murmur, "dear Rosalie," in his sleep; but the playful charge she brought was playfully answered, and the incident gave her no real uneasiness. The summer after their marriage, she proposed a residence at Sand-Hills; little aware what a whirlwind of emotion she excited in her husband's heart. The reasons he gave for rejecting the proposition appeared satisfactory; but she could not quite understand why he was never willing that their afternoon drives should be in the direction of those pleasant rural residences, which she had heard him praise so much. One day, as their barouche rolled along a winding road that skirted Sand-Hills, her attention was suddenly attracted by two figures among the trees by the way-side; and touching Edward's arm, she exclaimed, "Do look at that beautiful child!" He turned, and saw Rosalie and Xarifa. His lips

quivered, and his face became deadly pale. His young wife looked
at him intently, but said nothing. There were points of resemblance
in the child, that seemed to account for his sudden emotion. Suspicion
was awakened, and she soon learned that the mother of that lovely
girl bore the name of Rosalie; with this information came recollections
of the "dear Rosalie," murmured in uneasy slumbers. From gossiping
tongues she soon learned more than she wished to know. She wept,
but not as poor Rosalie had done, for she never had loved, and been
beloved, like her; and her nature was more proud. Henceforth a
change came over her feelings and her manners; and Edward had
no further occasion to assume a tenderness in return for hers.
Changed as he was by ambition, he felt the wintry chill of her
polite propriety, and sometimes in agony of heart, compared it with
the gushing love of her who was indeed his wife.

But these, and all his emotions, were a sealed book to Rosalie, of
which she could only guess the contents. With remittances for her
and her child's support, there sometimes came earnest pleadings
that she would consent to see him again; but these she never
answered, though her heart yearned to do so. She pitied his fair
young bride, and would not be tempted to bring sorrow into her
household by any fault of hers. Her earnest prayer was that she
might never know of her existence. She had not looked on Edward
since she watched him under the shadow of the magnolia, until his
barouche passed her in her rambles some months after. She saw
the deadly paleness of his countenance, and had he dared to look
back, he would have seen her tottering with faintness. Xarifa
brought water from a little rivulet, and sprinkled her face. When
she revived, she clasped the beloved child to her heart with a
vehemence that made her scream. Soothingly she kissed away her
fears, and gazed into her beautiful eyes with a deep, deep sadness
of expression, which Xarifa never forgot. Wild were the thoughts
that pressed around her aching heart, and almost maddened her
poor brain; thoughts which had almost driven her to suicide the
night of that last farewell. For her child's sake she conquered the
fierce temptation then; and for her sake, she struggled with it now.
But the gloomy atmosphere of their once happy home overclouded
the morning of Xarifa's life.

> "She from her mother learnt the trick of grief,
> And sighed among her playthings."

Rosalie perceived this; and it gave her gentle heart unutterable pain. At last, the conflicts of her spirit proved too strong for the beautiful frame in which it dwelt. About a year after Edward's marriage, she was found dead in her bed, one bright autumnal morning. She had often expressed to her daughter a wish to be buried under a spreading oak, that shaded a rustic garden-chair, in which she and Edward had spent many happy evenings. And there she was buried; with a small white cross at her head, twined with the cypress vine. Edward came to the funeral, and wept long, very long, at the grave. Hours after midnight, he sat in the recess-window, with Xarifa folded to his heart. The poor child sobbed herself to sleep on his bosom; and the convicted murderer had small reason to envy that wretched man, as he gazed on the lovely countenance, that so strongly reminded him of his early and his only love.

From that time, Xarifa was the central point of all his warmest affections. He employed an excellent old negress to take charge of the cottage, from which he promised his darling child that she should never be removed. He employed a music master, and dancing master, to attend upon her; and a week never passed without a visit from him, and a present of books, pictures, or flowers. To hear her play upon the harp, or repeat some favorite poem in her mother's earnest accents and melodious tones, or to see her flexile figure float in the garland-dance, seemed to be the highest enjoyment of his life. Yet was the pleasure mixed with bitter thoughts. What would be the destiny of this fascinating young creature, so radiant with life and beauty? She belonged to a proscribed race; and though the brown color on her soft cheek was scarcely deeper than the sunny side of a golden pear, yet was it sufficient to exclude her from virtuous society. He thought of Rosalie's wish to carry her to France; and he would have fulfilled it, had he been unmarried. As it was, he inwardly resolved to make some arrangement to effect it, in a few years, even if it involved separation from his darling child.

But alas for the calculations of man! From the time of Rosalie's death, Edward had sought relief for his wretched feelings in the free use of wine. Xarifa was scarcely fifteen, when her father was found dead by the road-side; having fallen from his horse, on his way to visit her. He left no will; but his wife with kindness of heart worthy of a happier domestic fate, expressed a decided reluctance to change any of the plans he had made for the beautiful child at Sand-Hills.

Xarifa mourned her indulgent father; but not as one utterly desolate. True she had lived "like a flower deep hid in rocky cleft;" but the sunshine of love had already peeped in upon her. Her teacher on the harp was a handsome and agreeable young man of twenty, the only son of an English widow. Perhaps Edward had not been altogether unmindful of the result, when he first invited him to the flowery cottage. Certain it is, he had more than once thought what a pleasant thing it would be, if English freedom from prejudice should lead him to offer legal protection to his graceful and winning child. Being thus encouraged, rather than checked, in his admiration, George Elliot could not be otherwise than strongly attracted toward his beautiful pupil. The lonely and unprotected state in which her father's death left her, deepened this feeling into tenderness. And lucky was it for her enthusiastic and affectionate nature; for she could not live without an atmosphere of love. In her innocence, she knew nothing of the dangers in her path; and she trusted George with an undoubting simplicity, that rendered her sacred to his noble and generous soul. It seemed as if that flower-embossed nest was consecreated by the Fates to Love. The French have well named it *La Belle Passion;* for without it life were "a year without spring, or a spring without roses." Except the loveliness of infancy, what does earth offer so much like Heaven, as the happiness of two young, pure, and beautiful beings, living in each other's hearts?

Xarifa inherited her mother's poetic and impassioned temperament; and to her, above others, the first consciousness of these sweet emotions was like a golden sunrise on the sleeping flowers.

> "Thus stood she at the threshold of the scene
> Of busy life.
> How fair it lay in solemn shade and sheen!
> And he beside her, like some angel, posted
> To lead her out of childhood's fairy land,
> On to life's glancing summit, hand in hand."

Alas, the tempest was brooding over their young heads. Rosalie, though she knew it not, had been the daughter of a slave; whose wealthy master, though he remained attached to her to the end of her days, had carelessly omitted to have papers of manumission recorded. His heirs had lately failed, under circumstances, which greatly exasperated their creditors; and in an unlucky hour, they discovered their claim on Angelique's grand-child.

The gentle girl, happy as the birds in springtime, accustomed to the fondest indulgence, surrounded by all the refinements of life, timid as a young fawn, and with a soul full of romance, was ruthlessly seized by a sheriff, and placed on the public auction-stand in Savannah. There she stood, trembling, blushing, and weeping; compelled to listen to the grossest language, and shrinking from the rude hands that examined the graceful proportions of her beautiful frame. "Stop that," exclaimed a stern voice, "I bid two thousand dollars for her, without asking any of their d—d questions." The speaker was probably about forty years of age, with handsome features, but a fierce and proud expression. An older man, who stood behind him, bid two thousand five hundred. The first bid higher; then a third, a dashing young man, bid three thousand; and thus they went on, with the keen excitement of gamblers, until the first speaker obtained the prize, for the moderate sum of five thousand dollars.

And where was George, during this dreadful scene? He was absent on a visit to his mother, at Mobile. But, had he been at Sand-Hills, he could not have saved his beloved from the wealthy profligate, who was determined to obtain her at any price. A letter of agonized entreaty from her brought him home on the wings of the wind. But what could he do? How could he ever obtain a sight of her, locked up as she was in the princely mansion of her master? At last by bribing one of the slaves, he conveyed a letter to her, and received one in return. As yet, her purchaser treated her with respectful gentleness, and sought to win her favor, by flattery and presents; but she dreaded every moment, lest the scene should change, and trembled at the sound of every footfall. A plan was laid for escape. The slave agreed to drug his master's wine; a ladder of ropes was prepared, and a swift boat was in readiness. But the slave, to obtain a double reward, was treacherous. Xarifa had scarcely given an answering signal to the low, cautious whistle of her lover, when the sharp sound of a rifle was followed by a deep groan, and a heavy fall on the pavement of the court-yard. With frenzied eagerness she swung herself down by the ladder of ropes, and, by the glancing light of lanthorns, saw George, bleeding and lifeless at her feet. One wild shriek, that pierced the brains of those who heard it, and she fell senseless by his side.

For many days she had a confused consciousness of some great agony, but knew not where she was, or by whom she was surrounded. The slow recovery of her reason settled into the most intense melancholy, which moved the compassion even of her cruel purchaser. The beautiful eyes, always pleading in expression, were now so heart-piercing in their sadness, that he could not endure to look upon them. For some months, he sought to win her smiles by lavish presents, and delicate attentions. He bought glittering chains of gold, and costly bands of pearl. His victim scarcely glanced at them, and the slave laid them away, unheeded and forgotten. He purchased the furniture of the cottage at Sand-Hills, and one morning Xarifa found her harp at the bed-side, and the room filled with her own books, pictures, and flowers. She gazed upon them with a pang unutterable, and burst into an agony of tears; but she gave her master no thanks, and her gloom deepened.

At last his patience was exhausted. He grew weary of her obstinacy, as he was pleased to term it; and threats took the place of persuasion.

In a few months more, poor Xarifa was a raving maniac. That pure temple was desecrated; that loving heart was broken; and that beautiful head fractured against the wall in the frenzy of despair. Her master cursed the useless expense she had cost him; the slaves buried her; and no one wept at the grave of her who had been so carefully cherished, and so tenderly beloved.

Reader, do you complain that I have written fiction? Believe me, scenes like these are of no unfrequent occurence at the South. The world does not afford such materials for tragic romance, as the history of the Quadroons.

Elizabeth Stuart Phelps

No News
1868

By 1868, when Elizabeth Stuart Phelps (1844–1911) wrote "No News," her father, the Reverend Austin Phelps, a Congregational minister and faculty member at Andover Theological Seminary in Massachusetts, had been married for ten years to his third wife. His first wife, the writer Elizabeth Wooster Stuart Phelps (1815–1952) had died in her daughter's eighth year, leaving the child with a permanent sense of loss. After her mother's death, this daughter, who had been christened Mary Gray, assumed her mother's name.

Less than two years after her mother's death, her father married his dead wife's tubercular sister. Elizabeth witnessed her death within eighteen months. The third wife added two more sons to the family. Elizabeth Stuart Phelps had already decided never to marry.

However, she became quite ill before the publication of her novel, The Story of Avis (1877), which portrays the life of a brilliant painter from adolescence through a marriage whose demands destroy her ability to work. Phelps's illness was apparently both physical and emotional. As her health failed, she began to lose confidence in her independent lifestyle and, in 1888, at the age of forty-four, she married a man seventeen years younger than herself. Herbert Dickinson Ward, the son of an old friend, had apparently expected to use her literary reputation and connections to establish her own. As his career languished and her health deteriorated, however, he abandoned their marriage in all ways except legally. She died alone.

Phelps was more fortunate in her work life. Her literary career lasted almost half a century. When The Gates Ajar, one of her three utopian novels, was published in 1868, it was immediately successful, becoming a best-seller that made her famous and financially independent.

Harriet Beecher Stowe, another minister's wife and daughter, had been a neighbor in Andover and, a generation older than Phelps, had provided her with a model of a successful literary woman. Annie Fields, wife of the editor of the Atlantic *and hostess of one of the most influential literary salons in United States history, had been the one to decide to publish* The Gates Ajar *and draw Phelps into the great literary network of women writers that included Stowe, Sarah Orne Jewett, Helen Hunt Jackson, Rose Terry Cooke, and others.*

Much of Phelps's fiction focuses on conventional middle class white married life from the perspective of the women for whom it becomes a form of destructive servitude. She wrote about her mother,

> Genius was in her and would out. She wrote because she could not help it . . . a wife, a mother, a housekeeper, a hostess, in delicate health, on an academic salary, undertakes a deadly load when she starts on a literary career . . . she fell beneath it.

Surely it is no accident that the daughter of such a mother defended women who were overburdened and undervalued in marriage. She also championed women who chose never to marry. The lives of independent women who support themselves and share close relationships with other independent women is another major focus of her fiction.

In "No News" Phelps portrays a husband's infidelity as recreation or distraction, arising out of emotional shallowness, selfishness, and self-indulgence. The irony of the story arises from the Old Maid narrator's fastidious unwillingness to portray Dr. Sharpe as other than one of the best of husbands. He is a man not without provocation. Because of her exhaustion from overwork, multiple pregnancies, and her personal assumption of major economies, his wife, Harrie, is no longer his social equal. She serves him and their family out of love and a sense of duty; she lives the life her husband believes a wife should live. He not only takes her services for granted, never thinking to share or return them, but ceases to care for (and to take care of) her. He has lost his "best earthly friend" because to cope with the outcome of that earthly friendship, his wife had become a servant. He feels abandoned, lonely, and ready for distraction and comfort.

Many nineteenth-century women writers came from clerical households since clerical men were most likely to marry educated women and to educate their daughters. However, while the uncontrolled pregnancies, household demands, and economic stringencies imposed on these women were no less than those of other women in the same class, the role of "helpmeet" to a minister made additional demands. Ministers' wives were expected to participate in the life of the parish or seminary, to attend church services and lectures, to teach Sunday school, perform "good works" in the community, and keep up with the theological issues that were the subject matter of their husband's professional lives. Phelps refers metaphorically to these conditions in her writing, replacing ministers, healers of souls, with doctors, healers of bodies. "No News" depicts domestic life as women in her family knew it.

This story, originally published in the Atlantic *in 1868 and later collected in her 1869 volume,* Men, Women, and Ghosts, *was radical in its espousal of birth control, subtle as the mention seems today. "Three innocent babies—and how many more . . ." is as far as Phelps dared spell it out.*

An additional irony is the role of Pauline Dallas, the still-single member of the wedding party. Only two lines are used to indict her:

> Pauline had been one of [Harrie's] eternal friendships at
> school. . . . She had come to Lime to enjoy herself.

Pauline could not have expected to pursue and further develop her "eternal friendship" with Harrie if she didn't help with the housework and the child care. For feminists of Phelps's generation, criticism of the abuses of women by men did not absolve women of responsibility to perform traditionally defined duties. The sharing of household work was a major element in the friendships of women. When unmarried Susan B. Anthony visited her married friend Elizabeth Cady Stanton, Anthony helped with the domestic chores and the child care while they planned the overthrow of the patriarchy. Their revolution was rooted in an understanding that meals had to be prepared, dishes washed, diapers changed and boiled, clothes cut out, sewed, laundered, and mended.

None at all. Understand that, please, to begin with. That you will at once, and distinctly, recall Mr. Sharpe—and his wife, I make no doubt. Indeed, it is because the history is a familiar one, some of the unfamiliar incidents of which have come into my possession, that I undertake to tell it.

My relation to the Doctor, his wife, and their friend, has been in many respects peculiar. Without entering into explanations which I am not at liberty to make, let me say, that those portions of their story which concern our present purpose, whether or not they fell under my personal observation, are accurately, and to the best of my judgment impartially, related.

Nobody, I think, who was at the wedding, dreamed that there would ever be such a story to tell. It was such a pretty, peaceful wedding! If you were there, you remember it as you remember a rare sunrise, or a peculiarly delicate May-flower, or that strain in a simple old song which is like orioles and butterflies and dew-drops.

There were not many of us; we were all acquainted with one another; the day was bright, and Harrie did not faint nor cry. There were a couple of bridesmaids,—Pauline Dallas, and a Miss—Jones, I think,—besides Harrie's little sisters; and the people were well dressed and well looking, but everybody was thoroughly at home, comfortable, and on a level. There was no annihilating of little country friends in gray alpacas by city cousins in point and pearls, no crowding and no crush, and, I believe, not a single "front breadth" spoiled by the ices.

Harrie is not called exactly pretty, but she must be a very plain woman who is not pleasant to see upon her wedding day. Harrie's eyes shone,—I never saw such eyes! and she threw her head back like a queen whom they were crowning.

Her father married them. Old Mr. Bird was an odd man, with odd notions of many things, of which marriage was one. The service was his own. I afterwards asked him for a copy of it, which I have preserved. The Covenant ran thus:—

"Appealing to your Father who is in heaven to witness your sincerity, you . . . do now take this woman whose hand you hold—choosing her alone from all the world— to be your lawfully wedded wife. You trust her as your best earthly friend. You promise to love, to cherish, and to protect her; to be considerate of her happiness in your plans of life; to cultivate for her sake all manly virtues; and in all things to seek her welfare as you seek your own. You pledge yourself thus honorably to her, to be her husband in good faith, so long as the providence of God shall spare you to each other.

"In like manner, looking to your Heavenly Father for his blessing, You . . t. do now receive this man, whose hand you hold, to be your lawfully wedded husband. You choose him from all the world as he has chosen you. You pledge your trust to him as your best earthly friend. You promise to love, to comfort, and to honor him; to cultivate for his sake all womanly graces; to guard his reputation, and assist him in his life's work! and in all things to esteem his happiness as your own. You give yourself thus trustfully to him, to be his wife in good faith, so long as the providence of God shall spare you to each other."

When Harrie lifted her shining eyes to say, "I *do!*" the two little happy words ran through the silent room like a silver bell; they would have tinkled in your ears for weeks to come if you had heard them.

I have been thus particular in noting the words of the service, partly because they pleased me, partly because I have since had some occasion to recall them, and partly because I remember having wondered, at the time, how many married men and women of your and my acquaintance, if honestly subjecting their union to the test and full interpretation and remotest bearing of such vows as these, could live in the sight of God and man as "lawfully wedded" husband and wife.

Weddings are almost always very sad things to me; as much sadder than burials as the beginning of life should be sadder than the end of it. The readiness with which young girls will flit out of a tried, proved, happy home into the sole care and keeping of a man whom they have known three months, six, twelve, I do not profess to understand. Such knowledge is too wonderful for me; it is high, I cannot attain unto it. But that may be because I am fifty-five, an old maid, and have spent twenty years in boarding-houses.

A woman reads the graces of a man at sight. His faults she cannot thoroughly detect till she has been for years his wife. And his faults are so much more serious a matter to her than hers to him!

I was thinking of this the day before the wedding. I had stepped in from the kitchen to ask Mrs. Bird about the salad, when I came abruptly, at the door of the sitting-room, upon as choice a picture as one is likely to see.

The doors were open through the house, and the wind swept in and out. A scarlet woodbine swung lazily back and forth beyond the window. Dimples of light burned through it, dotting the carpet and the black-and-white marbled oilcloth of the hall. Beyond, in the little front parlor, framed in by the series of doorways, was Harrie, all in a cloud of white. It floated about her with an idle, wavelike motion. She had a veil like fretted pearls through which her tinted arm shone faintly, and the shadow of a single scarlet leaf trembled through a curtain upon her forehead.

Her mother, crying a little, as mothers will cry the day before the wedding, was smoothing with tender touch a tiny crease upon the cloud; a bridesmaid or two sat chattering on the floor; gloves, and favors, and flowers, and bits of lace like hoar frost, lay scattered about; and the whole was repictured and reflected and reshaded in the great old-fashioned mirrors before which Harrie turned herself about.

It seemed a pity that Myron Sharpe should miss that, so I called him in from the porch where he sat reading Stuart Mill on Liberty.

If you form your own opinion of a man who might spend a livelong morning,—an October morning, quivering with color, alive with light, sweet with the breath of dropping pines, soft with the caress of a wind that had filtered through miles of sunshine,—and that the morning of the day before his wedding,—reading Stuart Mill on Liberty,—I cannot help it.

Harrie, turning suddenly, saw us,—met her lover's eyes, stood a moment with lifted lashes and bright cheeks,—crept with a quick, impulsive movement into her mother's arms, kissed her, and floated away up the stairs.

"It's a perfect fit," said Mrs. Bird, coming out with one corner of a very dingy handkerchief—somebody had just used it to dust the Parian vases—at her eyes.

And though, to be sure, it was none of my business, I caught myself saying, under my breath,—

"It's a fit for life; for a *life*, Dr. Sharpe."

Dr. Sharpe smiled serenely. He was very much in love with the little pink-and-white cloud that had just fluttered up the stairs. If it had been drifting to him for the venture of twenty lifetimes, he would have felt no doubt of the "fit."

Nor, I am sure, would Harrie. She stole out to him that evening after the bridal finery was put away, and knelt at his feet in her plain little muslin dress, her hair all out of crimp, slipping from her net behind her ears,—Harrie's ears were very small, and shaded off in the colors of a pale apple-blossom,—up-turning her flushed and weary face.

"Put away the book, please, Myron."

Myron put away the book (somebody on Bilious Affections), and looked for a moment without speaking at the up-turned face.

Dr. Sharpe had spasms of distrusting himself amazingly; perhaps most men have,—and ought to. His face grew grave just then. That little girl's clear eyes shone upon him like the lights upon an altar.

In very unworthiness of soul he would have put the shoes from off his feet. The ground on which he trod was holy.

When he spoke to the child, it was in a whisper:—"Harrie, are you afraid of me? I know I am not very good."

And Harrie, kneeling with the shadows of the scarlet leaves upon her hair, said softly, "How could I be afraid of you? It is *I* who am not good."

Dr. Sharpe would not have made much progress in Bilious Affections that evening. All the time that the skies were fading, we saw them wandering in and out among the apple-trees,—she with those shining eyes, and her hand in his. And when to-morrow had come and gone, and in the dying light they drove away, and Miss Dallas threw old Grandmother Bird's little satin boot after the carriage, the last we saw of her was that her hand was clasped in his, and that her eyes were shining.

Well, I believe that they got along very well till the first baby came. As far as my observation goes, young people usually get along very well till the first baby comes. These particular young people had a clear conscience,—as young people go,—fair health, a comfortable income for two, and a very pleasant home.

This home was on the coast. The townspeople made shoes, and minded their own business. Dr. Sharpe bought the dying practice of an antediluvian who believed in camomile and castor-oil. Harrie mended a few stockings, made a few pies, and watched the sea.

It was almost enough of itself to make one happy—the sea—as it tumbled about the shores of Lime. Harrie had a little seat hollowed out in the cliffs, and a little scarlet bathing-dress, which was surprisingly becoming, and a little boat of her own, moored in the little bay,—a pretty shell which her husband had had made to order, that she might be able to row herself on a calm water. He was very thoughtful for her in those days.

She used to take her sewing out upon the cliff; she would be demure and busy; she would finish the selvage seam; but the sun blazed, the sea shone, the birds sang, all the world was at play,— what could it matter about selvage seams? So the little gold thimble would drop off, the spool trundle down the cliff, and Harrie, sinking back into a cushion of green and crimson sea-weed, would open her wide eyes and dream. The waves purpled and silvered, and broke into a mist like powdered amber, the blue distances melted softly, the white sand glittered, the gulls were chattering shrilly. What a world it was!

"And he is in it!" thought Harrie. Then she would smile and shut her eyes. "And the children of Israel saw the face of Moses, that Moses' face shone, and they were afraid to come nigh him." Harrie wondered if everybody's joy were too great to look upon, and wondered, in a childish, frightened way, how it might be with sorrow if people stood with veiled faces before it, dumb with pain as she with peace,—and then it was dinner-time, and Myron came down to walk up the beach with her, and she forgot all about it.

She forgot all about everthing but the bare joy of life and the sea, when she had donned the pretty scarlet suit, and crept out into the surf,—at the proper medicinal hour, for the Doctor was very particular with her,—when the warm brown waves broke over her face, the long sea-weeds slipped through her fingers, the foam sprinkled her hair with crystals, and the strong wind was up.

She was a swift swimmer, and as one watched from the shore, her lithe scarlet shoulders seemed to glide like a trail of fire through the lighted waters; and when she sat in shallow foam with sunshine on her, or flashed through the dark green pools among the rocks, or floated with the incoming tide, her great bathing-hat dropping shadows on her wet little happy face, and her laugh ringing out, it was a pretty sight.

But a prettier one than that, her husband thought, was to see her in her boat at sunset; when sea and sky were aflame, when every flake of foam was a rainbow, and the great chalk-cliffs were blood-red; when the wind blew her net off, and in pretty petulance she pulled her hair down, and it rippled all about her as she dipped into the blazing West.

Dr. Sharpe used to drive home by the beach, on a fair night, always, that he might see it. Then Harrie would row swiftly in, and spring into the low, broad buggy beside him, and they rode home together in the fragrant dusk. Sometimes she used to chatter on these twilight drives; but more often she crept up to him and shut her eyes, and was as still as a sleepy bird. It was so pleasant to do nothing but be happy!

I believe that at this time Dr. Sharpe loved his wife as unselfishly as he knew how. Harrie often wrote me that he was "very good."

She was sometimes a little troubled that he should "know so much more" than she, and had fits of reading the newspapers and reviewing her French, and studying cases of hydrophobia, or some other pleasant subject which had a professional air. Her husband laughed at her for her pains, but nevertheless he found her so much the more entertaining. Sometimes she drove about with him on his calls, or amused herself by making jellies in fancy moulds for his poor, or sat in his lap and discoursed like a bobolink of croup and measles, pulling his whiskers the while with her pink fingers.

All this, as I have said, was before the first baby came.

It is surprising what vague ideas young people in general, and young men in particular, have of the rubs and jars of domestic life; especially domestic life on an income of eighteen hundred, American constitutions and country servants thrown in.

Dr. Sharpe knew something of illness and babies and worry and watching; but that his own individual baby should deliberately lie and scream till two o'clock in the morning, was a source of perpetual astonishment to him; and that it,—he and Mrs. Sharpe had their first quarrel over his peristence in calling the child an "it,"—that it should *invariably* feel called upon to have the colic just as he had fallen into a nap, after a night spent with a dying patient, was a phenomenon of the infant mind for which he was, to say the least, unprepared.

It was for a long time a mystery to his masculine understanding, that Biddy could not be nursery-maid as well as cook. "Why, what has she to do now? Nothing but to broil steaks and make tea for two people!" That whenever he had Harrie quietly to himself for a peculiarly pleasant tea-table, the house should resound with sudden shrieks from the nursery, and there was *always* a pin in that baby, was forever a fresh surprise; and why, when they had a house full of company, no "girl," and Harrie down with a sick-headache, his son and heir should of *necessity* be threatened with scarlatina, was a philosophical problem over which he speculated long and profoundly.

So gradually, in the old way, the old sweet habits of the long honeymoon were broken. Harrie dreamed no more on the cliffs by the bright noon sea; had no time to spend making scarlet pictures in the little bathing-suit; had seldom strength to row into the sunset, her hair loose, the bay on fire, and one to watch her from the shore.

There were no more walks up the beach to dinner; there came an end to the drives in the happy twilight; she could not climb now upon her husband's knee, because of the heavy baby on her own.

The spasms of newspaper reading subsided rapidly; Corinne and Racine gathered the dust in peace upon their shelves; Mrs. Sharpe made no more fancy jellies, and found no time to inquire after other people's babies.

One becomes used to anything after a while, especially if one happens to be a man. It would have surprised Dr. Sharpe, if he had taken the pains to notice,—which I believe he never did,—how easily he became used to his solitary drives and disturbed teas; to missing Harrie's watching face at door or window; to sitting whole evenings by himself while she sang to the fretful baby overhead with her sweet little tired voice; to slipping off in the "spare room" to sleep when the child cried at night, and Harrie, up and down with him by the hour, flitted from cradle to bed, or paced the room, or sat and sang, or lay and cried herself, in sheer despair of rest; to wandering away on lonely walks; to stepping often into a neighbor's to discuss the election or the typhoid in the village; to forgetting that his wife's conversational capacities could extend beyond Biddy and teething; to forgetting that she might ever hunger for a twilight drive, a sunny sail, for the sparkle and freshness, the dreaming, the petting, the caresses, all the silly little lovers' habits of their early married days; to going his own ways, and letting her go hers.

Yet he loved her, and loved her only, and loved her well. That he never doubted, nor to my surprise, did she. I remember once, when on a visit there, being fairly frightened out of the proprieties by hearing her call him "Dr. Sharpe." I called her away from the children soon after, on pretence of helping me unpack. I locked the door, pulled her down upon a trunk tray beside me, folded both her hands in mine, and studied her face; it had grown to be a very thin little face, less pretty than it was in the shadow of the woodbine, with absent eyes and a sad mouth. She knew that I loved her, and my heart was full for the child; and so, for I could not help it, I said,—

"Harrie, is all well between you? Is he quite the same?"

She looked at me with a perplexed and musing air. "The same? O yes, he is quite the same to me. He would always be the same to me. Only there are the children, and we are so busy. He—why, he loves me, your know,—"she turned her head from side to side wearily, with the puzzled expression growing on her forehead,— "he loves me just the same,—just the same. I am *his wife;* don't you see?"

She drew herself up a little haughtily, said that she heard the baby crying, and slipped away.

But the perplexed knot upon her forehead did not slip away. I was rather glad that it did not. I liked it better than the absent eyes. That afternoon she left her baby with Biddy for a couple of hours, went away by herself into the garden, sat down upon a stone and thought.

Harrie took a great deal of comfort in her babies, quite as much as I wished to have her. Women whose dream of marriage has faded a little have a way of transferring their passionate devotion and content from husband to child. It is like anchoring in a harbor,—a pleasant harbor, and one in which it is good to be,—but never on shore and never at home. Whatever a woman's children may be to her, her husband should be always something beyond and more; forever crowned for her as first, dearest, best, on a throne that neither son nor daughter can usurp. Through mistake and misery the throne may be left vacant or voiceless: but what man cometh after the king?

So, when Harrie forgot the baby for a whole afternoon, and sat out on her stone there in the garden thinking, I felt rather glad than sorry.

It was when little Harrie was a baby, I believe, that Mrs. Sharpe took that notion about having company. She was growing out of the world, she said; turning into a fungus; petrifying; had forgotten whether you called your seats at the Music Hall pews or settees, and was as afraid of a well-dressed woman as she was of the croup.

So the Doctor's house at Lime was for two or three months overrun with visitors and vivacity. Fathers and mothers made fatherly and motherly stays, with the hottest of air-tights put up for their benefit in the front room; sisters and sisters-in-law brought the fashions and got up tableaux; cousins came on the jump; Miss Jones, Pauline Dallas, and I were invited in turn, and the children had the mumps at cheerful intervals between.

The Doctor was not much in the mood for entertaining Miss Dallas; he was a little tired of company, and had had a hard week's work with an epidemic down town. Harrie had not seen her since her wedding day, and was pleased and excited at the prospect of the visit. Pauline had been one of her eternal friendships at school.

Miss Dallas came a day earlier than she was expected, and, as chance would have it, Harrie was devoting the afternoon to cutting out shirts. Anyone who has sat from two till six at that engaging occupation will understand precisely how her back ached and her temples throbbed, and her fingers stung, and her neck stiffened; why her eyes swam, her cheeks burned, her brain was deadened, the children's voices were insufferable, the slamming of a door an agony, the past a blot, the future unendurable, life a burden, friendship a myth, her hair down, and her collar unpinned.

Miss Dallas had never cut a shirt, nor, I believe, had Dr. Sharpe.

Harrie was groaning over the last wristband but one, when she heard her husband's voice in the hall.

"Harrie, Harrie, your friend is here. I found her, by a charming accident, at the station, and drove her home." And Miss Dallas, gloved, perfumed, rustling, in a very becoming veil and travelling-suit of the latest mode, swept in upon her.

Harrie was too much of a lady to waste any words on apology, so she ran just as she was, in her calico dress, with the collar hanging, into Pauline's stately arms, and held up her little burning cheeks to be kissed.

But her husband looked annoyed.

He came down before tea in his best coat to entertain their guest. Biddy was "taking an afternoon" that day, and Harrie bustled about with her aching back to make tea and wash the children. She had no time to spend upon herself, and, rather than keep a hungry traveller waiting, smoothed her hair, knotted a ribbon at the collar, and came down in her calico dress.

Dr. Sharpe glanced at it in some surprise. He repeated the glances several times in the course of the evening, as he sat chatting with his wife's friend. Miss Dallas was very sprightly in conversation; had read some, had thought some; and had the appearance of having read and thought about twice as much as she had.

Myron Sharpe had always considered his wife a handsome woman. That nobody else thought her so had made no difference to him. He had often looked into the saucy eyes of little Harrie Bird, and told her that she was very pretty. As a matter of theory, he supposed her to be very pretty, now that she was the mother of his three children, and breaking her back to cut out his shirts.

Miss Dallas was a generously framed, well-proportioned woman, who carried long trains, and tied her hair with crimson velvet. She had large, serene eyes, white hands, and a very pleasant smile. A delicate perfume stirred as she stirred, and she wore a creamy lace about her throat and wrists.

Calicoes were never becoming to Harrie, and that one with the palm-leaf did not fit her well,—she cut it herself, to save expense. As the evening passed, in reaction from the weariness of shirt-cutting she grew pale, and the sallow tints upon her face came out; her features sharpened, as they had a way of doing when she was tired and she had little else to do that evening than think how tired she was, for her husband observing, as he remarked afterwards, that she did not feel like talking, kindly entertained her friend himself.

As they went up stairs for the night, it struck him, for the first time in his life, that Harrie had a snubbed nose. It annoyed him, because she was his wife, and he loved her, and liked to feel that she was as well looking as other women.

"Your friend is a bright girl," he said, encouragingly, when Harrie had hushed a couple of children, and sat wearily down to unbutton her boots.

"I think you will find her more easy to entertain than Cousin Mehitabel."

Then, seeing that Harrie answered absently, and how exhausted she looked, he expressed his sorrow that she should have worked so long over the shirts, and kissed her as he spoke; while Harrie cried a little, and felt as if she would cut them all over again for that.

The next day Miss Dallas and Mrs. Sharpe sat sewing together; Harrie cramping her shoulders and blackening her hands over a patch on Rocko's rough little trousers; Pauline playing idly with purple and orange wools,—her fingers were white, and she sank with grace into the warm colors of the arm-chair; the door was opened into the hall, and Dr. Sharpe passed by, glancing in as he passed.

"Your husband is a very intelligent man, Harrie," observed Miss Dallas, studying her lavenders and lemons thoughtfully. "I was much interested in what he said about pre-Adamic man, last evening."

"Yes," said Harrie, "He knows a great deal. I always thought so." The little trousers slipped from her black fingers by and by, and her eyes wandered out of the window absently.

She did not know anything about pre-Adamic man.

In the afternoon they walked down the beach together,—the Doctor, his wife, and their guest,—accompanied by as few children as circumstances would admit of. Pauline was stately in a beach-dress of bright browns, which shaded softly into one another; it was one of Miss Dallas's peculiarities, that she never wore more than one color, or two, at the same time. Harrie, as it chanced, wore over her purple dress (Rocko had tipped over two ink-bottles and a vinegar-cruet on the sack which should have matched it) a dull gray shawl; her bonnet was blue,—it had been a present from Myron's sister, and she had no other way than to wear it. Miss Dallas bounded with pretty feet from rock to rock. Rocko hung heavily to his mother's finger; she had no gloves, the child would have spoiled them; her dress dragged in the sand,—she could not afford two skirts, and one must be long,—and between Rocko and the wind she held it up awkwardly.

Dr. Sharpe seldom noticed a woman's dress; he could not have told now whether his wife's shawl was sky-blue or pea-green; he knew nothing about the ink-spots; he had never heard of the unfortunate blue bonnet, or the mysteries of short and long skirts. He might have gone to walk with her a dozen times and thought her very pretty and "proper" in her appearance. Now, without the vaguest idea what was the trouble, he understood that something was wrong. A woman would have said, Mrs. Sharpe looks dowdy and old-fashioned; he only considered that Miss Dallas had a pleasant air, like a soft brown picture with crimson lights let in, and that it was an air which his wife lacked. So, when Rocko dragged heavily and more heavily at his mother's skirts, and the Doctor and Pauline wandered off to climb the cliffs, Harrie did not seek to follow or to call them back. She sat down with Rocko on the beach, wrapped herself with a savage hug in the ugly shawl, and wondered with a bitterness with which only woman can wonder over such trifles, why God should send Pauline all the pretty beach-dresses and deny them to her,—for Harrie, like many another "dowdy" woman whom you see upon the street, my dear madam, was a woman of fine, keen tastes, and would have appreciated the soft browns no less than yourself. It seemed to her the very sting of poverty, just then, that one must wear purple dresses and blue bonnets.

At the tea-table the Doctor fell to reconstructing the country, and Miss Dallas, who was quite a politician in Miss Dallas's way, observed that the horizon looked brighter since Tennessee's admittance, and that she hoped that the clouds,—and what *did* he think of Brownlow?

"Tennessee!" exclaimed Harrie; why, how long has Tennessee been in? I didn't know anything about it."

Miss Dallas smiled kindly. Dr. Sharpe bit his lip, and his face flushed.

"Harrie, you really *ought* to read the papers," he said, with some impatience; "it's no wonder you don't know anything."

"How should I know anything, tied to the children all day?" Harrie spoke quickly, for the hot tears sprang. "Why didn't you tell me something about Tennessee? You never talk politics with *me*."

This began to be awkward; Miss Dallas, who never interfered—on principle—between husband and wife, gracefully took up the baby, and gracefully swung her dainty Geneva watch for the child's amusement, smiling brilliantly. She could not endure babies, but you would never have suspected it.

In fact, when Pauline had been in the house four or five days, Harrie, who never thought very much of herself, became so painfully alive to her own deficiencies, that she fell into a permanent fit of low spirits, which did not add either to her appearance or her vivacity.

"Pauline is so pretty and bright!" she wrote to me. "I always knew I was a little fool. You can be a fool before you're married, just as well as not. Then, when you have three babies to look after, it is too late to make yourself over. I try very hard to read the newspapers, only Myron does not know it."

One morning something occurred to Mrs. Sharpe. It was simply that her husband had spent every evening at home for a week. She was in the nursery when the thought struck her, rocking slowly in her low sewing-chair, holding the baby on one arm and trying to darn stockings with the other.

Pauline was—she did not really know where. Was not that her voice upon the porch? The rocking-chair stopped sharply, and Harrie looked down through the blinds. The Doctor's horse was tied at the gate. The Doctor sat fanning himself with his hat in one of the garden chairs; Miss Dallas occupied the other; she was chatting, and twisting her golden wools about her fingers,—it was noticeable that she used only golden wools that morning; her dress was pale blue, and the effects of the purples would not have been good.

"I thought your calls were going to take till dinner, Myron," called Harrie, through the blinds.

"I thought so too," said Myron, placidly, "but they do not seem to. Won't you come down?"

Harrie thanked him, saying, in a pleasant *nonchalant* way, that she could not leave the baby. It was almost the first bit of acting that the child had ever been guilty of, —for the baby was just going to sleep, and she knew it.

She turned away from the window quietly. She could not have been angry, and scolded; or noisy, and cried. She put little Harrie into her cradle, crept upon the bed, and lay perfectly still for a long time.

When the dinner-bell rang, and she got up to brush her hair, that absent, apathetic look of which I have spoken had left her eyes. A stealthy brightness came and went in them, which her husband might have observed if he and Miss Dallas had not been deep in the Woman question. Pauline saw it; Pauline saw everything.

"Why did you not come down and sit with us this morning?" she asked, reproachfully, when she and Harrie were alone after dinner. "I don't want your husband to feel that he must run away from you to entertain me."

"My husband's ideas of hospitality are generous," said Mrs. Sharpe. "I have always found him as ready to make it pleasant here for my company as for his own."

She made this little speech with dignity. Did both women know it for the farce it was? To do Miss Dallas justice,—I am not sure. She was not a bad-hearted woman. She was a handsome woman. She had come to Lime to enjoy herself. Those September days and nights were fair there by the dreamy sea. On the whole I am inclined to think that she did not know exactly what she was about.

"*My* perfumery never lasts," said Harrie, once, stooping to pick up Pauline's fine handkerchief, to which a faint scent like unseen heliotrope clung; it clung to everything of Pauline's; you would never see a heliotrope without thinking of her, as Dr. Sharpe had often said. "Myron used to like good cologne, but I can't afford to buy it, so I make it myself, and use it Sundays, and it's all blown away by the time I get to church. Myron says he is glad of it, for it is more like Mrs. Allen's Hair Restorer than anything else. What do you use, Pauline?"

"Sachet powder of course," said Miss Dallas, smiling.

That evening Harrie stole away by herself to the village apothecary's. Myron should not know for what she went. If it were the breath of a heliotrope, thought foolish Harrie, which made it so pleasant for people to be near Pauline, that was a matter easily remedied. But sachet powder, you should know, is a dollar an ounce, and Harrie must needs content herself with "the American," which could be had for fifty cents; and so, of course, after she had spent her money, and made her little silk bags, and put them away into her bureau drawers, Myron never told *her*, for all her pains, that she reminded him of a heliotrope with the dew on it. One day a pink silk bag fell out from under her dress, where she had tucked it.

"What's all this nonsense, Harrie?" said her husband, in a sharp tone.

At another time, the Doctor and Pauline were driving upon the beach at sunset, when, turning a sudden corner, Miss Dallas cried out, in real delight,—

"See! That beautiful creature! Who can it be?"

And there was Harrie, out on a rock in the opal surf,—a little scarlet mermaid, combing her hair with her thin fingers, from which the water almost washed the wedding ring. It was—who knew how long, since the pretty bathing-suit had been taken down from the garret nails? What sudden yearning for the wash of waves, and the spring of girlhood, and the consciousness that one is fair to see, had overtaken her? She watched through her hair and her fingers for the love in her husband's eyes.

But he waded out to her, ill-pleased.

"Harrie, this is very imprudent,—very! I don't see what could have possessed you!"

Myron Sharpe loved his wife. Of course he did. He began, about
this time, to state the fact to himself several times a day. Had she
not been all the world to him when he wooed and won her in her
rosy, ripening days? Was she not all the world to him now that a
bit of searness had crept upon her, in a married life of eight hard-
working years?

That she *had* grown a little sear, he felt somewhat keenly of late.
She had a dreary, draggled look at breakfast, after the children had
cried at night, —and the nights when Mrs. Sharpe's children did
not cry were like angels' visits. It was perhaps the more noticeable,
because Miss Dallas had a peculiar color and coolness and sparkle
in the morning, like that of opening flowers. *She* had not been up
till midnight with a sick baby.

Harrie was apt to be too busy in the kitchen to run and meet
him when he came home at dusk. Or, if she came, it was with her
sleeves rolled up and an apron on. Miss Dallas sat at the window;
the lace curtain waves about her; she nodded and smiled as he
walked up the path. In the evening Harrie talked of Rocko, or the
price of butter; she did not venture beyond, poor thing! since her
experience with Tennessee.

Miss Dallas quoted Browning, and discussed Goethe, and talked
Parepa: and they had no lights, and the September moon shone in.
Sometimes Mrs. Sharpe had mending to do, and, as she could not
sew on her husband's buttons satisfactorily by moonlight, would
slip into the dining-room with kerosene and mosquitoes for company.
The Doctor may have noticed, or he may not, how comfortably he
could, if he made the proper effort, pass the evening without her.

But Myron Sharpe loved his wife. To be sure he did. If his wife
doubted it,—but why should she doubt it? Who thought she doubted
it? If she did, she gave no sign. Her eyes, he observed, had
brightened of late; and when they went to her from the moonlit
parlor, there was such a pretty color upon her cheeks, that he used
to stoop and kiss them, while Miss Dallas discreetly occupied herself
in killing mosquitoes. Of course he loved his wife!

It was observable that, in proportion to the frequency with which
he found it natural to remark his fondness for Harrie, his attentions
to her increased. He inquired tenderly after her headaches; he
brought her flowers, when he and Miss Dallas walked in the autumn
woods; he was particular about her shawls and wraps; he begged

her to sail and drive with them; he took pains to draw his chair beside hers on the porch; he patted her hands, and played with her soft hair.

Harrie's clear eyes puzzled over this for a day or two; but by and by it might have been noticed that she refused his rides, shawled herself, was apt to be with the children when he called her, and shrank, in a quiet way, from his touch.

She went into her room one afternoon, and locked the children out. An east wind blew, and the rain fell drearily. The Doctor and Pauline were playing chess down stairs; she should not be missed. She took out her wedding-dress from the drawer where she had laid it tenderly away; the hoar-frost and fretted pearl fell down upon her faded morning-dress; the little creamy gloves hung loosely upon her worn fingers. Poor little gloves! Poor little pearly dress! She felt a kind of pity for their innocence and ignorance and trustfulness. Her hot tears fell and spotted them. What if there were any way of creeping back through them to be little Harrie Bird again? Would she take it?

Her children's voices sounded crying for her in the hall. Three innocent babies—and how many more?—to grow into life under the shadow of a wrecked and loveless home! What had she done? What had they done?

Harrie's was a strong, healthy little soul, with a strong, healthy love of life: but she fell down there that dreary afternoon, prone upon the nursery floor, among the yellow wedding lace, and prayed God to let her die.

Yet Myron Sharpe loved his wife, you understand. Discussing elective affinities down there over the chessboard with Miss Dallas,— he loved his wife, most certainly; and, pray, why was she not content?

It was quite late when they came up for Harrie. She had fallen into a sleep or faint, and the window had been open all the time. Her eyes burned sharply, and she complained of a chill, which did not leave her the next day nor the next.

One morning, at the breakfast-table, Miss Dallas calmly observed that she should go home on Friday.

Dr. Sharpe dropped his cup; Harrie wiped up the tea.

"My dear Miss Dallas—surely—we cannot let you go yet? Harrie! Can't you keep your friend?"

Harrie said the proper thing in a low tone. Pauline repeated her determination with much decision, and was afraid that her visit had been more of a burden than Harrie, with all her care, was able to bear. Dr. Sharpe pushed back his chair noisily, and left the room. He went and stood by the parlor window. The man's face was white. What business had the days to close down before him like a granite wall, because a woman with long trains and white hands was going out of them? Harrie's patient voice came in through the open door:—

"Yes, yes, yes, Rocko: mother is tired to-day; wait a minute."

Pauline, sweeping by the piano, brushed the keys a little, and sang:—

> "Drifting, drifting on and on,
> Mast and oar and rudder gone,
> Fatal danger for each one,
> We helpless as in dreams."

What had he been about?

The air grew sweet with the sudden scent of heliotrope, and Miss Dallas pushed aside the curtain gently.

"I may have that sail across the bay before I go? It promises to be fair to-morrow."

He hesitated.

"I suppose it will be our last," said the lady, softly.

She was rather sorry when she had spoken, for she really did not mean anything, and was surprised at the sound of her own voice.

But they took the sail.

Harrie watched them off—her husband did not invite her to go on that occasion—with that stealthy sharpness in her eyes. Her lips and hands and forehead were burning. She had been cold all day. A sound like the tolling of a bell beat in her ears. The children's voices were choked and distant. She wondered if Biddy were drunk, she seemed to dance about so at her ironing-table, and wondered if she must dismiss her, and who could supply her place. She tried to put my room in order, for she was expecting me that night by the last train, but gave up the undertaking in weariness and confusion.

In fact, if Harrie had been one of the Doctor's patients, he would have sent her to bed and prescribed for brain-fever. As she was not a patient, but only his wife, he had not found out that anything ailed her.

Nothing happened while he was gone, except that a friend of Biddy's "dropped in," and Mrs. Sharpe, burning and shivering in her sewing-chair, dreamily caught through the open door, and dreamily repeated to herself, a dozen words of compassionate Irish brogue:—

"Folks as laves folks cryin' to home and goes sailin' round with other women—"

Then the wind latched the door.

The Doctor and Miss Dallas drew in their oars, and floated softly.

There were gray and silver clouds overhead, and all the light upon the sea slanted from low in the west: it was a red light, in which the bay grew warm; it struck across Pauline's hands, which she dipped, as the mood took her, into the waves, leaning upon the side of the boat, looking down into the water. One other sail only was to be seen upon the bay. They watched it for a while. It dropped into the west, and sunk from sight.

They were silent for a time, and then they talked of friendship, and nature, and eternity, and then were silent for a time again, and then spoke—in a very general and proper way—of separation and communion in spirit, and broke off softly, and the boat rose and fell upon the stong outgoing tide.

"Drifting, drifting on and on,"

hummed Pauline.

The west, paling a little, left a haggard look upon the Doctor's face.

"An honest man," the Doctor was saying, —"an honest man, who loves his wife devotedly, but who cannot find in her that sympathy which his higher nature requires, that comprehension of his intellectual needs, that—"

"I always feel a deep compassion for such a man," interrupted Miss Dallas, gently.

"Such a man," questioned the Doctor in a pensive tone, "need not be debarred, by the shallow conventionalities of an unappreciative world, from a friendship which will rest, strengthen, and ennoble his weary soul?"

"Certainly not," said Pauline, with her eyes upon the water; dull yellow, green, and indigo shades were creeping now upon its ruddiness.

"Pauline,"—Dr. Sharpe's voice was low,—"Pauline!"

Pauline turned her beautiful head.

"There are marriages for this world; true and honorable marriages, but for this world. But there is a marriage for eternity,—a marriage of souls."

Now Myron Sharpe is not a fool, but that is precisely what he said to Miss Pauline Dallas, out in the boat on that September night. If wiser men than Myron Sharpe never uttered more unpardonable nonsense under similar circumstances, cast your stones at him.

"Perhaps so," said Miss Dallas, with a sigh: "but see! How dark it has grown while we have been talking. We shall be caught in a squall; but I shall not be at all afraid—with you."

They were caught indeed, not only in a squall, but in a steady force of a driving northeasterly storm setting in doggedly with a very ugly fog. If Miss Dallas was not at all afraid—with him, she was nevertheless not sorry when they grated safely on the dull white beach.

They had had a hard pull in against the tide. Sky and sea were black. The fog crawled like a ghost over flat and cliff and field. The rain beat upon them as they turned to walk up the beach.

Pauline stopped once suddenly.

"What was that?"

"I heard nothing."

"A cry,—I fancied a cry down there in the fog."

They went back, and walked down the slippery shore for a space. Miss Dallas took off her hat to listen.

"You will take cold." said Dr. Sharpe, she put it on; she heard nothing,—she was tired and excited, he said.

They walked home together. Miss Dallas had sprained her white wrist, trying to help at the oars; he drew it gently through his arm.

It was quite dark when they reached the house. No lamps were lighted. The parlor window had been left open, and the rain was beating in. "How careless in Harrie!" said her husband, impatiently.

He remembered those words, and the sound of his own voice in saying them, for a long time to come; he remembers them now, indeed, I fancy, on rainy nights when the house is dark.

The hall was cold and dreary. No table was set for supper. The children were all crying. Dr. Sharpe pushed open the kitchen door with a stern face.

"Biddy! Biddy! what does all this mean? Where is Mrs. Sharpe?"

"The Lord only knows what it manes, or where is Mrs. Sharpe," said Biddy, sullenly. "It's high time, in me own belafe, for her husband to come ashkin' and inquirin', her close all in a hape on the floor upstairs, with her bath-dress gone from the nails, and the front door swingin',—me never findin' of it out till it cooms tay-time, with all the children cryin' on me, and me head shplit with the noise, and—"

Dr. Sharpe strode in a bewildered way to the front door. Oddly enough, the first thing he did was to take down the thermometer and look at it. Gone out to bathe in a temperature like that! His mind ran like lightning, while he hung the thing back upon its nail, over Harrie's ancestry. Was there not a traditionary great-uncle who died in an asylum? The whole future of three children with an insane mother spread itself out before him while he was buttoning his overcoat.

"Shall I go and help you find her?" asked Miss Dallas, tremulously; "or shall I stay and look after hot flannels and—things? What shall I do?"

"*I* don't care what you do!" said the Doctor, savagely. To his justice be it recorded that he did not. He would not exchange one glimpse of Harrie's little homely face just then for an eternity of sunset-sailing with the "friend of his soul." A sudden cold loathing of her possessed him; he hated the sound of her soft voice; he hated the rustle of her garments, as she leaned against the door with her handkerchief at her eyes. Did he remember at that moment an old vow, spoken on an old October day, to that little missing face? Did he comfort himself thus, as he stepped out into the storm, "You have trusted her, 'Myron Sharpe, as your best earthly friend' "?

As luck, or providence, or God—whichever word you prefer—decreed it, the Doctor had but just shut the door when he saw me driving from the station through the rain. I heard enough of the story while he was helping me down the carriage steps. I left my bonnet and bag with Miss Dallas, pulled my waterproof over my head, and we turned our faces to the sea without a word.

The Doctor is a man who thinks and acts rapidly in emergencies, and little time was lost about help and lights. Yet when all was done which could be done, we stood there upon the slippery weed-strewn sand, and looked in one another's faces helplessly. Harrie's little boat was gone. The sea thundered out beyond the bar. The fog hung, a dead weight, upon a buried world. Our lanterns cut it for a foot or two in a ghostly way, throwing a pale white light back upon our faces and the weeds and bits of wreck under our feet.

The tide had turned. We put out into the surf not knowing what else to do, and called for Harrie; we leaned on our oars to listen, and heard the water drip into the boat, and the dull thunder beyond the bar; we called again, and heard a frightened sea-gull scream.

"*This* yere's wastin' valooable time," said Hansom, decidedly. I forgot to say that it was George Hansom whom Myron had picked up to help us. Anybody in Lime will tell you who George Hansom is,—a clear-eyed, open-hearted sailor; a man to whom you would turn in trouble as instinctively as a rheumatic man turns to the sun.

I cannot accurately tell you what he did with us that night. I have confused memories of searching shore and cliffs and caves; of touching at little islands and inlets that Harrie fancied; of the peculiar echo which answered our shouting; of the look that settled little by little about Dr. Sharpe's mouth; of the sobbing of the low wind; of the flare of lanterns on gaping, green waves; of spots of foam that writhed like nests of white snakes; of noticing the puddles in the bottom of the boat, and of wondering confusedly what they would do with my travelling-dress, at the very moment when I saw—I was the first to see it—a little empty boat; of our hauling alongside of the tossing, silent thing; of a bit of a red scarf that lay coiled in its stern; of our drifting by, and speaking never a word; of our coasting along after that for a mile down the bay, because there was nothing in the world to take us there but the dread of seeing the Doctor's eyes when we should turn.

It was there that we heard the first cry.

"It's shoreward!" said Hansom.

"It is seaward!" cried the Doctor.

"It is behind us!" said I.

Where was it? A sharp, sobbing cry, striking the mist three or

four times in rapid succession,—hushing suddenly,—breaking into
shrieks like a frightened child's—dying plaintively down.

We struggled desperately after it, through the fog. Wind and
water took the sound up and tossed it about. Confused and
bewildered, we beat about it and about it; it was behind us, before
us, at our right, at our left,—crying on in a blind, aimless way,
making us no replies,—beckoning us, slipping from us, mocking us
utterly.

The Doctor stretched his hands out upon the solid wall of mist;
he groped with them like a man struck "To die there,—in my very
hearing,—without a chance—"

And while the words were upon his lips the cries ceased.

He turned a gray face slowly around, shivered a little, then smiled
a little, then began to argue with ghastly cheerfulness:—

"It must be only for a moment, you know. We shall hear it
again,—I am quite sure we shall hear it again, Hansom!"

Hansom, making a false stroke, I believe for the first time in his
life, napped an oar and overturned a lantern. We put ashore for
repairs. The wind was rising fast. Some drift-wood, covered with
slimy weeds, washed heavily up at our feet. I remember that a little
disabled ground-sparrow, chased by the tide, was fluttering and
drowning just in sight, and the Myron drew it out of the water,
and held it up for a moment to his cheek.

Bending over the ropes, George spoke between his teeth to me:—

"It may be a night's job on't, findin' of the body."

"The WHAT?"

The poor little sparrow dropped from Dr. Sharpe's hand. He
took a step backward, scanned our faces, sat down dizzily, and fell
over upon the sand.

He is a man of good nerves and great self-possession, but he fell
like a woman, and lay like the dead.

"It's no place for him," Hansom said, softly. "Get him home.
Me and the neighbors can do the rest. Get him home, and put his
baby into his arms, and shet the door, and go about your business."

I had left him in the dark on the office floor at last. Miss Dallas
and I sat in the cold parlor and looked at each other.

The fire was low and the lamp dull. The rain beat in an uncanny
way upon the windows. I never like to hear the rain upon the

windows. I liked it less than usual that night, and was just trying to brighten the fire a little, when the front door blew open.

"Shut it, please," said I, between the jerks of my poker.

But Miss Dallas looked over her shoulder and shivered.

"Just look at that latch!" I looked at that latch.

It rose and fell in a feeble fluttering way,—was still for a minute,—rose and fell again.

When the door swung in and Harrie—or the ghost of her—staggered into the chilly room and fell down in a scarlet heap at my feet, Pauline bounded against the wall with a scream which pierced into the dark office where the Doctor lay with his face upon the floor.

It was long before we knew how it happened. Indeed, I suppose we have never known it all. How she glided down, a little red wraith, through the dusk and damp to her boat; how she tossed about, with some dim, delirious idea of finding Myron on the ebbing waves; that she found herself stranded and tangled at last in the long, matted grass of that muddy cove, started to wade home, and sunk in the ugly ooze, held, chilled, and scratched by the sharp grass, blinded and frightened by the fog, and calling, as she thought of it, for help; that in the first shallow wash of the flowing tide she must have struggled free, and found her way home across the field,—she can tell us, but she can tell no more.

This very morning on which I write, an unknown man, imprisoned in the same spot in the same way overnight, was found by George Hansom dead there from exposure in the salt grass.

It was the walk home, and only that, which could have saved her.

Yet for many weeks we fought, her husband and I, hand to hand with death, seeming to *see* the life slip out of her, and watching for wandering minutes when she might look upon us with sane eyes.

We kept her—just. A mere little wreck, with drawn lips, and great eyes, and shattered nerves,—but we kept her.

I remember one night, when she had fallen into her first healthful nap, that the Doctor came down to rest a few minutes in the parlor where I sat alone. Pauline was washing the tea-things.

He began to pace the room with a weary abstracted look,—he was much worn by watching—and, seeing that he was in no mood

for words, I took up a book which lay upon the table. It chanced
to be one of Alger's, which somebody had lent to the Doctor before
Harrie's illness; it was a marked book, and I ran my eye over the
pencilled passages. I recollect having been struck with this one; "A
man's best friend is a wife of good sense and good heart, whom he
loves and who loves him."

"You believe that?" said Myron, suddenly, behind my shoulder.

"I believe that a man's wife ought to be his best friend,—in every
sense of the word, his *best friend*,—or she ought never to be his
wife."

"And if—there will be differences of temperament, and—other
things. If you were a man now, for instance, Miss Hannah—"

I interrupted him with hot cheeks and sudden courage.

"If I were a man, and my wife were *not* the best friend I had or
could have in the world, *nobody should ever know it,—she, least of
all,—Myron Sharpe!*"

Young people will bear a great deal of impertinence from an old
lady, but we had both gone further than we meant to. I closed Mr.
Alger with a snap, and went up to Harrie.

The day that Mrs. Sharpe sat up in the easy-chair for two hours,
Miss Dallas, who had felt called upon to stay and nurse her dear
Harrie to recovery, and had really been of service, detailed on duty
among the babies, went home.

Dr. Sharpe drove her to the station. I accompanied them at his
request. Miss Dallas intended, I think, to look a little pensive, but
had her lunch to cram into a very full travelling-bag, and forgot it.
The Doctor, with clear, courteous eyes, shook hands, and wished
her a pleasant journey.

He drove home in silence, and went directly to his wife's room.
A bright blaze flickered on the old-fashioned fireplace, and the walls
bowed with pretty dancing shadows. Harrie, all alone, turned her
face weakly and smiled.

Well, they made no fuss about it, after all. Her husband came
and stood beside her; a cricket on which one of the baby's dresses
had been thrown, lay between them; it seemed, for a moment, as
if he dared not cross the tiny barrier. Something of that old fancy
about the lights upon the altar may have crossed his thought.

"So Miss Dallas has fairly gone, Harrie," said he, pleasantly,
after a pause.

"Yes. She has been very kind to the children while I have been sick."

"Very."

"You must miss her," said poor Harrie, trembling; she was very weak yet.

Th Doctor knocked away the cricket, folded his wife's two shadowy hands into his own, and said:—

"Harrie we have no strength to waste, either of us, upon a scene; but I am sorry, and I love you."

She broke all down at that, and, dear me! they almost had a scene in spite of themselves. For O, she had always known what a little goose she was; and Pauline never meant any harm, and how handsome she was, you know! only *she* didn't have three babies to look after, nor a snubbed nose either, and the sachet powder was only American, and the very servants knew, and O Myron! she *had* wanted to be dead so long, and then—"

"Harrie!" said the Doctor, at his wit's end, this will never do in the world. I believe—I declare!—Miss Hannah!—I believe I must send you to bed."

"And then I'm SUCH a little skeleton!" finished Harrie, royally, and with a great gulp.

Dr. Sharpe gathered the little skeleton all into a heap in his arms,—it was a very funny heap, by the way, but that doesn't matter,—and to the best of my knowledge and belief he cried just about as hard as she did.

Helen Hunt Jackson

How One Woman
Kept Her Husband
1872

For almost one hundred years, Helen Maria Fiske Hunt Jackson (1830–1885) has occupied an honorable place in the history of the struggle for Native American rights. She has been called a minor Harriet Beecher Stowe because her pamphlet, A Century of Dishonor *(1881), and her novel,* Ramona *(1884), were said to have stirred the national conscience about the attempt to slowly exterminate the American Indians. She is also a significant figure in the history of women's relationships with each other. "H.H." (and sometimes "Rip Van Winkle"), as she signed herself at the end of her articles and poems when they were published in the* Nation, *the* New York Independent, *the* Post, Galaxy, *and the* Atlantic Monthly, *and in book form, detested celebrity and may have had a genius for friendship. Her name is beginning to appear frequently in the new studies of friendship networks among women in the twentieth-century United States.*

Like Elizabeth Stuart Phelps, Helen Fiske was the daughter of a minister who believed in and imitated a stern, demanding, and punishing idea of God. Her mother—sweet, happy, loving, and nurturant—felt pulled between the demand that she be "good" by being loyal and obedient to the patriarchy as it was embodied in her husband, and the impulse to be warm, generous with her love, forgiving, and fun. It appears from contemporary descriptions of Jackson as a child—"boisterous, rebellious, sturdy and stubborn"—that she was difficult to "feminize." As an adult, she was a passionate, risk-taking traveler.

Her mother died when she was thirteen and Helen was returned to the network of female relatives who had reared her mother. When she married for the first time, she immediately became enmeshed in the female network of her husband's family, and she maintained loving contact with those women after her husband's early death, the deaths of their two sons, during the years of her widowhood, and through her second marriage until her own death.

Jackson turned to writing at the urging of mostly male literary friends who worried about her sanity and will to survive when her nine-year-old and only surviving son died less than two years after his father.

"How One Woman Kept Her Husband" was published under the name of Saxe Holm in Scribner's Monthly Magazine *in February 1872, the third in a series of fifteen stories published under that* nom de plume. *In this story Jackson uses a device similar to Phelps's in "No News." An Old Maid narrator tells a cautionary tale about dangers in the way of even the most deserving of wives. In both stories, the other woman comes into the husband's life through her original friendship with the wife. Both narrators feel affection for the husbands. In both stories, the wife regains her husband's loyalty. But in "No News" the other woman is portrayed as a misdemeanant, not mysteriously evil as in "Her Story." In "How One Woman Kept Her Husband," as in "The Quadroons," both other women are presented as innocent of any intention to get involved with a previously committed man.*

Most daring, however, is the narrator's attitude toward the three members of the triangle in "How One Woman Kept Her Husband"; for the first time, a writer offers a "no fault" triangle. Helen Hunt Jackson had been a widow for eight years when she published this story. She had come to live in Newport in 1866, three years after her husband's death, and had reestablished many old ties. Although the time frame is somewhat different, these are essentially the same circumstances of the other woman, Emma Long, in this story.

Why my sister married John Gray, I never could understand. I was twenty-two and she was eighteen when the marriage took place. They had known each other just one year. He had been passionately in love with her from the first day of their meeting. She had come more slowly to loving him: but love him she did, with a love of such depth and fevor as are rarely seen. He was her equal in nothing except position and wealth. He had a singular mixture of faults of opposite temperaments. He had the reticent, dreamy, procrastinating inertia of the bilious melancholic man, side by side with the impressionable sensuousness, the sensitiveness and sentimentalism of the most sanguine-nervous type. There is great charm in such a combination, especially to persons of a keen, alert nature. My sister was earnest, wise, resolute. John Gray was nonchalant, shrewd, vacillating. My sister was exact, methodical, ready. John Gray was careless, spasmodic, dilatory. My sister had affection. He had tenderness. She was religious of soul; he had a sort of transcendental perceptivity, so to speak, which kept him more alive to the comforts of religion than to its obligations. My sister would have gone to the stake rather than tell a lie. He would tell a lie unhesitatingly, rather than give anybody pain. My sister lived earnestly, fully, actively, in each moment of the present. It never seemed quite clear whether he were thinking of to-day, yesterday, or to-morrow. She was upright because she could not help it. He was upright,—when he was upright —because of custom, taste, and the fitness of things. What fatal discrepancies! what hopeless lack of real moral strength, enduring purpose, or principle in such a nature as John Gray's! When I said these things to my sister, she answered always, with a quiet smile, "I love him." She neither admitted nor denied my accusations. The strongest expression she ever used, the one which came nearest to being an indignant repelling of what I had said, was one day, when I exclaimed—

"Ellen, I would die before I'd risk my happiness in the keeping of such a man."

"My happiness is already in his keeping," said she in a steady voice, "and I believe his is in mine. He is to be my husband and not yours, dear; you do not know him as I do. You do not understand him."

But it is not to give an analysis of her character or of his, nor to give a narrative of their family history, that I write this tale. It is only one episode of their life tha I shall try to reproduce here and I do it because I believe that its lesson is of priceless worth to women.

Ellen had been married fourteen years, and was the mother of five children, when my story begins. The years had gone in the main peacefully and pleasantly. The children, three girls and two boys, were fair and strong. Their life had been a very quiet one, for our village was far removed from excitements of all kinds. It was one of the suburban villages of ———, and most of the families living there were the families of merchants or lawyers doing business in the town, going in early in the morning, and returning late at night. There is usually in such communities a strange lack of social intercourse; whether it be that the daily departure and return of the head of the family keeps up a perpetual succession of small crises of interest to the exclusion of others, or that the night finds all the fathers and brothers too tired to enjoy anything but slippers and cigars, I know not; but certain it is that all such suburban villages are unspeakably dull and lifeless. There is barely feeling enough of good neighborhood to keep up the ordinary interchange of the commonest civilities.

Except for long visits to the city in the winter, and long journeys in the summer, I myself should have found life insupportably tedious. But Ellen was absolutely content. Her days were unvaryingly alike, a simple routine of motherly duties and housekeeping cares. Her evenings were equally unvaried, being usually spent in sewing or reading, while her husband, in seven evenings out of ten, dozed, either on the sofa, or on one of the children's little beds in the nursery. His exquisite tenderness to the children, and his quiet delight in simply being where they were, were the brightest points in John Gray's character and life.

Such monotony was not good for either of them. He grew more and more dreamy and inert. She insensibly but continually narrowed and hardened, and, without dreaming of such a thing, really came to be less and less a part of her husband's inner life. Faithful, busy, absorbed herself in the cares of each day, she never observed that he was living more and more in his children and his reveries, and withdrawing more and more from her. She did not need constant play and interchange of sentiment as he did. Affectionate, loyal, devoted as she was, there was a side of husband's nature which she did not see nor satisfy, perhaps, never could. But neither of them knew it.

At this time Mr. Gray was offered a position of importance in the city, and it became necessary for them to move there to live. How I rejoiced in the change. How bitterly I regretted it before two years had passed.

Their city home was a beautiful one, and their connections and associations were such as to surround them at once with the most desirable companionships. At first it was hard for Ellen to readjust her system of living and to accustom herself to the demands of even a moderately social life. But she was by nature very fond of all such pleasures, and her house soon became one of the pleasantest centres, in a quiet way, of the comparatively quiet city. John Gray expanded and brightened in the new atmosphere; he had always been a man of influence among men. All his friends, —even his acquaintances,— loved him, and asked his advice. It was a strange thing that a man so inert and procrastinating in his own affairs, should be so shrewd and practical and influential in the affairs of others, or in public affairs. This, however, was no stranger than many other puzzling incongruities in John Gray's character. Since his college days he had never mingled at all in general society until this winter, after their removal to town; and it was with delight that I watched his enjoyment of people, and their evident liking and admiration for him. His manners were singularly simple and direct; his face, which was not wholly pleasing in repose, was superbly handsome when animated in conversation; its inscrutable reticence which baffled the keenest observation when he was silent, all disappeared and melted in the glow of cordial good-fellowship which lighted every feature when he talked. I grew very proud of my brother as I watched him in his new sphere and surroundings; and I also enjoyed most keenly seeing Ellen in a wider and more appreciative circle. I spent a large part of the first winter in their house, and shared all their social pleasures, and looked forward to ever increasing delight, as my nieces should grow old enough to enter into society.

Early in the spring I went to the West and passed the entire summer with relatives; I heard from my sister every week; her letters were always cheerful and natural, and I returned to her in the autumn, full of anticipations of another gay and pleasant winter.

They met me in New York, and I remembered afterwards, though in the excitement of the moment I gave it no second thought, that when John Gray's eyes first met mine, there was in them a singular and indefinable expression, which roused in me an instant sense of distrust and antagonism. He had never thoroughly liked me. He had always had an undercurrent of fear of me. He knew I thought him weak: he felt that I had never put full confidence in him. That I really and truly loved him was small offset for this. Would it not be so to all of us?

This part of my story is best told in few words. I had not been at home one week before I found that rumor had been for some months coupling John Gray's name with the name of Mrs. Emma Long, a widow who had but just returned to ———, after twelve years of married life in Cuba. John had known her in her girlhood, but there had never been any intimacy or even friendship between them. My sister, however, had known her well, had corresponded with her during all her life at the South, and had invited her to her house immediately upon her return to ———. Emma Long was a singularly fascinating woman. Plain and sharp and self-asserting at twenty-two, she had become at thirty-five magnetic and winning, full of tact, and almost beautiful. We see such surprising developments continually: it seems as if nature did her best to give every woman one period of triumph and conquest; perhaps only they know its full sweetness to whom it comes late. In early youth it is accepted unthinkingly, as is the sunshine,—enjoyed without deliberation, and only weighed at its fullness when it is over. But a woman who begins at thirty to feel for the first time what it is to have power over men, must be more or less than woman not to find the knowledge and the consciousness dangerously sweet.

I never knew—I do not know to-day, whether Emma Long could be justly called a coquette. That she keenly enjoyed the admiration of men, there was no doubt. Whether she ever were conscious of even a possible harm to them from their relation to her, there was always doubt, even in the minds of her bitterest enemies. I myself have never doubted that in the affair between her and John Gray she was the one who suffered most; she was the one who had a true, deep sentiment, and not only never meant a wrong, but would have shrunk, for his sake, if not for her own, from the dangers which she did not foresee, but which were inevitable in their intimacy. I think that her whole life afterward proved this. I think that even my sister believed it.

Mrs. Long had spent six weeks in my sister's house, and had then established herself in a very beautiful furnished house on the same street. Almost every day Mrs. Long's carriage was at my sister's door, to take my sister or the children to drive. Almost every evening Mrs. Long came with the easy familiarity of an habituated guest in the house, to sit in my sister's parlor, or sent with the easy familiarity of an old friend for my sister and her husband to come to her, or to go with her to the theatre or to the opera.

What could be more natural?—what could be more delightful, had the relation been one which centred around my sister instead of around my sister's husband? What could be done, what offense could be taken, what obstacle interposed, so long as the relation appeared to be one which included the whole family? Yet no human being could see John Gray five minutes in Emma Long's presence without observing that his eyes, his words, his consciousness were hers. And no one could observe her in his presence without seeing that she was kindled, stimulated, as she was in no other companionship.

All this the city had been seeing and gossiping over for four months. All this, with weary detail, was poured into my ears by kind friends.

My sister said no word. For the first time in my life there was a barrier between us I dared not pass. Her every allusion to Mrs. Long was in the kindest and most unembarrassed manner. She fell heartily and graciously into every plan which brought them together: she not only did this, she also fully reciprocated all entertainments and invitations; it was as often by Ellen's arrangement as by Mrs. Long's that an evening or a day was spent by the two families together. Her manner to Mrs. Long was absolutely unaltered. Her manner to John was absolutely unaltered. When during an entire evening he sat almost motionless and often quite speechless, listening to Mrs. Long's conversation with others, Ellen's face never changed. She could not have seemed more unconscious if he had been blind. There were many bonds of sympathy between John Gray and Emma Long, which had never existed between him and his wife. They were both passionately fond of art and had studied it. Ellen's taste was undeveloped, and her instinctive likings those of a child. But she listened with apparent satisfaction and pleasure to long hours of conversation, about statues, pictures, principles of art, of which she was as unable to speak as one of her own babies would have been. Mrs. Long was also a woman who understood affairs; and one of her great charms to men of mind was the clear, logical, and yet picturesque and piquant way in which she talked of men and events. Ellen listened and laughed as heartily as any member of the circle at her repartee, her brilliant characterization, her offhand description.

To John Gray all this was a new revelation. He had never known this sort of woman. That a woman would be clever as men are clever, and also be graceful, adorned, and tender with womanliness, he had not supposed.

Ah, poor Emma Long! not all my loyalty to my sister ever quite stifled in my heart the question whether there was not in Mrs. Long's nature something which John Gray really needed—something which Ellen, affectionate, wise, upright, womanly woman as she was, could never give to any man.

The winter wore on. Idle and malicious tongues grew busier and busier. Nothing except the constant presence of my sister wherever her husband and Mrs. Long were seen together, prevented the scandal from taking the most offensive shape. But Ellen was so wise, so watchful, that not even the most malignant gossipmonger, could point to anything like a clandestine intercourse between the two.

In fact, they met so constantly either in Mrs. Long's house or my sister's that there was small opportunity for them to meet elsewhere. I alone knew that on many occasions when Mrs. Long was spending the evening at our house, Ellen availed herself of one excuse or another to leave them alone for a great part of the time. But she did this so naturally, that is, with such perfect art, that not until long afterward did I know that it had been intentional. This was one great reason for my silence during all these months. In her apparent ignorance and unsuspiciousness of the whole thing, she seemed so gay, so happy, so sweet and loving, how could I give her a pain? And if she did not see it now, she might never see it. It could never surely become any more apparent. No man could give, so far as simple manner was concerned, more unmistakable proof of being absorbed in passionate love for a woman, than John Gray gave in Emma Long's presence. I began to do Ellen injustice in my thoughts. I said, "After all, she has not much heart; no woman who loved a man passionately could look on unmoved and see him so absorbed in another."

How little I knew! Towards spring Ellen suddenly began to look ill. She lost color and strength, and a slight cough which she had had all winter became very severe. Her husband was alarmed. We all were distressed. Our old family physician, Dr. Willis, changed color when he felt Ellen's pulse, and said, involuntarily,—

"My dear child, how long have you had such fever as this?"

Ellen changed color too under his steady look, and replied,—

"I think, doctor, I have had a little fever for some weeks. I have not felt really well since the autumn, and I have been meaning for some time to have a long consultation with you. But we will not have it now," she added playfully, "I have a great deal to tell you which these good people are not to hear. We will talk it over some other time," and she looked at him so meaningly that he understood the subject must be dropped.

That night she told me that she wished me to propose to John to go over with me and spend the evening at Mrs. Long's; that she had sent for Dr. Willis, and she wished to have a long talk with him without John's knowing it.

"Dear," said I hastily, "I will not go to Mrs. Long's with John. I hate Mrs. Long."

"Why, Sally, what do you mean! I never heard you so unjust. Emma is one of the very sweetest women I ever saw in my life. How can you say such a thing! Everybody loves and admires her. Don't go if you feel so. I never dreamed that you disliked her. But I thought John would be less likely to suspect me of any desire to have him away, if you proposed going there; and I must have him out of the house. I cannot talk with the doctor if he is under the roof." She said these last words with an excited emphasis so unlike her usual manner, that it frightened me. But I thought only of her physical state; I feared that she suspected the existence of some terrible disease.

I went with John to Mrs. Long's almost immediately after tea. He accepted the proposal with unconcealed delight; and I wondered if Ellen observed the very nonchalant way in which he replied when she said she did not feel well enough to go. He already like better to see Mrs. Long without his wife's presence, cordial and unembarrassed as her manner always was. His secret consciousness was always disturbed by it.

When we reached Mrs. Long's house, we learned that she had gone out to dinner. John's face became black with the sudden disappointment, and quite forgetting himself, he exclaimed: "Why, what does that mean? She did not tell me she was going."

The servant stared, but made no reply. I was confused and indignant; but John went on: "We will come in and wait. I am sure it is some very informal dinner, and Mrs. Long will soon be at home."

I made no remonstrance, knowing that it might annoy and disturb Ellen to have us return. John threw himself into a chair in front of the fire, and looked moodily into the coals, making no attempt at conversation. I took up a book. Very soon John rose, sauntered abstractedly about the room, took up Mrs. Long's work-basket, and examined every article in it, and at last sat down before her little writing-desk, which stood open. Presently I saw that he was writing. More than an hour passed. I pretended to read; but I watched my brother-in-law's face. I could not mistake its language. Suddenly there came a low cry of delight from the door, "Why, John!"

Mrs. Long had entered the house by a side door, and having met no servant before reaching the drawing-room, was unprepared for finding any one there. From the door she could see John, but could not see me, except in the long mirror, to which she did not raise her eyes, but in which I saw her swift movement, her outstretched hands, her look of unspeakable gladness. In less than a second, however, she had seen me, and with no perceptible change of manner had come rapidly towards me, holding out her left hand familiarly to him, as she passed him. Emma Long was not a hypocrite at heart, but she had an almost superhuman power of acting. It was all lost upon me, however, on that occasion. I observed the quick motion with which John thrust into a compartment of the desk, the sheet on which he had been writing; I observed the clasp of their hands as she glided by him; I observed her face; I observed his; and I knew as I had never fully known before how intensely they loved each other.

My resolution was taken. Cost what it might, come what might, I would speak fully and frankly to my sister the next day. I would not longer stand by and see this thing go on. At that moment I hated both John Gray and Emma Long. No possible pain to Ellen seemed to me to weigh for a moment against my impulse to part them.

I could not talk. I availed myself of the freedom warranted by the intimacy between the families, and continued to seem absorbed in my book. But I lost no word, no look, which passed between the two who sat opposite me. I never saw Emma Long look so nearly beautiful as she did that night. She wore a black velvet dress, with fine white lace ruffles at the throat and wrists. Her hair was fair, and her complexion of that soft pale tint, with a slight undertone of brown in it, which is at once fair and warm, and which can kindle in moments of excitement into a brilliance far outshining any

brunette skin. She talked rapidly with much gesture. She was giving
John an account of the stupidity of the people with whom she had
been dining. Her imitative faculty amounted almost to genius. No
smallest peculiarity of manner or speech escaped her, and she could
become a dozen different persons in a minute. John laughed as he
listened, but not so heartily as he was wont to laugh at her humorous
sayings. He had been too deeply stirred in the long interval of
solitude before she returned. His cheeks were flushed and his voice
unsteady. She soon felt the effect of his manner, and her gayety
died away; before long they were sitting in silence, each looking at
the fire. I knew I ought to make the proposition to go home, but I
seemed under a spell: I was conscious of a morbid desire to watch
and wait. At length Mrs. Long rose, saying,—

"If it will not disturb Sally's reading, I will play for you a lovely
little thing I learned yesterday."

"Oh, no," said I. "But we must go as soon as I finish this chapter."

She passed into the music-room and looked back for John to
follow her; but he threw himself at full length on the sofa, and
said,—

"No, I will listen here."

My quickened instinct saw that he dared not go; also that he had
laid his cheek in the abandonment of ecstasy on the arm of the sofa
on which her hand had been resting. Even in that moment I had a
sharp pang of pity for him, and the same old misgiving of question,
whether my good and sweet and almost faultless Ellen could be
loved just in the same way in which Emma Long would be!

As soon as she had finished the nocturne, a sad, low sweet strain,
she came back to the parlor. Not even for the pleasure of giving
John the delight of the music he loved would she stay where she
could not see his face.

But I had already put down my book, and was ready to go. Our
good-nights were short and more formal than usual. All three were
conscious of an undefined constraint in the air. Mrs. Long glanced
up uneasily in John's face as we left the room. Her eyes were
unutterably tender and childlike when a look of grieved perplexity
shadowed them. Again my heart ached for her and for him. This
was no idle caprice, no mere entanglement of senses between two
unemployed and unprincipled hearts. It was a subtle harmony,
organic, spiritual, intellectual, between two susceptible and intense

natures. The bond was as natural and inevitable as any other fact of nature. And in this very fact lay the terrible danger.

We walked home in silence. A few steps from our house we met Dr. Willis walking very rapidly. He did not recognize us at first. When he did, he half stopped as if about to speak, then suddenly changed his mind, and merely bowing, passed on. A bright light was burning in Ellen's room.

"Why, Ellen has not gone to bed!" exclaimed John.

"Perhaps some one called," said I, guiltily.

"Oh, I dare say," replied he; "perhaps the doctor has been there. But it is half-past twelve," added he, pulling out his watch as we entered the hall. "He could not have stayed until this time."

I went to my own room immediately. In a few moments I heard John come up, say a few words to Ellen, and then go down-stairs, calling back, as he left her room,—

"Don't keep awake for me, wifie, I have a huge batch of letters to answer. I shall not get through before three o'clock."

I crept noiselessly to Ellen's room. It was dark. She had extinguished the gas as soon as she had heard us enter the house! I knew by the first sound of her voice that she had been weeping violently and long. I said—

"Ellen, I must come in and have a talk with you."

"Not to-night, dear. To-morrow I will talk over everything. All is settled. Good-night. Don't urge me to-night. Sally. I can't bear any more."

It is strange—it is marvellous what power there is in words to mean more than words. I knew as soon as Ellen had said, "Not to-night, dear," that she divined all I wanted to say, that she knew all I knew, and that the final moment, the crisis, had come. Whatever she might have to tell me in the morning, I should not be surprised. I did not sleep. All night I tossed wearily, trying to conjecture what Ellen would do, trying to imagine what I should do in her place.

At breakfast Ellen seemed better than she had seemed for weeks. Her eyes were bright and her cheeks pink; but there was an ineffable, almost solemn tenderness in her manner to John, which was pathetic. Again the suspicion crossed my mind that she knew that she must die. He too was disturbed by it; he looked at her constantly with a lingering gaze as if trying to read her face; and when he bade us good-bye to go to the office, he kissed her over and over as I had not seen him kiss her for months. The tears came into her eyes, and she threw both arms around his neck for a second,—a very rare thing for her to do in the presence of others.

"Why, wifie," he said, "you musn't make it too hard for a fellow to get off!—Doesn't she look well this morning, Sally?" turning to me. "I was thinking last night that I must take her to the mountains as soon as it was warm enough. But such cheeks as these don't need it." And he took her face in his two hands with a caress full of tenderness, and sprang down the steps.

Just at this moment Mrs. Long's carriage came driving swiftly around the corner, and the driver stopped suddenly at sight of John.

"Oh, Mr. Gray, Mr. Gray!" called Emma, "I was just coming to take Ellen and the children for a turn, and we can leave you at the office on our way."

"Thank you, " said John, "but there are several persons I must see before going to the office, and it would detain you too long. I am already much too late," and without a second look he hurried on.

I saw a slight color rise in Mrs. Long's cheek, but no observer less jealous than I would have detected it; and there was not a shade less warmth than usual in her manner to Ellen.

Ellen told her that she could not go herself, but she would be very glad to have some of the children go; and then she stood for some moments, leaning on the carriage-door and talking most animatedly. I looked from one woman to the other. Ellen at that moment was more beautiful than Mrs. Long. The strong, serene, upright look which was her most distinguishing and characteristic expression, actually shone on her face. I wished that John Gray had stopped to see the two face side by side. Emma Long might be the woman to stir and thrill and entrance the soul; to give stimulus to the intellectual nature; to rouse passionate emotion; but Ellen was the woman on whose stead-fastness he could rest,—in the light of whose sweet integrity and transparent truthfulness he was a far safer, and would be a far stronger man than with any other woman in the world.

As the carriage drove away with all three of the little girls laughing and shouting and clinging around Mrs. Long, a strange pang seized me. I looked at Ellen. She stood watching them with a smile which had something heavenly in it. Turning suddenly to me, she said:

"Sally, if I were dying, it would make me very happy to know that Emma Long would be the mother of my children."

I was about to reply with a passionate ejaculation, but she interrupted me.

"Hush, dear, hush. I am not going to die,—I have no fear of any such thing. Come to my room now, and I will tell you all."

She locked the door, stood for a moment looking at me very earnestly, then folded me in her arms and kissed me many times; then she made me sit in the large arm-chair, and drawing up a low foot-stool, sat down at my feet, rested both arms on my lap, and began to speak. I shall try to tell in her own words what she said.

"Sally, I want to tell you in the beginning how I thank you for your silence. All winter I have known that you were seeing all I saw, feeling all I felt, and keeping silent for my sake. I never can tell you how much I thank you; it was the one thing which supported me. It was an unspeakable comfort to know that you sympathized with me at every point; but to have had the sympathy expressed even by a look would have made it impossible for me to bear up. As long as I live, darling, I shall be grateful to you. And, moreover, it makes it possible for me to trust you unreservedly now. I had always done you injustice, Sally. I did not think you had so much self-control."

Here she hesitated an instant. It was not easy for her to mention John's name; but it was only for a second that she hesitated. With an impetuous eagerness unlike herself, she went on.

"Sally you must not blame John. He has struggled as constantly and nobly as a man ever struggled. Neither must you blame Emma. They have neither of them done wrong. I have watched them both hour by hour. I know my husband's nature so thoroughly that I know his very thoughts almost as soon as he knows them himself. I know his emotions before he knows them himself. I saw the first moment in which his eyes rested on Emma's face as they used to rest on mine. From that day to this I have known every phase, every step, every change of his feeling towards her; and I tell you, Sally, that I pity John from the bottom of my heart. I understand it all far better than you can, far better than he does. He loves her at once far more and far less than you believe, and he loves me far more than you believe! You will say, in the absolute idealization of your inexperienced heart, that this is impossible. I know that it is not, and I wish I could make you believe it, for without believing it you cannot be just to John. He loves me to-day, in spite of all this, with a sort of clinging tenderness born of this very struggle. He would far rather love me with all his nature if he could, but just now he cannot. I see very clearly where Emma gives him what he needs, and has never had in me. I have learned many things from Emma Long this winter. I can never be like her. But I need not have been so unlike her as I was. She has armed me with weapons when she least suspected it. But she is not after all, on the whole, so nearly what John needs as I am. If I really believed that he would be a better man, or even a happier one with her as his wife, I should have but one desire, and that would be to die. But I think that it is not so. I believe that is is in my power to do for him, and to be to him, what she never could. I do not wonder that you look pityingly and incredulously. You will see. But in order to do this, I must leave him."

I sprang to my feet. "Leave him! Are you mad?"

"No, dear, not at all; very sane and very determined. I have been for six months coming to this resolve. I began to think of it in a very few hours after I first saw him look at Emma as if he loved her. I have thought of it day and night since, and I know I am right. If I stay, I shall lose his love. If I go, I shall keep it, regain it, compel it." She spoke here more hurriedly. "I have borne now all I can bear without betraying my pain to him. I am jealous of Emma. It almost kills me to see him look at her, speak to her."

"My poor, poor darling!" I exclaimed; "and I have been thinking you did not feel it!"

She smiled sadly, and tossed back the sleeve of her wrapper so as to show her arm to the shoulder. I started. It was almost emaciated. I had again and again in the course of the winter asked her why she did not wear her usual syle of evening dress, and she had replied that it was on account of her cough.

"It is well that my face does not show loss of flesh as quickly as the rest of my body does," she said quietly. "I have lost thirty-five pounds of flesh in four months, and nobody observed it! Yes, dear," she went on, "I have felt it. More than that, I have felt it increasingly every hour, and I can bear no more. Up to this time I have never by look or tone shown to John that I knew it. He wonders every hour what it means that I do not. I have never by so much as the slightest act watched him. I have seen notes in Emma's handwriting lying on his desk, and I have left the house lest I might be tempted to read them! I know that he has as yet done no clandestine thing, but at any moment I should have led them both into it by showing one symptom of jealousy. And I should have roused in his heart a feeling of irritation and impatience with me, which would have done in one hour more to intensify his love for her, and to change its nature from a pure involuntary sentiment into an acknowledged and guilty one, than years and years of free intercourse could do. But I have reached the limit of my physical endurance. My nerves are giving away. I am really very ill, but nothing is out of order in my body aside from the effects of this anguish. A month more of this would make me a hopelessly broken-down woman. A month's absence from the sight of it will almost make me well."

I could not refrain from interrupting her.

"Ellen, you are mad! you are mad! You mean to go away and leave him to see her constantly alone, unrestrained by your presence? It has almost killed you to see it. How can you bear imagining it, knowing it?"

"Better than I can bear seeing it, far better. Because I have still undiminished confidence in the real lastingness of the bond between John and me. Emma Long would have been no doubt a good, a very good wife for him. But I am the mother of his children, and just so surely as right is right, and wrong is wrong, he will return to me and to them. All wrong things are like diseases, self-limited. It is wrong for a man to love any woman better than he loves his wife; I don't deny that, dear," she said, half smiling through her tears at my indignant face; "but a man may seem to do it when he is really very far from it. He may really do it for days, for months— for years, perhaps; but if he be a true man, and his wife a true wife, he will return. John is a true husband and a still truer father: that I am the mother of his five children, he can never forget. If I had had no children, it would be different. If I had ever been for one moment an unloving wife, it would be different; but I am his; I believe that he is mine; and that I shall live to remind you of all these things, Sally, after time has proved them true."

I was almost dumb with surprise. I was astounded. To me it seemed that her plan was simply suicidal. I told her in the strongest words I could use of the scene of the night before.

I could tell you of still more trying scenes than that, Sally. I know far more than you. But if I knew ten times as much, I should still believe that my plan is the only one. Of course I may fail. It is all in God's hands. We none of us know how much discipline we need. But I know one thing: if I do not regain John in this way, I cannot in any. If I stay I shall annoy, vex, disturb, torture him! Once the barriers of my silence and concealment are broken down, I shall do just what all other jealous women have done since the world began. There are no torments on earth like those which a jealous woman inflicts, except those which she bears! I will die sooner than inflict them on John. Even if the result proves me mistaken, I shall never regret my course, for I know that the worst is certain if I remain. But I have absolute faith,"—and her face was transfigured with it as she spoke,—"John is mine. If I could stay by his side through it all and preserve the same relation with him which I have all winter, all would sooner or later be well. I wish I were strong enough. My heart is, but my body is not, and I must go."

When she told me the details of her plan, I was more astounded than ever. She had taken Dr. Willis into her full confidence. (He had been to us father and physician both ever since our father's death.) He entirely approved of her course. He was to say—which indeed he could do conscientiously—that her health imperatively required an entire change of climate, and that he had advised her to spend at least one year abroad. It had always been one of John's and Ellen's air-castles to take all the children to England and to Germany for some years of study. She proposed to take the youngest four, leaving the eldest girl, who was her father's special pet and companion, to stay with him. A maiden aunt of ours was to come and keep the house, and I was to stay with the family. This was the hardest of all.

"Ellen, I cannot!" I exclaimed. "Do not—oh, do not trust me. I shall never have strength. I shall betray all some day and ruin all your hopes."

"You cannot, you dare not, Sally, when I tell you that my life's whole happiness lies in your silence. John is unobservant and also unsuspicious. He has never had an intimate relation with you. You

will have no difficulty. But you must be here,—because, dear, there
is another reason," and here her voice grew very unsteady, and tear
ran down her cheeks.

"In spite of all my faith, I do not disguise from myself the
possibility of the worst. I cannot believe my husband would ever
do a dishonorable thing. I do not believe that Emma Long would.
And yet, when I remember what ruin has overtaken many men and
women whom we believed upright, I dare not be wholly sure. And
I must know that some one is here who would see and understand
if a time were approaching at which it would be needful for me to
make one last effort with and for my husband face to face with him.
Unless that comes, I do not wish you to allude to the subject in
your letters. I think I know how all things will go. I believe that in
one year, or less, all will be well. But if the worst is to come, you
with your instincts will foresee it, and I must be told. I should
return then at once. I should have power, even at the last moment,
I believe, to save John from disgrace. But I should lose his love
irrecoverably; it is to save that that I go."

I could say but few words. I was lifted up and borne out of
myself, as it were by my sister's exaltation. She seemed more like
some angel-wife than like a mortal woman. Before I left her room
at noon, I believed almost as fully as she did in the wisdom and
the success of her plan.

There was no time to be lost. Every day between the announce-
ment of her purpose and the carrying of it out, would be a fearful
strain on Ellen's nerves. Dr. Willis had a long talk with John in his
office while Ellen was talking with me. John came home to dinner
looking like a man who had received a mortal blow. Dr. Willis had
purposely given him to understand that Ellen's life was in great
danger. So it was, but not from the cough! At first John's vehement
purpose was to go with them. But she was prepared for this. His
business and official relations were such that it was next to impossible
for him to do it, and it would at best involve a great pecuniary
sacrifice. She overrulled and remonstrated, and was so firm in her
objections to every suggestion of his accompanying or following
her, that finally, in spite of all his anxiety, John seemed almost
piqued at her preference for going alone. In every conversation on
the subject I saw more and more clearly that Ellen was right. He
did love—love her warmly, devotedly.

Two weeks from the day of my conversation with her they sailed for Liverpool. The summer was to be spent in England, and the winter in Nice or Mentone.

Alice, the eldest daughter, a loving, sunshiny girl of twelve was installed in her mother's room. This was Ellen's special wish. She knew that in this way John would be drawn to the room constantly. All her own little belongings were given to Alice.

"Only think, Auntie," said she, "mamma has given me, all for my own, her lovely toilette set, and all the Bohemian glass on the bureau, and her ivory brushes! She says when she comes home she shall refurnish her room and papa's too!"

Oh, my wise Ellen. Could Emma Long have done more subtly!

Early on the first evening after John returned from New York, having seen them off, I missed him. I said bitterly to myself, "At Mrs. Long's, I suppose," and went up-stairs to find Alice. As I drew near her room I heard his voice, reading aloud. I went in. He and Alice were lying together on the broad chintz-covered lounge as I had so often seen him and Ellen.

"Oh, Auntie, come here," said Alice, "hear mamma's letter to me! She gave it to papa in New York. She says it is like the sealed orders they give to captains sometimes, not to be opened till they are out at sea. It is all about how I am to fill her place to papa. And there are ever so many little notes inside, more orders, which even papa himself is not to see! only I suppose he'll recognize the things when I do them!"

At that moment, as I watched John Gray's face, with Alice's nestled close, and his arms clasped tight around her, while they read Ellen's letter, a great load rolled off my heart. I went through many dark days afterwards, but I never could quite despair when I remembered the fatherhood and the husbandhood which were in his eyes and his voice that night.

The story of the next twelve months could be told in few words, so far as its external incidents are concerned. It could not be told in a thousand volumes, if I attempted to reproduce the subtle undercurrents of John Gray's life and mine. Each of us was living a double life; he more or less unconsciously; I with such sharpened senses, such overwrought emotions, that I only wonder that my health did not give way. I endured vicariously all the suspense and torment of the deepest jealousy, with a sense of more than vicarious responsibility added, which was almost more than human nature could bear. Ellen little knew how heavy would be the burden she laid upon me. Her most express and explicit direction was that the familiar intimacy between our family and Mrs. Long's was to be preserved unaltered. This it would have been impossible for me to do if Mrs. Long had not herself recognized the necessity of it, for her own full enjoyment of John's society. But it was a hard thing; my aunt, the ostensible head of our house, was a quiet woman who had nothing whatever to do with society, and who felt in the outset a great shrinking from the brilliant Mrs. Long. I had never been on intimate terms with her, so that John and Alice were really the only members of the household who could keep up precisely the old relation. And so it gradually came about that to most of our meetings under each other's roofs, strangers were asked to fill up the vacant places, and in spite of all Emma Long's efforts and mine, there was a change in the atmosphere of our intercourse. But there was intimacy enough to produce the effect for which Ellen was most anxious, *i.e.*, to extend the shelter of our recognition to the friendship between John and Emma, and to remove from them both all temptation to anything clandestine or secret. They still saw each other almost daily; they still shared most of each other's interests and pleasures; they still showed most undisguised delight in each other's presence. Again and again I went with them to the opera, to the theatre, and sat through the long hours, watching, with a pain which seemed to me hardly less than Ellen's would have been, their constant sympathy with each other in every point of enjoyment, their constant forgetfulness of every one else.

But there was, all this time, another side to John Gray's life, which I saw, and Emma Long did not see. By every steamer came packages of the most marvelous letters from Ellen: letters to us all; but for John, a diary of every hour of her life. Each night she spent two hours in writing out the record of the day. I have never seen letters which so reproduced the atmosphere of the day, the scene, the heart. They were brilliant and effective to a degree that utterly astonished me; but they were also ineffably tender and loving, and so natural in their every word, that it was like seeing Ellen face to face to read them. At first John did not show them even to me; but soon he began to say, "These are too rare to be kept to myself; I must just read you this account;" or, "Here is a page I must read," until it at last became his habit to read them aloud in the evenings to the family, and even to more intimate friends who chanced to be with us. He grew proud beyond expression of Ellen's talent for writing; and well he might. No one who listened to them but exclaimed, "There never were such letters before!!" I think there never were. And I alone knew the secret of them.

But these long, brilliant letters were not all. In every mail came also packages for Alice—secret, mysterious things which nobody could see, but which proved to be sometimes small notes, to be given to papa at unexpected times and places; sometimes little fancy articles, as a pen-wiper, or a cigar-case, half worked by Ellen, to be finished by Alice, and given to papa on some especial day, the significance of which "only mamma knows;" sometimes a pressed flower, which was to be put by papa's plate at breakfast, or put in papa's button-hole as he went out in the morning. I was more and more lost in astonishment at the subtle and boundless art of love which could so contrive to reach across an ocean, and surround a man's daily life with its expression. There were also in every package, letters to John from all the children: even the baby's little hand was guided to write by every mail, "Dear papa, I love you just as much as all the rest do!" or, "Dear papa, I want you to toss me up!" More than once I saw tears roll down John's face in spite of him, as he slowly deciphered these illegible little scrawls. The older children's notes were vivid and living like their mother's. It was evident that they were having a season of royal delight in their journey, but also evident that their thoughts and their longings were constantly reverting to papa. How much Ellen really indited of these apparently spontaneous letters I do not know; but no doubt their tone was in part created by her. They showed, even more than did her own letters, that papa was still the centre of the family life. No sight was seen without the wish—"Oh, if papa were here!" and even little Mary, aged five, was making a collection of pressed leaves for papa, from all the places they visited. Louise had already great talent for drawing, and in almost every letter came two or three childish but spirited little pictures, all labelled "Drawn for papa!" "The true picture of our courier in a rage, for papa to see." "The washerwoman's dog, for papa," etc., etc. Again and again I sat by, almost trembling with delight, and saw John spend an entire evening in looking over these little missives and reading Ellen's letters. Then again I sat alone and anxious through an entire evening, when I knew he was with Emma Long. But even after such an evening, he never failed to sit down and write pages in his journal-letter to Ellen—a practice which he began of his own accord, after receiving the first journal-letter from her.

"Ha! little Alice," he said, "we'll keep a journal too, for mamma, won't we! She shall not out-do us that way." And so, between Alice's letters and his, the whole record of our family life went every week to Ellen; and I do not believe, so utterly unaware was John Gray of any pain in his wife's heart about Emma Long, I do not believe that he ever in a single instance omitted to mention when he had been with her, where, and how long.

Emma Long wrote too, and Ellen wrote to her occasional affectionate notes; but referring her always to John's diary-letters for the details of interest. I used to study Mrs. Long's face while these letters were read to her. John's animated delight, his enthusiastic pride, must, it seemed to me, have been bitter to her. But I never saw even a shade of such a feeling in her face. There was nothing base or petty in Emma Long's nature, and, strange as it may seem, she did love Ellen. Only once did I ever see a trace of pique or resentment in her manner to John, and then I could not wonder at it. A large package had come from Ellen, just after tea one night, and we were all gathered in the library, reading our letters and looking at the photograph— (she always sent unmounted photographs of the place from which she wrote, and, if possible, of the house in which they were living, and the children often wrote above the windows, "*Papa's* and mamma's room," etc, etc.)—hour after hour passed. The hall clock had just struck ten, when the dooor-bell rang violently. "Good heavens!" exclaimed John, spring-ing up, "That must be Mrs. Long; I totally forgot that I had promised to go with her to Mrs. Willis's party. I said I would be there at nine; tell her I am up-stairs dressing," and he was gone before the servant had had time to open the door. Mrs. Long came in, with a flushed face and anxious look. "Is Mr. Gray ill?" she said. "He promised to call for me at nine, to go to Mrs. Willis's and I have been afraid he might be ill."

Before I could reply, the unconscious Alice exclaimed,—

"Oh, no; papa isn't ill; he is so sorry, but he forgot all about the party till he heard you ring the bell. We were so busy over mamma's letters."

"John will be down in a moment," added I. "He ran up-stairs to dress as soon as you rang."

For one second Emma Long's face was sad to see. Such astonishment, such pain, were in it, my heart ached for her. Then a look of angry resentment succeeded the pain, and merely saying "I am very sorry; but I really cannot wait for him. It is now almost too late to go," she had left the room and closed the outer door before I could think of any words to say.

I ran up to John's room, and told him through the closed door. He made no reply for a moment, and then said,—

"No wonder she is vexed. It was unpardonable rudeness. Tell Robert to run at once for a carriage for me."

In a very few moments he came down dressed for the party, but with no shadow of disturbance on his face. He was still thinking of the letters. He took up his own, and putting it into the inside breast-pocket, said as he kissed Alice, "Papa will take mamma's letter to the party, if he can't take mamma!"

I shed grateful tears that night before I went to sleep. How I longed to write to Ellen of the incident; but I had resolved not once to disregard her request that the whole subject be a sealed one. And I trusted that Alice would remember to tell it. Well I might! At breakfast Alice said,—

"Oh, papa, I told mamma that you carried her to the party in your breast-pocket; that is, you carried her letter!"

I fancied that John's cheek flushed a little as he said,—

"You might tell mamma that papa carries her everywhere in his breast-pocket, little girlie, and mamma would understand."

I think from that day I never feared for Ellen's future. I fancied, too, that from that day there was a new light in John Gray's eyes. Perhaps it might have been only the new light in my own; but I think when a man knows that he has once, for one hour, forgotten a promise to meet a woman whose presence has been dangerously dear to him, he must be aware of his dawning freedom.

The winter was nearly over. Ellen had said nothing to us about returning.

"Dr. Willis tells me that, from what Ellen writes to him of her health, he thinks it would be safer for her to remain abroad another year," said John to me one morning at breakfast.

"Oh, she never will stay another year!" exclaimed I.

"Not unless I go out to stay with her," said John, very quietly.

"Oh, John, could you?" and "Oh, papa, will you take me?" exclaimed Alice and I in one breath.

"Yes," and "yes," said John, laughing, "and Sally too, if she will go."

He then proceeded to tell me that he had been all winter contemplating this; that he believed they would never again have so good an opportunity to travel in Europe, and that Dr. Willis's hesitancy about Ellen's health had decided the question. He had been planning and deliberating as silently and unsuspectedly as Ellen had done the year before. Never once had it crossed my mind that he desired it, or that it could be. But I found that he had for the last half of the year been arranging his affairs with a view to it, and had entered into new business connections which would make it not only easy, but profitable, for him to remain abroad two years. He urged me to go with them, but I refused. I felt that the father and the mother and the children ought to be absolutely alone in this blessed reunion, and I have never regretted my decision, although the old world is yet an unknown world to me.

John Gray was a reticent and undemonstrative man, in spite of all the tenderness and passionateness in his nature. But when he bade me good-by on the deck of the steamer, as he kissed me he whispered:—

"Sally, I shall hold my very breath till I see Ellen. I never knew how I loved her before." And the tears stood in his eyes.

I never saw Emma Long after she knew that John was to go abroad to join Ellen. I found myself suddenly without courage to look in her face. The hurry of my preparations for Alice was ample excuse for my not going to her house, and she did not come to ours. I knew that John spent several evenings with her, and came home late, with a sad and serious face, and that was all. A week before he sailed she joined a large and gay party for San Francisco and the Yosemite. In all the newspaper accounts of the excursion, Mrs. Long was spoken of as the brilliant centre of all festivities. I understood well that this was the first reaction of her proud and sensitive nature under an irremediable pain. She never returned to

————, but established herself in a Southern city, where she lived in great retirement for a year, doing good to all poor and suffering people, and spending the larger part of her fortune in charity. Early in the second year there was an epidemic of yellow fever: Mrs. Long refused to leave the city, and went as fearlessly as the physicians to visit and nurse the worst cases. But after the epidemic had passed by, she herself was taken ill, and died suddenly in a hospital ward, surrounded by the very patients whom she had nursed back to health.

Nothing I could say in my own words would give so vivid an idea of the meeting between John Gray and his wife, as the first letter which I received from little Alice:—

"DARLING AUNTIE,—

"It is too bad you did not come too. The voyage was horrid. Papa was so much sicker than I, that I had to take care of him all the time; but my head ached so that I kept seeing black spots if I stooped over to kiss papa; but papa said, I was just like another mamma.

"Oh, Auntie, only think, there was a mistake about the letters, and mamma never got the letter to tell her that we were coming; and she was out on the balcony of the hotel when we got out of the carriage, and first she saw me; and the lady who was with her said she turned first red and then so white the lady thought she was sick; and then the next minute she saw papa, and she just fell right down among all the people, and looked as if she was dead; and the very first thing poor papa and I saw, when we got up-stairs, was mamma being carried by two men, and papa and I both thought she was dead; and papa fell right down on his knees, and made the men put mamma down on the floor, and everybody talked out loud, and papa never spoke a word, but just looked at mamma, and nobody knew who papa was till I spoke, and I said,—

"That's my mamma, and papa and I have just come all the way from America,"—and then a gentleman told me to kiss mamma, and I did; and then she opened her eyes; and just as soon as she saw papa, she got a great deal whiter and her head fell back again, and I was so sure she was dying, that I began to cry out loud, and I do think there were more than a hundred people all round us; but Louise says there were only ten or twelve; and then the same gentleman that told me to kiss mamma took hold of papa, and made him go away; and they carried mamma into a room, and laid her on a bed, and said we must all go out; but I wouldn't: I got right under the bed, and they didn't see me; and it seemed to me a thousand years before anybody spoke; and at last I heard mamma's voice, just as weak as a baby's—but you know nobody could mistake mamma's voice; and she said, 'Where is John—I saw John;' and then the gentleman said,—oh, I forgot to tell you he was a doctor, —he said,—

"My dear madam, calm yourself'—and then I cried right out again, and crept out between his legs and almost knocked him down; and said I, 'Don't you try to calm my mamma; it is papa—and me too, mamma!' and then mamma burst out crying; and then the old gentleman ran out, and I guess papa was at the door, for he came right in; and then he put his arms round mamma, and they didn't speak for so long, I thought I should die; and all the people were listening, and going up and down in the halls outside, and I felt so frightened and ashamed, for fear people would think mamma wasn't glad to see us. But papa says that is always the way when people are more glad than they can bear; and the surprise, too, was too much for anybody. But I said at the tea-table that I hoped I should never be so glad myself as long as I lived; and then the old gentleman,—he's a very nice old gentleman, and a great friend of mamma's and wears gold spectacles,—he said 'My dear little girl, I hope you *may* be some day just as glad,' and then he looked at papa and mamma and smiled,—and mamma almost cried again! Oh, altogether it was a horrid time; the worst I ever had; and so different from what papa and I thought it would be.

"But it's all over now, and we're all so happy, we laugh so all the time, that papa says it is disgraceful; that we shall have to go off and hide ourselves somewhere where people can't see us.

"But Auntie, you don't know how perfectly splendid mamma is. She is the prettiest lady in the hotel, Louise says. She is ever so much fatter than she used to be. And the baby has grown so I did not know her, and her curls are more than half a yard long. Louise and Mary have got their hair cut short like boys, but their gowns are splendid; they say it was such a pity you had any made for me at home. But oh, dear Auntie, don't think I shall not always like the gowns you made for me. Charlie isn't here; he's at some horrid school a great way off; I forget the name of the place. But we are all going there to live for the summer. Mamma said we should keep house in an 'apartment,' and I was perfectly horrified, and I said, 'Mamma, in one room?' and then Louise and Mary laughed till I was quite angry; but mamma says that here an 'apartment' means a set of a good many rooms, quite enough to live in. I don't believe you can have patience to read this long letter; but I haven't told you half; no, not one half of half. Goodby, you darling aunty.

ALICE."

"P.S.—I wish you could just see mamma. It isn't only me that thinks she is so pretty; papa thinks so too. He just sits and looks, and looks at her, till mamma doesn't quite like it, and asks him to look at baby a little!"

Ellen's first letter was short. Her heart was too full. She said at the end,—

"I suppose you will both laugh and cry over Alice's letter. At first I thought of suppressing it. But it gives you such a graphic picture of the whole scene that I shall let it go. It is well that I had the excuse of the surprise for my behavior, but I myself doubt very much if I should have done any better, had I been prepared for their coming.

"God bless and thank you, dear Sally, for this last year, as I cannot.

ELLEN."

These events happened many years ago. My sister and I are now old women. Her life has been from that time to this, one of the sunniest and most unclouded I ever knew.

John Gray is a hale old man; white-haired and bent, but clear-eyed and vigorous. All the good and lovable and pure in his nature have gone on steadily increasing: his love for his wife is still so full of sentiment and romance that the world remarks it.

His grandchildren will read these pages, no doubt, but they will never dream that it could have been their sweet and placid and beloved old grandmother who, through such sore straits in her youth, kept her husband!

Harriet Prescott Spofford

Her Story
1872

Harriet Elizabeth Prescott Spofford (1835–1921), during a prolific sixty-year career, wrote and published successfully in many literary genres: short stories, poems, novels, literary criticism, biography, memoirs, articles on domestic management, articles on travel, and literature for children in many of those genres. Although she had only six years of formal education, faculty at both schools she attended encouraged the development of literary talent and skill among their students. By the time she was sixteen, her talent had been recognized and encouraged by Thomas Wentworth Higginson, the Unitarian minister, editor, abolitionist, man of letters, and life-long supporter of women's rights and women writers. The well-received publication in the Atlantic Monthly *in 1859 of her story "In a Cellar," along with Higginson's sponsorship, led to her introduction to the Boston literary elite.*

In 1865 she married Richard Spofford, a young lawyer from her home town of Newburyport, Massachusetts, where the couple maintained a home among the homes of the members of their extended families for the rest of their lives. Their only child, a son, died in infancy. Spofford's husband, enthusiastic about her talent and her literary career, was devoted and supportive, often imaginatively so, taking the initiative to plan trips that would help her work.

Spofford's involvement with other women writers of her time and her interest in earlier women writers led her to write a biography of Charlotte Brontë and a critical introduction for an 1898 reprinting of Jane Eyre. *Spofford collaborated with Alice Brown and Louise Imogen Guiney on* Three Heroines of New England Romance *in 1895 and wrote the introduction to the 1909 collection of Louise Chandler Moulton's poetry. In 1916, Spofford published a collection of essays memorializing some of her friends, among whom were Annie Fields, Celia Thaxter, Gail Hamilton,*

Rose Terry Cooke, and Sarah Orne Jewett. There is also evidence of friendships with Harriet Beecher Stowe and Helen Hunt Jackson.

While she is generally considered most successful as a writer of short stories, many of her stories appeared in women's periodicals, which have not yet been indexed. Hence, a great many remain unnumbered, uncollected, and unknown today. Spofford's two most famous stories were "Amber Gods" and "Circumstance," both published in the Atlantic Monthly *in 1860. "Circumstance," mentioned by Emily Dickinson in her letters, was included in William Dean Howells's famous 1920 anthology,* The Great Modern American Stories.

"Her Story" was first published in Lippincott's Magazine *in December 1872 and reprinted in Spofford's twenty-second published volume,* Old Madame and Other Tragedies *(Boston: R. G. Badger and Co., 1900). Literary commentators on her work have pointed out the seeming alternation between her gothic stories— rich with colors, fabrics, sounds, and exotic plots and settings—and her local color ones with spare, realistic New England characters and situations. This story combines elements she had otherwise been thought to have kept separate. By confining the narration to the woman locked in a madhouse, the author creates the uncertainty later to be celebrated in Charlotte Perkins Gilman's 1892 story, "The Yellow Wallpaper." We cannot know for sure whether we are reading the ravings of a madwoman, or an account of victimization by an unscrupulous husband permitted by a patriarchal legal and medical system to abuse his wife for his own convenience. Spofford returned to this theme of the man and two women triangle many times, treating it from different perspectives, and trying out different tones, including humor.*

This is a story of chronic grief. The narrator seems to be caught in a perpetual loop, from grief, to denial, anger, bargaining, depression, and then back to grief. Those betrayed who become the victims of chronic grief—Rosalie of "The Quadroons," Chayah, and the narrator of this story—are women who have had the least power over their own lives. The connection between victimization, despair, and chronic grief is central to some of these stories.

Wellnigh the worst of it all is the mystery.

If it was true, that accounts for my being here. If it wasn't true, then the best thing they could do with me was to bring me here. Then, too, if it was true, they would save themselves by hurrying me away; and if it wasn't true—You see, just as all roads lead to Rome, all roads led me to this Retreat. If it was true, it was enough to craze me; and if it wasn't true, I was already crazed. And there it is! I can't make out, sometimes, whether I am really beside myself or not; for it seems that whether I was crazed or sane, if it was true, they would naturally put me out of sight and hearing—bury me alive, as they have done, in this Retreat. They? Well, no—he. She stayed at home, I hear. If she had come with us doubtless I should have found reason enough to say to the physician at once that she was the made woman, not I—she, who, for the sake of her own brief pleasure, could make a whole after-life of misery for three of us. She—Oh no, don't rise, don't go. I am quite myself, I am perfectly calm. Mad! There was never a drop of crazy blood in the Ridgleys or the Bruces, or any of the generations behind them, and why should it suddenly break out like a smothered fire in me? That is one of the things that puzzle me—why should it come to light all at once in me if it wasn't true?

Now, I am not going to be incoherent. It was too kind in you to be at such trouble to come and see me in this prison, this grave. I will not cry out once; I will just tell you the story of it all exactly as it was, and you shall judge. If I can, that is—oh, if I can! For sometimes, when I think of it, it seems as if Heaven itself would fail to take my part if I did not lift my own voice. And I cry, and I tear my hair and my flesh, till I know my anguish weighs down their joy, and the little scale that holds that joy flies up under the scorching of the sun, and God sees the festering thing for what it is. Ah, it is not injured reason that cries out in that way: it is a breaking heart!

How cool your hand is, how pleasant you face is, how good it is to see you! Don't be afraid of me: I am as much myself, I tell you, as you are. What an absurdity! Certainly any one who heard me make such a speech would think I was insane and without benefit of clergy. To ask you not to be afraid of me because I am myself!—isn't it what they call a vicious circle? And then to cap the climax by adding that I am as much myself as you are myself! But no matter—you know better. Did you say it was ten years? Yes, I knew it was as much as that—oh, it seems a hundred years!But we hardly show it: your hair is still the same as when we were at school; and mine—Look at this lock—I cannot understand why it is only sprinkled here and there: it ought to be white as the driven snow. My babies are almost grown women, Elizabeth. How could he do without me all this time? Hush now! I am not going to be disturbed at all; only that color of your hair puts me so in mind of his: perhaps there was just one trifle more of gold in his. Do you remember that lock that used to fall over his forehead and he always tossed back so impatiently? I used to think that the golden Apollo of Rhodes had just such massive, splendid locks of hair as that; but I never told him, I never had the face to praise him: she had. She could exclaim how like ivory the forehead was—that great wide forehead—how that keen aquiline was to be found in the portrait of the Spencer of two hundred years ago. She could tell of the proud lip, of the fire burning in the hazel eye: she knew how, by a silent flattery, as she shrank away and looked up at him, to admire his haughtly stature, and make him feel the strength and glory of his manhood and the delicacy of her womanhood.

She was a little thing—a little thing, but wondrous fair. Fair, did I say? No: she was dark as an Egyptian, but such perfect features, such rich and splendid color, such great soft eyes—so soft, so black—so superb a smile; and then such hair! When she let it down, the backward curling ends lay on the ground and she stood on them, or the children lifted them and carried them behind her as pages carry a queen's train. If I had my two hands twisted in that hair! Oh, how I hate that hair! It would make as good a bowstring for her neck as ever any Carthaginian woman's made. Ah, that is too wicked! I am sure you think so. But living all these lonesome years as I have done seems to double back one's sinfulness upon one's self. Because one is sane it does not follow that one is a saint. And when I think of my innocent babies playing with that hair that once I saw him lift and pass across his lips! But I will not think of it!

Well, well! I was a pleasant thing to look at myself once on a time, you know, Elizabeth. He used to tell me so: those were his very words. I was tall and slender, and if my skin was pale it was clear, and the lashes of my gray eyes were black as shadows; but now those eyes are only the color of tears.

I never told any one anything about it—I never could. It was so deep down in my heart, that love I had for him: it slept there so dark and still and full, for he was all I had in the world. I was alone, an orphan—if not friendless, yet quite dependent. I see you remember it all. I did not even sit in a pew with my cousin's family, that was so full, but down in one beneath the gallery, you know.

And altogether life was a thing to me that hardly seemed worth the living. I went to church one Sunday. I recollect, idly and dreamingly as usual. I did not look off my book till a voice filled my ear—a strange new voice, a deep sweet voice, that invited you and yet commanded you—a voice whose sound divided the core of my heart, and sent thrills that were half joy, half pain, coursing through me. And then I looked up and saw him at the desk. He was reading the first lesson "Fear not, for I have redeemed thee, I have called thee by thy name: thou art mine." And I saw the bright hair, the bright upturned face, the white surplice, and I said to myself, It is a vision, it is an angel; and I cast down my eyes. But the voice went on, and when I looked again he was still there. Then I bethought me that it must be the one who was coming to take the place of our superannuated rector—the last of a fine line, they had been saying the day before, who, instead of finding his pleasure otherwise, had taken all his wealth and prestige into the Church.

Why will a trifle melt you so—a strain of music, a color in the sky, a perfume? Have you never leaned from the window at evening, and had the scent of a flower float by and fill you with as keen a sorrow as if it had been disaster touching you Long ago, I mean— ee never lean from any windows here. I don't know how, but it was in that same invisible way that this voice melted me and when I heard it saying "But thou hast not called upon me, O Jacob, but thou hast been weary of me, O Israel," I was fairly crying. Oh, nervous tears, I dare say. The doctor here would tell you so, at any rate. And that is what I complain of here: they give a physiological reason for every emotion—they would give you a chemical formula for your very soul, I have no doubt. Well, perhaps they were nervous tears, for certainly there was nothing to cry for, and the mood went as suddenly as it came—changed to a sort of exaltation, I suppose—and when they sang the psalm, and he had swept in, in his black gown, and had mounted the pulpit stairs, and was resting that fair head on the big Bible in his silent prayer, I too was singing—singing like one possessed:

> Awake, my glory; harp and lute,
> No longer let your strains be mute;
> And I, my tuneful part to take,
> Will with the early dawn awake!

And as he rose I saw him searching for the voice unconsciously, and our eyes met. Oh, it was a fresh young voice, let it be mine or whose. I can hear it now as if it were somebody else singing. Ah, ah, it has been silent so many years! Does it make you smile to hear me pity myself? It is not myself I am pitying; it is that fresh young girl that loved so. But it used to rejoice me to think that I loved him before I laid eyes on him.

He came to my cousin's in the week—not to see Sylvia or to see Laura: he talked of church-music with my cousin, and then crossed the room and sat down by me. I remember how I grew cold and trembled—how glad, how shy I was; and then he took me into the music-room to sing; and at first Sylvia sang with us, but by and by we sang alone—I sang alone. He brought me yellow old church music, written in quaint characters; he said those characters, those old square breves, were a text guarding secrets of enchantment as much as the text of Merlin's book did; and so we used to find it. Once he brought a copy of an old Roman hymn, written only in the Roman letters; he said it was a hymn which the ancients sang to Maia, the mother-earth, and which the Church fathers adopted, singing it stealthily in the hidden places of the Catacombs: and together we translated it into tones. A rude but majestic thing it was.

And once—The sunshine was falling all about us in the bright lonely music-room, and the shadows of the rose leaves at the window were dancing over us. I had been singing the Gloria while he walked up and down the room, and he came up behind me: he stooped and kissed me on the mouth. And after that there was no more singing, for, lovely as the singing was, the love was lovelier yet. Why do I complain of such a hell as this is now? I had my heaven once—oh, I had my heaven once! And as for the other, perhaps I deserve it all, for I saw God only through him: it was he that waked me up to worship. I had no faith but Spencer's faith: if he had been a heathen, I should have been the same, and creeds and systems might have perished for me had he only been spared from the wreck. And he had loved me from the first moment that his eyes met mine. "When I looked at you" he said, "Singing that Easter hymn that day, I felt as I do when I look at the evening star leaning out of the clear sunset lustre; there is something in your face as pure, as remote, as shining. It will always be there," he said, "though you should live a hundred years." He little knew, he little knew!

But he loved me then—oh yet, I never doubted that. There were no happier lovers trod the earth. We took our pleasure as lovers do: we walked in the field; we sat on the river's side; together we visited the poor and sick; he read me the passages he liked best in his writing from week to week; he brought me the verse from which he meant to preach, and up in the organ-loft I improvised to him the thoughts that it inspired in me. I did that timidly indeed: I could not think my thoughts were worth his hearing till I forgot myself, and only thought of him and the glory I would have revealed to him, and then the great clustering chords and the full music of the diapason swept out beneath my hands—swept along the aisles and swelled up the raftered roof as if they would find the stars, and sunset and twilight stole around us there as we sat still in the succeeding silence. I was happy: I was humble too. I wondered why I had been chosen for such a blest and sacred lot. It seemed *that* to be allowed to be the minister of one delight to him. I had a little print of the angel of the Lord appearing to Mary with the lily of annunciation his hand, and I thought—I dare not tell you what I thought. I made an idol of my piece of clay.

When the leaves had turned we were married, and he took me home. Ah, what a happy home it was! Luxury and beauty filled it. When I first went into it and left the chill October night without, fires blazed upon the hearths; flowers bloomed in every room; a marble Eros held a light up, searching for his Psyche. "Our love has found its soul," said he. He led me to the music-room—a temple in itself, for its rounded ceiling towered to the height of the house. There were golden organ-pipes and banks of keys fit for St. Cecilia's hand; and there were all the delightful outlines of violin and piccolo and horn for any comers who knew how to use them; there was a pianoforte near the door for me—one such as I had never touched before; and there were cases on all sides filled with the rarest musical works. The floor was bare and inlaid; the windows were latticed in stained glass, so that no common light of day ever filtered through, but light bluer than the sky, gold as the dawn, purple as the night; and then there were vast embowering chairs, in any of which he could hide himself away while I made my incantation, as he sometimes called it, of the great spirits of song. As I tried the piano

that night he tuned the old Amati which he now and then played
upon himself, and together we improvised our own epithalamium.
It was the violin that took the strong assuring part with strains of
piercing sweetness, and the music of the piano flowed along in a
soft cantabile of undersong. It seemed to me as if his part was like
the flight of some white and strong-winged bird above a sunny
brook.

But he had hardly created this place for the love of me alone. He
adored music as a regenerator; he meant to use it so among his
people: here were to be pursued those labors which should work
miracles when produced in the open church. For he was building
a church with the half of his fortune—a church full of restoration
of the old and creation of the new; the walls within were to be a
frosty tracery of vines running to break into the gigantic passion-
flower that formed the rose-window; the lectern was a golden globe
upon a tripod, clasped by a silver dove holding on out-stretched
wings the book.

I have feared, since I have been here, that Spencer's piety was
less piety than partisanship: I have doubted if faith was so much
alive in him as the love of a perfect system, and the pride in it I
know he always felt. But I never thought about it then: I believed
in him as I would have believed in an apostle. So stone by stone
the church went up, and stone by stone our lives followed it—lives
of such peace, such bliss! Then fresh hopes came into it—sweet
trembling hopes; and by and by our first child was born. And if I
had been happy before, what was I then? There are come compen-
sations in this world; such happiness ought not to come twice as
there was in that moment when I lay, painless and at peace, with
the little cheek nestled beside my own, while he bent above us both,
proud and glad and tender. It was a dear little baby—so fair, so
bright! and when she could walk she could sing. Her little sister
sang earlier yet; and what music their two shrill little voices made
as they sat in their little chairs together at twilight before the fire,
their curls glistening and their red shoes glistening, while they sang
the evening hymn, Spencer on one side of the hearth and I upon
the other! Sometimes we let the dear things sit up for a later hour
in the music-room—for many a canticle we tried and practiced there
that hushed hearts and awed them when the choir gave them on
succeeding Sundays—and always afterward I heard them singing

in their sleep, just as a bird stirs in his nest and sings his stave in the night. Oh, we were happy then; and it was then she came.

She was the step-child of his uncle, and had a small fortune of her own, and Spencer had been left her guardian; and so she was to live with us—at any rate, for a while. I dreaded her coming, I did not want the intrusion; I did not like the things I heard about her, I knew she would be a discord in our harmony. But Spencer, who had only seen her once in her childhood, had been told by some one who traveled in Europe with her that she was delightful and had a rare intelligence. She was one of those women often delightful to men indeed, but whom other women—by virtue of their own kindred instincts, it may be, perhaps by virtue of temptations overcome—see through and know for what they are. But she had her own way of charming: she was the being of infinite variety—to-day glad, to-morrow sad, freakish, and always exciting you by curiosity as to her next caprice, and so moodish that after a season of the lowering weather of one of her dull humors you were ready to sacrifice something for the sake of the sunshine that she knew how to make so vivid and so sweet. Then, too, she brought forward her forces by detachment. At first she was the soul of domestic life sitting at night beneath the light and embossing on weblike muslin designs of flower and leaf which she had learned in her convent, listening to Spencer as he read, and taking from the little wallet of her work-basket apropos scraps which she had preserved from the sermon of some Italian father of the Church or of some French divine. As for me, the only thing I knew was my poor music; and I used to burn with indignation when she interposed that unknown tongue between my husband and myself. Presently her horses came, and then, graceful in her dark riding-habit, she would spend a morning fearlessly breaking in one of the fiery fellows, and dash away at last with plume and veil streaming behind her. In the early evening she would dance with the children—witch-dances they were—with her round arms linked above her head, and her feet weaving the measure in and out as deftly as any flashing-footed Bayadere might do—only when Spencer was there to see; at other times I saw she pushed the little hindering things aside without a glance.

By and by she began to display a strange dramatic sort of power. She would rehearse to Spencer scenes that she had met with from

day to day in the place, giving now the old churchwarden's voice
and now the sexton's, their gestures and very faces; she could tell
the ailments of half the old women in the parish who came to see
me with them, in their own tone and manner to the life; she told
us once of a street-scene, with the crier crying a lost child, the
mother following with lamentations, the passing strangers questioning, the boys hooting, and the child's reappearance, followed by a
tumult, with kisses and blows and cries, so that I thought I saw it
all; and presently she had pierced the armor and found the secret
and vulnerable spot of every friend we had, and could personate
them all as vividly as if she did it by necromancy.

One night she began to sketch our portraits in charcoal: the
likenesses were not perfect; she exaggerated the careless elegance of
Spencer's attitude, perhaps the primness of my own; but yet he
saw there the ungraceful trait for the first time, I think. And so
much led to more: she brought out her portfolios, and there were
her pencil-sketches from the Rhine and from the Guadalquivir, rich
water-colors of Venetian scenes, interiors of old churches, and sheet
after sheet covered with details of church architecture. Spencer had
been admiring all the others—in spite of something that I thought
I saw in them, a something that was not true, a trait of her own
identity, for I had come to criticise her sharply—but when his eye
rested on those sheets I saw it sparkle, and he caught them up and
pored over them one by one.

"I see you have mastered the whole thing," he said; "you must
instruct me here." And so she did. And there were hours, while I
was busied with servants and accounts or with the children, when
she was closeted with Spencer in the study, criticising, comparing,
making drawings, hunting up authorities; other hours when they
walked away together to the site of the new church that was building,
and here an arch was destroyed, and there an aisle was extended,
and here a row of cloisters sketched into the plan, and there a row
of windows, till the whole design was reversed and made over. And
they had a thing between them, for, admire and sympathize as I
might, I did not *know*. At first Spencer would repeat the day's
achievement to me, but the contempt for my ignorance which she
did not deign to hide soon put an end to it when she was present.

It was this interest that now unveiled a new phase of her character:
she was devout. She had a little altar in her room; she knew all

about albs and chasubles; she would have persuaded Spencer to burn candles in the chancel; she talked of a hundred mysteries and symbols; she wanted to embroider a stole to lay across his shoulders. She was full of small church sentimentalities, and as one after another she uttered them, it seemed to me that her belief was no sound fruit of any system—if it were belief, and not a mere bunch of fancies—but only, as you might say, a rotten windfall of the Romish Church: it had none of the round splendor of the Church's creed, none of the pure simplicity of ours; it would be no stay in trouble, no shield in temptation. I said as much to Spencer.

"Your are prejudiced," said he: "her belief is the result of long observation abroad, I think. She has found the need of outward observances: they are, she had told me, a shrine to the body of her faith, like that commanded in the building of the tabernacle, where the ark of the covenant was enclosed in the holy of holies."

"And you didn't think it profane in her to speak so? But I don't believe it, Spencer," I said. "She has no faith: she has some sentimentalisms."

"You are prejudiced," he repeated. "She seems to me a wonderful and gifted being."

"Too gifted," I said. "Her very gifts are unnatural in their abundance. There must be scrofula there, to keep such a fire in the blood and sting the brain to such action: she will die in a madhouse, depend upon it." Think of my saying such a thing as that!

"I have never heard you speak so before," he replied coldly. "I hope you do not envy her her powers."

"I envy her nothing," I cried, "for she is as false as she is beautiful." But I did—oh I did!

"Beautiful?" said Spencer. "Is she beautiful? I never thought of that."

"You are very blind, then," I said with a glad smile.

Spencer smiled too. "It is not the kind of beauty I admire," said he.

"Then I must teach you, sir," said she. And we both started to see her in the doorway, and I, for one, did not know till shortly before I found myself here how much or how little she had learned of what we said.

"Then I must teach you, sir," said she again. And she came deliberately into the firelight and paused upon the rug, drew out

the silver arrows and shook down all her hair about her, till the
great snake-like coils unrolled upon the floor.

"Hyacinthine," said Spencer.

"Indeed it is," said she—"the very color of the jacinth, with that
red tint in its darkness that they call black in the shade and gold in
the sun. Now look at me."

"Shut your eyes, Spencer," I cried, and laughed.

But he did not shut his eyes. The firelight flashed over her: the
color in her cheeks and on her lips sprang ripe and red in it as she
held the hair away from them with her rosy finger-tips; her throat
curved small and cream-white from the beautiful half-bare bosom
that the lace of her dinner-dress scarcely hid; and the dark eyes
glowed with a great light as they lay full on his.

"You mustn't call it vanity," said she. "It is only that it is
impossible, looking at the picture in the glass, not to see it as I see
any other picture. But for all that, I know it is not every fool's
beauty: it is no daub for the vulgar gaze, but a masterpiece that it
needs the educated eye to find. I could tell you how this nostril is
like that in a famous marble, how the curve of this cheek is that of
a certain Venus, the line of this forehead like the line in the dreamy
Antinous' forehead. Are you taught? Is it beautiful?"

Then she twisted her hair again and fastened the arrows, and
laughed and turned away to look over the evening paper. But as for
Spencer, as he lay back in his lordly way, surveying the vision from
crown to toe, I saw him flush—I saw him flush and start and quiver,
and then he closed his eyes and pressed his fingers on them, and
lay back again and said not a word.

She began to read aloud something concerning the services at the
recent dedication of a church. I was called out as she read. When
I came back, a half hour afterward, they were talking. I stopped at
my work-table in the next room for a skein of floss that she had
asked me for, and I heard her saying, "You cannot expect me to
treat you with reverence. You are a married priest, and you know
what opinion I necessarily must have of married priests." Then I
came in and she was silent.

But I knew, I always knew, that if Spencer had not felt himself
weak, had not found himself stirred, if he had not recognized that,
when he flushed and quivered before her beauty, it was the flesh
and not the spirit that tempted him, he would not have listened to

her subtle invitation to unnatural austerity. As it was, he did. He did—partly in shame, partly in punishment; but to my mind the listening was confession. She had set the wedge that was to sever our union—the little seed in a mere idle cleft that grows and grows and splits the rock asunder.

Well, I had my duties, you know. I never felt my husband's wealth a reason why I should neglect them any more than another wife should neglect her duties. I was wanted in the parish, sent for here and waited for there; the dying liked to see me comfort their living, the living liked to see me touch their dead; some wanted help, and others wanted consolation; and where I felt myself too young and unlearned to give advice, I could at least give sympathy. Perhaps I was the more called upon for such detail of duty because Spencer was busy with the greater things, the church-building and the sermons—sermons that once on a time lifted you and held you on their strong wings. But of late Spencer had been preaching old sermons. He had been moody and morose too; sometimes he seemed oppressed with melancholy. He had spoken to me strangely, had looked at me as if he pitied me, had kept away from me. But she had not regarded his moods; she had followed him in his solitary strolls, had sought him in his study; and she had ever a mystery or symbol to be interpreted, the picture of a private chapel that she had heard of when abroad, or the ground-plan of an ancient one, or some new temptation to his ambition, as I divine; and soon he was himself again.

I was wrong to leave him so to her, but what was there else for me to do? And as for those duties of mine, as I followed them I grew restive; I abridged them, I hastened home; I was impatient even with the detentions the children caused. I could not leave them to their nurses, for all that, but they kept me away from him, and he was alone with her.

One day at last he told me that his mind was troubled by the suspicion that his marriage was a mistake; that on his part at least it had been wrong; that he had been thinking a priest should have the Church only for his bride, and should wait at the altar mortified in every affection; that it was not for hands that were full of caresses and lips that were covered with kisses to break sacramental bread and offer praise. But for answer I brought my children and put them in his arms. I was white and cold and shaking, but I asked

him if they were not justification enough; and I told him that he
did his duty better abroad for the heartening of a wife at home,
and that he knew better how to interpret God's love to men through
his own love for his children; and I laid my head on his breast
beside them, and he clasped us all and we cried together, he and I.

But that was not enough, I found; and when our good bishop
came, who had always been like a father to Spencer, I led the
conversation to that point one evening, and he discovered Spencer's
trouble, and took him away and reasoned with him. The bishop
was the power with Spencer, and I think that was the end of it.

The end of that, but only the beginning of the rest. For she had
accustomed him to the idea of separation from me—the idea of
doing without me. He had put me away from himself once in his
mind: we had been one soul, and now we were two.

One day, as I stood in my sleeping-room with the door ajar, she
came in. She had never been there before, and I cannot tell you
how insolently she looked about her. There was a bunch of flowers
on a stand that Spencer himself placed there for me every morning;
he had always done so, and there had been no reason for breaking
off the habit; and I had always worn one of them at my throat. She
advanced a hand to pull out a blossom. "Do not touch them," I
cried: "my husband puts them there."

"Suppose he does?" said she lightly. "What devotion!" Then she
overlooked me with the long sweeping glance of search and contempt,
shrugged her shoulders, and with a French sentence that I did not
understand turned back and coolly broke off the blossom she had
marked and hung it in her hair. I could not take her by the shoulders
and put her from the room; I could not touch the flowers that she
had desecrated. I left the room myself, and left her in it, and went
down to dinner for the first time without the flower at my throat.
I saw Spencer's eye note the omission: perhaps he took it as a release
from me, for he never put the flowers in my room again after that
day.

Nor did he ask me any more into his study, as he had been used,
or read his sermons to me; there was no need of his talking over
the church-building with me—he had her to talk it over and as for
our music, that had been a rare thing since she arrived, for her
conversation had been such as to leave but little time for it, and
somehow when she came into the music-room and began to dictate

to me the time in which I should take an Inflamatus and the spirit
in which I should sing a ballad, I could not bear it. Then, too, to
tell you the truth, my voice was hoarse and choked with tears full
half the time.

It was some weeks after the flowers ceased that our youngest
child fell ill. She was very ill—I don't think Spencer knew how ill.
I dared not trust her with any one, and Spencer said no one could
take such care of her as her mother could; so, though we had nurses
in plenty, I hardly left the room by night or day. I heard their
voices down below, I saw them go out for their walks. It was a
hard fight, but I saved her.

But I was worn to a shadow when all was done—worn with
anxiety for her, with alternate fevers of hope and fear, and with the
weight of my responsibility as to her life; and with anxiety for
Spencer too, with a despairing sense that the end of peace had
come, and with the total sleeplessness of many nights. Now when
the child was mending and gaining every day, I could not sleep if
I would.

The doctor gave my anodynes, but to no purpose; they only
nerved me wide awake. My eyes ached, and my brain ached, and
my body ached, but it was of no use; I could not sleep. I counted
the spots on the wall, the motes upon my eyes, the notes on all the
sheets of music I could recall; I remembered the Eastern punishment
of keeping the condemned awake till they die, and wondered what
my crime was; I thought if I could but sleep I might forget my
trouble, or take it up freshly and master it. But no, it was always
there—a heavy cloud, a horror of foreboding. As I heard that
woman's step go by the door I longed to rid the house of it, and I
dinted my palms with my nails till she had passed.

I did not know what to do. It seemed to me that I was wicked
in letting the thing go on, in suffering Spencer to be any longer
exposed to her power; but then I feared to take a step lest I should
thereby rivet the chains she was casting on him. And then I longed
so for one hour of the old dear happiness—the days when I and the
children had been all and enough. I did not know what to do; I had
no one to counsel with; I was wild within myself, and all distraught.
Once I thought if I could not rid the house of her I could rid it of
myself; and as I went through a dark passage and chanced to look
up where a bright-headed nail glittered, I questioned if it would

bear my weight. For days the idea haunted me. I fancied that when I was gone perhaps he would love me again, and at any rate I might be asleep and at rest. But the thought of the children prevented me, and one other thought—I was not certain that even my sorrows would excuse me before God.

I went down to dinner again at last. How she glowed and abounded in her beauty as she sat there! And I—I must have been very thin and ghastly: perhaps I looked a little wild in all my bewilderment and hurt. His heart smote him, it may be, for he came round to where I sat by the fire afterward and smoothed my hair and kissed my forehead. He could not tell all I was suffering then—all I was struggling with; for I thought I had better put him out of the world than let him, who was once so pure and good, stay in it to sin. I could have done it, you know. For though I slept still with the little girl, I could have stolen back into our own room with the chloroform, and he would never have known. I turned the handle of the door one night, but the bolt was slipped. I never thought of killing her, you see; let her live and sin, if she would. She was the thing of slime and sin, a splendid tropical growth of passionate heat and slime; it was only her nature. But then we think it no harm to kill reptiles, however splendid.

But it was by that time that the spirits had begun to talk with me—all night long, all day. It was they, I found, that had kept me so sleepless. Go where I might, they were ever before me. If I went to the woods, I heard them in the whisper of every pine tree; if I went down to the seashore, I heard them in the plash of every wave; I heard them in the wind, in the singing of my ears, in the children's breath as I hung above them, for I had decided that if I went out of the world I would take the children with me. If I sat down to play, the things would twist the chords into discords; if I sat down to read, they would come between me and the page. Then I could see them: they had wings like bats. I did not dare to speak of them, though I fancied she suspected me, for once she said, as I was kissing my little girl, "When you are gone to the madhouse, don't think they'll have many such kisses." I did not answer her, I did not look up: I suppose I should have flown at her throat if I had.

I took the children out with me on my long rambles: we went for miles; sometimes I carried one, sometimes the other. I took such long, long walks to escape those noisome things: they would never leave me till I was quite tired out. Now and then I was gone all day; and all the time that I was gone he was with her, I knew, and she was tricking out her beauty and practicing her arts.

I went to a little festival with them, for Spencer insisted. And she made shadow-pictures on the wall, wonderful things with her perfect profile and her perfect arms and her supple curves—she out of sight, the shadow only seen. Now it was Isis, I remember, and now it was the head and shoulders and trailing hair of a floating sea-nymph. And then there were charades in which she played; and I can't tell you the glorious things she looked when she came on as Helen of Troy with all her "beauty shadowed in white veils," you know—that brown and red beauty with its smiles and radiance under the wavering of the flower-wrought veil. I sat by Spencer, and I felt him shiver. He was fighting and struggling too within himself, very likely; only he knew that he was going to yield after all—only he longed to yield while he feared. But as for me, I saw one of those bat-like things perched on her ear as she stood before us, and when she opened her mouth to speak I saw them flying in and out. And I said to Spencer, "She is tormenting me, I cannot stay and see her swallowing the souls of men in this way." And I would have gone, but he held me down fast in my seat. But if I was crazy then—as they say I was, I suppose—it was only with the metaphor, for she was sucking Spencer's soul out of his body.

But I was not crazy. I should admit I might have been if I alone had seen those evil spirits. But Spencer saw them too. He never exactly told me so, but I knew he did; for when I opened the church door late, as I often did at that time after my long walks, they would rush in past me with a whizz, and as I sat in the pew I would see him steadily avoid looking at me; and if he looked by any chance, he would turn so pale that I have thought he would drop where he stood, and he would redden afterward as though one had struck him. He knew then what I endured with them, but I was not the one to speak of it. Don't tell me that his color changed and he shuddered so because I sat there mumbling and nodding to myself: it was because he saw those things mopping and mowing beside me and whispering in my ear. Oh what loathsomeness the obscene creatures whispered!—foul quips and evil words I had never heard before, ribald songs and oaths; and I would clap my hands over my mouth to keep from crying out at them. Creatures of the imagination, you may say. It is possible, but they were so vivid that them seem real to me even now; I burn and tingle as I recall them. And how could I have imagined such sounds, such shapes, of things I had never heard or seen or dreamed?

And Spencer was very unhappy, I am sure. I was the mother of his children, and if he loved me no more, he had an old kindness for me still, and my distress distressed him. But for all that the glamour was on him, and he could not give up that woman and her beauty and her charm. Once or twice he may have thought about sending her away, but perhaps he could not bring himself to do it—perhaps he reflected it was too late, and now it was no matter. But every day she stayed he was the more like wax in her hands. Oh, he was weaker than water that is poured out. He was abandoning himself, and forgetting earth and heaven, and hell itself, before a passion—a passion that soon would cloy, and then would sting.

It was the spring season then: I had been out several hours. The sunset fell while I was in the wood, and the stars came out; and at one time I thought I would lie down there on last year's leaves and never get up again; but I remembered the children, and went home to them. They were both in bed and asleep when I took off my shoes and opened the door of their room—breathing so sweetly and evenly, the little yellow heads close together on one pillow, their hands tossed about the coverlid, their parted lips, their rosy cheeks. I knelt to feel the warm breath on my own cold cheek, and then the spirits began whispering again: "If only they never waked! They never waked!"

And all I could do was to spring to my feet and run from the room. I ran shoeless down the great staircase and through the long hall. I thought I would go to Spencer and tell him all my sorrows, all the suggestions of the spirits, and maybe in the endeavor to save me he would save himself. And I ran down the long dimly-lighted drawing-room, led by the sound I heard, to the music-room, whose doors were open just beyond. It was lighted only by the pale glimmer from the other room and by the moonlight through the painted panes. And I paused to listen to what I had never listened to there—the sound of the harp and a voice with it. Of course they had not heard me coming, and I hesitated and looked, and then I glided within the door and stood by the open piano there.

She sat at the harp singing—the huge gilded harp. I did not know she sang—she had kept that for her last reserve—but she struck the harp so that it sang itself, like some great prisoned soul, and her voice followed it—oh so rich a voice! My own was white and thin, I felt, beside it. But mine had soared, and hers still clung to earth—a contralto sweet with honeyed sweetness—the sweetness of un-strained honey that has the earth-taste and the heavy blossom-dust yet in it—sweet, though it grew hoarse and trembling with passion. He sat in one of the great arm-chairs just before her; he was white with feeling, with rapture, with forgetfulness; his eyes shone like stars. He moved restlessly, a strange smile kindled all his face: he bent toward her, and the music broke off in the middle as they threw their arms around each other, and hung there lip to lip and heart to heart. And suddenly I crashed down both my hands on the keyboard before me and stood and glared upon them.

And I never knew anything more till I woke up here. And that is the whole of it. That is the puzzle of it—was it a horrid nightmare, an insane vision, or was it true? Was it true that I saw Spencer, my white, clean lover, my husband, a man of God, the father of our spotless babies,—was it true that I saw him so, or was it only some wild, vile conjuration of disease? Oh, I should be willing to have been crazed a lifetime, a whole lifetime, only to wake one moment before I died and find that that had never been!

Well, well, well! When time passed and I became more quiet, I told the doctor here about the spirits—I never told him of Spencer or of her—and he bade me dismiss care; he said I was ill—excitement and sleeplessness had surcharged my nerves with that strange magnetic fluid that has worked so much mischief in the world. There was no organic disease, you see; only when my nerves were rested and right, my brain would be. And the doctor gave me medicines and books and work, and when I saw the spirits again I was to go instantly to him. And after a little while I was not sure that I did see them; and in a little while longer they had ceased to come altogether, and I had had no more of them. I was on my parole then in the parlor, at the table, in the grounds. I felt that I was cured of whatever had ailed me; I could escape at any moment that I wished.

And it came Christmas-time. A terrible longing for home overcame me—for my children. I thought of them at this time when I had

been used to take such pains for their pleasure; I thought of the
little empty stockings, the sad faces; I fancied I could head them
crying for me. I forgot all about my word of honor. It seemed to
me that I should die, that I might as well die, if I could not see my
little darlings, and hold them on my knees, and sing to them while
the chimes were ringing in the Christmas Eve; and winter was here
and there was so much to do for them. And I walked down the
garden, and looked out the gate, and opened it and went through.
And I slept that night in a barn—so free, so free and glad; and the
next day an old farmer and his sons, who thought they did me a
service, brought me back, and of course I shrieked and raved; and
so would you.

But since then I have been in this ward and a prisoner. I have
my work, my amusements. I send such little things as I can make
to my girls; I read; sometimes of late I sing in the Sunday service.
The place is a sightly place; the grounds, when we are taken out
are fine; the halls are spacious and pleasant. Pleasant—but ah, when
you have trodden them ten years! And so, you see, if I were a clod,
if I had no memory, no desires, if I had never been happy before,
I might be happy now. I am confident the doctor thinks me well,
but he has no orders to let me go. Sometimes it is so wearisome;
and it might be worse if lately I had not been allowed a new service,
and that is to try to make a woman smile who came here a year
ago. She is a little woman, swarthy as a Malay, but her hair, that
grows as rapidly as a fungus grows in the night, is whiter than
leprosy; her eyebrows are so long and white that they veil and
blanch her dark dim eyes, and she has no front teeth. A stone from
a falling spire struck her from her horse, they say—the blow battered
her and beat out reason and beauty. Her mind is dead; she remembers
nothing, knows nothing, but she follows me about like a dog; she
seems to want to do something for me to propitiate me. All she
ever says is to beg me to do her no harm. She will not go to sleep
without my hand in hers. Sometimes, after long effort, I think there
is a gleam of intelligence, but the doctor says there was once too
much intelligence, and her case is hopeless. Hopeless, poor thing!—
that is an awful word; I could not wish it said for my worst enemy.
In spite of these ten years I cannot feel that it has yet been said for
me. If I am strange just now, it is only the excitement of seeing
you, only the habit of the strange sights and sounds here. I should

be calm and well enough at home. I sit and picture to myself that some time Spencer will come for me—will take me home to my girls, my fireside, my music. I shall hear his voice, I shall rest in his arms, I shall be blest again. For, oh, Elizabeth, I do forgive him all! Or if he will not dare to trust himself at first, I picture to myself how he will send another—some old friend who knew me before my trouble—who will see me and judge, and carry back report that I am all I used to be—some friend who will open the gates of heaven to me, or close the gates of hell upon me—who will hold my life and my fate. If—oh if it should be you, Elizabeth!

Mary E. Wilkins Freeman

A Moral Exigency
1884

Mary Eleanor Wilkins Freeman (1852–1930), after an adolescence unsettled by increasing financial hardship, moved with her family from their familiar Randolph, Massachusetts home to Brattleboro, Vermont. There, attempts to recoup economic stability ended with the successive deaths of her only sibling, her younger sister Nan, in 1876, her mother in 1880, and her father in 1883. She was left alone with the need to support herself in a time when the only careers open to young women of her class were teaching and literature. She returned to Randolph to live with the family of her life-long friend, Mary Wales, and stayed through the years of her literary apprenticeship and the years of her greatest literary success until her ill-fated marriage to Charles Freeman, a New Jersey physician, in 1902. (Their marriage was soon disrupted by Dr. Freeman's increasing alcoholism and its associated disorders.)

Freeman lived most of her domestic life in a world of women and, when she became restless, her literary earnings provided the means to travel. Her first success came with the acceptance in 1883 by Harper's Bazaar *of her story, "Two Old Lovers." By 1887 enough of her stories had been published in that periodical and in* Harper's New Monthly Magazine *to compile her first collection:* A Humble Romance. *It included "A Moral Exigency," first published July 26, 1884, in* Harper's Bazaar, *a magazine whose contents were dominated by fashion news, pictures, sewing patterns, and recipes. That volume was followed four years later by* A New England Nun. *Both of these volumes have been reprinted recently, as well as other volumes of stories, including the 1927 collection,* The Best Stories of Mary E. Wilkins. *She also published many novels and a historical tragedy.*

She was part of the network of literary women whose hub was Annie Fields, the wife of Henry Fields, publisher and editor of the Atlantic Monthly. *Among these*

*women was Sarah Orne Jewett, who had been the young Wilkins's literary inspiration
and teacher.*

*Freeman's genius lay in her ability to penetrate and illuminate the conjunction
between necessity and desire in a woman's life. She tells her truths in ways that
pierce the reader's heart as if with a boning knife. Her stories often focus on that
moment when a woman must act in the face of conflict between her personal values
and the demands being made by the "real" world, whether social or natural, or
between personal happiness and personal values. Her heroines must make choices in
no-win situations.*

*The New England villages after the Civil War, for a variety of economic, social,
and technological reasons, had fewer young unmarried men than women. And often
the young men who did remain in their native villages were not the pick of the local
crop. Recently, philosopher, biologist, and ecologist Garret Hardin has defined ethics
as "the study of ways to allocate scarce resources." (See* Promethean Ethics: Living
with Death, Competition, and Triage. *Seattle: Univ. of Washington Press,
1980). That definition serves well to highlight the dilemma represented in this story.
Marriageable men, however, are not the only scarce resource in this story; scarce
also are the moments of intimacy between female friends in the life of this minister's
daughter.*

*Many of Freeman's stories are characterized by intense and supportive relationships
between women. The characteristic pair in much of her work is either a mother and
daughter, two sisters (one almost old enough to be the mother of the younger), or
two women who stand in the stead of mother and daughter to each other. Such is
the case, although briefly, for Eunice and Ada.*

*This is the first other woman story to introduce the mother-daughter motif that
will become increasingly a feature of stories about two women involved with the
same man. It surfaces in "Turned," "The Difference," "Gal Young Un," and, more
subtly, in "A Happening in Barbados," and "The Girl Who Was Plugged In." In
some stories where the other woman theme is a motif subordinate to the main theme,
the mother-daughter overtones become even stronger, as in Fannie Hurst's "Oats for
the Woman" (in* Between Mothers and Daughters: Stories Across a Generation, *ed. by Susan Koppelman. Old Westbury, N.Y.: The Feminist Press, 1984)
and in Catharine Maria Sedgwick's germinal 1834 story, "Old Maids" (in* Old
Maids: Short Stories by Nineteenth-Century Women Writers, *ed. by Susan
Koppelman. New York: Pandora Press, Routledge & Kegan Paul, 1984).*

*The three themes—the other woman, the mother-daughter relationship, and the
unmarried woman—are not only frequently addressed in Freeman's fiction, they are
often interwoven. As Freeman grew older, so, frequently, did her characters, and
her stories increasingly focused on a rapprochement between the two women, with
the man often entirely absent.*

At five o'clock, Eunice Fairweather went up-stairs to dress herself for the sociable and Christmas-tree to be given at the parsonage that night in honor of Christmas Eve. She had been very busy all day, making preparations for it. She was the minister's daughter, and had, of a necessity, to take an active part in such affairs.

She took it, as usual, loyally and energetically, but there had always been seasons from her childhood—and she was twenty-five now—when the social duties to which she had been born seemed a weariness and a bore to her. They had seemed so to-day. She had patiently and faithfully sewed up little lace bags with divers-colored worsteds, and stuffed them with candy. She had strung pop-corn, and marked the parcels which had been pouring in since daybreak from all quarters. She had taken her prominent part among the corps of indefatigable women always present to assist on such occasions, and kept up her end of the line as minister's daughter bravely. Now, however, the last of the zealous, chattering women she had been working with had bustled home, with a pleasant importance in every hitch of her shawled shoulders, and would not bustle back again until half-past six or so; and the tree, fully bedecked, stood in unconscious impressiveness in the parsonage parlor.

Eunice had come up-stairs with the resolution to dress herself directly for the festive occasion, and to hasten down again to be in readiness for new exigencies. Her mother was delicate, and had kept to her room all day in order to prepare herself for the evening, her father was inefficient at such times, there was no servant, and the brunt of everything came on her.

But her resolution gave way; she wrapped herself in an old plaid shawl and lay down on her bed to rest a few minutes. She did not close her eyes, but lay studying idly the familiar details of the room. It was small, and one side ran in under the eaves; for the parsonage was a cottage. There was one window, with a white cotton curtain trimmed with tasselled fringe, and looped up on an old porcelain knob with a picture painted on it. That knob, with its tiny bright landscape, had been one of the pretty wonders of Eunice's childhood. She looked at it even now with interest, and the marvel and the beauty of it had not wholly departed her eyes. The walls of the little room had a scraggly-patterned paper on them. The first lustre of it had departed, for that too was one of the associates of Eunice's childhood, but in certain lights there was a satin sheen and a blue line visible. Blue roses on a satin ground had been the original pattern. It had never been pretty, but Eunice had always had faith in it. There was an ancient straw matting on the floor, a homemade braided rug before the cottage bedstead, and one before the stained-pine bureau. There were a few poor attempts at adornment on the walls; a splint letter-case, a motto worked in worsteds, a gay print of an eminently proper little girl holding a faithful little dog.

This last, in its brilliant crudeness, was not a work of art, but Eunice belived in it. She was a conservative creature. Even after her year at the seminary, for which money had been scraped together five years ago, she had the same admiring trust in all the revelations of her childhood. Her home, on her return to it, looked as fair to her as it had always done; no old ugliness which familiarity had caused to pass unnoticed before gave her a shock of surprise.

She lay quietly, her shawl shrugged up over her face, so only her steady, light-brown eyes were visible. The room was drearily cold. She never had a fire; one in a sleeping-room would have been sinful luxury in the poor minister's family. Even her mother's was only warmed from the sitting-room.

In sunny weather Eunice's room was cheerful, and its look, if not actually its atmosphere, would warm one a little, for the windows faced southwest. But to-day all the light had come through low, gray clouds, for it had been threatening snow ever since morning, and the room had been dismal.

A comfortless dusk was fast spreading over everything now. Eunice rose at length, thinking that she must either dress herself speedily or go down-stairs for a candle.

She was a tall, heavily-built girl, with large, well-formed feet and hands. She had a full face, and a thick, colorless skin. Her features were coarse, but their combination affected one pleasantly. It was a stanch, honest face, with a suggestion of obstinacy in it.

She looked unhappily at herself in her little square glass, as she brushed out her hair and arranged it in a smooth twist at the top of her head. It was not becoming, but it was the way she had always done it. She did not admire the effect herself when the coiffure was complete, neither did she survey her appearance complacently when she had gotten into her best brown cashmere dress, with its ruffle of starched lace in the neck. But it did not occur to her that any change could be made for the better. It was her best dress, and it was the way she did up her hair. She did not like either, but the simple facts of them ended the matter for her.

After the same fashion she regarded her own lot in life, with a sort of resigned disapproval.

On account of her mother's ill-health, she had been encumbered for the last five years with the numberless social duties to which the wife of a poor country minister is liable. She had been active in Sunday-school picnics and church sociables, in mission bands and neighborhood prayer-meetings. She was a church member and a good girl, but the *role* did not suit her. Still she accepted it as inevitable, and would no more have thought of evading it than she would have thought of evading life altogether. There was about her an almost stubborn steadfastness of onward movement that would forever keep her in the same rut, no matter how disagreeable it might be, unless some influence outside of herself might move her.

When she went down-stairs, she found her mother seated beside the sitting-room stove, also arrayed in her best—a shiny black silk, long in the shoulder-seams, the tops of the sleeves adorned with pointed caps trimmed with black velvet ribbon.

She looked up at Eunice as she entered, a complacent smile on her long, delicate face; she thought her homely, honest-looking daughter charming in her best gown.

A murmur of men's voices came from the next room, whose door was closed.

"Father's got Mr. Wilson in there," explained Mrs. Fairweather, in response to Eunice's inquiring glance. "He came just after you went up-stairs. They've been talking very busily about something. Perhaps Mr. Wilson wants to exchange."

Just at that moment, the study door opened and the two men came out, Eunice's father, tall and round-shouldered, with grayish sandy hair and beard, politely allowing his guest to precede him. There was a little resemblance between the two, though there was no relationship. Mr. Wilson was a younger man by ten years; he was shorter and slighter; but he had similarly sandy hair and beard, though they were not quite so gray, and something the same cast of countenance. He was settled over a neighboring parish; he was a widower with four young children; his wife had died a year before.

He had spoken to Mrs. Fairweather on his first entrance, so he stepped directly toward Eunice with extended hand. His ministerial affability was slightly dashed with embarrassment, and his thin cheeks were crimson around the roots of his sandy beard.

Eunice shook the proffered hand with calm courtesy, and inquired after his children. She had not a thought that his embarrassment betokened anything, if, indeed, she observed it at all.

Her father stood by with an air of awkward readiness to proceed to action, waiting until the two should cease the interchanging of courtesies.

When the expected pause came he himself placed a chair for Mr. Wilson. "Sit down, Brother Wilson," he said, nervously, "and I will consult with my daughter concerning the matter we were speaking of. Eunice, I would like to speak with you a moment in the study."

"Certainly sir," said Eunice. She looked surprised, but she followed him into the study "Tell me as quickly as you can what it is, father," she said, "for it is nearly time for people to begin coming, and I shall have to attend to them."

She had not seated herself, but stood leaning carelessly against the study wall, questioning her father with her steady eyes.

He stood in his awkward height before her. He was plainly trembling. "Eunice," he said, in a shaking voice, "Mr. Wilson came—to say—he would like to marry you, my dear daughter."

He cleared his throat to hide his embarrassment. He felt a terrible constraint in speaking to Eunice of such matters; he looked shame-faced and distressed.

Eunice eyed him steadily. She did not change color in the least. "I think I would rather remain as I am, father," she said quietly.

Her father roused himself then. "My dear daughter," he said, with restrained eagerness, "don't decide this matter too hastily, without giving it all the consideration it deserves. Mr. Wilson is a good man; he would make you a worthy husband, and he needs a wife sadly. Think what a wide field of action would be before you with those four little motherless children to love and care for! You would have a wonderful opportunity to do good."

"I don't think," said Eunice, bluntly, "that I should care for that sort of an opportunity."

"Then," her father went on, "you will forgive me if I speak plainly, my dear. You—are getting older; you have not had any other visitors. You would be well provided for in this way—"

"Exceedingly well," replied Eunice, slowly. "There would be six hundred a year and a leaky parsonage for a man and woman and four children, and—nobody knows how many more." She was almost coarse in her slow indignation, and did not blush at it.

"The Lord would provide for his servants."

"I don't know whether he would or not. I don't think he would be under any obligation to if his servant deliberately encumbered himself with more of a family than he had brains to support."

Her father looked so distressed that Eunice's heart smote her for her forcible words. "You don't want to get rid of me, surely, father," she said, in a changed tone.

Mr. Fairweather's lips moved uncertainly as he answered: "No, my dear daughter; don't ever let such a thought enter your head. I only—Mr. Wilson is a good man, and a woman is best off married, and your mother and I are old. I have never laid up anything. Sometimes—Maybe I don't trust the Lord enough, but I have felt anxious about you, if anything happened to me." Tears were standing in his light-blue eyes, which had never been so steady and keen as his daughter's.

There came a loud peal of the door-bell. Eunice started. "There! I must go," she said. "We'll talk about this another time. Don't worry about it, father dear."

"But, Eunice, what shall I say to him?"

"Must something be said to-night?"

"It would hardly be treating him fairly otherwise."

Eunice looked hesitatingly at her father's worn, anxious face. "Tell him," said at length, "that I will give him his answer in a week."

Her father looked gratified. "We will take it to the Lord, my dear."

Eunice's lip curled curiously, but she said, "Yes, sir" dutifully, and hastened from the room to answer the door-bell.

The fresh bevies that were constantly arriving after that engaged her whole attention. She could do no more than give a hurried "Good-evening" to Mr. Wilson when he came to take leave, after a second short conference with her father in the study. He looked deprecatingly hopeful.

The poor man was really in a sad case. Six years ago, when he married, he had been romantic. He would never be again. He was not thirsting for love and communion with a kindred spirit now, but for a good, capable woman who would take care of his four clamorous children without a salary.

He returned to his shabby, dirty parsonage that night with, it seemed to him, quite a reasonable hope that his affairs might soon be changed for the better. Of course he would have preferred that the lady should have said yes directly; it would both have assured him and shortened the time until his burdens should be lightened; but he could hardly have expected that, when his proposal was so sudden, and there had been no preliminary attention on his part. The week's probation, therefore, did not daunt him much. He did not really see why Eunice should refuse him. She was plain, was getting older; it probably was her first, and very likely her last, chance of marriage. He was a clergyman in good standing, and she would not lower her social position. He felt sure that he was now about to be relieved from the unpleasant predicament in which he had been ever since his wife's death, and from which he had been forced to make no effort to escape, for decency's sake, for a full year. The year, in fact, had been up five days ago. He actually took credit to himself for remaining quiescent during those five days. It was rather shocking, but there was a good deal to be said for him. No wife and four small children, six hundred dollars a year, moderate brain, and an active conscience, are a hard combination of circumstances for any man.

To-night, however, he returned thanks to the Lord for his countless blessings with pious fervor, which would have been lessened had he known of the state of Eunice's mind just at that moment.

The merry company had all departed, the tree stood dismantled in the parlor, and she was preparing for bed, with her head full, not of him, but another man.

Standing before her glass, combing out her rather scanty, lustreless hair, her fancy pictured to her, beside her own homely, sober face, another, a man's, blond and handsome, with a gentle, almost womanish smile on the full red lips, and a dangerous softness in the blue eyes. Could a third person have seen the double picture as she did, he would have been struck with a sense of the incongruity, almost absurdity, of it. Eunice herself, with her hard, uncompromising common-sense, took the attitude of a third person in regard to it, and at length blew her light out and went to bed, with a bitter amusement in her heart at her own folly.

There had been present that evening a young man who was a comparatively recent aquisition to the village society. He had been in town about three months. His father, two years before, had purchased one of the largest farms in the vicinity, moving there from an adjoining state. This son had been absent at the time; he was reported to be running a cattle ranch in one of those distant territories which seem almost fabulous to New-Englanders. Since he had come home he had been the cynosure of the village. He was thirty and a little over, but he was singularly boyish in his ways, and took part in all the town frolics with gusto. He was popularly supposed to be engaged to Ada Harris, Squire Harris's daughter, as she was often called. Her father was the prominent man of the village, lived in the best house, and had the loudest voice in public matters. He was a lawyer, with rather more pomposity than ability, perhaps, but there had always been money and influence in the Harris family, and these warded off all criticism.

The daughter was a pretty blonde of average attainments, but with keen wits and strong passions. She had not been present at the Christmas-tree, and her lover, either on that account, or really from some sudden fancy he had taken to Eunice, had been at her elbow the whole evening. He had a fashion of making his attentions marked: he did on that occasion. He made a pretence of assisting her, but it was only a pretence, and she knew it, though she thought it marvellous. She had met him, but had not before exchanged two words with him. She had seen him with Ada Harris, and he had seemed almost as much out of her life as a lover in a book. Young men of his kind were unknown quantities heretofore to this steady, homely young woman. They seemed to belong to other girls.

So his devotion to her through the evening, and his asking permission to call when he took leave, seemed to her well-nigh incredible. Her head was not turned, in the usual acceptation of the term—it was not an easy head to turn—but it was full of Burr Mason, and every thought, no matter how wide a starting-point it had, lost itself at last in the thought of him.

Mr. Wilson's proposal weighed upon her terribly through the next week. Her father seemed bent upon her accepting it; so did her mother, who sighed in secret over the prospect of her daughter's remaining unmarried. Either through unworldliness, or their conviction of the desirability of the marriage in itself, the meagreness of the financial outlook did not seem to influence them in the least.

Eunice did not once think of Burr Mason as any reason for her reluctance, but when he called the day but one before her week of probation was up, and when he took her to drive the next day, she decided on a refusal of the minister's proposal easily enough. She had wavered a little before.

So Mr. Wilson was left to decide upon some other worthy, reliable woman as a subject for his addresses, and Eunice kept on with her new lover.

How this sober, conscientious girl could reconcile to herself the course she was now taking, was a question. It was probable she did not make the effort; she was so sensible that she would have known its futility and hypocrisy beforehand.

She knew her lover had been engaged to Ada Harris; that she was encouraging him in cruel and dishonorable treatment of another woman; but she kept steadily on. People even came to her and told her that the jilted girl was breaking her heart. She listened, her homely face set in an immovable calm. She listened quietly to her parents' remonstrance, and kept on.

There was an odd quality in Burr Mason's character. He was terribly vacillating, but he knew it. Once he said to Eunice, with the careless freedom that would have been almost insolence in another man: "Don't let me see Ada Harris much, I warn you, dear. I mean to be true to you, but she has such a pretty face, and I meant to be true to her, but you have—I don't know just what, but something she has not."

Eunice knew the truth of what he said perfectly. The incomprehensibleness of it all to her, who was so sensible of her own disadvantages, was the fascination she had for such a man.

A few days after Burr Mason had made that remark, Ada Harris came to see her. When Eunice went into the sitting-room to greet her, she kept her quiet, unmoved face, but the change in the girl before her was terrible. It was not wasting of flesh or pallor that it consisted in, but something worse. Her red lips were set so hard that the soft curves in them were lost, her cheeks burned feverishly, her blue eyes had a fierce light in them, and, most pitiful thing of all for another woman to see, she had not crimped her pretty blond hair, but wore it combed straight back from her throbbing forehead.

When Eunice entered, she waited for no preliminary courtesies, but sprang forward, and caught hold of her hand with a strong, nervous grasp, and stood so, her pretty, desperate face confronting Eunice's calm, plain one.

"Eunice!" she cried, "Eunice! why did you take him away from me? Eunice! Eunice!" Then she broke into a low wail, without any tears.

Eunice released her hand, and seated herself. "You had better take a chair, Ada," she said, in her slow, even tones. "When you say *him*, you mean Burr Mason, I suppose."

"You know I do. Oh, Eunice, how could you? how could you? I thought you were so good!"

"You ask me why *I* do this and that, but don't you think he had anything to do with it himself?"

Ada stood before her, clinching her little white hands. "Eunice Fairweather, you know Burr Mason, and I know Burr Mason. You know that if you gave him up, and refused to see him, he would come back to me. You know it."

"Yes, I know it."

"You know it; you sit there and say you know it, and yet you do this cruel thing—you, a minister's daughter. You understood from the first how it was. You knew he was mine, that you had no right to him. You knew if you shunned him ever so little, that he would come back to me. And yet you let him come and make love to you. You knew it. There is no excuse for you: you knew it. It is no better for him. You have encouraged him in being false. You have dragged him down. You are a plainer girl than I, and a soberer one, but you are no better. You will not make him a better wife. You cannot make him a good wife after this. It is all for yourself— yourself!"

Eunice sat still.

Then Ada flung herself on her knees at her side, and pleaded, as for her life. "Eunice, O Eunice, give him up to me! It is killing me! Eunice, dear Eunice, say you will!"

As Eunice sat looking at the poor, dishevelled golden head bowed over her lap, a recollection flashed across her mind, oddly enough, of a certain recess at the village school they two had attended years ago, when she was among the older girls, and Ada a child to her:

how she had played she was her little girl, and held her in her lap, and that golden head had nestled on her bosom.

"Eunice, O Eunice, he loved me first. You had better have stolen away my own heart. It would not have been so wicked or so cruel. How could you? O Eunice, give him back to me, Eunice, *won't* you?

"No."

Ada rose, staggering, without another word. She moaned a little to herself as she crossed the room to the door. Eunice accompanied her to the outer door, and said good-bye. Ada did not return it. Eunice saw her steady herself by catching hold of the gate as she passed through.

Then she went slowly up-stairs to her own room, wrapped herself in a shawl, and lay down on her bed, as she had that Christmas Eve. She was very pale, and there was a strange look almost of horror, on her face. She stared, as she lay there, at all the familiar objects in the room, but the most common and insignificant of them had a strange and awful look to her. Yet the change was in herself, not in them. The shadow that was over her own soul overshadowed them and perverted her vision. But she felt also almost a fear of all those inanimate objects she was gazing at. They were so many reminders of a better state with her, for she had gazed at them all in her unconscious childhood. She was sickened with horror at their dumb accusations. There was the little glass she had looked in before she had stolen another woman's dearest wealth away from her, the chair she had sat in, the bed she had lain in.

At last Eunice Fairweather's strong will broke down before the accusations of her own conscience, which were so potent as to take upon themselves material shapes.

Ada Harris, in her pretty chamber, lying worn out on her bed, her face buried in the pillow, started at a touch on her shoulder. Some one had stolen into the room unannounced—not her mother, for she was waiting outside. Ada turned her head, and saw Eunice. She struck at her wildly with her slender hands. "Go away!" she screamed.

"Ada!"

"Go away!"

"Burr Mason is down-stairs. I came with him to call on you."

Ada sat upright, staring at her, her hand still uplifted.

"I am going to break my engagement with him."

"Oh, Eunice! Eunice! you blessed—"

Eunice drew the golden head down on her bosom, just as she had on that old school-day.

"Love me all you can, Ada," she said. "I want—something."

Alice Brown

Natalie Blayne
1902

Alice Brown (1856–1948), a New Englander who became one of the most acclaimed short story writers of her time during the peak years of her literary career, has been lost to readers for many decades. Although her brilliant stories were identified as among the best of those labeled "local color," she wrote during the years of declining interest in literary regionalism. Despite inclusion in a few fine collections of local color fiction, she has presented difficulties for the literary historian. Although the best were written in the early twentieth century, her stories seem to belong to the nineteenth century because of their style and focus on women of middle age and older who had lived the first half of their lives during the nineteenth century in rural settings. For them, life did not change significantly when the new century began.

Brown published 17 novels, 4 volumes of plays, 3 of poetry, and 4 miscellaneous volumes of criticism, personal essays, and works for children during her career, which began in the early 1890s and continued for close to half a century. But it is the 115 stories collected in 8 volumes that justify claims for her literary greatness. She is very much the inheritor of the literary tradition of Catharine Maria Sedgwick, Lydia Maria Child, Harriet Beecher Stowe, and the "regionalists" who befriended her and welcomed her as their youngest colleague.

Many of Alice Brown's stories focus on women in community and in communication with each other, very often across the generations. "Natalie Blayne," originally published in Harper's Magazine *in September 1902, was reprinted in her third volume of short stories,* High Noon, *in 1904. This story, like Alice Walker's "Her Sweet Jerome," published more than sixty years later, represents another type of other woman story: one in which there is no other woman. Stories such as these lay bare some of the most degrading elements of heterosexual romances between people who, because of inappropriate gender-related ideas, are valued by each other and value themselves differently. This story, told with gentle compassion and humor that in no way minimizes the strong passions of both the younger and the older woman, does not directly address, let alone resolve, the underlying issues of self-sacrifice, stifled anger, and the presumption of different rights to happiness for women and men. It merely portrays them as conditions of the characters' reality.*

Brown never married. She spent her professional literary life as a respected member of a community and network of creative women: among them, Sarah Orne Jewett, Mary E. Wilkins Freeman, Elizabeth Stuart Phelps, Harriet Prescott Spofford, and Helen Hunt Jackson. Louise Imogen Guiney, the poet, was central to Alice Brown's life.

All eight volumes of her stories have been reprinted in recent years. The other seven are: Meadow-Grass: Tales of New England Life, *1895;* Tiverton Tales, *1899;* The Country Road, *1906;* Country Neighbors, *1910;* Vanishing Points, *1913;* The Flying Teuton, *1918; and* Homespun and Gold, *1920.*

It was a gentle autumn day, full of beguiling promise. The earth smelled good from ripened chalices. The mist hung in the distance like an enchanted censer-cloud, and no air stirred. This was the top note of fruition, so subtly mingled with hope that the human heart had to be heavy indeed not to rejoice in it.

Old Madam Gilbert lay in an upper chamber sick nearly to death; and no one knew her ailment. She had taken to her bed two weeks before, and languished there, not saying a word beyond quiet commonplaces, but with her dark eyes following her husband piteously, as he walked about the room doing little services for her. As time went on he seemed to be superseding the nurse, because, as he and his wife both knew, he could translate her wishes better than anybody else. Now she was growing swiftly weaker, as if unseen wings were wafting her out of life.

"Is there anything on her mind?" the doctor asked her husband, when he took his leave that day.

"No! no!" said old Ralph Gilbert, with all the certainty of his gentle heart. It hardly seemed worth while to fret either of them by asking that. He knew her life from sunrising to dusk through these difficult days, as he had known it every day for forty years. At night they had slept in like security of unison, one wrinkled hand clasped upon the other. Their hours had been like precious fragments welded into one.

"No," said he, "there is nothing on her mind."

"Queer!" muttered the doctor, with a puzzled frown. "There's nothing the matter with her, yet she's slipping downhill. I'll come tomorrow."

Ralph Gilbert stood for a moment in the doorway, looking out on the sweep of lawn and the noble trees that were all his—and hers. A sob came into his throat, and the air wavered before him. It was not possible that the final word had been spoken to their blended life together. The doubt, the hint of change, at once made that life ineffably precious to him, and he turned and went up the stairs in haste, like a boy, knowing there would be time enough for grieving afterwards. Delia, his wife, lay high upon the pillows in the great south room where the sun slept placidly on the chintz-covered chairs and old-fashioned settings. Her delicate profile looked sharp, and the long black lashes softened her eyes pathetically. Her gray hair went curling in a disordered mass up from the top of her head like a crown. She was a wonderful old creature, with a beauty full of meaning, transcending that of bloom and color. Her husband, standing there by the bedside, subtly resembled her. He was rather slight, and his fine old face, though it lacked the intensity of hers, had a mobile charm. He put one hand on hers, lying in ringed distinction outside the sheet.

"Dear," said he, an extremity of love in his voice, "Don't you feel any better?"

"I feel very well, dear," answered the old wife, in a tone as thrilling as her face.

"But you don't eat, dear!"

"I eat all I can. I need very little, lying here."

"Diana will be here to-night."

"Yes. That will be good."

He sat down by the bedside, and, like a faithful dog, refused to leave her, though she besought him not to miss his dinner. The nurse came and brought her a glass of something, but after a few teaspoonfuls she refused to swallow.

"I can't," she said. "It chokes me. Ralph, won't you go down to dinner?"

"No, dear," said the old man; "if you can't eat, I can't."

He bowed his head upon her hand, and she felt his tears. So, to please him, she tried again to drink; and seeing what poor work she made of it, and how it distressed her to try, he yielded and went down. Then she rested while the light faded, and in the early evening he brought Diana up to her. Diana, entering the room, dwarfed them both by her size, her deep-chested, long-limbed majesty, her goddess walk. She was a redundant creature in all that pertains to the comforts of life. She looked wifehood and motherhood in one. Her shoulder was a happy place for a cheek. Her brown eyes were full of fun and sorrow. Her crisping hair was good for baby hands to pull. She went swiftly up to Madam Gilbert, and touching her very gently, seemed to take her into her heart and arms.

"You lamb!" said she.

"There, Delia, now!" cried Ralph Gilbert, as if it were an efficacious thing to be called a lamb. Aunt Delia put up a languid hand to the firm red cheek.

"Diana!" said she, "that's nice."

"I expect you'd like to have her stay with you an hour or two to-night," suggested the old man. "I shall be here too, Delia. Right round the corner." He pointed to the dressing-room where he had lain ever since she fell ill, stirring at a breath.

"Yes," said his wife "You stay, Diana. Yes, Ralph, I know you'll be here."

"It puzzles me," said Diana later to her uncle, when they stood in the hall below, while the nurse made ready for the night. "There's nothing the matter with her, but she seems struck with—she seems strange."

The old man's face fell into the lines of a grief she could hardly meet.

"That's like Delia," said he solemnly. "She won't go like anybody else. It won't be sickness. She'll waste away."

"But I don't see," began Diana perplexedly.

"Well, never mind. I'll stay with her to-night, and maybe in the morning we can tell."

At nine o'clock she was installed with full prerogative in the chintz-gardened room. The nurse went to bed, and Uncle Gilbert camped on his temporary couch. He was very tired, and when Diana heard the breathing that betokened sleep, she softly shut the door upon him and returned to her great high-shouldered chair, just beyond Aunt Delia's gaze. The lamp burned low, a pin-speck in the moonlight, and the few embers broke and fell together on the hearth. The time went on for an hour, and she was conscious that Aunt Delia did not sleep, but lay there in an acute watchfulness like her own. At eleven Diana stole out of her chair to feed her, and found the great eyes wide open in the half light as if they had lost all power of closing. Diana never failed to enrich the life about her through lack of words. To her mind the gracious and living thing must be said, lest there remain no time for saying it.

"Dear heart!" she whispered. "What's the matter with you? The doctor doesn't know. You do. I know you do. You tell. Tell Diana, dearie. Diana's nobody."

"Move your chair a little nearer," said the old lady. "Towards the foot. There, so! Maybe I'll tell you, if I can. How long were you married, dear?"

Diana's hand went to her throat, where the blue wrapper fell away and showed a noble contour. She had never got used to her grief, that unmated mourning like the bird bereft when summer is at flood and the other creature is mysteriously lost in a clear heaven.

"Only two years," she said.

"Two years," repeated the old lady musingly. "And I have been married forty-one. You missed a great deal, Diana."

"Yes, I missed a great deal."

"You had the happiness of it; but you missed growing into his likeness and finding him growing into yours. I have had forty-one years."

"We won't have a golden wedding," said Diana, at random. "That's too much publicity. But I'll come and crown both of you with vine leaves in the garden, and uncle will reel off Horace, and we'll drink Hippocrene. I don't know what Hippocrene is, but it sounds very delirious, and it's none too good for wedding-days."

It was a change indeed when Aunt Delia forbore to smile at foolishness; but the dark eyes still looked solemnly forth into the shadows, and she said musingly:—

"I hoped it would be a good many more years, so that one of us wouldn't have long to stay alone. But we can't tell, we can't tell."

Diana felt the unyieldingness of the situation. Here was a difficulty which was no difficulty, and yet it seemed impervious.

"Dear," said she, "you tell Diana all about it."

She put her warm hand over the frail old one, and Aunt Delia turned a little on her pillow, and, as it seemed, snuggled into a confidential frame of mind.

"I was not very young when I met your uncle, dear," said she, "not as things went then. I was twenty-seven. Now, I believe it is different. Women are as old as they behave now. It wasn't the same in my day."

"We're as old as our ambitions now," said Diana. "However, we're not very partial to crowsfeet and double chins, I've noticed. Well, dear?"

"Your uncle was very attractive. You know that, of course?"

"Yes, auntie. He's always been an old dear."

"He wasn't an *old* dear then," said her aunt, in delicate reproof. "He was a very high-spirited young man, working hard at the law, and singing a great deal, and reading the classics in the evening. I am proud of your uncle's youth. He was a poor boy, and he made himself a name."

"Yes, dear," said Diana tentatively, in the pause that followed. "Take a sup of wine. You mustn't talk too much."

"It does me good," said the old lady, with zest. "I'm going to tell you something that has lain in my mind for over forty years. They say women can't keep secrets. I've kept this one. You'll keep it too, Diana. You'll understand, and see you can't ever tell. You know, my dear, your uncle has a very poetic mind. He is full of fun, but never to the detriment of his ideals."

Diana stopped herself in time from saying again that he was an old dear. She thought she knew exactly what kind of a youth Uncle Ralph's had been,—hot-headed, erratic, full of impossible ambitions trained into working forces by his mate.

"When we met," said Aunt Delia, "it was like the great stories We recognized each other. We saw it had got to be. Your uncle was too poor to marry, but—my dear, I felt from the first as if I were his wife already."

"I know," agreed Diana softly. "I know."

"I was perfectly happy until a week before our wedding-day. Then one evening we were sitting in the garden. It was just such weather as this. I could smell the grapes.—I hoped to put up my own preserves this year.—Well! well! Somehow—I don't know how it came about—I mentioned Natalie Blayne. She was a girl a good deal younger than I, and she came here for a visit. I had seen her two or three times, but she never made much impression on me. Well I spoke her name. 'Natalie Blayne!' said your uncle. 'Natalie Blayne!'" Madam Gilbert sat up in bed, and her voice rang dramatically. Diana saw that she was forgotten, and that the other woman was acting out a scene which had played itself in her memory many a time. "'Do you know her?' said I. His eyes grew very bright. His face changed, my dear. 'Natalie Blayne!' said he. 'I saw her for an hour, a year and a half ago. She came into Judge Blayne's office, and he sent me out with her to find columbines in the meadow. I liked her better at first sight than any woman I ever saw.'"

"But, auntie!"

"No, dear," said Madam Gilbert conclusively, as one who has long ago settled that disputed point, "he didn't even know he said it. Somehow we were on such terms that he never had to put a guard upon his lips. 'But didn't you try to see her again?' said I. 'No, said he; how could I? I was a poor boy in Judge Blayne's office. Besides, she was going abroad the next week.' 'So you lost her!' said I. He took my hand, and said the fingers were cold. Then he went on talking about what he calls potential mates. You know, my dear, he thinks there are many people we recognize instinctively when we meet them. They have a kinship with us. Sometimes it is explained. Sometimes it never is. These are our potential mates. You've heard him talk about it?"

"Of course I have," said Diana. "The dear old simpleton!"

"What, dear?"

"Yes, I've heard him talk. Go on."

"Well, I went to bed that night thinking my wedding-day was coming in a week, and that somehow, without any pain to him, I'd got to break it all off. Because he'd liked Natalie Blayne better than any girl he ever saw in his life, I knew I'd got to get her for him."

"But, auntie!" said Diana despairingly—"auntie!"

"Yes, my dear, I know. You think I was unreasonable. But those things have always been very sacred to me. I believe in the one true mate—there are many others too, my dear; I don't deny that—but one true one. And if it was Natalie Blayne!"

She sat there in her white bed, looking forward with eyes so moving in their childlike pathos that Diana's heart yearned over her. But she despaired of comforting anything so frail yet so invincible, so capable of pain.

"Aunt Delia," said she, in futile rallying, "Here you are, Uncle's commanding officer and mine, with power of life and death over us, and yet you're nothing but a baby. How can you suffer so?"

In her loneliness such conjuring seemed like tempting Heaven. If the man she loved could walk the earth again, he might moan over potential mates by the battalion, so that she only put the cup to his lips and touched his hand.

"I made up my mind to it," said Madam Gilbert, "and the next day—my dear, it was like a tragedy!—word came that Natalie Blayne was married. Whatever I did, he couldn't have her, after all."

"There!" Diana said whole-heartedly, "*she* was disposed of."

"I told him myself," continued the old lady. "I told him in the garden. I thought it might be a blow. 'I didn't want him to hear it from anybody else. 'Natalie Blayne is married,' I said. I couldn't look at him. Just then mother called from the window, and your uncle never had to answer me at all. But he went away quite early that day."

"Well, I should hope he did. Six days before his wedding! He went to buy the ring. *I* know!"

"Then I was tempted," continued the old lady fiercely, "and I yielded. What I really felt was this: 'If there is another woman in the world to whom he turns, I won't marry him.' But then I said, 'He can't have her. Let him take me. I'd rather be second best with him than first in heaven.' "

"Good for you, auntie! That's the way to talk."

"So we were married, and I kept on caring more and more and more and more—and so did he; and he was happy, and I was, too. But all the time Natalie Blayne stood between us. I had a terrible feeling as if I had stolen him from her, and the time must come when they would meet, in some other world, and he'd say, 'Why, here you are, my mate!' "

"O you poor little child!" cried Diana. "You poor little tragic, foolish child!"

"My dear, I have always held those things very sacred. But at last I began to forget her; and then, five years after she was married, her husband died, and the story ran that she was coming home to live with old Judge Blayne."

"But surely you didn't think"—"Oh no, my dear! He was too good, he was too honorable ever to have looked away from me. But don't you see, if he hadn't married me, he could have had her, after all."

Diana chafed a little under this theory of Uncle Ralph's invincibility. "You don't seem to consider," she ventured to suggest, "that Natalie Blayne may have been devoted to her husband's memory."

"I do, my dear, I do. But if they were mates, your uncle and she, why, she might recognize it this time, and that other marriage would have been only an episode."

"Now, I'll tell you," said Diana, "I begin to be a little sorry for Natalie Blayne. You bandied her about in a pretty fashion. She might as well have been that slave girl they wrangled over in the Trojan War."

"Well, she came, but only for a visit. Your uncle was away, it happened. I saw her. She was quite tall, with wonderful red hair. It curled. Red hair never turns gray, you know."

"It does worse," muttered Diana. "But never mind."

"I looked at her as I never had before. She had a lovely mouth. The upper lip was short and made a little pout, yet it wasn't a small mouth either. Her teeth were white as milk. Her hair grew in a little peak on her forehead. Her clothes were made in Paris. The long veil—my dear, she was slender, but that veil made her majestic."

Diana put her arms out and drew the rocking figure to her heart, but not to keep it there. Aunt Delia needed no woman's comforting: only that of the man who, in her despairing fancy, had been her soul and flesh and yet not wholly hers. Diana felt for her an agony of pity. Her grief seemed at once so tragic, so compounded of the spiritual jealousies and renunciations that take hold on life and death, and at the same time of the lesser pangs that make up sexual cruelties.

"Well, she went away," said Madam Gilbert, "but I heard about her. She studied music—she'd always played well—and now she went to Germany and worked very hard. She played quite wonderfully, sometimes in public. I never played. Your uncle was always fond of music. So there she stood between us until—she must have been forty then—she married again. Her name is Meredith."

"Oh, so she married again! Well, she seems not to have shrunk from experiments."

"Oh, but, my dear, doesn't that prove they were experiments? If she had married her true mate—and if I had not married your uncle, you see he would have been free—well! well!"

Diana thought she knew a good deal about womankind, but for the first time she began to penetrate the tortuous course of woman's jealousy.

"But, why on earth didn't you say this to uncle?" she urged, in one final despair. "I'd have said it to Jack. I'd have put my two hands on his shoulders and pinned him to the wall, and said; 'Out with it! Do you want Natalie Blayne? You can't have her; but be a man! speak up and tell! Do you want her?' "

"Your uncle was different, my dear. So am I different. And perhaps if you had been married longer you would have learned this: we must never let them see we can be hurt by what has happened. If they do, they keep things from us. They shut up certain chambers and lock the door. And it isn't that we want to go in there, dear; but it hurts us to think we have pushed them even a hair's-breadth away. We want to live so near them—so near—so near!"

"But, little Delia, don't you see you've been building up a wall between you all these years? Out of nothing, too!—a wall out of nothing! Uncle Ralph sat there in the garden and got mooning. I've heard him. He loves the sound of his own voice. He adores being a sort of Heine's lyric. And out of that innocent folly of his you pieced together a hair shirt, and you've been wearing it ever since!"

"He was quite honest," said Madam Gilhert solemnly. " 'I liked her better at first sight,' he said, 'than any woman I ever saw.' It meant so much to him that he quite forgot me when he said it. It was like saying it to himself."

"But dear heart, how many men have been bowled over by women they wouldn't take the gift of for keeps?"

"It may be so now, Diana, but it wasn't so in my day. We thought very differently of those things."

Diana pored again over the situation, which, as her amazed mind told her, was no situation at all. "But think of it!" she cried. "You're digging all this up now when you and Uncle Ralph are"—She was about to say "old people," but she stopped. The other woman seemed to be at that moment pathetically young. "Why not forget it?"

Again Madam Gilbert rose up in bed. Her pale cheeks wore each a tiny fever spot.

"Because she's coming here!"

"Natalie Blayne?"

"Natalie Meredith. She's a widow, and she's coming here to see the Blaynes."

"A widow! History repeats itself. But, auntie, in the name of Heaven! Why, the woman must be"—Still, as she instantly reminded herself, this drama had nothing to do with years, and she forebore.

"It's only that I haven't the spirit to meet it now," said Madam Gilbert faintly. "I hardly had it years ago; but now I am an old woman. I realize it. My hair is white. See how big the veins are in my hands!"

"Never mind! Uncle is older than you are!"

But this was no answer, and Diana knew it. She was talking to a woman whose passion was welling from the exhaustless fountain it had sprung from in her youth.

"Well," said Diana, "We're sure of one thing. You must go to sleep. Drink this. Yes, you must. You don't want uncle to behead me in the morning."

When the old lady was settling down among the pillows, she opened her eyes wide again, and said fiercely: "But it's unjust. It's one of God's injustices. I gave everything I had. He is my husband. I want him in this world, in the world to come. And she's always stood between us."

"Don't think of it now, dear. Don't try to account for anything. Let it all go."

"That's why I told you, Diana. And don't let me see her. I'm not strong enough. Let your uncle see her, if she comes—all he can, dear, all he can. But keep her away from me."

She fell into fluttering sleep, and Diana, watching while the cold dawn painted the sky, reflected upon the strangeness of life. Diana never split hairs. Again it seemed to her incredible that any woman who could live beside the man she loved should treasure cobwebs such as these. To sit at table with a man, to see him come home at night—these were the solid joys she coveted. Then with a sigh she began to muse again over this flimsy tissue woven from a dream.

Next morning Uncle Ralph came in in haste, so renewed by sleep that it seemed amazing not to find his Delia better. He regarded her with some pathos of rebuke, and she smiled wanly back at him.

"It's really ridiculous," said she. "I am an old fool, but I can't help it."

Diane breakfasted with him, and then put on her hat without delay. It took more than one night's wakefulness to destroy her bloom, and she was sweet and wholesome as she stood at the front door surveying the morning, her uncle sadly there beside her.

"I'm going to have a little walk," she said. "That will set me up. Better than sleep—oh, dear, yes! Don't tell her I'm out of the house, will you? As for you, uncle—well, if I were you, I'd spend most of my time making love to her."

"I always have done that," declared the old man simply. "I suppose you mean I'd better make the most of every minute now."

Diana turned upon him. "Don't let yourself think of such a thing!" she said angrily. "Die! Aunt Delia die! She's good for twenty years, if we've got any sense about us. But I tell you this; we've got to clutch her petticoats and drag her back."

Diana went down the garden walk, looking very splendid, as if she and the morning were in league together. In an hour she came back, all radiance and bloom. Her brown hair was curled the tighter from her haste, the red in her cheeks had deepened as if the sun had sunken into it. Little darts had awakened in her eyes and played about her mouth.

"Heavens, Diana! what's happened?" asked her uncle when she walked into the sick-room. "Who's left you a fortune?"

"Nobody," said Diana, in great tenderness, putting her cheek to the invalid's hand. "They've left it to Aunt Delia. It's a pot of gold."

"Enough to make her very rich?" asked Uncle Ralph. He liked to play at fairytales.

"Rich! I should think so. Not a competency, not your old annuities, but rich forever and two days after."

Then she sent her uncle out to walk, exiled the nurse, and assumed her reign again. All that forenoon she took perfect care of the invalid. She gave her food by the smallest quantities, and left her long intervals in quiet. After luncheon she sat down by the bedside and held Aunt Delia's hand.

"Sweetheart," said she, "what do you think I did this morning?

I took a walk. My shoe hurt me, so I went in to the Blayne girls to rest. They were just getting up from the breakfast table. I saw Natalie Meredith."

"Diana!"

"Yes, dear, I did. I couldn't help it, could I? Didn't my shoe pinch me? Dear, I could have wept. I did laugh. I went into a gale. They said you must find me excellent company."

"So you have seen Natalie Blayne!" said the old lady, wonderingly.

"Yes, I've see Natalie Blayne, and she's no sight at all. I hoped to find her a monster, rotund, busked, glittering in jet,—but she's not. No: she's simply a very well-preserved woman, with great evidence of facial massage and a look of exquisite care. Oh, she was pretty! I can see that. She's pretty still. Her hair isn't the glory as you describe, but it's lovely hair. She's got white hands that look as if they could play anything anybody ever wrote, and a great many rings on them. But, dear me, sweetheart! she's only a woman, after all. You've exalted her into something between a Cleopatra and a seraph. She's nothing of the kind."

Aunt Delia was looking steadily out at the red and gold maple-tops, a solemn sadness on her face. Diane began to wish she had caricatured Natalie Blayne.

"Well, dear," said Madam Gilbert presently, "I'm glad you've seen her. I hope it won't come in my way. And we mustn't talk about her any more."

That afternoon at four o'clock Diana sent the nurse to walk, and left her uncle in the sick-room. She took up her own station on the veranda, and sat there until Natalie Meredith came up the garden path. Diana went to meet her, and the stately woman greeted her with a simple grace.

"I feel as if I had deceived you," said Diana sweetly. "I told you Aunt Delia would be cheered by visitors, and now she proves to be too tired. I'm so sorry. But Uncle Ralph wants cheering, too, poor dear! Let me call him. Talk to him, do! Draw him out of himself!"

Natalie Meredith was exactly what Diana had painted her, save, perhaps, a shade more telling. She was the product of a high civilization, charming by nature, and with another charm added to that. She talked well, yet with a sympathetic regard to her listener; she was one of the women who take upon themselves the active share of entertainment. Presently Diana rose, with a pretty air of apology.

"You must let me call uncle,"said she.

When she entered the upper room he was sitting by his Delia's side, pathetically essaying the nonsense that in lighter seasons, made his joy.

"Uncle," said Diana, "I wish you'd come down and talk to a caller. I don't know what to do with her. She is a Mrs. Meredith. She's visiting at the Blaynes'."

A hot look throbbed into Madam Gilbert's eyes, but she kept them steadfastly on the tree-tops.

"Meredith? Meredith?" said Uncle Ralph fractiously. "I don't know any Meredith."

"Why, yes, Ralph, yes!" put in his wife eagerly. "You know her—Natalie Blayne!"

"Natalie Blayne? Oh, yes! She was one of the granddaughters. Heavens, Diana! didn't you tell her your aunt is sick and we're not seeing people?"

"Why, it's Natalie Blayne!" insisted the old lady. Her voice had a piercing quality he had never heard in it, her sombre eyes besought him. "Why, you remember, Ralph! It was summer, and you walked with her in the columbine meadow."

The old man turned on her a look of piteous apprehension. Then he spoke very gently, as we speak to those in pain, "Yes, dear, yes! I don't remember, but I dare say I did."

"You don't remember?"

"No, dear, but I've no doubt it's just as you say. Diana, you run down and tell her to go home. She must be a fool to come at a time like this."

"No! no!" cried Madam Gilbert. "No! you go down, Ralph. You must go. I insist upon it."

Diana got him out of the room and down the stairs. Meantime she whispered to him, "Does she seem to you as well, uncle? Is she sinking?"

"Don't say that!" cried the old man sharply. "Don't say that! Let me get rid of this Meredith woman"—

Natalie Meredith stayed a long time. She liked to talk, and, as she justly thought, these two people needed cheering. She told them a great deal about Germany and the music there, the charted freedom and atmosphere of pleasure. She did it very gracefully and sweetly, while Uncle Ralph rumpled his hair and fidgeted. So it went on until Diana, warned by the sympathetic tension of her own mind, grew keenly alive to the troubled spirit in that upper room.

"Uncle," she said, with her innocent air of sudden thought, "We've forgotten Aunt Delia's little powder. It's ten minutes late."

Uncle Ralph flew out of the room and up the stairs. Whe he saw his wife she was sitting up in bed, her eyes turned toward the door. She seemed to be watching in an agonized apprehension for what a step might bring. The old man hurried to her side and put his arms about her. He forgot the powder, for looking at her face. She was his Delia.

"There, there, honey!" he smoothed her, as he had for over forty years. "You lie down. Diana'll be up in a minute, as soon as that woman knows enough to go."

He laid her back on the pillow and gave her the medicine. She took it obediently, looking at him all the time in an incredulous seeking.

"There, Ralph!" she whispered. "Now go down again."

"Go down? I won't! Her tongue's hung in the middle. She talks a blue streak."

"But, Ralph, it's Natalie Blayne!"

"I don't care if it's old Judge Blayne himself. She's a bore."

"Dear, how does she look?"

"Well enough, I guess. Too much rigged out for a widow. Sheep dressed lamb fashion."

"But, Ralph, shouldn't you have know her? Does she remind you—Oh, you remember Natalie Blayne!"

"Why, yes, of course I do. The old judge sent me to the depot to meet her, or something. How he used to rope me in! I went there to study law, and he made me black his boots. But I should have said that girl had brown hair and brown eyes something like yours, dear, only not so pretty. This one's hair is copper-color. I dare say she does some ungodly thing to it."

Upon the silence that followed this, Diana came in. "She's gone," announced Diana.

"Thank God!" rejoined her uncle fevently.

Diana looked at Madam Gilbert for one solemn moment, and then the two women began to laugh. Aunt Delia laughed until she cried a little, in a happy fashion, and Diana put her arms about her, cooing and calling her a lamb.

"Here, uncle," said Diana, "You've got her back. In a week she'll be putting up preserves."

Madam Gilbert looked extraordinarily pretty and shy, and flushed like a girl.

"You lay out my clothes, Diana," said she happily; "I'm going to get up to dinner."

Martha Wolfenstein

Chayah
1905

Martha Wolfenstein (1869–1905) was born in Insterburg, Prussia. She came as an infant with her parents Bertha Brieger (1844–1885) and Rabbi Samuel Wolfenstein (1841–1921) to the United States.The family originally settled in St. Louis, Missouri, where Dr. Wolfenstein had accepted a call to the congregation of B'nai El through the influence of Dr. Isaac M. Wise. He simultaneously served as vice-president of the Hebrew Relief Association. The family moved to Cleveland, Ohio, in 1878, where Dr. Wolfenstein assumed the superintendency of the Cleveland Jewish Orphan Asylum. By this time, the family, which made its home at the orphanage, included six children. Dr. Wolfenstein stressed the principle of maintaining a home-like atmosphere for all the children under his care.

Martha Wolfenstein received her education in the Cleveland public schools.After her mother's death, Martha, then sixteen, assumed the duties of housekeeper for her father and younger siblings. She also served for a brief time as matron of the orphanage. She began to publish short stories in both Anglo-Jewish and secular periodicals. She appears to have been the first Jewish American woman to publish stories with Jewish characters and settings in secular, general readership magazines. her stories from Lippincott's Magazine *and* Outlook *were collected and published under the title of one of them,* Idyls of the Gass (The Alley) *by the Jewish Publication Society of America in 1901. The society also published her stories from the* Cleveland Jewish Review and Observer, *of which "Chayah" is one, as* The Renegade and Other Stories *in 1905. She received praise and encouragement from Henrietta Szold, the famous American Jewish leader and woman of letters, and Israel Zangwill, prominent English Jewish novelist and Zionist.*

By 1900, she had already been rendered frail by the tuberculosis from which her mother had died and that was to kill her six years later. The play she struggled to complete before her death has never been produced. Although she died in the same year that her second collection of short stories was published, there was no obituary in the secular Cleveland papers.

Most of her stories were said to have been based on her father's reminiscences of his life as a child in a Moravian ghetto, but "Chayah" and a few others seem to reflect a different voice, a different memory, and a different vision from these. The narrator of "Chayah" makes no attempt to hide the fact that she is telling this tragic story as a cautionary tale. A woman is safest among her own kind, with a man of her own people who is bound by the constraints of custom and community scrutiny to treat her less cavalierly than a stranger might. Within their shared culture she has value as an incubator of desired children, a worker for community survival, and a participant in the preservation of community tradition and identity.

As was true in "The Quadroons" for Rosalie, Chayah (whose name means "life"), as a member of a group of people whose oppression and victimization are sanctioned by the secular and religious law of the land, can only choose what attitude she will assume toward her "suitor." As women, both Rosalie and Chayah are doubly oppressed. In neither case does the young woman's innocence and trusting nature protect her. Both women are defenseless, betrayed, and destroyed. Both tragic stories are told by writers safe from the kind of victimization that claimed their central characters. "The Quadroons" was written by a white woman and "Chayah" was written by a Jewish woman in the United States where, at the turn of the century, Jews lived in greater safety than they had known for centuries in Eastern Europe.

The structure of this story, a "story within a story," is typical of writing from a culture in transition from an oral to a written tradition, as was Yiddish culture in this period. Each culture has its own literary history, but the literary histories of all cultures seem to follow a similar pattern in terms of the development of the short story. Whether Native American, black, or women's writing, the earliest stories reflect the history of storytelling. The narrator is most often an older woman—grandmother, aunt, mentor—telling stories to a girl on the cusp of womanhood, although sometimes the narrator is represented by an elderly man (usually a servant) addressing a group of children. To the modern reader, there is sometimes a clear distinction between the "moral" inherent in the storyteller's story and the "lesson" pointed out by the storyteller to the listener.

Tell thee of olden times? Now, what shall I tell thee? Thou hast heard all my old Maisselè [tales] a dozen times, and usser can you young people of nowadays understand. A world nowadays! They say it has grown better. Perhaps. To be sure, nowadays a girl has a silk dress at six years old, that we got first when we were married; and grown-ups they are at ten. My word, Mrs. Cohn's Mildred is only ten and belongs already to two clubs. And learning they have, that God have mercy! In my day a decent Jewish girl learned to read her prayer book, to cook and knit and manage a household, but nowadays!

There is Rosa Weinstein. I knew her father when he was a poor Bochur [Talmud student]—she is learned, no joke that, her learning! All day she watches fleas and worms and frogs and suchlike vermin and writes about them in a book. Pui! But Reb Weinstein would rejoice if he could arise out of his grave and see how his dear child Resel puts on a big pair of spectacles and watches how a cockroach wriggles his legs! A learning that! Natural geography or some such name they call it. Meshuggas [madness]! As if anything could be more un-natural. Natural is when a woman has a home, a husband, and children. But these are trifles nowadays. Rather would she stand in the school-room and teach, "See, Kinderlech [little ones], thus and thus is the manner in which a pinchbug scratches his ear, and now take this well to heart, that you all may grow up pious and learned men and women."

And how does that come? I will tell thee how. Nowadays the children know everything better than their elders. If a father finds a good match for his daughter, she will say, "I do not want him." "Why?" "I do not love him," she says. Is not that the purest nonsense! In my day it was not considered even decent to love a man before one was married to him. So they go on, and wait until they are dried-up old maids, and no one will have them. Serves them right, too. What is the good of parents, if they cannot know what is best for their children?

I also had some foolish notions when I was young,—I don't deny it,—and that came through an acquaintance I had with a Mamselle, who was employed at the palace of our Count, at home, in the old country. She told me so many stories about grand gentlemen, that I thought I also must have one, and when my father—peace be to him—made a match for me with thy dear grandfather, I didn't want him. He was small, was Yaikew, and not handsome to look at, I thought (though a finer looking man than my husband is now one need not wish to see). So I told my mother, who rests in Paradise, that I didn't want him. And dost know what my mother did? She slapped my face, big and stout as I was.

"Has anyone asked thee yet whether thou wantest him or not?" she said. And was she not right, and have I not been a happy woman in the forty-five years that I have been married?

We had no trouble at all, for my mother had said to me "Thou must be patient with thy husband. A man has many cares and perplexities in business, and if he comes home sometimes cross and scolding, thou must not mind. "Tis a woman's business to be patient and hold her tongue."

And his mother also had instructed him, he told me later.

"Do thou be patient with thy young wife," she had said. "A woman has many worries and annoyances in her household, and if sometimes she is cross, or the potatoes are a little burnt, or the meat tough, do thou not notice it, but be kind to her."

And so we had patience with each other, and learned to love each other, and have a happy life together. But nowadays they love each other so that they could eat each other up before the wedding, and six months thereafter they are tearing each other's hair out.

At home, in the old country, I also knew a girl after the fashion of nowadays. Chayah was her name. We lived in the same house with them for years; we in back, they in front.

Her mother had died when she was a baby, and she never liked Zirl, their old housekeeper, but clung to me, and used to call me Aunt Mindel from the time she was ten years old. She was the apple of Reb Lippman's eye, and if she had said, "Tate Leben [daddy dear], fetch me the moon down to play with," he would have found a way to get it.

The teachers at home were not good enough for her, Reb Lippman thought, so he got her one from the city; and she learned everything except what she should have learned, and grew up with her head full of foolish notions.

One day I came upon her as she was learning out of a book wherein were frightful pictures of bones and people cut in pieces, like a calf in the butcher-shop!

"Shema!—Chayah Leben," I said, "what terrible book is that?"

"This," she said, "is a physiognomy, and it is not terrible at all, for therein is written about one's liver and one's kidneys, and how one shall be well and healthy."

"Wie haisst?" I said to Reb Lippman. "Is that a learning for a girl, to learn about her inwards? It is not even decent," I said. "I tell you if she were my daughter, she would also learn about bones, but about the kind that go into the soup-pot," I said.

"What shall I do?" said Reb Lippman. "She wants to learn those things."

"And if she wants to dance around on the roof, will you also permit that?" I said. But what did it help? I might just as well have talked to the wall.

Thou must not think that I am of those foolish ones who think that learning is not a good thing. God forbid! But everything in its place. What is the good, I ask thee, if a woman knows about her inwards, when her children go dirty, and her husband has to eat bad dinners; or if, perchance, what is worse, she gets no husband at all?

Chayah could have made many a good match, although she had not much of a dowry, for Reb Lippman's business was going backward in those days already. She was a great beauty,—even envy had to admit that,—tall and strong, her skin like milk and roses, her hair black as night, and eyes she had, as blue as the heavens; but she could not find a man to suit her.

"For whom dost thou wait?" I used to say to her, "for a prince perhaps?" But she would only laugh and say, "Whether a prince or a beggar, I do not know. I wait for him whom I shall love," just like the girls of nowadays.

So she got to be twenty-three years old,—a very old maid in those days,—and still she had no husband. Then my nephew Mordché wanted to marry her—he was a step-son of thy great-aunt Veile,—and a nice young man he was, too; honest, diligent, thrifty, and no fool, either. He would have given his right hand for a kind word from Chayah, but she only laughed at him. I tried to persuade her to have him, but she said: "Mordché is a dolt! He is just like my cousin Belé's husband."

"Dovid?" I said. "And what is the matter with him? Is he not a good man, and is thy cousin Belé not a happy wife and mother?"

The Chayah looked at me with big eyes.

"And that thou callest happiness?" she said. "All day he works like a beast of burden, and when he comes home at night, his first word is, 'Wife, is the supper ready?' Then they eat; and when he speaks, it is of the hides he bought, and when she speaks, it is of

Maierlè's torn shoes, or Voegelè's tooth-ache. My God! and that thou callest happiness?"

That made me angry.

"Nu, of what should man and wife speak if not of their children and their business?" I said. "With all respect for thy learning," I said, "the more thou learnest the less sense thou hast. Dost think that everything is written in those books of thine? I tell thee, life is also a book, wherein one learns what is written in no other book, and therefore it behooves thee to listen to the voice of thy elders. Thou mayest live to regret that thou didst not," I said. But she only smiled to herself and said, kind of sadly, "Thou dost not understand, Aunt Mindel."

She was a strange girl.

We had war that year, and we Jews, nebbich, were pestered and worried to death. What they did not squeeze out of us in taxes, the soldiers ate up. For more than two months we had a regiment quartered on us; every one three or four, some as many as six soldiers. We also had our share, four common soldiers. The officers stopped with the rich Goyim; some of them were at the inn. My nephew Mordché used to see a good deal of these officers, for he used to get them their hair-oil and moustache-wax and cigarettes and suchlike stuff.

One evening he came to me in great anger.

"Why does Chayah run about the streets when they are full of soldiers?" he said..

"Is it thy business?" I said.

"Well, I cannot bear that these officers should make their filthy sport over her," he said, and then he told me that he had heard them speak her name over their wine, and so he had listened.

One of them swore, she was the most beautiful girl he had ever seen and that he meant to *conquer* her,—and what the wretches mean by that everyone knows. Then another had said that she looks like those who are not to be conquered, and then they had made a wager of it,—a large sum of money against a horse,—that he would conquer the beautiful Jew-girl before they left the town.

Mordché was in a great rage, and was for telling her father at once, but thy grandfather advised him not to.

"Reb Lippman has a weak heart," he said, "it will only anger him, and can do no good."

But I said I would speak to Chayah, and I told her that Mordché had heard the officers talking about her at the inn. She was much hurt, for she was modest and proud, and she said she would no longer walk on the streets while the soldiers were in the town.

A few days later Reb Lippman received notice that the soldiers who were quartered on him would be removed, and an officer, Baron von Hohenfels, would come in their place.

Thou canst imagine Reb Lippman's excitement. No other Jew had an officer in his house, and moreover a baron! Whatever there was that was fine and beautiful in the household, we carried into the best room, and made it ready for him, and in the evening he came. He was handsome man of thirty-five or thereabouts; tall and built like an oak, with yellow hair and moustache, bold and jolly, yet with the nicest, politest manners.

Reb Lippman asked him to what he owed the honor of so grand a guest, and the baron said that he had grown tired of that gypsy camp of an inn, that he had commissioned the quartermaster to find him a quiet family, so that he might have repose, since he wished to study. He did pack out a lot of books, too, and he began to read in them, but I was uneasy. That tale of Mordché's kept going through my head.

Mordché was away on business, and he did not get back for a week, and when he came I told him about Reb Lippman's grand guest. He wanted at once to see the man, so I took him into their kitchen, through the door of which one could look into the living room Therein sat the baron reading aloud. Reb Lippman had fallen asleep over it, but Chayah was listening, and her cheeks were burning red.

Mordché turned white as chalk when he saw the baron. "Tis he who made the wager," he said.

I had suspected it from the beginning.

Mordché was wild. "Reb Lippman must throw him out of the house!" he stormed.

"God forbid!" cried my husband. "Reb Lippman must not even be told. He might in his anger put him out, and bring misery not alone on himself but on the whole Gass."

You people who are born in America cannot imagine how it is over there. An insult to a baron, an officer! For less than that whole Jewish communities have been plundered and murdered.

Then Mordché thought of another way. "I shall report it to his superiors," he said.

"Fool!" said my husband, "what do they care? And what if the baron should deny it? Whom will they believe, thee, a Jew, or him?"

Mordché saw the sense of this, and he was silenced, but he insisted that Chayah be warned, so I told her what I knew.

Then one should only have seen her. "Tis a lie!" she cried. "Mordché is vexed, because the baron is kind to me. He should be ashamed to talk scandal, just because he is angry that I will not marry him. The baron is a gentleman, a kinder gentleman never lived. And even if he were what Mordché says he is, does he think I do not know what I owe to myself? His doubts are an impudence and an insult!" and off she walked with her head in the air, like an offended princess.

What could we do? Nothing at all. I made up my mind to watch the baron, and I did, but I saw nothing wrong. Not that I feared any harm could come to Chayah. God forbid! She was pure as snow and as proud and distant with him as with everyone; but I wanted to see what was going on. They were together all the time. When she sewed, he sat winding her thread upon bits of paper, and in the evening he read to her out of German books.

But after a while I gave up suspecting any wrong. I thought that Mordché, being jealous, had laid too much weight on what he had heard in the inn, and that the officers were only jesting, as in the manner with young noblemen. The baron was the nicest man one could imagine. It was not possible to think evil of him. Reb Lippman, too, could not say enough in praise of his noble guest, and Chayah went about with an exalted air, like one who has been granted a vision of Gan Eden.

One day, when I went into Reb Lipman's living room, I found the baron holding Chayah in his arms. The moment she saw me, she threw herself on my neck, trembling and crying. "He loves me,—he loves me, and I am to be his wife."

I thought that I should swoon, but I had enough sense left to see that the baron was embarrassed and angry. He had intended that they should keep it secret, and he asked me not to speak of it. I had heard that the Goyim do such things, but I was not used to that. Why should one keep a betrothal secret? I told it at once to Reb Lippman and his relations, and it went through the Gass like wildfire.

One should only have seen Reb Lippman then. He acted like one who has lost his senses. One moment he was tearing his hair and weeping; "My only child, to marry a Goy!" and the next moment he would say to himself as with wonder, "baroness—a baroness!"

"Nu," I said to my nephew Mordché, "what sayest thou now?"

"What should I say? His sport has become earnest. He has fallen in love with her," Mordché said. "But a rascal he is anyhow."

"Shah!" I said, "thou art jealous,"—but I was miserable. What kind of a match was that, a Gentile, a baron, and a Jewish girl? Such a thing had never been heard of.

"There can no good come of it," I said, and God knows I was right and Mordché was right, too.

This was on a Friday. The next day, Sabbath,—just as the people were coming out of Schul,—there came word that the regiment was ordered to the front, and by dark the village was empty of soldiers.

Chayah made no outcry when the baron went, but she could not sleep that night, so I let her talk to me, for I thought it might comfort her. Far into the night she talked, and only of her betrothed.

"Thou didst not believe it, Aunt Mindel," she said, "when I told thee that some day he would come,—he for whom my heart was yearning. But I believed it. I knew that God would not put that precious hope into my soul and not bring it to fulfilment. I knew that God would guide him to me if it were from the other end of the world. And I knew that when he came,—whether Jew or Gentile, whether rich or poor, whether high or low,—I should leave all else to follow him; for love is greater than all else," and then she wept softly to herself.

It was strange talk; more like a page out of the books which the baron used to read aloud, than what a sensible person would speak; but to tell the truth, I wept also. It would have melted a heart of stone to see her in her happiness.

The next day we began to hear the cannons, and frightened peasants came hurrying to the village, saying that a great battle was raging just above the Black Marsh. From the moment the shooting began, Chayah was a changed being. She walked the floor like a caged beast; she would not eat nor rest, but she only moaned to herself. Along toward evening she suddenly gave a great shriek. "My God, he is wounded—I know he is wounded," she cried, and fell to weeping and wringing her hands. We comforted her as best we could, and I persuaded her to go to bed.

Early next morning,—it was not yet light,—Reb Lippman came pounding on our door, crying that she was gone. He held a bit of paper on which was written: "I have gone to find him. I must know how he fares. If he is wounded, I shall bring him home."

Nu, she was gone, and we could but sit down and wait. The second day thereafter she came back. In an open farm-wagon she came, in which lay the baron, and his head was resting in her lap. We put him to bed, and got the doctor, for he was quite unconscious, and then we learned all that Chayah had done.

Into the battlefield she had gone, into the battlefield, while yet the shells were splitting open the ground at her feet. For a whole day and a whole night, far ahead of the ambulance corps, among the dead and the dying, through blood and a thousand horrors, without food or shelter, without help or protection, this tenderly nurtured girl had sought him. And she had found him and brought him out alive. He was unconscious and bleeding to death from a wound in his side; and she had staunched the blood, bound up the wound, and with the aid of a peasant lad carried him away, and brought him home.

It was days before the baron could even speak, and when he heard how Chayah had saved his life, he wept like a child.

"I was not worth it," he said again and again, "better I had died on the field."

God knows, it was the truth he was speaking, but Chayah would kiss him and stop his mouth when he spoke thus. She nursed and fed and petted him, as she would a child. She who had always been so shy of showing her feelings, now caressed and fondled him openly. She was a changed being.

And the baron also was changed. He was no longer bold and jolly, but humble and sad. It was most strange to behold. He talked all the time about how he would repay everything we did, and every day he begged the doctor to let him go.

Chayah was grieved that he should be so eager to go away, but he said he must, and every day he gave a more urgent reason why he must.

One day at dusk,—I remember it as if it were to-day, we had just lighted the there came a knock at the street door. Chayah answered. When she returned, she looked frightened, still she was laughing.

"There is a strange lady outside," she said, "she is entirely mad. She says," and then she threw her arms around the baron's neck and laughed aloud, "she says, she is thy wife!"

The lady had followed Chayah and now stood in the door-way. She was a tall, thin young woman, with a proud face, and she held a little boy by the hand. The baron turned white as death when he saw her.

"Pardon me," she said in a proud voice, "I see I am intruding. We received word that you were dying. Your mother thought that you might wish to see your wife and child. I see, however, that you are quite well, since you are at your usual business of deceiving women."

With that she went, but the little one hung back. "I have a new colt at home, papa," he said, but she dragged the child away.

Chayah had stared at the baron all the time. He sat pale-faced and guilty. Then she looked at us one after the other, with a face— may Heaven defend me from seeing such a face again!—and then she laughed,—'tis the God's truth, I'm telling thee—she *laughed* and walked quietly into her room.

Reb Lippman had not spoken a word. Now he suddenly dropped to the floor like a log. I ran to him; he lay as one dead.

"Wa geschrieen!" I cried. "Run for the doctor. Reb Lippman is dying."

For hours we worked over him, until he showed a sign of life, and when he opened his eyes, he asked for Chayah. I went to her room to get her, but she was not there. We looked for her all through the house; she was not to be found. She was gone. We asked the neighbors, but no one had seen her go.

May God defend everyone from the terrors we went through in the days that followed!

They sought her everywhere. They dragged the river, and sounded every well. High and low they sought her, and the baron— wretched scamp though he was, he must have had a conscience, for he sent out a searching party of his own.

On the fourth day thereafter they found her. She was wandering about the country full fifteen miles from home, and she had utterly lost her reason.

Nu, they brought her back. If I had not seen her with my own eyes, I would not have believed that a living being could change so in four days. She was wasted to a bone—bent and shrunken and haggard. One would have thought that a woman of fifty stands before one. She seemed not to know us, but stared straight before her, always with frightened eyes, and when one approached, she would shrink together, and gasp as with terror, "My God! My God!" No other word did she speak.

Reb Lippman had his death of it. He had, alas, a weak heart, and lived only two weeks thereafter, and Chayah was a forlorn creature, helpless and utterly mad.

Woe is me! It was a wretched business. But so it goes when children will know better than their elders. She might have been a happy woman. My nephew Mordché would have given his right hand for a kind word from her.

Charlotte Perkins Gilman

Turned
1911

"Turned" was first published in The Forerunner, *September 1911, a monthly periodical written, edited, and published by Charlotte Perkins Gilman (1860–1935) from November 1909 through December 1916. She founded the publication when she was fifty years old. The estimated 1,764,000 words written entirely by Gilman during its seven years existence included theoretical essays, book reviews, an advice column, short stories, seven serialized novels, and reports and commentary on relevant current events. (For a short time, she even wrote advertisements for products she personally used and could fully endorse). All of these writings expressed, illustrated, and supported Gilman's life-long commitments: feminism and an early humanitarian, non-Marxist form of economic socialism.*

"Turned" turns on contemporary vestiges of the droit du seigneur, *the legal claim of the feudal lord to sexual use of the female serfs who lived on his estate, a custom that has metamorphosed today in the United States into the sexual harassment of employees by some bosses and of students by some faculty members. Mr. Marroner has sexually used Gerta, the young Swedish maid, "the defenseless, unformed character" whose "docility and habit of obedience . . . made her so attractive—and so easily a victim."*

Mrs. Marroner, Marion, is as morally sickened by her husband's use of Gerta and subsequent callous, detached caution about the coming child as she is heartbroken by the fact of his betrayal of her. A man who could take pleasure in a defenseless girl's meek compliance is a man whose betrayal of his wife predates the actual consummation of his dilatory lust. He has violated the innocence of both women: "This is the sin of man against . . . womanhood." When she realizes the universal political implications of what she had originally felt "only" as a paralyzing personal violation,

Marion takes healing action. This story is the first clear articulation we have of the alliance that will become increasingly frequent in women's stories on this theme in ensuing years.

That Gilman had a humorous, often ironic side to her is evident in the multiple levels of meaning in the title "Turned." Mr. Marroner's name is also richly suggestive: a marron *is a chestnut. Webster's* Collegiate Dictionary *defines a chestnut as "an old joke or story; something repeated to the point of staleness." In other words, as Elizabeth Stuart Phelps asserts in the title of her story, such husbands as these are "No News."*

The complex life of Charlotte Perkins Stetson Gilman, feminist, sociologist, socialist, writer, editor, publisher, lecturer, and social change theorist and advocate, has not yet been fully explored. Some of her books have been reissued, including Women and Economics: A Study of the Economic Relations between Men and Women as a Factor in Social Evolution *(1898) in 1966;* The Forerunner *in 1968;* The Man-Made World; or, Our Androcentric Culture *(1911) in 1971; her 1935 autobiography,* The Living of Charlotte Perkins Gilman, *in 1972; "The Yellow Wallpaper," an acknowledged literary masterpiece since its original publication in 1892, published in book form in 1973 (The Feminist Press); the 1923 volume* His Religion and Hers: A Study of the Faith of Our Fathers and the Work of Our Mothers *in 1976;* Herland, *her feminist utopian novel published serially in* The Forerunner *in 1915 and only first published in book form in 1978; and the 1980 publication of the* Charlotte Perkins Gilman Reader, *containing sixteen stories, including "Turned."*

Her father was a member of the famous New England Beecher family of theologians, preachers, educators, social reformers, and authors, including his aunt Harriet Beecher Stowe, author of Uncle Tom's Cabin. *Frederic Beecher Perkins, writer, editor, and librarian, left his wife and the two surviving (out of four) children soon after Charlotte's birth, returning for only occasional visits and sending reading lists to his children. He contributed so little to their support that his wife, Mary Fitch Westcott, and the children lived in desperate poverty, moving nineteen times in eighteen years, living on the fruits of hard labor and the inadequate charity of relatives. Her parents were divorced when Charlotte was thirteen years old.*

Her mother withheld all expression of physical affection from her children, evidently hoping to help them achieve independent and invulnerable adult lives. However, sometimes while they slept—or she thought they did—she would caress them.

After a brief period of formal education at the Rhode Island School of Design, Charlotte began while still in her teens to support herself as a commercial artist, art teacher, and governess. She led a Spartan life both by necessity and by choice, maintaining an interest in physical fitness all her life.

At twenty-four she married a fellow artist, Charles Stetson, and a year later gave birth to her only child, their daughter Katharine Beecher. Gilman became deeply and increasingly despondent and finally suffered a complete nervous collapse.

After the medical mal-ministrations of the famous specialist, S. Weir Mitchell, failed to heal her, she took a trip to California alone in 1885 and discovered that alone, her symptoms receded. Three years later she moved with her daughter to Pasadena and in 1894 the couple was divorced. Soon after, Stetson married the writer Grace Ellery Channing, Charlotte's closest friend. Gilman remained close to her friend and her ex-husband and, when it seemed beneficial for Katharine to live with them, she sent her to them. Gilman was castigated for these choices and called an "unnatural" mother.

She supported herself for the next ten years as she was to support herself for most of her life, by giving public lectures which were, in the time before radio, movies, and television, almost the only form of public entertainment, education, and gathering, rivaled only by church- or synagogue-going. Gilman married a second time, in 1900, at the age of forty, this time to her first cousin, another Beecher descendent, George Houghton Gilman, a man seven years her junior.

In her soft-carpeted, thick-curtained, richly furnished chamber, Mrs. Marroner lay sobbing on the wide, soft bed.

She sobbed bitterly, chokingly, despairingly; her shoulders heaved and shook convulsively; her hands were tight-clenched. She had forgotten her elaborate dress, the more elaborate bedcovers; forgotten her dignity, her self-control, her pride. In her mind was an overwhelming, unbelievable horror, an immeasurable loss, a turbulent, struggling mass of emotion.

In her reserved, superior, Boston-bred life, she had never dreamed that it would be possible for her to feel so many things at once, and with such trampling intensity.

She tried to cool her feelings into thoughts; to stiffen them into words; to control herself—and could not. It brought vaguely to her mind an awful moment in the breakers at York Beach, one summer in girlhood when she had been swimming under water and could not find the top.

In her uncarpeted, thin-curtained, poorly furnished chamber on the top floor, Gerta Petersen lay sobbing on the narrow, hard bed.

She was of larger frame than her mistress, grandly built and strong; but all her proud young womanhood was prostrate now, convulsed with agony, dissolved in tears. She did not try to control herself. She wept for two.

If Mrs. Marroner suffered more from the wreck and ruin of a longer love—perhaps a deeper one; if her tastes were finer, her ideals loftier; if she bore the pangs of bitter jealousy and outraged pride, Gerta had personal shame to meet, a hopeless future, and a looming present which filled her with unreasoning terror.

She had come like a meek young goddess into that perfectly ordered house, strong, beautiful; full of goodwil and eager obedience, but ignorant and childish—a girl of eighteen.

Mr. Marroner had frankly admired her, and so had his wife. They discussed her visible perfections and as visible limitations with that perfect confidence which they had so long enjoyed. Mrs. Marroner was not a jealous woman. She had never been jealous in her life—till now.

Gerta had stayed and learned their ways. They had both been fond of her. Even the cook was fond of her. She was what is called "willing," was unusually teachable and plastic; and Mrs. Marroner, with her early habits of giving instruction, tried to educate her somewhat.

"I never saw anyone so docile," Mrs. Marroner had often commented. "It is perfection in a servant, but almost a defect in character. She is so helpless and confiding."

She was precisely that: a tall, rosy-cheeked baby; rich womanhood without, helpless infancy within. Her braided wealth of dead-gold hair, her grave blue eyes, her mighty shoulders and long, firmly moulded limbs seemed those of a primal earth spirit; but she was only an ignorant child, with a child's weakness.

When Mr. Marroner had to go abroad for his firm, unwillingly, hating to leave his wife, he had told her he felt quite safe to leave her in Gerta' hands—she would take care of her.

"Be good to your mistress, Gerta," he told the girl that last morning at breakfast. "I leave her to you to take care of. I shall be back in a month at latest."

Then he turned, smiling to his wife. "And you must take care of Gerta, too," he said, "I expect you'll have her ready for college when I get back."

This was seven months ago. Business had delayed him from week to week, from month to month. He wrote to his wife, long, loving, frequent letters, deeply regretting the delay, explaining how necessary, how profitable it was, congratulating her on the wide resources she had, her well-filled, well-balanced mind, her many interests.

"If I should be eliminated from your scheme of things, by any of those 'acts of God' mentioned on the tickets, I do not feel that you would be an utter wreck," he said. "That is very comforting to me. Your life is so rich and wide that no one loss, even a great one, would wholly cripple you. But nothing of the sort is likely to happen, and I shall be home again in three weeks—if this thing gets settled. And you will be looking so lovely, with that eager light in your eyes and the changing flush I know so well—and love so well! My dear wife! We shall have to have a new honeymoon-other moons come every month, why shouldn't the mellifluous kind?"

He often asked after "little Gerta," sometimes enclosed a picture postcard to her, joked his wife about her laborious efforts to educate "the child," was so loving and merry and wise—

All this was racing through Mrs. Marroner's mind as she lay there with the broad, hemstiched border of fine linen sheeting crushed and twisted in one hand, and the other holding a sodden handkerchief.

She had tried to teach Gerta, and had grown to love the patient, sweet-natured child, in spite of her dullness. At work with her hands, she was clever, if not quick, and could keep small accounts from week to week. But to the woman who held a Ph.D., who had been on the faculty of a college, it was like baby-tending.

Perhaps having no babies of her own made her love the big child the more, though the years between them were but fifteen.

To the girl she seemed quite old, of course; and her young heart was full of grateful affection for the patient care which made her feel so much at home in this new land.

And then she had noticed a shadow on the girl's bright face. She looked nervous, anxious, worried. When the bell rang, she seemed startled, and would rush hurriedly to the door. Her peals of frank laughter no longer rose from the area gate as she stood talking with the always admiring tradesmen.

Mrs. Marroner had labored long to teach her more reserve with men, and flattered herself that her words were at last effective. She suspected the girl of homesickness, which was denied. She suspected her of illness, which was denied also. At last she suspected her of something which could not be denied.

For a long time she refused to believe it, waiting. Then she had to believe it, but schooled herself to patience and understanding. "The poor child," she said. "She is here without a mother—she is so foolish and yielding—I must not be too stern with her." And she tried to win the girl's confidence with wise, kind words.

But Gerta had literally thrown herself at her feet and begged her with streaming tears not to turn her away. She would admit nothing, explain nothing, but frantically promised to work for Mrs. Marroner as long as she lived—if only she would keep her.

Revolving the problem carefully in her mind, Mrs. Marroner thought she would keep her, at least for the present. She tried to repress her sense of ingratitude in one she had so sincerely tried to help, and the cold, contemptuous anger she had always felt for such weakness.

"The thing to do now," she said to herself, "is to see her through this safely. The child's life should not be hurt any more than is unavoidable. I will ask Dr. Bleet about it—what a comfort a woman doctor is! I'll stand by the poor, foolish thing till it's over, and then get her back to Sweden somehow with her baby. How they do come where they are not wanted—and don't come where they are wanted!" And Mrs. Marroner, sitting alone in the quiet spacious beauty of the house, almost envied Gerta.

Then came the deluge.

She had sent the girl out for needed air toward dark. The late mail came; she took it in herself. One letter for her—her husband's letter. She knew the postmark, the stamp, the kind of typewriting. She impulsively kissed it in the dim hall. No one would suspect Mrs. Marroner of kissing her husband's letters—but she did, often.

She looked over the others. One was for Gerta, and not from Sweden. It looked precisely like her own. This struck her as a little odd, but Mr. Marroner had several times sent messages and cards to the girl. She laid the letter on the hall table and took hers to her room.

"My poor child," it began. What letter of hers had been sad enough to warrant that?

"I am deeply concerned at the news you sent." What news to so concern him had she written? "You must bear it bravely, little girl. I shall be home soon, and will take care of you, of course. I hope there is not immediate anxiety—you do not say. Here is money, in case you need it. I expect to get home in a month at latest. If you have to go, be sure to leave your address at my office. Cheer up—be brave—I will take care of you."

The letter was typewritten, which was not unusual. It was unsigned, which was unusual. It enclosed an American bill—fifty dollars. It did not seem in the least like any letter she had ever had from her husband, or any letter she could imagine him writing. But a strange, cold feeling was creeping over her, like a flood rising around a house.

She utterly refused to admit the ideas which began to bob and push about outside her mind, and to force themselves in. Yet under the pressure of these repudiated thoughts she went downstairs and brought up the other letter—the letter to Gerta. She laid them side by side on a smooth dark space on the table; marched to the piano and played, with stern precision, refusing to think, till the girl came back. When she came in, Mrs. Marroner rose quietly and came to the table. "Here is a letter for you," she said.

The girl stepped forward eagerly, saw the two lying together there, hesitated, and looked at her mistress.

"Take yours, Gerta. Open it, please."

The girl turned frightened eyes upon her.

"I want you to read it, here," said Mrs. Marroner.

"Oh, ma'am—No! Please don't make me!"

"Why not?"

There seemed to be no reason at hand, and Gerta flushed more deeply and opened her letter. It was long; it was evidently puzzling to her; it began "My dear wife." She read it slowly,

"Are you sure it is your letter?" asked Mrs. Marroner. "Is not this one yours? Is not that one—mine?"

She held out the other letter to her.

"It is a mistake," Mrs. Marroner went on, with a hard quietness. She had lost her social bearings somehow, lost her usual keen sense of the proper thing to do. This was not life; this was a nightmare.

"Do you not see? Your letter was put in my envelope and my letter was put in your envelope. Now we understand it."

But poor Gerta had no antechamber to her mind, no trained forces to preserve order while agony entered. The thing swept over her, resistless, overwhelming. She cowered before the outraged wrath she expected; and from some hidden cavern that wrath arose and swept over her in pale flame.

"Go and pack your trunk," said Mrs. Marroner. "You will leave my house tonight. Here is your money."

She laid down the fifty-dollar bill. She put with it a month's wages. She had no shadow of pity for those anguished eyes, those tears which she heard drop on the floor.

"Go to your room and pack,"said Mrs. Marroner. And Gerta, always obedient, went.

Then Mrs. Marroner went to hers, and spent a time she never counted, lying on her face on the bed.

But the training of the twenty-eight years which had elapsed before her marriage; the life at college, both as student and teacher; the independent growth which she had made, formed a very different background for grief from that in Gerta's mind.

After a while Mrs. Marroner arose. She administered to herself a hot bath, a cold shower, a vigorous rubbing. "Now I can think," she said.

First she regretted the sentence of instant banishment. She went upstairs to see if it had been carried out. Poor Gerta! The tempest of her agony had worked itself out at last as in a child, and left her sleeping, the pillow wet, the lips still grieving, a big sob shuddering itself off now and then.

Mrs. Marroner stood and watched her, and as she watched she considered the helpless sweetness of the face; the defenseless, unformed character; the docility and habit of obedience which made her so attractive—and so easily a victim. Also she thought of the mighty force which had swept over her; of the great process now working itself out through her; of how pitiful and futile seemed any resistance she might have made.

She softly returned to her own room, made up a little fire, and sat by it, ignoring her feelings now, as she had before ignored her thoughts.

Here were two women and a man. One woman was a wife: loving, trusting, affectionate. One was a servant: loving, trusting, affectionate—a young girl, an exile, a dependent; grateful for any kindness; untrained, uneducated, childish. She ought, of course, to have resisted temptation! but Mrs. Marroner was wise enough to know how difficult temptation is to recognize when it comes in the guise of friendship and from a source one does not suspect.

Gerta might have done better in resisting the grocer's clerk; had, indeed, and with Mrs. Marroner's advice, resisted several. But where respect was due, how could she criticize? Where obedience was due, how could she refuse—with ignorance to hold her blinded—until too late?

As the older, wiser woman forced herself to understand and extenuate the girl's misdeed and foresee her ruined future, a new feeling rose in her heart, strong, clear, and overmastering: a sense of measureless condemnation for the man who had done this thing. He knew. He understood. He could fully foresee and measure the consequences of his act. He appreciated to the full the innocence, the ignorance, the grateful affection, the habitual docility, of which he deliberately took advantage. Mrs. Marroner rose to icy peaks of intellectual apprehension, from which her hours of frantic pain seemed far indeed removed. He had done this thing under the same roof with her—his wife. He had not frankly loved the younger woman, broken with his wife, made a new marriage. That would have been heart-break pure and simple. This was something else.

That letter, that wretched, cold, carefully guarded, unsigned letter, that bill—far safer than a check—these did not speak of affection. Some men can love two women at one time. This was not love.

Mrs. Marroner's sense of pity and outrage for herself, the wife, now spread suddenly into a perception of pity and outrage for the girl. All that splendid, clean young beauty, the hope of a happy life, with marriage and motherhood, honorable independence, even—these were nothing to that man. For his own pleasure he had chosen to rob her of her life's best joys.

He would "take care of her," said the letter. How? In what capacity?

And then, sweeping over both her feelings for herself, the wife, and Gerta, his victim, came a new flood, which literally lifted her to her feet. She rose and walked, her head held high. "This is the sin of man against woman," she said. "The offense is against womanhood. Against motherhood. Against—the child."

She stopped.

The child. His child. That, too, he sacrificed and injured—doomed to degradation.

Mrs. Marroner came of stern New England stock. She was not a Calvinist, hardly even a Unitarian, but the iron of Calvinism was in her soul: of that grim faith which held that most people had to be damned "for the glory of God."

Generations of ancestors who both preached and practiced stood behind her; people whose lives had been sternly moulded to their highest moments of religious conviction. In sweeping bursts of feeling, they achieved "conviction," and afterward they lived and died according to that conviction.

When Mr. Marroner reached home a few weeks later, following his letters too soon to expect an answer to either, he saw no wife upon the pier, though he had cabled, and found the house closed darkly. He let himself in with his latch-key, and stole softly upstairs, to surprise his wife.

No wife was there.

He rang the bell. No servant answered it.

He turned up light after light, searched the house from top to bottom; it was utterly empty. The kitchen wore a clean, bald, unsympathetic aspect. He left it and slowly mounted the stairs, completely dazed. The whole house was clean, in perfect order, wholly vacant.

One thing he felt perfectly sure of—she knew.

Yet was he sure? He must not assume too much. She might have been ill. She might have died. He started to his feet. No, they would have cabled him. He sat down again.

For any such change, if she had wanted him to know, she would have written. Perhaps she had, and he, returning so suddenly, had missed the letter. The thought was some comfort. It must be so. He turned to the telephone and again hesitated. If she had found out—if she had gone—utterly gone, without a word—should he announce it himself to friends and family?

He walked the floor; he searched everywhere for some letter, some word of explanation. Again and again he went to the telephone—and always stopped. He could not bear to ask: "Do you know where my wife is?"

The harmonious, beautiful rooms reminded him in a dumb,

helpless way of her—like the remote smile on the face of the dead. He put out the lights, could not bear the darkness, turned them all on again.

It was a long night—

In the morning he went early to the office. In the accumulated mail was no letter from her. No one seemed to know of anything unusual. A friend asked after his wife—"Pretty glad to see you, I guess?" He answered evasively.

About eleven a man came to see him: John Hill, her lawyer. Her cousin, too. Mr. Marroner had never liked him. He liked him less now, for Mr. Hill merely handed him a letter, remarked, "I was requested to deliver this to you personally," and departed, looking like a person who is called on to kill something offensive.

"I have gone. I will care for Gerta. Good-bye. Marion."

That was all. There was no date, no address, no postmark, nothing but that.

In his anxiety and distress, he had fairly forgotten Gerta and all that. Her name aroused in him a sense of rage. She had come between him and his wife. She had taken his wife from him. That was the way he felt.

At first he said nothing, did nothing, lived on alone in his house, taking meals where he chose. When people asked him about his wife, he said she was traveling—for her health. He would not have it in the newspapers. Then, as time passed, as no enlightenment came to him, he resolved not to bear it any longer, and employed detectives. They blamed him for not having put them on the track earlier, but set to work, urged to the utmost secrecy.

What to him had been so blank a wall of mystery seemed not to embarrass them in the least. They made careful inquiries as to her "past," found where she had studied, where taught, and on what lines; that she had some little money of her own, that her doctor was Josephine L. Bleet, M.D., and many other bits of information.

As a result of careful and prolonged work, they finally told him that she had resumed teaching under one of her old professors, lived quietly, and apparently kept boarders; giving him town, street, and number as if it were a matter of no difficulty whatever.

He had returned in early spring. It was autumn before he found her.

A quiet college town in the hills, a broad, shady street, a pleasant house standing in its own lawn, with trees and flowers about it. He had the address in his hand, and the number showed clear on the white gate. He walked up the straight gravel path and rang the bell. An elderly servant opened the door.

"Does Mrs. Marroner live here?"

"No, sir."

"This is number twenty-eight?"

"Yes, sir."

"Who does live here?"

"Miss Wheeling, sir."

Ah! Her maiden name. They had told him, but he had forgotten. He stepped inside. "I would like to see her," he said.

He was ushered into a still parlor, cool and sweet with the scent of flowers, the flowers she had always loved best. It almost brought tears to his eyes. All their years of happiness rose in his mind again—the exquisite beginnings; the days of eager longing before she was really his; the deep, still beauty of her love.

Surely she would forgive him—she must forgive him. He would humble himself; he would tell her of his honest remorse—his absolute determination to be a different man.

Through the wide doorway there came in to him two women. One like a tall Madonna, bearing a baby in her arms.

Marion, calm, steady, definitely impersonal, nothing but a clear pallor to hint of inner stress.

Gerta, holding the child as a bulwark, with a new intelligence in her face, and her blue, adoring eyes fixed on her friend—not upon him.

He looked from one to the other dumbly.

And the woman who had been his wife asked quietly:

"What have you to say to us?"

Helen Reimensnyder Martin

A Poet Though Married
1911

There is scant biographical information available about Helen Reimensnyder Martin (1868–1939). She was born in Lancaster, Pennsylvania, to Henrietta Thurman and the Reverend Cornelius Reimensnyder, an immigrant German Lutheran pastor. Educated as a special student in English at Swarthmore and Radcliffe, she taught at a fashionable private school in New York City where she came in contact with the wealthy. After her marriage to Frederic C. Martin, a music teacher, in 1899, they settled in Harrisburg, Pennsylvania, where Helen Martin began to write. She published a novel a year, eventually producing thirty-six novels and two volumes of short stories. The couple had one daughter and one son. Martin wrote for middle class popular audiences, publishing stories in McClure's, Century, Cosmopolitan, *and other periodicals. Her husband died in 1936 and she died three years later, at the age of seventy, in her daughter's home.*

She had one subject—the oppression of women—which she explored in two settings: sophisticated high society and rural Pennsylvania Dutch society. Her high-society novels were not well received until after she had achieved recognition and success with her ethnic material.

Her work was successfully translated to the stage and screen. Her most famous and frequently reprinted novel, the 1904 Tillie: A Mennonite Maid, *was made into a film in 1922 and produced on stage in 1924. Her 1914 Mennonite novel,* Barnabetta, *was turned into a play at the request of Minnie Maddern Fiske (1865– 1932), one of the greatest theatrical artists in U.S. history. After a two-year absence from the stage during which she filmed the earliest cinematic version of Thomas Hardy's* Tess of the D'Urbervilles *(1913) and William Thackeray's* Vanity

Fair *(1915)*, *Fiske, who had introduced Henrik Ibsen to American audiences, returned to the stage in the starring role in* Erstwhile Susan *(1916), the theatrical version of* Barnabetta. *It was later made into a film. Finally, two of Martin's high-society novels became films:* The Parasite *(1913) in 1925 with Owen Moore and Madge Bellamy and* The Snob *(1924) in 1924 with John Gilbert and Norma Shearer.*

Martin has been variously praised for the authenticity of her portrayals of the Pennsylvania German ethnic community and for the comic exaggerations of characteristics presumed to be typical of its members. She had also been castigated for those same exaggerations, which have been labeled extreme, unfair, and cruel caricatures. In a 1916 interview published in the New York Evening Post, *to defend herself from these attacks, she said, "The Pennsylvania Dutchman is parsimonious with everything but the labor of his women. He'll buy modern plows, an automobile to take his products to market, modern harness to save his horse. Up-to-dateness in the barn means more money in his pocket. But he won't spend a cent to save his wife or daughter a bit of work. That is what they are for—to work for men folk in the kitchen or near it."*

She campaigned actively for women's suffrage and for socialism. She saw significant connections between capitalism and the organized church, and she opposed them both. Beverly Seaton, a modern critic, has written about Martin that her central message was "The absolute necessity for a person to be independent of others, educated, able to earn a living, free to choose a vocation," adding that, for women, "money of her own is the key to control of her own life."

"A Poet Though Married" was originally published in Hampton's Magazine, *September 1911, and later collected in Martin's 1930 volume of short stories,* Yoked with a Lamb *which, along with her 1907 collection,* The Betrothal of Elypholate and Other Tales of the Pennsylvania Dutch, *has recently been reprinted. This story focuses on her most constant themes, although it is free of the extreme ethnic stereotyping for which she has been criticized: Benny Glick is a "special case" in his community. Additionally, Martin in this story echoes the theme of sisterhood and women's solidarity first suggested in Mary E. Wilkins Freeman's story "A Moral Exigency" and elaborated in Charlotte Perkins Gilman's story "Turned," published in 1911, the same year as was "A Poet Though Married."*

Maggie Glick, in the flush of unwanted indignation that colored her mild, delicate face and brightened her soft, patient eyes, looked almost as young as she really was and almost as pretty as on the day, six years ago, when Bennie Glick had fallen in love with her, written a poem to her and then proceeded to marry her. Six years—during which she had borne him four children and supported the whole family, at the cost of her youth and beauty, while he—*ach, Himmel!*—wrote "pomes" for the Lebanon *Intelligencer* and the county *New Era*, his sole compensation for which consisted in the glory of seeing himself in print. And now, in the very face of her loving sacrifices for him, he sat at their table in their tiny dining-room and made love—"or next thing *to*"—to their boarder, the brazen, pretty young "towner" who had come out to teach the village school!

"She's as crazy after Bennie as he is after her!" thought Maggie, tears of self-pity filling her eyes as she bent over her baby girl's plate to cut her meat. Never in all her married life had she grudged slaving for Bennie Glick that he might be free to write his "po-try" so long as he *loved* her. But only to *hear* the way he and that teacher were going on at each other! Bennie was telling the teacher, in effect, that not until he had known *her* had he written as he was capable of writing, that *her* appreciation, *her* understanding, had inspired his masterpiece. No one else, he said, had ever really appreciated his talents.

"But," wondered Maggie, bewildered, "if workin' day and night fur six years yet to support him and his children ain't 'preciation, what *is*? I certainly wouldn't of did it fur no *common* man!"

The teacher herself looked like an exotic in this neat little painted frame house at the end of the one long street of the Pennsylvania Dutch villlage. The cheap varnished dining-room suite—which was the proud and triumphant result of a year's secret saving on Maggie's part—the two luridly colored chromos which hung over the sideboard, representing a variety of fruits never known to appear simultaneously, and so perfect in form and color as to be monstrosities, a ghastly picture of the dying Garfield hanging over the refrigerator—these details made an odd setting for the radiant and extremely stylish young lady who sat at the poet's side and daintily sipped her tea.

"Of course I recognize," she was saying with that air of elegance which both awed and cowed poor Maggie, "that your poetry—*yours*—wouldn't be appreciated here."

Bennie—incapable of the least suspicion that she was saying to herself, "Or they'd publish it in the joke column!"—gazed at her with his soul in his eyes.

"Till I'm through dinner I'll read you what I wrote off this morning," he eagerly announced.

"Now you've taken away my appetite, I'm so eager to hear it!"

"I hope it *is* my pome and not these here scorched turnips that has took your appetite," he returned as, having helped himself abundantly to the turnips and tasted them, he cast a reproving glance at his wife.

"Oh!" exclaimed Miss De Ford, "You are different from *some* of the great poets—Shakespeare, you remember, never knew *what* Anne put before him," she improvised. "And as for Virgil and Whittier and Alfred Austin and all those—well, plain living and high thinking, you know."

Maggie looked up in astonishment. "Why! I conceited it was just the other way about—that the po-try workin' in 'em made 'em so wonderful choicy about their wittles!"

"Och, Maggie, what do you know about it?"

"But that's what you always *told* me, Bennie! And that's why my cookin' worries me so—for fear you can't write your po-try if I don't feed you up wholesome and hearty!" she insisted.

"These here scorched turnips don't look as if your cookin' worried you!"

"They stuck fur me while baby was nursin'—and I didn't call you to stir 'em because I seen you was deep in it—with that new pome."

"But I assure you, Mrs. Glick, that a true poet's delicate sensibilities are revolted by the grossness of rich or heavy food," Miss De Ford affirmed dogmatically, helping herself deliberately (to Maggie's consternation) to a second cream puff, the last on the dish, the one intended for Bennie's dessert. "I would know merely to look at Mr. Glick that that was the case with *him*," she added, her bright eyes moving appreciatively from Bennie's greasy visage to his double chin and hat, overfed body.

"But it ain't!" cried Maggie. "It ain't!"

"You don't understand him, Mrs. Glick," Miss De Ford returned with a patronizing smile which made Maggie long to rise up in her wrath and tell her she could suit herself with another boarding place, that *this* house was "full-up" and that her room was needed.

But the sad truth was she did not even dare to show the claws with which she yearned to scratch her rival; for since the death of one of their two cows, the teacher's board was almost their only income, and so they needed not only what she paid, but the money she was going to pay Bennie for acting as janitor of the schoolhouse— a function which all her predecessors had performed themselves. But *this* teacher, it seemed, was "too tony" to do such work, you had only to look at her hands. Maggie had never seen such hands. And such was her unbelievable power over Bennie, with her pretty looks and flattering ways, that she had actually got him to *work*— at least an hour a day!—to keep the schoolroom fire, wash the windows, sweep the floor and dust the desks!

"I would be takin' the bread out of my chil'ren's mouths, to send her off!" the poor wife thought. "And not even to keep Bennie's love to myself will I hurt my babies!"

It really looked as if Miss De Ford had helped herself to that cream puff just because she didn't think such rich things good for poets, for after taking only one bite of it, she was leaving it on her plate. Maggie was sure Bennie would reproach her for not having had more of them on the table, he was so fond of them. But they cost "two for five," and though the children, too, loved them, she could not afford to buy such luxuries for any one but Bennie and the boarder.

"Ben!" Miss De Ford suddenly spoke to the five-year-old boy opposite her at the table. "Will you finish my cream puff?"

"You bet you!" Ben quickly responded, his face beaming at this unexpected windfall. His mother had warned him not to ask for any.

"Now," the teacher turned brightly to the poet, who was sadly following the course of the cream puff which should have been his, "we will go into the parlor and hear the poem."

"They don't ask me to come hear it, too—they just want to be by theirselves!" thought Maggie as, with a speed expressive of her heated mind, she took the children down from the table and proceeded to "clear off" and "wash up." "It's Saturday and she ain't got nothin' to do but set in there and spoon with Bennie!"

The sound of Bennie's voice, thick with the emotion called up by his poem as he read, came to her as she moved to and from between the boxlike dining-room and kitchen of the little village cottage.

This is what Bennie was reading:

LINES ON A LADY'S VISIT TO A FORMER LADY FRIEND

> On a summer eve a lady strayed,
> In charity perchance a call she paid.
>
> Her host in other days she had known:
> She found her in sadness, neglect and forlorn.
>
> Happy, oh, how happy once was she,
> Oh, how great a change she did see!
>
> Now she was married, wan, and pale,
> The story of many an ofttold tale.
>
> There squalor and penury and want and misery
> Stalked as handmaids in full mastery.
>
> Her husband to her unkind and poor,
> No cheer was there and bare was the floor
>
> As long as the aunt's bounty did last
> They had drove a pace exceedingly fast.
>
> Once they most lavishly did entertain,
> Now one room all their effects doth contain.
>
> Now they sit upon the stool of repentance
> Bewailing their want of sustenance.
>
> They drank the cup of violence:
> Now they eat the bread of bitterness.
>
> And my lady far in silence withdrew,
> And in pity bade her former friend adieu.

The poet finished and looked up—the flush of emotion on his broad, oily face deepened. His visitor was so overcome that she sat with her mouth and eyes buried in her handkerchief.

Maggie, who had hovered near the parlor door to listen, was saying to herself "He kin write off such pitiful things as them and yet he never stops to think that our own house would be just so bare and poor if I didn't do the double work that's rightly mine *and* his'n!"

Miss De Ford raised her face at last and wiped her eyes. "Mr. Glick, there is money in your poetry."

"I wisht I knew how to get it out!" he answered facetiously.

"*I* could get it out. Let me have your poems to copy!"

"I'll be pleased to oblige!" he returned beamingly. "I'll get 'em together for you."

"Thanks. By the way, this is the day your pay is due for cleaning the schoolroom."

"It's a week to-day," he agreed, benignly expectant, though his wife was always ready to supply him with what small sums he required for stationery, tobacco, perfumery and the other trifling necessities of a poet's life. But this money from Miss De Ford, earned by work distastefully beneath him save for the extenuating circumstance that it brought him into closer relations with the radiant lady who appreciated his poems—*this* money he would save up for a new suit of clothes, for he was rather ashamed of his shabbiness in contrast with her daintiness.

Miss De Ford drew a bank check from the jaunty little pocket of her blouse, and Bennie was smilingly about to hold out his hand for it.

"Mrs. Glick!" the teacher's pleasant voice called, and Maggie, surprised at being summoned to their *tête-a-tête*, appeared in the doorway.

"Have you time to come in a minute?" inquired Miss De Ford.

Maggie silently came forward. Miss DeFord handed her the check.

"Mr. Glick's money for the week. A check for three dollars. You are the family cashier, I believe."

Maggie looked at it, puzzled. It was made out to *her*.

Bennie laughed. "You are so used to see my wife handle the money that you think mebby, I don't know how to cash a check! Give it here, Maggie."

He glanced at it as Maggie obeyed, then handed it back to her. "You'll have to indorse it for me."

"But you see," explained Miss De Ford, "I've made it out, not to Mrs. Glick's order, but to herself. No one else can cash it. Of course," she added flatteringly, "*I* understand, Mr. Glick, that you don't want your writing interrupted with such trivial matters."

"It makes nothing," he answered lightly, endeavoring to meet her peculiar idea of a poet's temperament. "It's neither here nor there. You can just gimme three dollars, then, Maggie, and keep the check."

"I ain't got no three dollars."

"Why ain't you?" Bennie asked, off his guard. "Miss De Ford paid you her board yesterday."

"I paid the store bill with what she gimme. If I didn't keep our store bill paid, Jake Esh would *soon* say he don't give us no credit no more!"

"If it's all the same to you, Miss De Ford, you can pay me in cash instead of a check," Bennie suggested.

"I never keep more loose money about me than what I absolutely need and I always pay everything by check, Mr. Glick." Miss De Ford's tone was firm.

"Then Maggie, you go to the store and cash that check for me.

"But, Bennie," Maggie faltered, "I got the kitchen to clean and a cake to bake and supper to get. You know it would take me a good hour to go and come from the store."

"*Let* some of the work. Or finish it after supper. I got to have the money, Maggie."

"What fur, Bennie?"

He glanced at her in surprise. She was not in the habit of asking him to account to her for the use of money; why should she expect him to account to her for what he himself had earned?

"That's neither here nor there, Maggie," he answered with dignity. "I'll take care of that. You just go get me the money."

Before this tone and air of dignified reproof, Maggie yielded perforce. "Will you mind baby fur me that she don't crawl near the stove till I get back a'ready?" she asked. He hated to be bothered with the care of the children.

"Better take her along."

"I was a-goin' to take Ben and Flossie. The baby would be better manageable fur you than them."

"It would do 'em all good to get out fur a walk. I won't have time to mind any of 'em."

"But, Bennie, till I got 'em all cleaned up and dressed, it would take the whole afternoon yet! I *can't* Bennie! Miss De Ford," she appealed to the teacher, "could you make out another check—to Bennie instead of me?"

I have used up the last page of my check book. I'll tell you what I will do, Mrs. Glick! Let *me* bake the cake and mind the children and you go alone. It will do you good to get out if you go without *them*. I can make such good cake!"

"Oh!" thought Maggie distraught. "It's a plot she's made up so she and Bennie kin spoon, that's what it is!"

But she acted on the suggestion, carrying with her a picture of Bennie's adoring gaze upon this angel in the house who could make him delicious cake, admire his poems, pay him money, make herself beautiful in dainty clothes for his pleasure—how could poor, faded, soiled, overworked Maggie hope to hold her own against such a creature?

It was an hour later when, looking more puzzled over life's problems than ever, Maggie returned home. She found Bennie and the teacher at the kitchen table eating from a plate of beautiful chocolate cakes, the baby asleep in its basket in the corner, and Ben and Flossie peacefully playing in the dining-room with some building blocks which Miss De Ford had brought them from town a few days ago.

"Well, did you cash the check?" asked the lady.

"No, I didn't. Jake Esh he acted awful funny about it. He just grinned at me and sayed he had took all his money to the bank a'ready and couldn't spare me none. He'd give me credit on the check, he sayed, but he couldn't cash it."

"Well, then, did you bring me some tobacco?" Bennie inquired testily, in a tone of disappointment.

"You didn't say that's what you wanted," Maggie lamented.

"My goodness!" cried Bennie. "I ain't got tobacco enough to do me over Sunday! I'll have to go myself, I guess!"

"But I doubt, Mr. Glick," said Miss De Ford, "whether the shopkeeper will give *you* credit on that check, as it's made out to your wife. And I remember hearing you say that he never would give you tobacco unless you could pay cash for it. Never mind! Read me that poem again!" she smilingly exclaimed. "And the rest of your poems. *Please*, Mr. Glick!"

Maggie's simple heart would have overflowed with gratitude to

Miss De Ford for her generosity to the children had it not been for those burning suspicions that possessed her as to the wily creature's designs upon the gifted Bennie.

It was on the occasion of Miss De Ford's producing tickets for the circus in Lebannon for all the family except Maggie and the baby, together with the munificence of a book of trolley-car tickets, that, for the first time, Maggie "had words" with Bennie on the subject of his infatuation.

"Don't oversleep to-morrow," he advised his wife as they were preparing for bed the night before the circus, "for we'll have to leave on the eight o'clock trolley if we're going to see the parade, too."

"Bennie Glick!" Maggie suddenly turned upon him, dire trouble in her sweet voice as she stood half undressed, with her beautiful brown hair falling about her shoulders. Her hair was the only beauty that remained unmarred by the strain of her years of married life.

"What's the matter?" Bennie yawned.

"It ain't *appropriate* fur you to leave her take you to the circus— without me!" Maggie's effort to speak that last phrase unfalteringly, made her tone hard.

"Ben and Flossie will be along," her husband returned indifferently.

"It's a wonder you wouldn't think that *I'd* want to go oncet on a circus, too," Maggie forced herself to say, her back toward him that he might not see the trembling of her lips and the hot tears in her eyes.

"Who'd mind the baby?"

Maggie had no answer to this quite unanswerable argument.

"And anyhow," added Bennie, "she has bought only four tickets."

This, also, seemed to Maggie to leave nothing to be said.

"What's more," Bennie pursued his advantage, "you haven't no clothes fit to go to the city."

"Do I ever have any money to buy clo'es fur myself yet?" she asked in a muffled voice.

"Don't Miss De Ford earn all her'n?" he demanded triumphantly.

"She has only herself to keep," said Maggie—which retort was so out of character that Bennie was startled, and for an instant subdued.

But presently he rallied. "If you was a better manager you wouldn't go about so unkempt still." He could always awe her by introducing into common conversation a word proper to poetry.

Maggie furtively wiped her eyes, then again turned to face her lord as he sat on the side of the bed to draw off his shoes.

"Look-a-here, Bennie, I've often heard that when girls in town that are earnin' their own livin' seem to spend so much more'n they earn, it's well knowed *how* they get their extra money. Now you know what the teacher's wages is here, and you know how free she spends. Why, only this after when I was tryin' Ben's little pants on him to see if he'd overgrowed 'em too much to wear to the circus, and he sayed they was so tight they choked his legs—and when I tried to stretch 'em bigger, he hollered, 'You're makin' 'em too worser!'—she thought it so comic that she told me she'd buy him a whole new suit in town to-morrow! And her no relation to us! So, Bennie Glick, can't you *see* what she must be when she can spend so freehanded? And," Maggie affirmed conclusively, "she says the *De* in her name is French! Now, think! Nothin' but a French woman!"

"Och, Maggie, you're dumm!" Bennie drawled.

"Them French is bad people, Bennie Glick!"

"How do *you* know?" Bennie scoffed.

"They stand up to be drawed without any clothes on!—fur twenty-five cents a time!" she said in a scandalized tone. "A Mennonite preacher tole me."

"Well, I guess the whole French nation don't stand up to be drawed without any clothes on! You're wonderful dumm, Maggie!"

"I ain't so dumm, Bennie, but I can see she spends more'n she earns!"

"All there is to it is that she's a good manager. If you was as good a manager as her we could live enough better'n we do. It ain't becomin' in you to hint such mean things about her when she's livin' here with us and bein' so kind to us."

And thus silenced, Maggie climbed into their high feather bed and cried herself to sleep.

But the next morning the surprise of husband and wife was equal to find when Miss De Ford came down to breakfast that she was clad merely in her school garb of white blouse and dark cloth skirt! Surely she would put on her best to go to a circus. And she had a frock that was so "appropriate," too; an "Alice blue" silk with lace yoke and elbow sleeves, which Maggie considered the "ressiest" frock she had ever seen.

"Is it that she ain't *goin'?* Maggie marveled, hope rising in her aching heart, as she hastened the bringing in of the sausage, fried potatoes and coffee.

"Why, Mrs. Glick!" The teacher stopped short, halfway across the room and surveyed her landlady in astonishment. "Why aren't you dressed? You'll be too late!"

"*Me?* Why, *I* ain't a-gon'. Am I?" she lamely inquired.

"Why of course you are going! What an idea! Run along this minute and get into your other gown. I'll give the children their breakfast."

"But I can't go! Who'd take care of the baby?"

"The baby's father, of course. Who else?" cheerfully announced Miss De Ford.

"But he's all dressed to *go!*" said Maggic chokingly, her hopes dashed as she realized that the denouement was to get her off to the circus and out of the way with the two elder children that the coast might be clear at home for a long day's *tête-a-tête* between this Jezebel and the lawful husband of another woman!

"Oh!" Miss De Ford cried as her eyes fell upon Bennie's spruce attire. "How very unselfish of you, Mr. Glick, to think of sacrificiing the whole day for your children's pleasure! But it so unnecessary. Mrs. Glick will *enjoy* going—while, of course, to you it would be a waste of time and a bore!"

Her assumption that he was superior to the frivolity of circuses and his realization that she also would be at home, alone with him; that her desire for his society had probably led her to plan this excursion for his wife and children—so flattered him that he rose to her bait straightway, though he had never missed a circus day in town in the past twenty years, and nothing short of this strong appeal to his vanity could have made him do it now.

"To be sure, I'd sooner leave Maggie go," he readily assented, though the statement sounded affected even to himself.

"It would be such a very unnecessary sacrifice for you to make," reiterated Miss De Ford. "though I think it was lovely of vou to be *willing* to do it, Mr. Glick. Now do hurry, Mrs. Glick. Dear me!" she cried as she lifted Ben and Flossie to their places and began to help them to their breakfast, while Maggie slowly and with infinite uncertainty walked to the door, "how spick-and-span and shiny the dear babies look—all dressed up so fine to go to the circus! *Dear me!* And you know," she turned to Bennie as he drew up to the table, "you couldn't very well spare the time to go, as it is your day for cleaning the schoolroom, you remember—not to mention the poem you promised me—the one that is to be dedicated to me!" She smiled upon him beautifully. "Shan't I be proud of it!"

To have had one's mind adjusted to a day at the circus and suddenly to find, instead, that one was expected to stay at home, clean a schoolroom and mind a baby, would have been too much for Bennie to digest even under the goad of her "appreciation" if the prospect of a long day's solitude with her had not seemed almost as good a thing as the circus itself. He wondered, while eating his sausage and fried potatoes, whether, in view of the daily "encouragement" he received he could safely venture, when presenting her with the poem dedicated to her, to imprint a poetic kiss upon her brow. In spite of her undisguised admiration, he had an instictive, though surely unreasonable, apprehension that it would be a risk. For Bennie knew, in the depth of his soul, that he stood in awe of her.

"This ought to be a day of inspiration to you!" she went on. "The greatest poetry the world has ever known has been, as of course *you* know, inspired by sentiments of chivalry; and your consciousness to-day that you are chivalrously minding the baby in order to give your faithful little wife a bit of needed recreation— oh, I shall expect another masterpiece, Mr. Glick!"

"You shall not be disappointed!" he earnestly returned. "Your appreciation has not only brang out the best in me, it also reveals to me depths in myself I did not dream of. Semtiments of chivalry, for instance—"

The door opened and Maggie, dressed in the green sateen with white polka dots which had been her best dress ever since her marriage, came into the room. She did not look happy. In her anxiety and sorrow she had no heart for the vanities of a circus, and were it not that the children must not be disappointed nor those expensive tickets wasted, not a step would she have gone.

"I hadn't ought to have went," she feebly protested as Miss DeFord sprang to help her with the children's hats and coats.

"Bennie ain't used to a cold bite at dinner and it ain't to be expected that *you'd* cook him his dinner, Miss De Ford—"

"Now, then!" broke in Miss De Ford, "you're all ready but me." And before any one could say a word she had run into the hall and had come back instantly, her jacket over her arm and her leather bag hanging from her wrist as she raised her arms to pin on the jaunty brown hat which matched her suit, the stylishness of which impressed Maggie beyond words.

"You need not bother to see—them—on the car, Mr. Glick, I'll do it," she quickly spoke. "Just finish your breakfast and," she smiled at him archly, "see how much of the work you can have done by the time I get back!"

He laughed delightedly at her intimate playfulness, but she gave them no time for farewells. She hurried them out with the admonition that they had but five minutes to catch the trolley at the corner.

Never in her life had Maggie been called upon to readjust so violently a mental attitude as when, to the utter routing of her conception of the deep subtlety of Miss De Ford's machinations, that bewildering person boarded the car with her and the two children to go to town to the circus.

"But there ain't no car back till this after yet!" Maggie frantically explained as the car started.

"I know," was the serene reply as Miss De Ford turned Ben around on her lap to face the window. "Won't we have a good time to-day, Ben? I wouldn't exchange it for a day in Paris, would you, Bennie-man?"

Maggie sank back limply, nearly letting Flossie slide off her lap. She could not think—she was too confused. Miss De Ford had intended going all the time. She did vaguely wonder what Bennie would do about his noon meal; and his long, lonely day at home— Bennie hated so to be alone that he even objected to her running in for a half hour's chat of an evening with her sister who lived across the way; also his being obliged to mind the baby all day long and give her her bottle; not to mention the cleaning of the schoolhouse without her help—for having done it alone one Saturday, he had given his wife to understand that thereafter she must be on hand to help him—and of course that meant that Bennie had looked on while Maggie had done the work.

"Ain't, Mom," Ben was exclaiming as a long freight train passed the trolley car, "Ain't, Mom, when you're lookin' at a choo-choo train and the little red caboose comes along, then it's *all!*" (All gone.)

The state of bewilderment with which Maggie had started upon this excursion continued all day. By the time, however, that they had seen the parade, had bought Ben's new suit, had had dinner at the Eagle Hotel (at fifty cents apiece and, to Maggie's consternation, nothing deducted for the children!) a dinner the "stylishness" of which filled her soul with mingled awe and pleasure, and had at last found themselves in the circus tent seated in reserved chairs *not the common benches, mind you*—by this time, Maggie's general sense of well-being had softened her heart, smoothed out the puzzled pucker of her brow and loosened her tongue. For the first time since Miss De Ford had come among them, Mrs. Glick waxed friendly and communicative.

"Yes, this is the first time I went pleasure-seeking' yet since I am married a'ready," she said, while they comfortably waited for the performance to begin, the children being sufficiently absorbed in prize popcorn bags to leave the two women undisturbed. "Except, to be sure, on a funeral now and again. Me and Bennie was to a funeral the week before you come—my cousin's mister was the corp. Such a pretty corp he made, too!" she sighed, luxuriating in so congenial a theme. "Ach, such flowers as he had! Eight big sprays and two *de*-signs. One *de*-sign was a heart and one was Golden Gates. She took it awful hard, missus did. Him and her always got along so nice and happy together! Yes, she called him popper and he called her mommer, that way. That's always how it goes—them that gets along good together, one of 'em's always taken, it seems. Honest it does. Ach, she took it so hard. Right in front of all the people she flung herself on the corp and hollered, 'Oh, Popper, we've lived together seventeen years and this here's the first time we was separated!' I tell you, Miss De Ford, there wasn't a dry eye in them rooms! The undertaker had to drag her off!"

Miss De Ford nodded sympathetically. And Maggie forgot to wonder that so "high" a lady should show such interest in what *she* had to say. She could understand, of course, how one so superior would be interested in listening to her poet-husband. "But as common as what *I* am yet, it's a wonder she'd take such interest!"

"Your husband, Mrs. Glick, is the only Pennsylvania German I have encountered out here," remarked Miss De Ford, "who isn't what you call 'a hard worker and close saver.' How does it happen that, being a Pennsylvania German, he is—well, *what* he is?"

"It's on account of his bein' a poet that way," Mrs. Glick answered.

"But wasn't he trained into habits of thrift and industry as all Pennsylvania Germans seem to be?"

"His pop he died when Bennie was little yet and so his mom was a widdah woman. She brang Bennie up to work so hard that when he took the scarlet fever till he was ten a'ready, the doctor sayed how it was overwork that made him ketch it. He had it so bad he near died fur her yet! So, when he did pull through, why, after that, to be sure, she never made him do nothin' he didn't feel fur doin', even after he was growed—and her havin' nothin' but what she earnt. But she often sayed she felt paid fur all she done when first she seen Bennie's pomes printed in the noospapers!"

"Why did you marry a man with no means of support?"

"But when I married Bennie he was teachin' the school here—he had *your* job. You see, his mother had just died and he hadn't no one to keep him, so he *had* to get a job. But the teachin' was too hard on him. He sayed it didn't leave him no time nor strength to write pomes. So, till we was married a little while, he resigned," she sadly concluded with a little stifled sigh. "And so I kep' boarders when I could get 'em still, and sold milk."

"Suppose," suggested Miss De Ford, "That Mr. Glick wanted to get back the school—could he?"

"You needn't worry," Maggie smiled wanly, "He won't try to take your job off you."

"But could he get it if I resigned?"

"Oh, yes, he *could* get it all right he's so in with the political boss out here."

"So I thought," the teacher replied in a tone of satisfaction that mystified Maggie. But she had no time to wonder what that tone, with the accompanying little firm tightening of the lips, might mean, for at this moment the performance began.

"Now me," Maggie remarked during the course of the show, "I like a circus so much better than a dime waudewille. At them ten-cent shows the actors certainly do make remarks sometimes that give you a shamed face! They make remarks that ain't *appropriate!*"

It was not until they were again on the street that Mrs. Glick recalled the existence of her lonely and neglected lord and began to look anxious.

"I hope we get the five o'clock car—or what will Bennie do fur his supper?" she worried, trying to hasten their progress through the crowds on the sidewalk.

"We are going to have supper at the Eagle Hotel," Miss De Ford calmly announced. "You would be quite too tired to cook a supper for us when we get home. And we're all hungry *now*."

"But Bennie's supper!" gasped Maggie. "He can't cook his own *supper* too!"

"Why not?" Miss De Ford inquired innocently.

"He won't do it!" Maggie cried. "He'll set and go hungry first!"

"Yes," responded Miss De Ford cheerfully, "a poet is always indifferent to gross details like meals."

"The Bennie ain't no poet! Or else you don't know a lot of poets if you think that! *Do* you know many?"

"Many poets? None like Bennie."

"I guess then!" Maggie nodded proudly. "But ach, Miss De Ford," she added, "I'd sooner we went home on the five o'clock car. Bennie will have so cross if we don't!"

"Leave him to me. I'll manage—cheer him up," she amended it.

Maggie bridled at this usurpation of her prerogatives. But her sense of deep obligation for incredible favors kept her subdued.

"What time is it now?" she meekly though anxiously inquired.

"A quarter to five."

"A quarter '*to*'?" she repeated uncertainly. "Does that mean a quarter over or a quarter till?"

Miss De Ford considered. "A quarter 'till'," she decided. "We couldn't possibly catch the five o'clock car no matter how much we hurried."

"Ach, well then," Maggie gave it up with a long breath, "if we can't then would you mind if I stopped at the five-and-ten and got some individual hairpins?"

"'Individual' hairpins?"

"Them little thin ones you can't hardly see yet!"

"Invisible hairpins—yes; and we can get some toys for the children at the 'five-and-ten' and then have supper and take the six-thirty car home."

"Ach!" breathed Maggie, "it'll be a half over seven till we get home a'ready, ain't?"

"Yes; and what a good quiet day we've given Mr. Glick for his poems!"

Maggie wondered, as they neared home, whether even Miss De Ford could "manage" and "cheer up" a Bennie affronted by such a long day of loneliness and neglect; and upon their confronting him as he sat stolid and sulky in the dining-room, it looked like a formidable undertaking indeed, though Maggie was dumfounded to behold that he had cleared away the remains of the breakfast and had attended to the fires. The fact was he had done the former under the inspiration of Miss De Ford's parting words and the expectation of her immediate return; and the latter he had been obliged to do for his own comfort.

But even Maggie's jealousy could not withold some meed of admiration for the skill with which the feat of appeasing him was performed—though to her simple conscience it seemed luridly mixed with guile.

"Oh, you dear good man," Miss De Ford greeted him caressingly, "how I have envied your peaceful, quiet day! When it came to the point I was really afraid to let your three helpless treasures go alone; I knew," she continued as she bustled about taking off the sleepy children's wraps, "that your anxiety about them would disturb the Muse—the Muse, you know—and I did *so* want you to write the poem you're going to dedicate to me! I hope it's written! I see," she gave him no time to answer, "how beautifully you have thought of your wife in having cleared away the breakfast débris and attended to the fires! Chivalry, as I've before remarked, has inspired more great poetry—Ben!" she suddenly whirled the small boy about to face his fast-softening parent, "tell papa about the circus!"

"The big lion," said Ben, opening wide his sleepy eyes with reminiscent wonder, "roared as dreadful as he could!! An'—an'—"

"He will tell you more to-morrow when he is not so sleepy. Mrs. Glick, just *see* how thoughtful the dear man has been for our comfort!—the coal brought up and everything so clean and cozy! Now, then, baby boy," she suddenly deposited the astonished child on his astonished father's lap, "papa will carry you up and undress you and put you in your little bed for poor tired mamma! What a theme for a poem, Mr. Glick! You remember all the charming things the great poets have written about the little curly, sleepy head upon one's breast?"

"I ain't no curly head!" Ben protested, while the elder Bennie, under the spell of all this sentimental cajolery, proceeded, without more demur than a moment's questioning glance toward his wife, to perform, for the first time in his life, the poetic task of disrobing and putting his son to bed.

"Be sure to come down again!" Miss De Ford tenderly admonished him as he started, "and read me what you've written to-day. I can't sleep without hearing it!"

"I—I ain't wrote it—yet," Bennie faltered, pausing in the doorway with his burden. "But—but—"

"I know," she said sympathetically, "that one cannot force the Muse. Well, then let me hear again, before I sleep," she said softly, "those 'Lines on a Lady's Visit to a Former Lady Friend.'"

"All right," he answered, beaming, entirely mollified. "I'll be down till I get Ben to bed."

Maggie, following her husband with the sleeping Flossie, was trembling with the agitation of a tremendous idea that began to dawn upon her—*Was the teacher "jollying" her Bennie?* The thought appalled her.

But by the time the children were in bed her horror had changed, under the spell of Bennie's angelically forbearing to reproach her, to a hot indignation against the perfidy of the woman who could so lead her trusting man by the nose; whose subtle flattery (to Maggie it seemed infinitely subtle) so outweighed all her own devotion and sacrifice.

In the days that followed, however, it became manifest to Miss De Ford, to Bennie, and even to Maggie herself, that the extraordinary experience of that day in town had wonderfully emancipated the cowed little wife from the thraldom of her belief that Bennie could not work; that she herself could not ever take a bit of recreation at the price of his slight inconvenience.

The extent of this emancipation could be measured by the unprecedented event which occurred the very day after the mad dissipation of that memorable Saturday; Maggie, about to cook the Sunday dinner, walked into the dining-room where her husband sat in conversation with their boarder, and asked him to bring her a bucket of coal from the cellar. Never before in their married life had she requested such a menial service from the poet and she trembled inwardly now; but she was expressing the sudden passionate protest of her heart against the long morning's intimate intercourse between these two, sitting at ease while she worked.

Bennie looked first astonished, then indignant, then hurt, in quick succession, but his glance, meeting a certain look in the eye of the lady seated before him—a look that seemed to put him on a pedestal even higher than that on which his own self-esteem constantly held him—what could he do but act up to her ideal of him?

"Sure, sure!" he quickly consented, rising heavily and taking the bucket from her hands. "don't you ever carry the coal up yourself, Maggie."

"What I can't see," Maggie kept telling herself these days, "is what she's lookin' to *get* out of Bennie."

At last she found out. It was about ten days after the circus and Miss De Ford had asked that she might be permitted a half hour's conversation with Mrs. Glick alone in her room.

"Mrs. Glick," she announced as soon as they were alone behind the closed door, "I am going to give up the school and go away."

Maggie turned pale. The teacher's board was still almost their sole support, inasmuch as they had not been able to save enough out of it to buy another cow and so extend their milk business.

"Ain't you stayin' to finish out the term?" she demanded weakly.

"No. I go next week."

"Oh! Is some of your folks took sick?"

"No, I am going because I think I have got all I came for. Mr. Glick can finish out the term. They will pay a man fifty dollars a month."

"Oh! Think what that would be to us!" breathed Maggie. "But," she added dejectedly, "Bennie won't do it to take it."

"Yes, he will. It all depends on you."

"*I* can't make him do nothin'," Maggie returned almost resentfully.

Miss De Ford leaned forward confidentially. "If you will do as I suggest, he will have to take it."

Maggie shook her head. "Even you couldn't make Bennie take no steady job and keep it. He's all fur hisself, that way, and he don't like to work."

"It will be *you* that will make him take the school."

"Now are you jollyin' *me?*" demanded Maggie suspiciously.

Miss De Ford laughed. "Listen; I want to take you and the three children with me next week to my summer home at Point Pleasant where I live from the first of May to the first of November. You would live in the cottage on the grounds where every year I keep a family to help out with the work of the house. Your work would be the washing, ironing and mending. You would get your living and ten dollars a week. Meantime, Mr. Glick would have his fifty dollars for teaching during the month of May; and during the summer, until school opened again in the fall, he could get work with the farmers about. Then when you came back in November it would be to a comfortable income—fifty dollars a month."

"Bennie would never leave me go!"

"Pack your trunk and *go*," advised Miss De Ford.

"What fur do you want to separate me from my mister?" Maggie inquired darkly.

"To teach Mr. Glick to depend on himself."

"Yes, and when I was out the way, you'd mebby come back here to *him!*" Maggie, trembling at her own audacity, looked to see the teacher rise up in dire wrath to crush her.

To her utter astonishment, Miss De Ford shrieked with laughter. "Come back to Bennie Glick? Oh! no, no, *no*, Mrs. Glick! Hear me—I am a married woman!"

Maggie gazed at her in utter stupefaction.

"'Tis even so, Mrs. Glick I am *Mrs*. De Ford."

"Then where's your mister *anyhow?*"

He had to be in Europe for three months this winter and as I had to do *something* to drown my sorrow, I decided to use the time in experimenting—I am a suffragist, a socialist—and I wished to understand the conditions of women who are self-supporting. Incidentally, I think I've done out here—or am doing—the best bit of suffragist work I've ever done—though I've lectured all over the state—"

"Lekshured!" gasped Maggie. "A suffragist! Then is you husband a sufferer—or what do you call it when it's a male?"

"A sufferer? Yes, he is, though he doesn't know it! At all events—Mr. De Ford gets home next week, and believe me, *he'll* take care that I don't worry you and Bennie any more! Now, to come back to you—think of the advantage to your children of six months at

the seaside; and to *you* of freedom from worry about expenses. And
your work will be ridiculously light compared to what you do at
home." But she did not need to point out these advantages—they
loomed so large to Maggie's mind that even the astounding news
that this girl was a married woman seemed insignificant by com-
parison.

"No house rent for you to pay," Mrs. De Ford continued. "For
Mr. Glick would, of course, have to pay it. No pasture rent for your
cow, no tobacco, perfumery, or stationery to buy for Bennie—you
could *save*, Mrs. Glick!" she triumphantly announced, knowing the
powerful appeal of this to a Pennsylvania German soul.

"Mebby," Maggie said feebly, "Bennie would grow away from
me!"

"Mrs. Glick," spoke Mrs. De Ford impressively, "your husband
would learn to appreciate you so completely that you would have
him—" she paused to raise her hand and bend her thumb significantly—"that you would *have—him—right—there*, Mrs. Glick!"
Wriggling her thumb. "Right—there!"

Maggie stared at the thumb, fascinated.

"Mrs. Glick," Miss De Ford continued still more solemnly, "no
man ever *keeps on* loving a sheep—a creature he can use and bully.
Don't you *see* how much I can do with Bennie because I am *not* a
sheep? A serpent, if you will! Be any kind of a beast rather than a
sheep—be a rat-terrier. Try it. Look here, Maggie," she waxed very
earnest, "why hold yourself as cheap as an old shoe for a man who
turns from you for the first woman who flatters his egotism a bit?
If you do give yourself to him, make him be at least half-way
worthy of you. Why, Maggie, even if he were what you think him,
a poet and a superior being, *no* man would be worth all that *you*
give. Poet or no poet, make Bennie stand on his own feet. You've
been keeping him down on all fours ever since you married him.
Give the man a chance and if he proves he *can't* stand up, well
then," she concluded grimly, "if I were you I'd certainly let him
flop!"

Maggie gazed into the bright eyes of the young woman before
her and her own began to reflect their fire, while her shoulders
straightened and her bosom rose and fell in a long, deep breath.

"Miss—Mrs. De Ford! I will!"

Ellen Glasgow

The Difference
1923

Ellen Glasgow *(1873–1945), author of nineteen novels, one volume of short stories, a posthumously published autobiography,* The Woman Within *(1954), and various other works, was such a widely read and influential writer during the 1920s and 1930s that women named their daughters after the strong heroines in her novels, especially Dorinda Oakley of* Barren Ground *(1925). After years of best-selling popularity and financial success great enough to finance an unsuccessful world-wide search for a cure for her deafness, she began, after 1925, to receive the critical praise and honors (including the 1942 Pulitzer Prize for fiction) she had earlier yearned for and believed she deserved. Her novel* In This Our Life *(1941) was made into a film with Bette Davis and Olivia de Havilland.*

Always ambitious to create great work, Glasgow struggled all her life with no formal training and an absence of encouragement. She designed for herself a course in the discipline of her craft that would have made her as great a teacher for others as she was for herself. She learned early to translate life into art, and left behind her an important body of fiction.

While waiting for her first novel, The Descendant *(1897), to be published, she told herself she could die of happiness if only that one book would be published. In 1931, at the publication of* They Stooped to Folly, *she commented, "I've had seventeen published and I've never been happy and have not died," (Wilson Bulletin, Apr. 1, 1931, p. 424).*

Glasgow was the eighth of ten children (five born before and five after the Civil War) of Anne Jane Gholson, a descendant of colonial settlers of Virginia and a member of the Tidewater aristocracy, and Francis Thomas Glasgow, of a Scotch-Irish family of eighteenth-century settlers in the Shenandoah Valley. Her mother was apparently unquestioning of a traditional life of domesticity, maternity, and submissiveness to an authoritarian husband. Her father was a life-long managerial employee of the Tredegar Iron Works, a large, successful family foundry in Richmond, Virginia, where Ellen Glasgow grew up and lived all her life, except for brief periods of residence in New York City and long trips abroad.

Despite an income and lifestyle at least equivalent to Virginia Woolf's prescribed 500 pounds a year and a room of her own, Ellen Glasgow was never happy in any conventional way until she was over sixty years old. Her absolute commitment to her work as well as her life experiences, which repeatedly reinforced her conviction of women's moral superiority to men, limited the accommodation she was willing or able to make to conventional expectations about women's "place" and proper pursuits. She was isolated, grieved, and depressed by her increasing deafness, which began immediately after her mother's death in 1893 to encroach on her ability to interact independently with people. Her intellectual inclinations toward economic, scientific, and philosophical inquiry; her artistic ambition; and her inherited roots in southern "ladylikeness" created conflicts in her life, and her personal bereavements were many. Two particularly devastating ones are relevant to "The Difference."

Soon after the birth of her tenth child, Glasgow's mother had discovered the existence of her husband's black mistress. Her subsequent nervous breakdown is vividly described in The Woman Within, *although there is no mention of the precipitating event. This early encounter with major depression and the suffocating atmosphere it generated was devastating for the child Ellen. Life for much of her childhood was lived in the shadow of her mother's illness, which ended for her with her death, but continued to plague her daughter all her life.*

When Glasgow was twenty-seven years old, she fell in love with a married man. They carried on a secret romance for six or seven years. In her autobiography she represents "Gerald B." as dying at the end of this time; however, some of Glasgow's biographers have suggested otherwise: after his first marriage ended, he may have married yet a third woman. At any rate, he disappeared from Glasgow's life in 1906.

Although she claimed to have no interest in reading or writing short stories, the apprenticeship in her craft included a close study of the great short story writer, Guy de Maupassant. She deprecated herself as a short story writer, and most critics have taken that self-assessment at face value. Nevertheless, there is no question that many elements of her talent were well suited to the crafting of short stories. "The Difference" is an example of these skills at their finest: epigrammatic condensation, telling details, tight focus, and a perfect balance between internal conflict and external events. It was first published in Harper's Magazine *in June 1923.*

Most of Glasgow's stories were written between 1916 and 1923, a period during which her heretofore steady production of novels faltered. The novels written during the ten years after the stories are generally considered to be her best. Linda Wagner, a recent Glasgow critic, suggests that these stories allowed her to work out a new

approach to character and to begin to create the strong heroines who made her later
novels so important in the lives of the women who read them.

Outside, in the autumn rain, the leaves were falling.

For twenty years, every autumn since her marriage, Margaret Fleming had watched the leaves from this window; and always it had seemed to her that they were a part of her life which she held precious. As they fell she had known that they carried away something she could never recover—youth, beauty, pleasure, or only memories that she wanted to keep. Something gracious, desirable and fleeting; but never until this afternoon had she felt that the wind was sweeping away the illusion of happiness by which she lived. Beyond the panes, against which the rain was beating in gray sheets, she looked out on the naked outlines of the city: bleak houses, drenched grass in squares, and boughs of trees where a few brown or yellow leaves were clinging.

On the hearth rug the letter lay where it had fallen a few minutes—or was it a few hours ago? The flames from the wood fire cast a glow on the white pages; and she imagined that the ugly words leaped out to sting her like scorpions as she moved by them. Not for worlds, she told herself, would she stoop and touch them again. Yet what need had she to touch them when each slanting black line was etched in her memory with acid? Never, though she lived a hundred years, could she forget the way the letters fell on the white paper!

Once, twice, three times, she walked from window to door and back again from door to window. The wood fire burned cheerfully with a whispering sound. As the lights and shadows stirred over the familiar objects she had once loved, her gaze followed them hungrily. She had called this upstairs library George's room, and she realized now that every piece of furniture, every book it contained, had been chosen to please him. He liked the golden brown of the walls, the warm colours in the Persian rugs, the soft depth of the cushioned chairs. He liked, too, the flamboyant red lilies beneath the little Chippendale mirror.

After twenty years of happiness, of comradeship, of mutual

dependence, after all that marriage could mean to two equal spirits, was there nothing left except ashes? Could twenty years of happiness be destroyed in an afternoon, in an hour? Stopping abruptly, with a jerk which ran like a spasm through her slender figure, she gazed with hard searching eyes over the red lilies into the mirror. The grave beauty of her face, a beauty less of flesh than of spirit, floated there in the shadows like a flower in a pond.

"I am younger than he is by a year," she thought, "and yet he can begin over again to love, while a new love for me would be desecration."

There was the sound of his step on the stair. An instant later his hand fell on the door, and he entered the room.

Stooping swiftly, she picked up the letter from the rug and hid it in her bosom. Then turning toward him, she received his kiss with a smile. "I didn't wait lunch for you," she said.

"I got it at the club." After kissing her cheek, he moved to the fire and stood warming his hands. "Beastly day. No chance of golf, so I've arranged to see that man from Washington. You won't get out, I suppose?"

She shook her head. "No, I shan't get out."

Did he know, she wondered, that this woman had written to her? Did he suspect that the letter lay now in her bosom? He had brought the smell of rain, the taste of dampness, with him into the room; and this air of the outer world enveloped him while he stood there, genial, robust, superbly vital, clothed in his sanguine temperament as in the healthy red and white of his flesh. Still boyish at forty-five, he had that look of perennial innocence which some men carry untarnished through the most enlightening experiences. Even his moustache and his sharply jutting chin could not disguise the softness that hovered always about his mouth, where she noticed now, with her piercing scrutiny, the muscles were growing lax. Strange that she had never seen this until she discovered that George loved another woman! The thought flashed into her mind that she knew him in reality no better than if she had lived with a stranger for twenty years. Yet, until a few hours ago, she would have said, had any one asked her, that their marriage was as perfect as any mating between a man and a woman could be in this imperfect world.

"You're wise. The wind's still in the east, and there is no chance,

I'm afraid, of a change." He hesitated an instant, stared approvingly at the red lilies, and remarked abruptly, "Nice colour."

"You always liked red." Her mouth lost its softness. "And I was pale even as a girl."

His genial gaze swept her face. "Oh, well, there's red and red, you know. Some cheeks look best pale."

Without replying to his words, she sat looking up at him while her thoughts, escaping her control, flew from the warm room out into the rough autumn weather. It was as if she felt the beating of the rain in her soul, as if she were torn from her security and whirled downward and onward in the violence of the storm. On the surface of her life nothing had changed. The fire still burned; the lights and shadows still flickered over the Persian rugs; her husband still stood there, looking down on her through the cloudless blue of his eyes. But the real Margaret, the vital part of her, was hidden far away in that deep place where the seeds of mysterious impulses and formless desires lie buried. She knew that there were secrets within herself which she had never acknowledged in her own thoughts; that there were unexpressed longings which had never taken shape even in her imagination. Somewhere beneath the civilization of the ages there was the skeleton of the savage.

The letter in her bosom scorched her as if it were fire. "That was why you used to call me magnolia blossom," she said in a colourless voice, and knew it was only the superficial self that was speaking.

His face softened; yet so perfectly had the note of sentiment come to be understood rather than expressed in their lives that she could feel his embarrassment. The glow lingered in his eyes, but he answered only, "Yes, you were always like that."

An irrepressible laugh broke from her. Oh, the irony, the bitterness! "Perhaps you like them pale!" she tossed back mockingly, and wondered if this Rose Morrison who had written to her was coloured like her name?

He looked puzzled but solicitous. "I'm afraid I must be off. If you are not tired, could you manage to go over these galleys this afternoon? I'd like to read the last chapter aloud to you after the corrections are made." He had written a book on the history of law; and while he drew the roll of proof sheets from his pocket, she remembered, with a pang as sharp as the stab of a knife, all the work of last summer when they had gathered material together. He needed her for his work, she realized, if not for his pleasure. She stood, as she had always done, for the serious things of his life. This book could not have been written without her. Even his success in his profession had been the result of her efforts as well as his own.

"I'm never too tired for that," she responded, and though she smiled up at him, it was a smile that hurt her with its irony.

"Well, my time's up," he said. "By the way, I'll need my heavier golf things if it is fine to-morrow." To-morrow was Sunday, and he played golf with a group of men at the Country Club every Sunday morning.

"They are in the cedar closet. I'll get them out."

"The medium ones, you know. That English tweed."

"Yes, I know. I'll have them ready." Did Rose Morrison play golf? she wondered.

"I'll try to get back early to dinner. There was a button loose on the waistcoat I wore last evening. I forgot to mention it this morning."

"Oh, I'm sorry. I left it to the servants, but I'll look after it myself." Again this perverse humour seized her. Had he ever asked Rose Morrison to sew on a button?

At the door he turned back. "And I forgot to ask you this morning to order flowers for Morton's funeral. It is to be Monday."

The expression on her face felt as stiff as a wax mask, and though she struggled to relax her muscles, they persisted in that smile of inane cheerfulness. "I'll order them at once, before I begin the galleys," she answered.

Rising from the couch on which she had thrown herself at his entrance, she began again her restless pacing from door to window. The library was quiet except for the whispering flames. Outside in the rain the leaves were falling thickly, driven hither and thither by the wind which rocked the dappled boughs of the sycamores. In the gloom of the room the red lilies blazed.

The terror, which had clutched her like a living thing, had its fangs in her heart. Terror of loss, of futility. Terror of the past because it tortured her. Terror of the future because it might be empty even of torture. "He is mine, and I will never give him up," she thought wildly. "I will fight to the end for what is mine."

There was a sound at the door and Winters, the butler, entered.

"Mrs. Chambers, Madam. She was quite sure you would be at home." ·

"Yes, I am at home." She was always at home, even in illness, to Dorothy Chambers. Though they were so different in temperament, they had been friends from girlhood; and much of the gaiety of Margaret's life had been supplied by Dorothy. Now, as her friend entered, she held out her arms. "You come whenever it rains, dear," she said. "It is so good of you." Yet her welcome was hollow, and at the very instant when she returned her friend's kiss she was wishing that she could send her away. That was one of the worst things about suffering; it made one indifferent and insincere.

Dorothy drew off her gloves, unfastened her furs, and after raising her veil over the tip of her small inquisitive nose, held out her hand with a beseeching gesture.

"I've come straight from a committee luncheon. Give me a cigarette."

Reaching for the Florentine box on the desk, Margaret handed it to her. A minute later, while the thin blue flame shot up between them, she asked herself if Dorothy could look into her face and not see the difference?

Small, plain, vivacious, with hair of ashen gold, thin intelligent features, and a smile of mocking brilliance, Dorothy was the kind of woman whom men admire without loving and women love without admiring. As a girl she had been a social success without possessing a single one of the qualities upon which social success is supposed to depend.

Sinking back in her chair, she blew several rings of smoke from her lips and watched them float slowly upward.

"We have decided to give a bridge party. There's simply no other way to raise money. Will you take a table?"

Margaret nodded. "Of course." Suffering outside of herself made no difference to her. Her throbbing wound was the only reality.

"Janet is going to lend us her house." A new note had come into Dorothy's voice. "I haven't seen her since last spring. She had on a new hat, and was looking awfully well. You know Herbert has come back."

Margaret started. At last her wandering attention was fixed on her visitor. "Herbert? And she let him?" There was deep disgust in her tone.

Dorothy paused to inhale placidly before she answered. "Well, what else could she do? He tried to make her get a divorce, and she wouldn't."

A flush stained Margaret's delicate features. "I never understood why she didn't. He made no secret of what he wanted. He showed her plainly that he loved the other woman."

Dorothy's only reply was a shrug; but after a moment, in which she smoked with a luxurious air, she commented briefly, "But man's love isn't one of the eternal verities."

"Well, indifference is, and he proved that he was indifferent to Janet. Yet she has let him come back to her. I can't see what she is to get out of it."

Dorothy laughed cynically. "Oh, she enjoys immensely the attitude of forgiveness, and at last he has permitted her to forgive him. There is a spiritual vanity as well as a physical one, you know, and Janet's weakness is spiritual."

"But to live with a man who doesn't love her? To remember every minute of the day and night that it is another woman he loves?"

"And every time that she remembers it she has the luxury of forgiving again." Keenness flickered like a blade in Dorothy's gray eyes. "You are very lovely, Margaret," she said abruptly. "The years seem only to leave you rarer and finer, but you know nothing about life."

A smile quivered and died on Margaret's lips. "I might retort that you know nothing about love."

With an impatient birdlike gesture Dorothy tossed her burned-out cigarette into the fire. "Whose love?"she inquired as she opened the Florentine box, "Herbert's or yours?"

"It's all the same, isn't it?"

By the flame of the match she had struck Dorothy's expression appeared almost malign. "There, my dear, is where you are wrong," she replied. "When a man and a woman talk of love they speak two different languages. They can never understand each other because women love with their imagination and men with their senses. To you love is a thing in itself, a kind of abstract power like religion; to Herbert it is simply the way he feels."

"But if he loves the other woman, he doesn't love Janet; and yet he wants to return to her."

Leaning back in her chair, Dorothy surveyed her with a look which was at once sympathetic and mocking. Her gaze swept the pure grave features; the shining dusk of the hair; the narrow nose with its slight arch in the middle; the straight red lips with their resolute pressure; the skin so like a fading rose-leaf. Yes, there was beauty in Margaret's face if one were only artist or saint enough to perceive it.

"There is so much more in marriage than either love or indifference," she remarked casually. "There is, for instance, comfort."

"Comfort?" repeated Margaret scornfully. She rose, in her clinging draperies of chiffon, to place a fresh log on the fire. "If he really loves the other woman, Janet ought to give him up," she said.

At this Dorothy turned on her. "Would you, if it were George?" she demanded.

For an instant, while she stood there in front of the fire, it seemed to Margaret that the room whirled before her gaze like the changing colours in a kaleidoscope. Then a gray cloud fell over the brightness, and out of this cloud there emerged only the blaze of the red lilies. A pain struck her in the breast, and she remembered the letter she had hidden there.

"Yes," she answered presently. "I should do it if it were George."

A minute afterward she became conscious that while she spoke, a miracle occurred within her soul.

The tumult of sorrow, of anger, of bitterness, of despair, was drifting farther and farther away. Even the terror, which was worse than any tumult, had vanished. In that instant of renunciation she had reached some spiritual haven. What she had found, she understood presently, was the knowledge that there is no support so strong as the strength that enables one to stand alone.

"I should do it if it were George," she said again, very slowly.

"Well, I think you would be very foolish." Dorothy had risen and was lowering her veil. "For when George ceases to be desirable for sentimental reasons, he will still have his value as a good provider." Her mocking laugh grated on Margaret's ears. "Now, I must run away. I only looked in for an instant. I've a tea on hand, and I must go home and dress."

When she had gone, Margaret stood for a minute, thinking deeply. For a minute only, but in that space of time her decision was made. Crossing to the desk, she telephoned for the flowers. Then she left the library and went into the cedar closet at the end of the hall. When she had found the golf clothes George wanted, she looked over them carefully and hung them in his dressing room. Her next task was to lay out his dinner clothes and to sew the loose button on the waistcoat he had worn last evening. She did these things deliberately, automatically, repeating as if it were a formula, "I must forget nothing"; and when at last she she had finished, she stood upright, with a sigh of relief, as if a burden had rolled from her shoulders. Now that she had attended to the details of existence, she would have time for the problem of living.

Slipping out of her gray dress, she changed into a walking suit of blue homespun. Then, searching among the shoes in her closet, she selected a pair of heavy boots she had worn in Maine last summer. As she put on a close little hat and tied a veil of blue chiffon over her face, she reflected, with bitter mirth, that only in novels could one hide one's identity behind a veil.

In the hall downstairs she met Winters, who stared at her discreetly but disapprovingly.

"Shall I order the car, madam?"

She shook her head, reading his thoughts as plainly as if he had uttered them. "No, it has stopped raining. I want to walk."

The door closed sharply on her life of happiness, and she passed out into the rain-soaked world where the mist caught her like damp smoke. So this was what it meant to be deserted, to be alone on the earth! The smell of rain, the smell that George had brought with him into the warm room upstairs, oppressed her as if it were the odour of melancholy.

As the chill pierced her coat, she drew her furs closely about her neck, and walked briskly in the direction of the street car. The address on the letter she carried was burned into her memory not in numbers, but in the thought that it was a villa George owned in an unfashionable suburb named Locust Park. Though she had never been there, she knew that, with the uncertain trolley service she must expect, it would take at least two hours to make the trip and return. Half an hour for Rose Morrison; and even then it would be night, and Winters at least would be anxious, before she reached home. Well, that was the best she could do.

The street car came, and she got in and found a seat behind a man who had been shooting and carried a string of partridges. All the other seats were filled with the usual afternoon crowd for the suburbs—women holding bundles or baskets and workmen returning from the factories. A sense of isolation like spiritual darkness descended upon her; and she closed her eyes and tried to bring back the serenity she had felt in the thought of relinquishment. But she could remember only a phrase of Dorothy's which floated like a wisp of thistledown through her thoughts, "Spiritual vanity. With some women it is stronger than physical vanity." Was that her weakness, vanity, not of the body, but of the spirit?

Thoughts blew in and out of her mind like dead leaves, now whirling, now drifting, now stirring faintly in her consciousness with a moaning sound. Twenty years. Nothing but that. Love and nothing else in her whole life . . . The summer of their engagement. A rose garden in bloom. The way he looked. The smell of roses. Or was it only the smell of dead leaves rotting to earth? . . . All the long, long years of their marriage. Little things that one never forgot. The way he laughed. The way he smiled. The look of his hair when it was damp on his forehead. The smell of cigars in his clothes. The three lumps of sugar in his coffee. The sleepy look in his face when he stood ready to put out the lights while she went up the stairs. Oh, the little things that tore at one's heart!

The street car stopped with a jerk, and she got out and walked though the drenched grass in the direction one of the women had pointed out to her.

"The Laurels? That low yellow house at the end of this lane, farther on where the piles of dead leaves are. You can't see the house now, the lane turns, but it's just a stone's throw farther on."

Thanking her, Margaret walked on steadily toward the turn in the lane. Outside of the city the wind blew stronger, and the coloured leaves, bronze, yellow, crimson, lay in a thick carpet over the muddy road. In the west a thin line of gold shone beneath a range of heavy, smoke-coloured clouds. From the trees rain still dripped slowly; and between the road and the line of gold in the west there stretched the desolate autumn landscape.

"Oh, the little things!" her heart cried in despair. "The little things that make happiness!"

Entering the sagging gate of The Laurels, she passed among mounds of sodden leaves which reminded her of graves, and followed the neglected walk between rows of leafless shrubs which must have looked gay in summer. The house was one of many cheap suburban villas (George had bought it, she remembered, at an auction) and she surmised that, until this newest tenant came, it must have stood long unoccupied. The whole place wore, she reflected as she rang the loosened bell, a furtive and insecure appearance.

After the third ring the door was hurriedly opened by a dishevelled maid, who replied that her mistress was not at home.

"Then I shall wait," said Margaret firmly. "Tell your mistress, when she comes in, that Mrs. Fleming is waiting to see her." With a step as resolute as her words, she entered the house and crossed the hall to the living room where a bright coal fire was burning.

The room was empty, but a canary in a gilded cage at the window broke into song as she entered. On a table stood a tray containing the remains of tea; and beside it there was a half-burned cigarette in a bronze Turkish bowl. A book—she saw instantly that it was a volume of the newest plays—lay face downward beneath a pair of eyeglasses, and a rug, which had fallen from the couch, was in a crumpled pile on the floor.

"So she isn't out," Margaret reflected; and turning at a sound, she confronted Rose Morrison.

For an instant it seemed to the older woman that beauty like a lamp blinded her eyes. Then, as the cloud passed, she realized that it was only a blaze, that it was the loveliness of dead leaves when they are burning.

"So you came?" said Rose Morrison, while she gazed at her with the clear and competent eyes of youth. Her voice, though it was low and clear, had no softness; it rang like a bell. Yes, she had youth, she had her flamboyant loveliness; but stronger than youth and loveliness, it seemed to Margaret, surveying her over the reserves and discriminations of the centuries, was the security of one who had never doubted her own judgment. Her power lay where power usually lies in an infallible self-esteem.

"I came to talk it over with you," began Margaret quietly; and though she tried to make her voice insolent, the deep instinct of good manners was greater than her effort. "You tell me that my husband loves you."

The glow, the flame, in Rose Morrison's face make Margaret think again of leaves burning. There was no embarrassment, there was no evasion even, in the girl's look. Candid and unashamed, she appeared to glory in this infatuation, which Margaret regarded as worse than sinful, since it was vulgar.

"Oh, I am so glad that you did," Rose Morrison's sincerity was disarming. "I hated to hurt you. You can never know what it cost me to write that letter; but I felt that I owed it to you to tell you the truth. I believe that we always owe people the truth."

"And did George feel this way also?"

"George?" The flame mounted until it enveloped her. "Oh, he doesn't know. I tried to spare him. He would rather do anything than hurt you, and I thought it would be so much better if we could talk it over and find a solution just between ourselves. I knew if you cared for George, you would feel as I do about sparing him."

About sparing him! As if she had done anything for the last twenty years, Margaret reflected, except think out new and different ways of sparing George!

"I don't know," she answered, as she sat down in obedience to the other's persuasive gesture. "I shall have to think a minute. You see this has been—well, rather—sudden."

"I know, I know." The girl looked as if she did. "May I give you a cup of tea? You must be chilled."

"No, thank you. I am quite comfortable."

"Not even a cigarette? Oh, I wonder what you Victorian women did for a solace when you weren't allowed even a cigarette!"

You Victorian women! In spite of her tragic mood, a smile hovered on Margaret's lips. So that was how this girl classified her. Yet Rose Morrison had fallen in love with a Victorian man.

"Then I may?" said the younger woman with her fullthroated laugh. From her bright red hair, which was brushed straight back from her forehead, to her splendid figure, where her hips swung free like a boy's, she was a picture of barbaric beauty. There was a glittering hardness about her, as if she had been washed in some indestructible glaze; but it was the glaze of youth, not of experience. She reminded Margaret of a gilded statue she had seen once in a museum; and the girl's eyes, like the eyes of the statue, were gleaming, remote and impassive—eyes that had never looked on reality. The dress she wore was made of some strange "art cloth," dyed in brilliant hues, fashioned like a kimono, and girdled at the hips with what Margaret mistook for a queer piece of rope. Nothing, not even her crude and confident youth, revealed Rose Morrison to her visitor so completely as this end of rope.

"You are an artist?" she asked, for she was sure of her ground. Only an artist, she decided, could be at once so arrogant with destiny and so ignorant of life.

"How did you know? Has George spoken of me?"

Margaret shook her head. "Oh, I knew without any one's telling me."

"I have a studio in Greenwich Village, but George and I met last summer at Ogunquit. I go there every summer to paint."

"I didn't know." How easily, how possessively, this other woman spoke her husband's name.

"It began at once." To Margaret, with her inherited delicacy and reticence, there was something repellent in this barbaric simplicity of emotion.

"But you must have known that he was married," she observed coldly.

"Yes, I knew, but I could see, of course, that you did not understand him."

"And you think that you do?" If it were not tragic, how amusing it would be to think of her simple George as a problem!

"Oh, I realize that it appears very sudden to you; but in the emotions time counts for so little. Just living with a person for twenty years doesn't enable one to understand him, do you think?"

"I suppose not. But do you really imagine," she asked in what struck her as a singularly impersonal tone for so intimate a question, "that George is complex?"

The flame, which was revealed now as the illumination of some secret happiness, flooded Rose Morrison's features. As she leaned forward, with clasped hands, Margaret noticed that the girl was careless about those feminine details by which George declared so often that he judged a woman. Her hair was carelessly arranged; her finger nails needed attention; and beneath the kimonolike garment, a frayed place showed at the back of her stocking. Even her red morocco slippers were run down at the heels; and it seemed to Margaret that this physical negligence had extended to the girl's habit of thought.

"He is so big, so strong and silent, that it would take an artist to understand him," answered Rose Morrison passionately. Was this really, Margaret wondered, the way George appeared to the romantic vision?

"Yes, he is not a great talker," she admitted. "Perhaps if he talked more, you might find him less difficult." Then before the other could reply, she inquired sharply, "Did George tell you that he was misunderstood?"

"How you misjudge him!" The girl had flown to his defense; and though Margaret had been, as she would have said "a devoted wife," she felt that all this vehemence was wasted. After all, George, with his easy, prosaic temperament, was only made uncomfortable by vehemence. "He never speaks of you except in the most beautiful way," Rose Morrison was insisting. "He realizes perfectly what you have been to him, and he would rather suffer in silence all his life than make you unhappy."

"Then what is all this about?" Though she felt that it was unfair, Margaret could not help putting the question.

Actually there were tears in Rose Morrison's eyes. "I could not bear to see his life ruined," she answered. "I hated to write to you; but how else could I make you realize that you were standing in the way of his happiness? If it were just myself, I could have borne it in silence. I would never have hurt you just for my own sake; but, the subterfuge, the dishonesty, is spoiling his life. He does not say so, but, oh, I see it every day because I love him!" As she bent over, the firelight caught her hair, and it blazed out triumphantly like the red lilies in Margaret's library.

"What is it you want me to do?" asked Margaret in her dispassionate voice.

"I felt that we owed you the truth," responded the girl, "and I hoped that you would take what I wrote you in the right spirit."

"You are sure that my husband loves you?"

"Shall I show you his letters?" The girl smiled as she answered, and her full red lips reminded Margaret suddenly of raw flesh. Was raw flesh, after all, what men wanted?

"No!" The single word was spoken indignantly.

"I thought perhaps they would make you see what it means," explained Rose Morrison simply. "Oh, I wish I could do this without causing you pain!"

"Pain doesn't matter. I can stand pain."

"Well, I'm glad you aren't resentful. After all, why should we be enemies? George's happiness means more than anything else to us both."

"And you are sure you know best what is for George's happiness?"

"I know that subterfuge and lies and dishonesty cannot bring happiness." Rose Morrison flung out her arms with a superb gesture. "Oh, I realize that it is a big thing, a great thing, I am asking of you. But in your place, if I stood in his way, I should so gladly sacrifice myself for his sake I should give him his freedom. I should acknowledge his right to happiness, to self-development."

A bitter laugh broke from Margaret's lips. What a jumble of sounds these catchwords of the new freedom made! What was this self-development which could develop only through the sacrifice of others? How would these immature theories survive the compromises and concessions and adjustments which made marriage permanent?

"I cannot feel that our marriage has interfered with his development," she rejoined presently.

"You may be right," Rose Morrison conceded the point. "But to-day he needs new inspiration, new opportunities. He needs the companionship of a modern mind."

"Yes, he has kept young at my cost," thought the older woman. "I have helped by a thousand little sacrifices, by a thousand little cares and worries, to preserve this unnatural youth which is destroying me. I have taken over the burden of details in order that he might be free for the larger interests of life. If he is young to-day, it is at the cost of my youth."

For the second time that day, as she sat there in silence, with her eyes on the blooming face of Rose Morrison, a wave of peace, the peace of one who has been shipwrecked and then swept far off into some serene haven, enveloped her. Something to hold by, that at least she had found. The law of sacrifice, the ideal of self-surrender, which she had learned in the past. For twenty years she had given freely, abundantly, of her best; and to-day she could still prove to him that she was not beggared. She could still give the supreme gift of her happiness. "How he must love you!" she exclaimed. "How he must love you to have hurt me so much for your sake! Nothing but a great love could make him so cruel."

"He does love me," answered Rose Morrison, and her voice was like the song of a bird.

"He must." Margaret's eyes were burning, but no tears came. Her lips felt cracked with the effort she made to keep them from trembling. "I think if he had done this thing with any other motive than a great love, I should hate him until I died." Then she rose and held out her hand, "I shall not stand in your way," she added.

Joy flashed into the girl's eyes. "You are very noble," she answered. "I am sorry if I have hurt you. I am sorry, too, that I called you old-fashioned."

Margaret laughed. "Oh, I am old-fashioned. I am so old-fashioned that I should have died rather than ruin the happiness of another woman."

The joy faded from Rose Morrison's face. "It was not I," she answered. "It was life. We cannot stand in the way of life."

"Life to-day, God yesterday, what does it matter? It is a generation that has grasped everything except personal responsibility." Oh, if one could only keep the humour! A thought struck her, and she asked abruptly, "When your turn comes, if it ever does, will you give way as I do?"

"That will be understood. We shall not hold each other back."

"But you are young. You will tire first. Then he must give way?" Why in twenty years George would be sixty-five and Rose Morrison still a young woman!

Calm, resolute, uncompromising, Rose Morrison held open the door. "Whatever happens, he would never wish to hold me back."

Then Margaret passed out, the door closed behind her, and she stood breathing deep draughts of the chill, invigorating air. Well, that was over.

The lawn, with its grave-like mounds of leaves, looked as mournful as a cemetery. Beyond the bare shrubs the road glimmered; the wind still blew in gusts, now rising, now dying away with a plaintive sound; in the west the thread of gold had faded to a pale greenish light. Veiled in the monotonous fall of the leaves, it seemed to Margaret that the desolate evening awaited her.

"How he must love her," she thought, not resentfully, but with tragic resignation. "How he must love her to have sacrificed me as he has done."

This idea, she found as she walked on presently in the direction of the street car, had taken complete possession of her point of view. Through its crystal lucidity she was able to attain some sympathy with her husband's suffering. What agony of mind he must have

endured in these past months, these months when they had worked
so quietly side by side on his book! What days of gnawing remorse!
What nights of devastating anguish! How this newer love must have
rent his heart asunder before he could stoop to the baseness of such
a betrayal! Tears, which had not come for her own pain, stung her
eyelids. She knew that he must have fought it hour by hour, day
by day, night by night. Conventional as he was, how violent this
emotion must have been to have conquered him so completely.
"Terrible as an army with banners," she repeated softly, while a
pang of jealously shot through her heart. Was there in George, she
asked now, profounder depths of feeling than she had ever reached;
was there some secret garden of romance where she had never
entered? Was George larger, wilder, more adventurous in imagination, than she had dreamed? Had the perfect lover lain hidden in
his nature, awaiting only the call of youth?

The street car returned almost empty; and she found restfulness
in the monotonous jolting, as if it were swinging her into some
world beyond space and time, where mental pain yielded to the
sense of physical discomfort. After the agony of mind, the aching
of body was strangely soothing.

Here and there, the lights of a house flashed among the trees,
and she thought, with an impersonal interest, of the neglected villa,
surrounded by mounds of rotting leaves, where that girl waited
alone for happiness. Other standards. This was how the newer
generation appeared to Margaret—other standards, other morals.
Facing life stripped bare of every safeguard, of every restraining
tradition, with only the courage of ignorance, of defiant inexperience,
to protect one. That girl was not wilfully cruel. She was simply
greedy for emotion; she was gasping at the pretense of happiness
like all the rest of her undisciplined generation. She was caught by
life because she had never learned to give up, to do without, to
stand alone.

Her corner had come, and she stepped with a sensation of relief
on the wet pavement. The rain was dripping steadily in a monotonous
drizzle. While she walked the few blocks to her door, she forced
herself by an effort of will to go on, step by step, not to drop down
in the street and lose consciousness.

The tinkle of the bell and the sight of Winters's face restored her
to her senses.

"Shall I bring you tea, madam?"

"No, it is too late."

Goin upstairs to her bedroom, she took off her wet clothes and slipped into her prettiest tea gown, a trailing thing of blue satin and chiffon. While she ran the comb through her damp hair and touched her pale lips with colour, she reflected that even renunciation was easier when one looked desirable. "But it is like painting the cheeks of the dead," she thought, as she turned away from the mirror and walked with a dragging step to the library. Never, she realized suddenly, had she loved George so much as in this hour when she had discovered him only to lose him.

As she entered, George hurried to meet her with a anxious air. "I didn't hear you come in, Margaret. I have been very uneasy. Has anything happened?"

By artificial light he looked younger even than he had seemed in the afternoon; and this boyishness of aspect struck her as strangely pathetic. It was all a part, she told herself, of that fulfilment which had come too late, of that perilous second blooming, not of youth, but of Indian Summer. The longing to spare him, to save him from the suffering she had endured, pervaded her heart.

"Yes, something has happened," she answered gently. "I have been to see Rose Morrison."

As she spoke the name, she turned away from him, and walking with unsteady steps across the room, stood looking down into the fire. The knowledge of all that she must see when she turned, of the humiliation, the anguish, the remorse in his eyes, oppressed her heart with a passion of shame and pity. How could she turn and look on his wounded soul which she had stripped bare?

"Rose Morrison?" he repeated in an expressionless voice. "What do you know of Rose Morrison?"

At his question she turned quickly, and faced not anguish, not humiliation, but emptiness. There was nothing in his look except the blankness of complete surprise. For an instant the shock made her dizzy; and in the midst of the dizziness there flashed through her mind the memory of an evening in her childhood, when she had run bravely into a dark room where they told her an ogre was hiding, and had found that it was empty.

"She wrote to me." Her legs gave way as she replied, and, sinking into the nearest chair, she sat gazing up at him with an immobile face.

A frown gathered his eyebrows, and a purplish flush (he flushed so easily of late) mounted slowly to the smooth line of his hair. She watched the quiver that ran through his under lip (strange that she had not noticed how it had thickened) while his teeth pressed it sharply. Everything about him was acutely vivid to her, as if she were looking at him closely for the first time. She saw the furrow between his eyebrows, the bloodshot stain on one eyeball, the folds of flesh beneath his jutting chin, the crease in his black tie, the place where his shirt gave a little because it had grown too tight—all these insignificant details would exist indelibly in her brain.

"She wrote to you?" His voice sounded strained and husky, and he coughed abruptly as if he were trying to hide his embarrassment. "What the devil? But you don't know her."

"I saw her this afternoon. She told me everything."

"Everything?" Never had she imagined that he could appear so helpless, so lacking in the support of any conventional theory. A hysterical laugh broke from her, a laugh as utterly beyond her control as a spasm, and at the sound he flushed as if she had struck him. While she sat there she realized that she had no part or place in the scene before her. Never could she speak the words that she longed to utter. Never could she make him understand the real self behind the marionette at which he was looking. She longed with all her heart to say: "There were possibilities in me that you never suspected. I also am capable of a great love. In my heart I also am a creature of romance, of adventure. If you had only known it, you might have found in marriage all that you have sought elsewhere . . ." This was what she longed to cry out, but instead she said merely,

"She told me of your love. She asked me to give you up."

"She asked you to give me up?" His mouth fell open as he finished, and while he stared at her he forgot to shut it. It occurred to her that he had lost the power of inventing a phrase, that he could only echo the ones she had spoken. How like a foolish boy he looked as he stood there , in front of the sinking fire, trying to hide behind that hollow echo!

"She said that I stood in your way." The phrase sounded so grotesque as she uttered it that she found herself laughing again. She had not wished to speak these ugly things. Her heart was filled with noble words, with beautiful sentiments, but she could not make her lips pronounce them in spite of all the efforts she made. And she recalled suddenly the princess in the fairy tale who when she opened her mouth, found that toads and lizards escaped from it instead of pearls and rubies.

At first he did not reply, and it seemed to her that only mechanical force could jerk his jaw back into place and close the eyelids over his vacant blue eyes. When at last he made a sound it was only the empty echo again, "stood in my way!"

"She is desperately in earnest." Justice wrung this admission from her. "She feels that this subterfuge is unfair to us all. Your happiness, she thinks, is what we should consider first, and she is convinced that I should be sacrificed to your future. She was perfectly frank. She suppressed nothing."

For the first time George Fleming uttered an original sound. "O Lord!" he exclaimed devoutly.

"I told her that I did not wish to stand in your way," resumed Margaret, as if the exclamation had not interrupted the flow of her thoughts. "I told her I would give you up."

Suddenly, without warning, he exploded. "What, in the name of heaven, has it got to do with you?" he demanded.

"To do with me?" It was her turn to echo. "But isn't that girl—" she corrected herself painfully—"isn't she living in your house at this minute?"

He cast about helplessly for an argument. When at last he discovered one, he advanced it with a sheepish air, as if he recognized its weakness."Well, nobody else would take it, would they?"

"She says that you love her."

He shifted his ground nervously. "I can't help what she says, can I?"

"She offered to show me your letters."

"Compliments, nothing more."

"But you must love her, or you couldn't—you wouldn't—" A burning flush scorched Margaret's body.

"I never said that I . . ." Even with her he had always treated the word love as if it were a dangerous explosive, and he avoided touching it now, "that I cared for her in that way."

"Then you do in another way?"

He glanced about like a trapped animal. "I am not a fool, am I? Why, I am old enough to be her father! Besides, I am not the only

one anyway. She was living with a man when I met her, and he
wasn't the first. She isn't bad, you know. It's a kind of philosophy
with her. She calls it self. . ."

"I know." Margaret cut the phrase short. "I have heard what she
calls it." So it was all wasted; Nothing that she could do could lift
the situation above the level of the commonplace, the merely vulgar.
She was defrauded not only of happiness, but even the opportunity
to be generous. Her sacrifice was as futile as that girl's passion.
"But she is in love with you now," She said.

"I suppose she is." His tone had grown stubborn. "But how long
would it last? In six months she would be leaving me for somebody
else. Of course, I won't see her again," he added, with the manner
of one who is conceding a reasonable point. Then, after a pause in
which she made no response, his stubbornness changed into resentment. "Anybody would think that you are angry because I am
not in love with her!" he exclaimed. "Anybody would think—but
I don't understand women!"

"Then you will not—you do not mean to leave me?" she asked;
and her manner was as impersonal, she was aware, as if Winters
had just given her notice.

"Leave you?" He glanced appreciatively round the room. "Where
on earth could I go?"

For an instant Margaret looked at him in silence. Then she insisted
coldly, "To her, perhaps. She thinks that you are in love with her."

"Well, I suppose I've been a fool," he confessed, after a struggle,
"but you are making too much of it."

Yes, she was making too much of it; she realized this more
poignantly than he would ever be able to do. She felt like an actress
who has endowed a comic part with the gesture of high tragedy. It
was not, she saw clearly now, that she had misunderstood George,
but that she had overplayed life.

"We met last summer at Ogunquit." She became aware presently
that he was still making excuses and explanations about nothing.
"You couldn't go about much, you know, and we went swimming
and played golf together. I liked her, and I could see that she liked
me. When we came away I thought we'd break it off, but somehow
we didn't. I saw her several times in New York. Then she came
here unexpectedly, and I offered her that old villa nobody would
rent. You don't understand such things, Margaret. It hadn't any

more to do with you than—than—" He hesitated, fished in the stagnant waters of his mind, and flung out abruptly, "than golf has. It was just a sort of—well, sort of—recreation."

Recreation! The memory of Rose Morrison's extravagant passion smote her sharply. How glorified the incident had appeared in the girl's imagination, how cheap and tawdry it was in reality. A continual compromise with the second best, an inevitable surrender to the average, was this the history of all romantic emotion? For an instant, such is the perversity of fate, it seemed to the wife that she and this strange girl were united by some secret bond which George could not share—by the bond of woman's immemorial disillusionment.

"I wouldn't have had you hurt for worlds, Margaret," said George, bending over her. The old gentle voice, the old possessive and complacent look in his sleepy blue eyes, recalled her wandering senses. "If I could only make you see that there wasn't anything in it."

She gazed up at him wearily. The excitement of discovery, the exaltation, the anguish, had ebbed away, leaving only gray emptiness. She had lost more than love, more than happiness, for she had lost her belief in life.

"If there had been anything in it, I might be able to understand," she replied.

He surveyed her with gloomy severity. "Hang it all! You act as if you wanted me to be in love with her." Then his face cleared as if by magic. "You're tired out, Margaret and you're nervous. There's Winters now. You must try to eat a good dinner."

Anxious, caressing, impatient to have the discussion end and dinner begin, he stooped and lifted her in his arms. For an instant she lay there without moving, and in that instant her gaze passed from his face to the red lilies and the uncurtained window beyond.

Outside the leaves were falling.

Mary Austin

Papago Wedding
1925

"Papago Wedding" was originally published as one of a trio of short-short stories under the title "American Marriage" in the September 1925 issue of American Mercury, *H. L. Mencken's controversial monthly founded only eighteen months earlier. The other two stories, "The Way of a Woman" and "The Man Who Lied about a Woman" also centered on Native American characters. "Papago Wedding" was awarded the O. Henry Memorial Award Prize of 1925 for the best short-short story of the year. Blanche Colton Williams, chair of the award committee and editor of its annual volume of short stories, chose to include Austin's story in* Great American Short Stories 1919–1934, *one of 47 chosen from over 300 award-winning stories. It continued to be included in subsequent expanded volumes. In 1935 it appeared in* One Smoke Stories, *Mary Austin's collection of short stories about Native Americans. One of the most frequently reprinted stories in twentieth-century U.S. literature, it has appeared in a wide variety of collections reflecting many different special interests and themes, including women, marriage, the West, and short-short stories, as well as general American fiction and internationally distinguished short fiction.*

It is difficult to know how the story has been viewed by its many collectors. For some it seems to have been a quaint curiosity; to others a "race" story; others have treated it as an illuminating anthropological anecdote; still others have considered it a genuine work of art. As in Helen Reimensnyder Martin's Pennsylvania Dutch stories and novels, a culture different from the dominant white middle class U.S. majority culture is portrayed in order to disguise a feminist critique of male/female relationships.

Mary Austin (1868–1934) was a novelist, short story writer, political essayist, playwright, translator of Native American poetry, feminist, Fabian Socialist, naturalist, anthropologist, folklorist, lecturer, teacher, founder in 1894–1895 of the community theater movement, and mystic. She emigrated to a desert homestead at the edge of the San Joaquin Valley in California from Carlinville, Illinois at the age of twenty with her feminist mother and her brother, after the deaths of her father and only sister and after having completed a B.S. degree. She fell in love with the southwestern desert and began to write about it after her marriage and the birth of her only child. Her first book, The Land of Little Rain, *a collection of fourteen sketches published in 1903, brought her success and prestige as a naturalist. By this time she had separated from her husband and was living at Carmel, California, the artists' colony, among such other writers as Jack London and Ambrose Bierce. Willa Cather wrote the latter chapters of* Death Comes for the Archbishop *in Austin's home, La Casa Querida, in Sante Fe, New Mexico, where Austin spent the last sixteen years of her life, after years in New York and abroad as well as at Carmel. She maintained a friendship with Mabel Dodge Luhan, who was working to create an artists' colony in Taos. Their friendship had begun decades earlier, in New York, where Austin had met Emma Goldman, Elizabeth Gurley Flynn, Bill Haywood, and other radical revolutionaries at Mabel's Thursday evening salon.*

Austin published thirty-five books during her life. Among them is A Woman of Genius *(1912) the fictional autobiography of a midwestern woman's struggle to give expression to her theatrical genius as a tragedian in spite of an environment that militated against a woman giving expression to anything other than maternal and domestic impulses.*

Critical responses to Austin's work have often reflected her powerful personality, which seems to have evoked strong feelings, both positive and negative, in those who knew her. Too, she lived during a time when social constraints on a woman's private life were stringent and the public exposure of a public person's private life was an invitation to public censure. Therefore, judgments about decisions she made concerning her severely retarded daughter, the reasons adduced for the dissolution of her marriage, her personal conduct as a divorced member of the bohemian artists' colony at Carmel, and the feminist and socialist causes she espoused, all influenced judgments about her literary artistic achievement. Both her supporters and her detractors relied on ad feminum *arguments.*

In a sense Austin was the inheritor of Helen Hunt Jackson's role as Anglo spokeswoman for Native American women. In "Papago Wedding" and "How One Woman Kept Her Husband," the wandering husband returns to the woman to whom he has made an earlier commitment after the betrayed wife has apparently abandoned the fight to win him back. Successful manipulation of their children brings him home.

There was a Papago woman out of Panták who had a marriage paper from a white man after she had borne him five children, and the man himself was in love with another woman. This Shuler was the first to raise cotton for selling in the Gila Valley—but the Pimas and Papagos had raised it long before that—and the girl went with him willingly. As to the writing of marriage, it was not then understood that the white man is not master of his heart, but is mastered by it, so that if it is not fixed in writing it becomes unstable like water and is puddled in the lowest place. The Sisters at San Xavier de Bac had taught her to clean and cook. Shuler called her Susie, which was nearest to her Papago name, and was fond of the children. He sent them to school as they came along, and had carpets in the house.

In all things Susie was a good wife to him, though she had no writing of marriage and she never wore a hat. This was a mistake which she learned from the Sisters. They, being holy women, had no notion of the *brujería* which is worked in the heart of the white man by a hat. Into the presence of their God also, without that which passes for a hat they do not go. Even after her children were old enough to notice it, Susie went about the country with a handkerchief tied over her hair, which was long and smooth on either side of her face, like the shut wings of a raven.

By the time Susie's children were as tall as their mother, there were many white ranchers in the Gila country, with their white wives, who are like Papago women in this, that, if they see a man upstanding and prosperous, they think only that he might make some woman happy, and if they have a cousin or a friend, that she should be the woman. Also the white ones think it so shameful for a man to take a woman to his house without a writing that they have no scruple to take him away from her. At Rinconada there was a woman with large breasts, surpassing well-looking, and with many hats. She had no husband, and was new to the country, and when Shuler drove her about to look at it, she wore each time a different hat.

This the Papagos observed, and, not having visited Susie when she was happy with her man, they went now in numbers, and by this Susie understood that it was in their hearts that she might have need of them. For it was well known that the white woman had told Shuler that it was a shame for him to have his children going about with a Papago woman who had only a handkerchief to cover her head. She said it was keeping Shuler back from being the principal man among the cotton-growers of Gila Valley, to have in his house a woman who would come there without a writing. And when the other white women heard that she had said that, they said the same thing. Shuler said, 'My God, this is the truth, I know it,' and the woman said that she would go to Susie and tell her that she ought to go back to her own people and not be a shame to her children and Shuler. There was a man of Panták on the road, who saw them go, and turned in his tracks and went back in case Susie should need him, for the Papagos, when it is their kin against whom there is *brujería* made, have in-knowing hearts. Susie sat in the best room with the woman and was polite. 'If you want Shuler,' she said, 'you can have him, but I stay with my children.' The white woman grew red in the face and went out to Shuler in the field where he was pretending to look after something, and they went away together.

After that Shuler would not go to the ranch except of necessity. He went around talking to his white friends. 'My God,' he kept saying, 'what can I do, with my children in the hands of that Papago?' Then he sent a lawyer to Susie to say that if she would go away and not shame his children with a mother who had no marriage writing and no hat, he would give her money, so much every month. But the children all came in the room and stood by her, and Susie said, 'What I want with money when I got my children and this good ranch?' Then Shuler said, 'My God!' again, and, 'What can I do?'

The lawyer said he could tell the Judge that Susie was not a proper person to have care of his children, and the Judge would take them away from Susie and give them to Shuler. But when the day came for Susie to come into court, it was seen that, though she had a handkerchief on her hair, her dress was good, and the fringe of her shawl was long and fine. All the five children came also, with new clothes, well-looking. 'My God!' said Shuler, 'I must get those kids away from that Papago and into the hands of a white woman.' But the white people who had come to see the children taken away saw that, although the five looked like Shuler, they had their mouths shut like Papagos; so they waited to see how things turned out.

Shuler's lawyer makes a long speech about how Shuler loves his children, and how sorry he is in his heart to see them growing up like Papagos, and water is coming out of Shuler's eyes. Then the Judge asks Susie if she has anything to say why her children shall not be taken away.

'You want to take these children away and giff them to Shuler?' Susie asks him. 'What for you giff them to Shuler?' says Susie, and the white people are listening. She says, 'Shuler's not the father of them. Thees children all got different fathers,' says Susie. 'Shuler—'

Then she makes a sign with her hand. I tell you if a woman makes that sign to a Papago he could laugh himself dead, but he would not laugh off that. Some of the white people who have been in the country a long time know that sign and they begin to laugh.

Shuler's lawyer jumps up. . . 'Your Honor, I object—'

The Judge waves his hand. 'I warn you the court cannot go behind the testimony of the mother in such a case . . .'

By this time everybody is laughing, so that they do not hear what the lawyer says. Shuler is trying to get out of the side door, and the Judge is shaking hands with Susie.

'You tell Shuler,' she says, 'if he wants people to think hees the father of thees children he better giff me a writing. Then maybe I think so myself.'

'I *will*,' said the Judge, and maybe two-three days after that he takes Shuler out to the ranch and makes the marriage writing.

Then all the children come around Susie and say, 'Now, Mother, you will have to wear a hat.'

Susie, she says, 'Go, children, and ask your father.'

But it is not known to the Papagos what happened after that.

─A. R. Leach─

A Captain
Out of Etruria
1925

Three years of research, with the assistance of librarians who specialize in American history, literature, women's studies, and genealogy, as well as letters of inquiry to potential sources of information have brought no more information about A. R. Leach than I found when I discovered this story. "A Captain Out of Etruria" *was first published in* Harper's Magazine *in April 1925 and reprinted in* Prize Short Stories: The Twelve Prizewinning Short Stories in the 1924–25 Short Story Contest Conducted by Harper's Magazine *with an introduction by Bliss Perry (Harper & Bros., N.Y., 1925). At the back of the book are brief informational paragraphs about each of the authors. After the name A. R. Leach the following appears: "Lives in Parkersburg, W. Va. Has written some previous stories, but generally under a pen name. 'A Captain Out of Etruria' was her first* Harper's *story." Her second and last* Harper's *story was "Old Master, Unknown," published in January 1928. The possibility that the signature A. R. Leach is another pen name raises the possibility that the "her" is a pseudonymous authorial fiction. Might A. R. Leach have been a man?*

The story concerns Lucy, a committed artist, who believes that her greatest chance for a satisfactory life is in living alone with her art and her sense of identity unchallenged by someone who might think her or want her to be other than what she is. However, the shared perception of Emelie as an object has precipitated an apparent intimacy between Lucy and Lossing. Lucy thinks, slowly allows herself to think, that she has found a man who will provide her with autonomy, understanding, companionship, and love, who seems to be an ideal potential partner for her life. She discovers in herself capacities for joy, tenderness, and vulnerability she had previously avoided acknowledging or exploring. There was to have been no room for such in her life. But Lossing—note the symbolism of the name—does not fulfill her expectations. They have understood and valued very differently that shared perception of Emelie-as-object. The contrast between the meaning of a man seeing a woman as an object—the normal state of affairs, rendering Lossing a very common, ordinary man, after all—and the meaning of a woman seeing a woman as an object—which makes Lucy an artist—is the source of irony in the story. Lucy will never know whether Lossing deceived her or she deceived herself, whether he intentionally misled her or she invited the misunderstanding. Whichever is true, it is clear that for Lucy this has been a sentimental education, one that will enrich her vision as an artist, one from which she has already recovered by story's end.

Lucy Anderson, as Lucy Anderson, with no eulogies or criticism attached to her name, proved at the time of this story, that she, thiry-six years old, was not always perched aloft in the ivory tower of her art. She had been living in Europe since the War, moving freely in that agreeable society of compatriots and their foreign acquaintance which is so much envied by readers of the Paris *Herald*.

Miss Anderson, however, was not as these. She was painting, surreptitiously as it were. She had a small but sufficient income which, in francs, went a considerable distance beyond its capacity in dollars, and she had her banker uncle as a refuge and a background.

She worked constantly wherever she was, because she never looked into a face without seeing the problem it held for her— without wishing to take what struck her consciousness as its salient feature, and translate it, bring it into a harmony which would vibrate into the consciousness of humanity. She created (as the critics have taught us in these last few years) by the stroke of a brush, by the juxtaposition of colors, a sensation, an outthrust statement which a poet puts into meter, a musician into harmonies.

As Miss Anderson had no conversation about art, had never even learned its patter, she was not taken seriously even by her friends. She talked about anything, making herself so generally agreeable that there are old ladies of both sexes still hanging about who insist, with dark hints, that she employed some "real artist" who painted "those pictures," or at least "finished" them. "There was that portrait of Mrs. Burt, the one she behaved over so badly. Mrs. Burt, just out of good nature, and of course expecting she would give her the sketch or whatever it was, sat for days being painted; and when she saw the result it was a perfect daub. The loveliest frame ever fashioned couldn't have made it possible to hang on a wall. Mrs. Burt said she wouldn't have taken the thing home; and Lucy Anderson had the impertinence to sell it!—if you please, to the French government!"

But these were the days when Lucy was still a dear nice girl, Robert Anderson's niece and one of Paris' social fluxes. It was the season she painted the old woman shearing her dog on the river bank, the gray light on the Seine making sinister the cutting shears, the rebellious dog, and the cruel old woman. It was the first picture the critics were to see and gloat over, but the time had not arrived for opening the storehouse of wonders she had ready for them; and it is doubtful if it would have come in her lifetime had it not been for that autumn in Italy when her road turned.

It was at tea time in the garden of the largest hotel in Geneva, after the horse chestnuts had dropped their bloom in Paris, that Miss Anderson personally encountered Mrs. James T. Clevering and her pretty, slim daughter. When Miss Anderson saw them they were sitting at a table in the center of the chattering crowd, making a great show of talk and amusement, which did not disguise the fact that they were entirely alone. Miss Anderson, who took a very sane and human interest in gossip, of which she heard a great deal, had seen the Cleverings in Paris and had heard more thathan she had seen. The Cleverings had been very well advertised by the two little newspapers printed in English which exist for that purpose, and at the time Emelie Clevering was presented to the English Court, her dress (with the name of the Parisian maker) had been described and photographed and she had been placed in the gallery of international publicity. After that, gossip said, the mother and daughter had been bewildered. The presentation had been arranged for them long before, as long before as the time when Mr. Clevering had so generously contributed to a presidential campaign.

The pair first came into Miss Anderson's vision one day at the Pré Catalan when the band played and motors drew up to discharge the notables and those who came to look at them. The sweet Paris air was vibrating with the American music, the flash and color and small talk of a holiday gathering, when the Cleverings came in: happy in the company of a dark lady and one of the dyed-hair Grand Dukes who have made a profession of escape.

Kind Americans looked at the group with consternation, "Look at the poor things," Miss Anderson's hostess said over her cup. "Lucy, you haven't anything to do, why don't you write a social Baedeker? How can they know that they are in notorious society? They say that after the girl was presented they sat in their hotel and expected the Queen to ask them to dinner. I am not at all certain they did not invite her."

"Who are they anyway?" old Mrs. Varick asked, after everything had been laboriously repeated into her trumpet. Mrs. Black shook her head as though it were too dreadful to repeat. In reality, she told Lucy, the Cleverings were ordinary simple rich people who were said to be deadly dull. Miss Anderson thought that that might not be an insuperable barrier to association with royalty, but like a good many other thoughts whose edge might have cut the delicate frosting of her niceness, it was unexpressed.

"The girl," she said, "is rather a type." But that remark met with the inattention given to all conventional remarks. Lucy Anderson began to make a picture of Emelie—the fresh-faced, blank-eyed young creature, so certainly un-sophisticated in spite of her truly amazing clothes, her saucy hat, her knowing shoes. These were so plainly mere decorations laid on from the outside without any reference to the inner structure of taste. She was a ready-made problem for the artist.

"The second generation: the first has climbed out of its environment exactly as an earthworm climbs, and the second has no instinct to fit. It squirms. I must get her on canvas some day."

As the days went on and she saw more of the mother and daughter, she began to visualize them as distracted travelers caught in one of those old-fashioned mazes which the practical humor of an earlier time planted in gardens. The pavilion where the society they coveted disported itself with music and laughter was somewhere at the end of one of those paths, but when they rushed at the next turning—or rather the mother rushed, passive daughter in hand— they always found themselves in another blind alley.

When, on that idle afternoon in Geneva, Lucy Anderson saw them again she could not know that they were recovering from one of these false turnings, against whose blocking hedge they had flung themselves with such momentum that its thorns had left them smarting. The first days of their stay in London they had met an American citizen at the American Embassy, where he had come to pay his respects to the representative of the country under whose protection he lived while he roamed the world with the free conscience of a man who had done his whole duty to his country by fighting for her. Mrs. Clevering, misled by the sweetness of his manner, had confided in him as a compatriot and a brother. He had been charm itself; too charming, in his facile dexterous ease, for Mrs. Clevering's comprehension.

Emelie had basked in his gentle questionings. It had been a matter of angry puzzlement on the mother's part that men did not "flock" about Emelie. They had come abroad expecting to be beset, warned against the titled adverturer who would try to marry a beauty and an heiress, but they had had to make no rebuffs. So when Bertram Lossing had given them an hour of delight (the light talk, the gay assumption that they, too, were part of all this rushing to and fro, this steady brilliance in the midst of furious activity which was the London season) they felt that for this they had come to London.

Lossing was innocent of any wish to impress them. His thirty-eight years had only perfected his face, and every one of the had laid a softer patina on his manners. Poor little Emelie, unaccustomed to anything that he represented, turned him into one of the heroes who live in the mists of a young girl's fancy.

When they parted Mrs. Clevering took a card from the gold case with the diamond monogram that she habitually carried in her hand and gave it to him; and while he held it delicately and put it away carefully, she effusively begged him to come to tea. "We have our own parlor at the Ritz," she told him, "and we have tea every day at five o'clock." When he did not come they speculated over it, and Emelie was certain it was on account of an accident. If they had known his address they would have sent him a more formal invitation or, as Emelie felt sure that he was ill, possibly they would have sent flowers.

Then, when an opportunity came, they asked about him at the Embassy and were a little excited to learn that he more than fulfilled their dreams. He had a great villa on Lake Como which he called home, where he entertained his many friends. Everything added

their satisfaction in him. He would "do." And then they had gone
to Paris and met his sister-in-law at—of all places—their jeweler's
shop. Mrs. Clevering, over the counter where each was buying
lavishly, hesitatingly mentioned to the rather spectacular lady beside
her that she had accidentally heard her name spoken, and that they
knew her brother-in-law. "We met him in London at our Embassy,"
Mrs. Clevering said in the assured voice of one who offers a perfect
reference. Mrs. Digby-Lossing turned and looked at her specula-
tively.

"Oh! Bertram," carelessly, "he goes all over the shop." They
walked to the edge of the Avenue de L'Opéra together where the
two smart motors stood. Mrs. Digby-Lossing, tall, dark, flashing,
drawing all eyes, hesitated a moment and then, "Since you are
friends of my brother-in-law, my *dear* brother-in-law" (any note of
sarcasm was lost on the Cleverings) "why not come to Paillard's to
tea with me?" They had gone, and the next day the jeweler found
occasion to call at their hotel on some ostensible errand concerning
settings, and took the opportunity to tell them that Mrs. Digby-
Lossing had been too conspicuous a figure in Paris before a young
war-sick fool had married her.

The Parisian tradesman who had heard of the tea at Paillard's
felt that he could not have his shop come into bad social repute,
but he shrugged his shoulders over the density of his wealthy
customers. He had mentioned that Mr. Bernard Lossing was a
favorite in France, particularly in the old legitimist families. Mrs.
Clevering had said laughingly that she "didn't quite know what a
legitimist was, but it sounded exclusive."

Then the Cleverings turned their bewildered backs on that path
and were pacing between the rows in Geneva when Miss Anderson
went by and smiled. Mrs. Clevering had no idea who Lucy Anderson
might be (as that social arbiter, the Paris *Herald*, never mentioned
her name), but she had seen her many times between the columns
of the pavillion at the end of their social labyrinth, and when she
walked by their table, smiling and hesitating, her gentle distinction
so flattering, Mrs. Clevering—not quite as readily as she would
have done in May, her cordial instincts a little hampered by
experience—with some of the shrinking of the burnt child rose and
greeted her.

Miss Anderson, with the boldness of the hunter who means to

run down his prey without any reference to the game laws, murmured many politenesses and hoped that they were enjoying Geneva, although everybody seemed to find it a dull season.

"I suppose you came down with Mrs. Colmar" (mentioning the name of the wife of an American Secretary in Paris); "I have not seen you since the day of her reception," she added. Miss Anderson did not mention that she had not seen her that day but had heard one of those vociferous ladies, who pay their social way by giving amusing caricatures of all the people not present at the time, describe their costumes and entrance and exit at the patriotic gathering.

Presently she was sitting at the Cleverings' abundant table, making herself as agreeable as she knew how, and that was very agreeable indeed—bowing to her friends as they went by, and altogether giving the Cleverings the comfortable feeling of shelter from the cold world. That night at dinner in one of the villas near by, Bertram Lossing sat beside Miss Anderson—and then and there began one of those episodes which later was to add to the world's store of masterpieces.

Lucy and Lossing had met several times, but never had the cement of a mutual interest held them together for even a moment. To-night, after the two courses whose passing each felt it necessary to devote to the other side, they turned toward each other with animation. Lossing's high-nosed keen face was full of interest as he looked into Lucy's long, bright-brown eyes which shone like lamps behind the solidly carven olive features.

"I saw you having tea with some of our compatriots to-day," he said.

"I enjoyed meeting them very much," Miss Anderson replied.

"I am very sure you did," he said quickly. He would have been equally sympathetic to the vociferous chronicler of the doings of the Cleverings, but he found Miss Anderson's attitude more to his taste.

"I met them in London one afternoon when we were both calling at the Embassy." He made no attempt to keep the light note of amusement out of his voice. "I have never forgotten them."

"You should visit America some time," Miss Anderson said blandly, and put her fork into the *langouste mousse* on her plate with the interest of one who is in the years when food is food, after youth scorns and before age rejects.

Mr. Lossing smiled. He knew how to meet that remark. "I have been there," he said, "but—the 'Dollar Princesses,' as I believe they call them—were not so prominent as they appear to be now."

"To tell the truth, they are not so prominent in America as they are in Europe. But these people are not prominent, or rather important, anywhere—yet."

"Why 'yet'? Do they interest you so much?"

"The girl—enormously."

"Shall you take her about with you?"

"I am about to ask that privilege."

The impatient old French general on the other side of Miss Anderson claimed her again and they were getting into the salad when Lossing was able to go on. He began as though there had been no interval:

"Why, may I be pardoned for asking?"

Miss Anderson hesitated. She knew that if Lossing had ever heard that she painted portraits, or anything else, the fact had certainly not been impressed on his consciousness as a matter of consequence. He, with his intimate little collection of early Italian art—where every bit was a treasure at whose mention even dealers lowered their voices—would hardly remember an amateur, and it amused her to play with his state of mind and her own.

"I find her a stimulus," she said. "She gives me great thoughts."

"A stimulus? In what direction, pray?"

"Art," said Miss Anderson.

Lossing half turned on his chair in his real astonishment. "She— I had no idea that she knew anything about art. They—I am sorry to say that I was so obtuse. I like to think . . ." He hesitated.

"You like to think," Miss Anderson said, "that you are so accustomed to being let past the portals, as one might say, that you believe that you can inventory one's mental furnishings at the first glance and make up your mind whether it is worth while to come again."

Lossing looked at her helplessly and then smiled his incomparable smile: "At any rate, it is not often that I find a companion on my explorations," he said. "It is delightful to hear of secret rooms."

"I doubt if you talked to the girl at all." Lucy knew that if he had, he was amusing himself entirely after her fashion.

"I am certain I did not. The remarkable mother talked to me.

She told me that her father was the first Judge of the County Court somewhere."

"A most respectable ancestry," Miss Anderson said gravely, and they both smiled.

Later, when they spoke again in the drawing-room that overlooked the lake where little boats with gay lanterns on their bows were still passing, Lossing said:

"I think I was bewildered by the young lady's remarkably beautiful costume. She was—she reminded me—perhaps she did not remind me then, but she does now as I recall her—of a little white villa lost in very ornamental grounds. There were so many parterres to admire, so many jeweled fountains playing that perhaps I never reached the living apartments at all."

Miss Anderson's long eyes were lighted. "Exactly," she said.

When she reached home that night she put herself into the voluminous red robe diapered in gold, which Fortuny had made for her in Venice the year before, that satisfied the gorgeousness she repressed daily. She opened the glass doors to her balcony which her French maid had so carefully closed against the night air of the lake, and sat for a long time looking across the water toward the place where Mont Blanc sometimes lifts her icy shoulder through the clear air; and she was filled with a vast content. It is the most delightful of experiences to find a companion who travels your road and sees what you see, and a rare one when he sees as much as Lucy Anderson sees.

The next afternoon when Miss Anderson returned from her walk she found the foreign-looking bit of pasteboard on which Mr. Bertram Lossing's name was engraved. She was half glad and half sorry. At thirty-six one has grown to distrust the vision of the night. She threw the card into the china bowl by her door and went about making the composition for the portrait of Emelie Clevering that was possessing her thoughts.

Evidently Lossing had no intention of losing what he had found, for the next day brought an invitation to dine with him; and she discovered, when she arrived at the villa he was sharing with a friend on whose account he had come to Geneva, that the company was, in a manner, assembled about her own personality.

"I almost invited your friends—only . . ."

"Her mother doesn't talk as much as she did earlier in the season, I am told," Lucy said, and Lossing gazed at her with the fascinated delight we give to a mind reader.

The portrait was not so easy to arrive at as Miss anderson had expected. Taken about by Miss Anderson in the easy summer groups—the tennis-playing, dancing, passing crowd—the Cleverings began to have "a really good time"; and there was no propitious moment for a suggestion of painting Emelie's portrait.

Lossing and Miss Anderson were building a friendship as a coral island is made, by infinitesimal particles, and as it put its branches ever nearer the surface there came to at least one of them a fear of an unknown thing. If it were true that they were making each other into a habit—weaving that unbreakable tie, a dependent congeniality—Lucy at least knew that neither would remain as before. The precious individuality which each cherished would change by a process as subtle as the structural changes of chemistry to become, in a way, a part of the other. And while Lucy revolted, struggled against the change, she feared to look too closely at Lossing lest she should find him in the same struggle against what was, after all, to their sort a variety of personal death. And then a chance hand touched the kaleidoscope of their days and whirled the bits into a new pattern.

The old Duchessa of Valadino wrote to Lucy and asked her to take her apartment in Florence for three autumn months. The Duchessa had, she wrote her "dear young friend," two or three servants, her cockatoos, and her tapestries, as well as the plants she hoped to keep through the winter; and it was very expensive to pay for the care of all of these. Would Lucy come and live in the apartment and pay the bills while she went visiting? Nobody had any money now except Americans.

Miss Anderson went to see the Cleverings and asked if she could have Emelie for the autumn. She was careful to tell Mrs. Clevering that the apartment on the Lung' Arno was a Duchessa's apartment, and she said nothing at all about a portrait.

So, after Emelie had dutifully looked at Juliet's tomb in Verona, and added her visiting card to the heap of yellowing pasteboard that lies where the guides tell you the Flower of Verona fell to dust, and fed the pigeons and bought twisted glass in Venice, and forgotten all about the Titians in her naive appreciation of Favai's gondolas silhouetted against moonlit palaces—October saw them established in the great old apartment with its balconies and stone floors where the Duchessa, her hands in thick woolen gloves, sniffingly drank *tisane* on winter afternoons. And then Miss Anderson put out the iron hand and began to work on the canvas to which all this was the preliminary. She had put Bertram Lossing back in the last corner of her consciousness. "There are a number of things there that I have forgotten," she told herself, with the naivete of twenty.

The portrait "went" beautifully. It had been in the artist's mind so long that her facile hands put it on canvas as one writes a line that has been singing itself in one's ears with every cadence echoing true. That Emelie thought it nonsense and was more than sulky over taking the time from teas and lace shops, the more-or-less modern antiques, and the more-or-less perfect pearls of the Ponte Vecchio was no drawback to Miss Anderson's work. In some subtle way, all of that went into the inconsequent nothingness of the fresh-colored transparent little face with the fair hair above it, in its setting of garments for whose inspiration designers had sacked galleries. The picture was a series of beautiful harmonies, accented, broken into by the incongruities, the discords. Lucy Anderson was a great painter, as we all know now.

There came a stage in Miss Anderson's pictures where she let the sitter go. The last touches, the sweep of her own personality that she left on her canvases she put in bit by bit as the feeling for them came to her. The thing at which she looked was her motif, her theme. That they seldom saw their finished portraits was one reason why the sitters left them in her hands so lightly.

And now Emelie was generously given her reward in the perfect riot of little pleasures which she could understand. She was really sweet and gentle when she was happy, and her fondness for Miss Anderson sometimes gave that translator of life the feeling that a visisector must have when a doomed puppy licks his hand.

It was the day when Miss Anderson—from Emelie's point of view—gave up a bad job and turned a failure to the wall, that Bertram Lossing arrived in Florence as a guest in a villa on a hill. He was one of a very sophisticated company of English who had come together to comfort a very beautiful lady who was in deep mourning for an exalted friend whose name was never mentioned.

But the instant Lucy Anderson met Lossing, on the Lung' Arno one windy day when the afterglow was sending its first sheets of red gold over the river, she knew why he had come. And that thing she had hidden and bade herself forget burst its locks and walked blithely out into the open. She knew, and knowing she drew a long sigh of vast content. She even forgot her picture for a little while.

Lossing walked home with her and, halfway, led her on to one of the bridges where they stopped and looked up toward the hills, soft against the glory in the sky. The wind was dying with the setting sun and the rush of the water sang its scale over and over, while Lossing smiled at her as ingenuously as though they were twenty.

There had been few times in Lucy Anderson's life when the sense of humor entirely deserted her, and now with the flush of pleasure on her face she recalled in spite of herself that it had been at least a dozen years since any man had paid her the compliment of following her from one city to another. The last one had been a ridiculous widower whom she had likened to a bawling, skirt-catching child who had lost his nurse, and was deceived by her kind hesitations as to whether or not she could attempt a subject that would have delighted Franz Hals.

Recalling this, she had something of a thrill in realizing that she could never think of painting Lossing. He satisfied her supremely as he was.

"And I hear that you have little Miss Clevering with you."

"Yes, I have." She wondered how soon she could tell him why. She was going to rid herself of the girl presently, and she had a warm delight in the certainty that here was someone she could take past her reception room to the utmost confines of her domain. It would be one of her great moments when she could show him the portrait which was so perfectly the white dwelling place of a little incoherent spirit lost in its surroundings.

"I have thought many times of what you told me of the girl, and I am glad that she is here. It will interest me very much to see what you have found in her."

"I am certain it will interest you." Miss Anderson's long eyes gleamed. The wind had only added to her trimness, her fine dark face was looking its best, and she was glad of it; but beyond the moment she saw him coming back to her, after his explorations into the barren place that was Emelie's mind, to express his bewilderment. She saw herself dramatically—every woman makes a theatrical heroine of herself at times (whatever may die, that never does while she has strength for bare living)—showing him the all-explaining portrait. How much of it would be a feline triumph over a younger, prettier woman, and how much a delight in Lossing's nearness to herself, Miss Anderson's conscience was not morbid enough to ask.

She rejoiced single-hearted over the precious friend who could understand. She knew, because it is the gift of genius to know, what her work represented. She knew that when she was ready to send it forth finished, the criticism of authority would be the criticism she herself gave it; but here was one who had given her the assurance that he saw her point of departure.

She took him home to tea in the Duchessa's long-windowed salon. They found Emelie, exquisite as always, rather sulkily awaiting tea and cross that no one had come. She resented the tea guests being so entirely Miss Anderson's friends. She had been "in things" long enough to begin to make claims.

The girl's slender young figure was silhouetted half against the long pink-and-green striped curtains which the Duchessa was wont to show as the hangings of the room in which her great-grandfather had strangled her great-grandmother, her pale embroidered crepe frock very effective against the background of yellow river and striped silk. She turned at their entrance, and to Miss Anderson's surprise she flushed a brilliant rose when she saw Lossing and her face was tremulous with embarrassed smiles.

Lossing took her hand—not a very small nor delicate hand—with all the gentle reassuring charm in which he was so perfect, and sat down to talk to her while Miss Anderson busied herself with the Duchessa's heavy cups behind the branched candlesticks of the tea table.

"If you are able to support this—*tazza*—" she said to Lossing as she handed him the lumpy piece of imitation Capo da Monte with which the Duchessa had replaced her priceless treasures, serenely certain that "the Americans" would never know the difference. Lossing took the cup with a vague smile and went on listening to Emelie's halting recital of the joys of Florence.

"And the Pitti and Uffizi? I suppose you visit them every day."

"Not every day—" Emilie hesitated. "Some of the pictures are lovely, but some I find dreadful."

"So do I."

"Some I could look at forever."

Miss Anderson held her own cup poised to hear Emilie's oft-repeated views on "The baby," as she called the holy child of Raphael's depicting, and the "splendid" copy she was having made. Unfortunately at that moment a group of English girls came in and Emelie's art views waited.

They saw Lossing every day after this. The grief of the beautiful lady appeared to be assuaged in bridge and the winning of large sums, and Mr. Lossing left his friends to their fate and went quite happily about in the easy Florentine autumn society which was then at its high tide.

"I am beginning to see where you find the spring of inspiration in your young friend," he said one day. Lucy waited, with the anticipation with which she met all his beginnings.

"You may remember that one of those ladies who fled the plague in the year 1348 to make themselves 'innocently merry' in the meadows over yonder was named Emilia."

Lucy Anderson laughed.

"I cannot think of our Emelie providing Boccaccio with one of his tales."

"Why not? Boccaccio provided the tale. All he asked was the object on which to hang it. 'Our Emelie,' as you call her, would look in perfect keeping in a pearl net and a brocade robe, sitting on the green grass with that company. She might even have the gown now."

And Lucy Anderson gave one of her rare flushes. She felt that it was not necessary to show him that portrait; in some way he understood.

"There is some trace of the belated paganism of that time in her face," he continued, playing with the fancy.

"Remember the Judge," Lucy laughed.

"It is really an unawakened look," he went on.

"The sleeping beauty you mean, waiting to be awakened."

"Perhaps."

"Do awaken her!" Lucy happily jeered. "It should be interesting to hear her awakening cries."

Emelie had not talked to Lossing as much as he had hoped. As she realized him as a figure in the world around them, a world which filled her with respect, whose thinness she was incapable of seeing, her awe of him grew. She was much more impressed by his fluent Italian and French than by anything he could say in English: indeed, her lack of comprehension was almost as complete in one language as the other.

Her decorative, or decorated stillness grew complete, and there crept into the blank face a shadow—a shadow which Miss Anderson failed to see, a shadow that she would have doubtless refused to see because it would have meant the ruin of the glowing picture in the stone room behind her bedroom.

And the days moved on to their climax, as days are always moving to end something. Life carries a serial story for every one of us, and what we see as we go by is only the beginnings and the endings of her old, old plots tricked out in new accouterments.

One day at a Florentine house where the walls of the reception room were lively with old prints, Miss Anderson and Lossing, going over them, found a little old eighteenth-century print of the fair at Impruneta. The date hidden among the scrolls on the margin was that of the next day.

"I wonder if they still hold that festival," Lossing said.

Their host, so long tired of prints that he looked at them only as milestones on his journey into knowledge of Italian things, put up a languid glass to the yellowing old sheet where gentlemen in full coats and wigs elegantly composed themselves in a *piazza* before a little church. In his heart he thought Miss Anderson must be a very stupid woman when Lossing talked to her about the subject of a print. But he knew Tuscany.

"Impruneta is exactly like that now, and the little church still has its Della Robbia—and the peasants still have the fair—yes."

Miss Anderson was about to ask if there existed any reason for looking at the Della Robbia on the fair day, when Mrs. Dunallen, the Scotch woman who missed nothing—least of all any possibility of an "excursion"—had gathered the very young of the company by what Miss Anderson called her war-cry, and with Emelie wistfully in the midst of the questioning they found themselves committed to the fair at Impruneta.

Lucy Anderson never forgot that golden October morning. She put it away in the dark room from which Lossing had broken his way, but it has never lost its detail nor its vivid surfaces.

They took an old-fashioned barouche with two strong horses for the hill climbing, driven by a young Italian with the face of a Roman senator above the stiff collar of a livery left behind by some traveling milord of a long-past day. His gravity lent it a dignity which made it seem a new fashion instead of an old one. Emelie, in the smartest of tight Parisian walking costumes and a close hat, sat beside Miss Anderson; while facing them, Lossing talked gay nonsense.

They went up the hills and down the dales of Tuscany, beyond the line of the ancient walls; past the dusty green olive orchards where the old trees, like quarrelsome humans, split and writhed away from what had once been their common heart; past the smoky fields where great cream-colored oxen took their stately way unconscious of the inadequate plow that dragged behind them; through vineyards whose red and russet vines were losing the last of their grapes under the brown fingers of boys and girls clothed in the soft colors that use had given what was once their garish holiday dress.

To Lucy Anderson, exquisitely tuned to every impression, they rode through the land of romance—her romance. She was tender in her happiness. She was tender to poor little Emelie sitting quiet under her cuplike hat. She forgot that impressions were things to be recorded. The essence of the day was color, sun, glancing light, an atmosphere, a setting for life that she herself was living. She was drinking her wine, not pressing it into casks to be put away in storehouses.

They were the last to reach the village of Impruneta, and when they came down the hill to the *piazza* they were met by the indignant people from the forward carriages exclaiming over the horrors of the most sordid of ugly peasant fairs: a thing of cheap jacks, ready-made clothing to disfigure the peasants, chickens and calves, and not even a decent glass of wine or a place to drink it. The restaurants were foul. There was nothing to do but look at the Della Robbia, and there were "dozens better in Florence," and then go back somewhere for food, Mrs. Dunallen angrily told them.

They were surrounded when they left the carriage and it was only Miss Anderson who saw that Emelie was hanging back.

"I think that I shall not try to cross that crowded place," she said; "my head aches. I think I shall sit in the carriage until you come back."

"I am sorry," Miss Anderson said, and told the driver to wait. She crossed the square—tall strong, dominant as she had never been in her life before, but as she would always be in the future. The earth force which had been drawn up through her blood and nerves had awakened to life that strong thing on which the spirit lives, and while she lives it will live with her.

Emelie looked at them going away with a hurt self-pity. She felt miserably unhappy. How did people learn all the things they talked about? How could they read all the dull books after they had spent years and years learning the languages in which they were written? What made the difference between the thing they laughed at and the thing they discussed with enthusiasm? She would have felt as though she was still in that maze if she had been capable of visualizing the maze.

"He is just kind to me. He just talks to me"—"He" covering her horizon. "I shall go back to mother, I guess," she thought miserably.

A vagrant memory possessed her mind. Back there in the United States when they wer planning their "trip," that "trip" which had spun out in their vision as a vista of following delights, her mother had said that they must buy a "souvenir" of every place they visited. She luxuriated now in the misery of buying a reminder of what she felt was the most miserable day of her life.

Down beside the carriage sat a brown old woman eating roasted chestnuts from a withered claw of a hand. On the ground were set out some pieces of coarse pottery, and dotted here and there among them were rude little pottery figures of men on horseback, the horses with square stiff legs.

Emelie knew how to ask the cost of things in three languages; and now she lifted the nearest of the little figures with her timid "Quanto costa?"

The old woman rose hastily with floods of talk, gathering up bowls and plates and trying to press them into the girl's arms, running a horny finger round the rude decoration, ringing the bottoms with a snapping of thumbs. Emelie backed away, repeating her one question. Finally she bought one of the tiny horsemen for the lira which was twenty times its price. With it held tightly in her suede palm she climbed into the barouche and sat for the half hour Miss Anderson and Lossing gave to the church.

Lucy Anderson had passed many a miracle-working madonna and she was almost self-conscious as she put a piece of money into the box and lighted a candle in the dull little Impruneta church. She formulated no prayer. She was giving thanks that she had no prayer. Life was full of satisfactions.

They drifted back to the carriages and Emelie, missed for the first time, listened to polite regrets with a droop to her pretty pink mouth that was too pathetic for the self-pity it expressed. She sat silent, looking blankly, unseeing over the visions of old arranged beauty that ages had created.

They stopped at a wayside garden inn and ate *frittura* and half-dried figs while vine leaves fluttered into their plates. Lossing sat beside Emelie, and when she set the rude little figure of the horseman on the checked cloth, he took it in in his fingers and turned it round in the sun. "What is this?"

"I—bought it in the square," she said, flushing. "It is nothing; I thought—"

"A captain out of Etruria," he said and ran his forefinger down the curve that made a swagger in the tiny back, just as the peasant woman had marked the coarse green daubs on her plate.

"What is it?" Mrs. Dunallen asked crossly. "Do you mean to say there was something of value in that place after all?"

"That depends upon what you call valuable," Lossing said. "Miss Clevering appears to have the eye to see the characteristic thing while we are wasting our time on the banal. These little figures have doubtless been sold at that fair ever since it was a fair. The helmet of the captain is Etruscan. See the gallant poise of him! The mold has probably been recast a hundred times, and it is a poor thing now: but he rode out of Etruria."

The respect on all their faces was balm to the sore spirit of the girl. Tears came into her eyes and she held her face shaded under the cup hat so that they might not be seen. The trained conscience that would suggest a denial of taste or knowledge in buying the figure, which would tell that it was an accident, was as far from the girl's comprehension as the taste with which they were crediting her. In that at least she was surely pagan. But then, Nature is pagan.

They rode home in the blue smoke of the late afternoon, and the afterglow was again on the bland slow river, darkness coming furtively in the shadows of the palaces and churches, lurking like some storied forgotten thing in the narrow streets as they left their carriage.

The Duchessa's butler begged Miss Anderson to come into the recesses of the apartment where the telephone was in hiding, to answer an insistent call, and Lossing went up the stone stairs with Emelie. They turned into the great bare salon: dusky, smelling of the years. The girl took her close hat from her head with petulant twists and threw it on a couch. In the light from outside Lossing saw the tears on her white cheeks. He doesn't know—although he thinks he does; and she doesn't know, because all life is a mystery to her, as it must be to anything that Nature moves by instincts in primal ways—*why* or *how*—but there was a murmur, "My poor child!" and Emelie was sighing long sobbing sighs against Lossing's tweed coat.

Miss Anderson found them—and at the sight of her tall figure, her face white in the gloom, Emelie ran away leaving Lossing to explain. What he astonishingly said was, "How good you have been to us!"

He thanked her again, holding her strong hand. It was she, he told her, who had shown him the crystal depths of Emelie's beautiful nature. He had been blind at first. He had looked at her again, and then had confidently followed the sweet attractiveness of the dear girl when he saw that "my friend," as he called Miss Anderson with some emotion, had chosen Emelie to live with her, to be her constant companion.

How beautiful, how wonderful Emelie was! How unerring her feeling, her taste! He held out the figure of the Etruscan captain as proof of the last: "I shall keep it all my life."

The cut went so deep that it momentarily severed Lucy Anderson's sense of humor. It may be that it never rose again in its former brilliant strength. She had no inclination to twist her lip in the faintest smile, although she saw the situation in all its sharp contrasts. We are continually giving Nature credit for a sense of humor, because the devil has given it to us to divert us from our purposes and compensate us for their loss. Nature goes to the end of her road and cares not at all for the vehicle which carries her there.

Lucy did not jeer at herself then; that came later. Now she said, with sympathy, the word that fixed Lossing in supreme masculine satisfaction. She knew that he never would know, what all his world would smile over, that here was an old formula working: a man of thirty-eight who had become as simple as any Adam under the glance of a young pretty girl who had fallen in love with him. That she was stupid and incredible to his world was a mere detail.

It was Nature's everyday trick that is ever presented with new scenery.

That night after the apartment was still, like a Renaissance conspirator in her red-and-gold gown Miss Anderson took a branched silver candlestick from the Duchessa's dressing table and went as one reluctant into the stone room where Emelie's portrait stood on its easel. The picture was a brilliant thing. It was her child; not her only child but her youngest child. Into it was painted more than poor trifling Emelie in her trappings —more than she, its creator, had in herself: it was a work of art.

Lucy Anderson looked at her work for a long time.

And gradually, as delicately, as inevitably as a chemical reaction it worked its magic. The vibrations that had shaken her, that had brought her here carrying the banal purpose of a hurt woman who had the immemorial impulse of sacrifice, died. The pulse of creation throbbed unobstructed through her at last. She tapped the pool of understanding.

The strong right hand of the artist went against her mouth and then into the air with a high gesture.

"God! It is good!" she said.

Marjorie Kinnan Rawlings

Gal Young Un
1932

"Gal Young Un" is a profound narrative of a woman coming to consciousness through pain. Mattie starts out an alienated creature with no human ties, no sense of her own membership in the human community. Black men come to pick resin from the trees on her property, but the racism bred into her makes her unable to perceive those contacts as human contacts. She sees them as Other: creatures with whom she can coexist and exchange minimal animal kindness. As becomes clear from the way she relates to Trax from the beginning of their relationship, she also sees herself, woman, as Other. However, with Trax, her ability to experience both physical and emotional pleasure awakens.

Mattie is attracted to loving Trax because she can love him not only shamelessly, not only with his permission, but in concert with him. She learns to love him from the one person in the world with the greatest experience of loving Trax—Trax, himself. He exhibits a casual sense of entitlement, approving of everything about himself: his sensuality, his greed, his way of experiencing himself as the center of the universe.

She loves him, she gives him everything she has, time passes, and he demands more and more of her, moving beyond material and labor demands to a demand that she collaborate in her own humiliation. Mattie's new sullenness is the first evidence of stirring self-love and a sense of her own entitlement. The sullenness grows to blunt blind anger and then to a sense of justified rage. Her sense of membership in the human family, her sense of place in the human community, her sense of herself as a person and not as Other has become conscious. She asserts her newly owned self with an awesome power. Then, having spent that terrific emotional storm, she sleeps.

She will not sink again into the oblivion that characterized her life before Trax came.

When she awakens to hear the "gal young un," Mattie becomes conscious of the girl, for the first time, not as Enemy, not as Other, but as another woman like herself, used, discarded, alone. She embraces the girl and takes her into a life that will now be theirs, together. The story ends with the same formation of an alliance, with the same mother-daughter overtones, as in Charlotte Perkins Gilman's story "Turned." Here, too, the turning is not a turning from, but a turning to. Mattie rescues the girl, not because her husband was the most recent to hurt her, but because she, Mattie, has come to full consciousness of her self and her place in the world. Mattie understands that she has been punishing the girl because Trax was exploiting her; she has been blaming the victim.

When Mattie raises the girl from the ground, the mood of the story becomes exultant. Mattie has passed from unconsciousness through pain to self-possession. She has developed the courage to acknowledge her victimization and has acted to free herself. She will rear the girl to reject the role of victim when she grows to be a woman. Mattie has come to understand that a woman can care without being subservient, can nurture without being powerless.

Trax might have been an imaginative transformation of Marjorie Kinnan Rawlings's perception of her husband Charles Rawlings, whom she was in the process of divorcing during the writing of this story. In a letter to an old friend discussing both the divorce and this story she describes Charles as having

> always had an inferiority complex . . . about the whole
> world. . . . He never, in a way, matured. He kept a high
> school boy's philosophy and psychology to the end. That
> might have been rather touching if it had taken a touching or
> appealing form. But with me, he was completely the bully. I
> took constant abuse. And because I loved him so, and just
> couldn't admit, even to myself, that he was an utterly
> impossible person to live with, I kept on year after year
> kidding myself, thinking that if this was changed, or that
> was changed, he would be all right and we would be happy.

Marjorie Kinnan Rawlings (1896–1953) began her literary career as a journalist and became a literary artist of a high order. Her best writing is about the south Florida "crackers," a culture to which she did not belong, but which she chose, amid which she came to live and for which she became a chief literary image-maker, one of the first to follow in the early literary footsteps of Constance Fenimore Woolson (1840–1894).

Often described as a "local colorist," she is in fact an immigrant writer, like Joseph Conrad, writing about a world she came to know only as an adult. In adopting a new culture as her literary landscape, she adopted a gender-free persona as a literary artist.

With the release of the 1983 film Cross Creek *(based on Rawlings's 1942 memoir, starring Mary Steenburgen as Marjorie Kinnan Rawlings), the shape and details of much of Rawlings's life have become accessible. "Gal Young Un," originally published in* Harper's Magazine, *June and July, 1932, and an O. Henry Prize Award story in 1933 (for which she won $500), was translated movingly and accurately to the screen by Victor Nunez in 1979. The story has been reprinted in many anthologies and collected in her volume of short stories,* When the Whippoorwill, *published in 1940 by Scribner's, whose famous editor, Maxwell Perkins, was her literary mentor, inspiring what has been her most popular book,* The Yearling *(1938). It was a critical and financial success, released as an MGM movie in 1946 and awarded the Pulitzer Prize for fiction in 1939. Her first book,* South Moon Under *(1933), like a number of her later books, became a Book-of-the-Month Club selection.*

When Rawlings died, she was at work on a biography of Ellen Glasgow, a writer she admired enormously but with whom she corresponded only briefly before Glasgow's death.

The house was invisible from the road which wound, almost untraveled, through the flat-woods. Once every five days a turpentine wagon creaked down the ruts, and negroes moved like shadows among the pines. A few hunters in season came upon them chipping boxes, scraping aromatic gum from red pots into encrusted buckets; inquired the way and whether quail or squirrel or turkey had been seen. Then hunters and turpentiners moved again along the road, stepping on violets and yellow pitcher-plants that rimmed the edges.

The negroes were aware of the house. It stood a few hundred yards away, hidden behind two live oaks isolated and remote in a patch of hammock. It was a tall square two-stories. The woman who gave them water from her well when the near-by branch was dry looked to them like the house, tall and bare and lonely, weathered gray, like its unpainted cypress. She seemed forgotten.

The two white men, hunting lazily down the road, did not remember—if they had ever known—that a dwelling stood here. Flushing a covey of quail that flung themselves like feathered bronze discs at the cover of the hammock, their first shots flicked through the twin oaks. They followed their pointer dog on the trail of single birds and stopped short in amazement. Entering the north fringe of the hammock, they had come out on a sandy open yard. A woman was watching them from the back stoop of an old house.

"Shootin' mighty close, men," she called.

Her voice sounded unused, like a rusty iron hinge.

The older man whistled in the dog, ranging feverishly in the low palmettos. The younger swaggered to the porch. He pushed back the black slouch hat from his brazen eyes.

"Never knowed nobody lived in six miles o' here."

His tone was insolent. He drew a flattened package of cigarettes from his corduroy hunting jacket, lighted one, and waited for her to begin scolding. Women always quarreled with him. Middle-aged women, like this one, quarreled earnestly; young ones snapped at him playfully.

"It's a long ways from anybody, ain't it?" she agreed.

He stared at her between puffs.

"Jesus, yes."

"I don't keer about you shootin'," she said. "It's purely sociable, hearin' men-folks acrost the woods. A shot come thu a winder jest now, that's all the reason I spoke."

The intruders shifted their shotguns uneasily. The older man touched his finger to his cap.

"That's all right, ma'am."

His companion strolled to the stone curbing of an open well. He peered into its depths, shimmering where the sun of high noon struck vertically.

"Good water?"

"The finest ever. Leave me fetch you a clean cup."

She turned into the house for a white china coffee cup. The men wound up a bucket of water on creaking ropes. The older man drank politely from the proffered cup. The other guzzled directly from the bucket. He reared back his head like a satisfied hound, dripping a stream of crystal drops from his red mouth.

"Ain't your dog thirsty? Here—reckon my ol' cat won't fuss if he drinks outen his dish." The woman stroked the animal's flanks as he lapped. "Ain't he a fine feller."

The hunters began to edge away.

"Men, I jest got common rations, bacon an' biscuit an' coffee, but you're plumb welcome to set down with me."

"No thank you, Ma'am." They looked at the sun. "Got to be moseyin' home."

The younger man was already on his way, sucking a straw. The other fumbled in his game-pocket.

"Sorry we come so clost up on you, lady. How 'bout a bird for your dinner?"

She reached out a large hand for the quail.

"I'd shore thank you for it. I'm a good shot on squirrel, an' turkeys when I git 'em roosted. Birds is hard without no dog to point 'em. I gits hungry for quail . . ."

Her voice trailed off as the hunters walked through the pines toward the road. She waved her hand in case they should turn around. They did not look back.

The man was hunting alone because he had been laughed at. His cronies in the Florida village, to which he had returned after a few years' wandering, knew that he detested solitude. It was alien to him, a silent void into which he sank as into quicksand. He had stopped at the general store to pick up a hunting partner. The men lounging there hours at a time were usually willing to go with him. This time none was ready.

"Come go with me, Willy," he insisted. "I cain't go by myself."

The storekeeper called over his shoulder, weighing out a quarter's worth of water-ground meal for a negro.

"You'll git ketched out alone in the woods sometime, Trax, an' nobody won't know who 'tis."

The men guffawed.

"Trax always got to git him a buddy."

His smoldering eyes flared at them. He spat furiously across the rough pine floor of the store.

"I ain't got to git me none o' these sorry catbirds."

He had clattered down the wooden steps, spitting angrily every few feet. They were jealous, he thought, because he had been over on the east coast. He had turned instinctively down the south road out of the village. Old man Blaine had brought him this way last week. He hunted carelessly for two or three hours, taking pot shots at several coveys that rose under his feet. His anger made him miss the birds widely. It was poor sport without a companion and a dog.

Now he realized that he was lost. As a boy he had hunted these woods, but always with other boys and men. He had gone through them unseeing, stretching his young muscles luxuriously, absorbing lazily the rich Florida sun, cooling his face at every running branch. His shooting had been careless, avid. He like to see the brown birds tumble in midair. He liked to hunt with the pack, to gorge on the game dinners they cooked by lake shores under oak trees. When the group turned homeward, he followed, thinking of supper; of the 'shine his old man kept hidden in the smoke-house; of the girls he knew. Some one else knew north and south, and the cross patterns of the piney-woods roads. The lonely region was now as unfamiliar as though he had been a stranger.

It was an hour or two past noon. He leaned his 12-gauge shotgun against a pine and looked about him nervously. He knew by the sun that he had come continuously south. He had crossed and recrossed the road, and could not decide whether it now lay to the right or left. If he missed it to the right, he would come to cypress swamp. He licked his lips. If he picked the wrong road to the left, it would bring him out a couple of miles above the village. That would be better. He could always get a lift back. He picked up his gun and began to walk.

In a few minutes a flat gray surface flashed suddenly from a patch of hammock. He stopped short. Pleasure swept over him, cooling his hot irritation. He recognized the house where he and Blaine had drawn water. He had cursed Blaine for giving a quail to the woman. He wiped the sweat from his face. The woman would feed him and direct him out of the woods. Instinctively he changed his gait from a shuffling drag to his customary swagger.

He rapped loudly on the smooth cypress front door. It had a half-moon fanlight over it. The house was old but it was capacious and good. There was, for all its bareness, an air of prosperity. Clean white curtains hung at the windows. A striped cat startled him by rearing against his legs. He kicked it away. The woman must be gone. A twig cracked in the yard beyond the high piazza. He turned. The woman was stalking around the side of the house to see before she was seen. Her gray face lightened as she recognized him. She laughed.

"Mister, if you knowed how long it's been since I heerd a rap. Don't nobody knock on my front door. The turpentine niggers calls so's I won't shoot, and the hunters comes a-talkin' to the well."

She climbed the front steps with the awkwardness of middle age. She dried a hand on her flour-sacking apron and held it out to him.

He took it limply, interrupting the talk that began to flow from her. He was ugly with hunger and fatigue and boredom.

"How 'bout a mess o' them rations you was offerin' me last week?"

His impatience was tempered with the tone of casual intimacy in which he spoke to all women. It bridged time and space. The woman flushed.

"I'd be mighty well pleased—"

She opened the front door. It stuck at the sill, and she threw a strong body against it. He did not offer to help. He strolled in ahead of her. As she apologized for the moments it would take to fry bacon and make coffee, he was already staring about him at the large room. When she came to him from the kitchen half an hour later, her face red with her hurry, the room had made an impress in his mind, as roads and forest could not do. The size of the room, of the clay fireplace, the adequacy of chairs and tables of a frontier period, the luxury of a Brussels carpet, although ancient, over wood, the plenitude of polished, unused kerosene lamps—the details lay snugly in his mind like hoarded money.

Hungry, with the smell of hot food filling his breath, he took time to smooth his sleek black hair at a walnut-framed mirror on the varnished matchboard wall. He made his toilet boldly in front of the woman. A close watching of his dark face, of the quickness of his hands moving over his affectation of clipped side-burns, could only show her that he was good to look at. He walked to the kitchen with a roll, sprawling his long legs under the table.

With the first few mouthfuls of food good humor returned to him. He indulged himself in graciousness. The woman served him lavishly with fried cornbread and syrup, coffee, white bacon in thick slices, and fruits and vegetables of her own canning. His gluttony delighted her. His mouth was full, bent low over his heaped plate.

"You live fine, ma'am, for any one lives plumb alone."

She sat down opposite him, wiping back the wet gray hair from her forehead, and poured herself a convivial cup of coffee.

"Jim—that was my husband—an' Pa always did say if they was good rations in the house they'd orter be on the table. I ain't got over the habit."

"You been livin' alone quite some time?"

"Jim's fifteen year dead. Pa 'bout six."

"Don't you never go nowheres?"

"I got no way to go. I kep' up stock for two-three year after Pa died, but 'twa'n' wuth the worry. They's a family lives two mile closer to town than me, has a horse an' wagon. I take 'em my list o' things 'bout oncet a month. Seems like . . ."

He scarcely listened.

A change of atmosphere in her narrative indicated suddenly to him that she was asking him about himself.

"You a stranger?"

She was eager, leaning on the table waiting for his answer.

He finished a saucer of preserved figs, scraping at the rich syrup with relish. He tilted back in his chair luxuriously and threw the match from his cigarette in the general direction of the wood stove. He was entirely at home. His belly well filled with good food, his spirit touched with the unfailing intoxication to him of a woman's interest, he teetered and smoked and talked of his life, of his deeds, his dangers.

"You ever heerd the name o' Trax Colton?"

She shook her head. He tapped his chest significantly, nodding at her.

"That's me. You've heerd tell, if you on'y remembered, o' me leavin' here a few years back on account of a little cuttin' fuss. I been on the east coast—Daytona, Melbourne, all them places. The fuss blowed over an' I come back. Fixin' to take up business here."

He frowned importantly. He tapped a fresh cigarette on the table, as he had learned to do from his companions of the past years. He thought with pleasure of all that he had learned, of the sophistication that lay over his Cracker speech and ways like a cheap bright coat.

"I'm an A-1 bootlegger, ma'am."

For the time being he was a big operator from the east coast. He told her of small sturdy boats from Cuba, of signal flares on the St. Augustine beach at midnight, of the stream of swift automobiles moving in and out just before high tide. Her eyes shone. She plucked at the throat of her brown-checked gingham dress, breathing quickly. It was fitting that this dark glamorous young man should belong to the rocket-lit world of danger. It was ecstasy painful in its sharpness, that he should be tilted back at her table, flicking his fragrant ashes on her clean, lonely floor.

He was entirely amiable as he left her. Pleased with himself, he was for a moment pleased with her. She was a good woman. He laid his hand patronizingly on her shoulder. He stroked the striped cat on his way down the steps. This time he turned to lift his hand to her. She waved heartily as long as his lithe body moved in sight among the pines.

An impulse took her to the mirror where he had smoothed his hair, as though it would bring him within her vision again. She saw herself completely for the first time in many years. Isolation had taken the meaning from age. She had forgotten until this moment that she was no longer young. She turned from the mirror and washed the dishes soberly. It occurred to her that the young man had not even asked her name.

The hammock that had been always a friendly curtain about the old house was suddenly a wall. The flat-woods that had been sunny and open, populous with birds and the voice of winds, grew dense and dark. She had been solitary. She had grieved for Jim and for the old man her father. But solitude had kept her company in a warm natural way, sitting cozily at her hearth, like the cat. Now loneliness washed intolerably over her, as though she were drowning in a cold black pond.

The young man's complacency lasted a mile or two. As his feet began to drag, fact intruded on the fiction with which he had enraptured the gray-haired woman. Memories seeped back to him like a poison: memories of the lean years as ignorant hanger-on of prosperous bootleggers; of his peddling to small garages of lye-cut 'shine in ignominious pints. The world for which he considered himself fitted had evaded him. His condition was desperate. He thought of the woman who had fed him, whom he had entranced with his story. Distaste for her flooded him, as though it was her fault the story was a lie. He lifted his shotgun and blew the head from a redbird trilling in a wild plum tree.

The storekeeper in the village was the only person who recognized Mattie Syles. The store was packed with the Saturday-night buyers of rations. A layer of whites milled in front of the meat counter; a layer of blacks shifted behind them. At the far grocery counter along a side wall a wedge of negroes had worked in toward the meal and sugar barrels, where helpers weighed out the dimes' and quarters' worth with deliberately inaccurate haste. Two white women were buying percale of the storekeeper's wife at the dry-goods counter.

The woman came in defiantly, as though the store was a shameful place where she had no business. She looked searchingly from side to side. The storekeeper's wife called, "Evenin', Ma'am," and the two white women wheeled to stare and whisper after her. She advanced toward the meat counter. The negroes parted to let her in. The storekeeper poised his knife over a pork backbone to look at her. He laid it down, wiped his hands with a flourish on his front, and shook hands across the counter.

"If this ain't a surprise! Must be four-five years since you been to town! Meat I been sendin' you by Lantry's been all right? What kin I do for you? Butchered this mornin'—got fresh beef. How 'bout a nice thin steak?

She made her purchases slowly and moved to the staples counter. She insisted on being left until the last.

"I ain't in no hurry."

The store was almost empty and ready to close when she gathered her sacks together and climbed into the Lantrys' wagon, waiting outside the door. As Lantry clicked to his horse and they moved off she did not notice that the man she had hoped desperately to see was just strolling into the store.

"Gimme a couple o' packs o' Camels to tide me over Sunday."

"Fifteen cents straight now, Trax."

"Jest one, then,"

The storekeeper spoke across the vacant store to his wife, rolling up the bolts of cloth.

"Edna, you have better manners with the customers, or we'll be losing 'em. Why'n't you take up some time with Mis' Syles?"

"Who?"

"Mis' Syles—Jim Syles' widder—ol' man Terry's daughter—lives four-five miles south, out beyond Lantry's. You knew her, Edna. Lantry's been buyin' for her."

"I never knowed her. How'd I know her now? Why'n't you call her by name, so's I'd of knowed?"

"Well, you keep better track of her if she's goin' to take to comin' to town agin. She's rich."

Trax turned in the doorway.

"You talkin' about that gank-gutted woman left jest now?"

He had avoided going into the store until she left. He had not intended to bring her volubility upon him in public, have her refer to their meal together. He had half-guessed she had come looking for him. Women did.

"She live alone in a two-story house you cain't see from the road?"

"That's her," the storekeeper agreed. "That's Mis' Syles, a'right."

"She's rich?"

"I mean rich. Got her five dollars a week steady rent-money from turpentine, an' three thousand dollars insurance in the bank her daddy left her. An' then lives t'other end o' nowhere. Won't leave the old house."

" 'Bout time somebody was fixin' to marry all that, goin to waste."

"She wouldn't suit you, Trax. You didn't git a good look at her. You been used to 'em younger an' purtier."

The man Colton was excited. He walked out of the store without the customary "Well, evenin' " of departure. He hurried to Blaine's where he was boarding, but did not go in. It was necessary to sit alone on the bench outside and think. His luck had not deserted him. As he leaned his dark head back against the wall, the tropical stars glittering over him were the bright lights of city streets. Here and there a fat star flickered. These were the burnished kerosene lamps of the widow Syles. The big room—the fireplace that would heat it on the coolest nights—one by one he drew out the remembered details and tucked them into his plans.

The man courted the woman with the careless impatience of his quail hunting. He intended to be done with it as quickly as possible. There was, astonishingly, a certain pleasure in her infatuation. He responded to any woman's warmth as a hound does to a grate fire, stretching comfortably before it. The maternal lavishness of her emotion for him was satisfying. Younger women, pretty women, expected something of him, coaxed and coquetted.

On his several visits to the widow before he condescended to be married to her, he sprawled in the early spring nights before the big fireplace. He made it plain that he was not one to sit around the kitchen stove. His fastidiousness charmed her. She staggered into the room with her generous arms heaped with wood: live oak and hickory, and some cedar chips, because Trax liked the smell.

From his chair he directed the placing of the heavy logs. A fire must crackle constantly to please him. She learned to roll cigarettes for him, bringing them to him to lick flickeringly, like a snake, with his quick tongue. The process stirred her. When she placed the finished cigarette between his lips and lighted it with a blazing lighter'd splinter; when he puffed languidly on it and half-closed his eyes, and laid his fingers perhaps on her large-boned hand, she shivered.

The courting was needlessly protracted because she could not believe that he would have her. It was miracle enough that he should be here at all in these remote flat-woods. It was unbelievable that he should be willing to prolong the favor, to stay with her in this place forever.

She said, "Cain't be you raly wants me."

Yet she drank in his casual insistence.

"Why not? Ain't a thing the matter with you."

She understood sometimes—when she wakened with a clear mind in the middle of the night—that something strange had happened to her. She was moving in a delirium, like the haze of malaria when the fever was on. She solaced herself by thinking that Trax too might be submerged in such a delicious fog.

When he left her one night in the Blaine Ford he had borrowed, the retreating explosions of the car left behind a silence that terrified her. She ran to the beginning of the pines to listen. There was no sound but the breath of the south wind in the needles. There was no light but the endless flickering of stars. She knew that if the man did not come back again she would have to follow him. Solitude she had endured. She could not endure desolation.

When he came the next day she was ready to go to the village with him to the preacher. He laughed easily at her hurry and climbed ahead of her into the borrowed car. He drove zestfully, with abandon, bouncing the woman's big frame over the ruts of the dirt road.

As they approached the village he said casually, "I keep my money in Clark City. We'd orter do our business together. Where's yours?"

"Mine's there too. Some's in the post office an' some in the bank."

"Supposin' we go git married there. An' reckon you kin lend me a hundred till I add up my account?"

She nodded an assent to both questions.

"Don't you go spendin' no money on me, Trax, if you ain't got it real free to spend." She was alarmed for his interests. "You leave me pay for things a while."

He drew a deep breath of relief. He was tempted for a moment to get her cash and head for the east coast at once. But he had made his plans to stay. He needed the old house in the safe flat-woods to make his start. He could even use the woman.

When they came back through the village from the city she stopped at the store for supplies. The storekeeper leaned across the fresh sausage to whisper confidentially.

"Tain't my business, Mis' Syles, but folks is sayin' Trax Colton is sort o' courtin' you. You come of good stock, an' you'd orter step easy. Trax is purely trash, Mis' Syles."

She looked at him without comprehension.

She said, "Me an' Trax is married."

The gray of the house was overlaid with the tenderness of the April sun. The walls were washed with its thin gold. The ferns and lichens of the shingled roof were shot through with light, and the wren's nest under the eaves was luminous. The striped cat sprawled flattened on the rear stoop, exposing his belly to the soft warmth. The woman moved quietly at her work, for fear of awakening the man. She was washing. When she drew a bucket of water from the well she steadied it with one hand as it swung to the coping, so that there should be no sound.

Near the well stood bamboo and oleander. She left her bucket to draw her fingers along the satin stoutness of the fresh green bamboo shoots, to press apart the new buds of the oleander in search of the pale pinkness of the first blossoms. The sun lay like a friendly arm across her square shoulders. It seemed to her that she had been chilled, year on year, and that now for the first time she was warmed through to her marrow. Spring after the snapping viciousness of February; Trax sleeping in the bed after her solitude . . . When she finished her washing she slipped in to look at him. A boyish quiet wiped out the nervous shiftiness of his waking expression. She wanted to gather him up, sleeping, in her strong arms and hold him against her capacious breast.

When his breakfast was almost ready, she made a light clatter in the kitchen. It irritated him to be called. He liked to get up of his own accord and find breakfast smoking, waiting for him. He came out gaping, washed his face and hands in the granite basin on the water-shelf, combed his hair leisurely at the kitchen mirror, turning his face this way and that. Matt stood watching him, twisting her apron. When he was quite through, she came to him and laid her cheek against his.

"Mornin', Trax-honey."

Her voice was vibrant.

"Mornin'."

He yawned again as he dropped into his chair. He beat lightly on his down-turned plate with his knife and surveyed the table. He scowled.

"Where's the bacon?"

"Honey, I didn't think you'd want none with the squirrel an' eggs an' fish."

"My God, I cain't eat breakfast without bacon."

"I'm sorry, Trax.' 'Twon't take me but a minute now."

She was miserable because she had not fried bacon and he wanted it.

He slid eggs and meat and biscuits to his plate, poured coffee with an angry jerk so that it spilled on the table, shoveled the food in, chewing with his mouth open. When Matt put the crisp thick slices of white bacon before him, he did not touch them. He lighted a cigarette and strolled to the stoop, pushing off the cat so that he might sit down. He leaned back and absorbed the sun. This was fine.

He had deliberately allowed himself these few idle weeks. He had gone long without comfort. His body needed it. His swaggering spirit needed it. The woman's adoration fed him. He could have had no greater sense of well-being, of affluence, if she had been a nigger servant. Now he was ready for business. His weasel mind was gnawing its hole into the world he longed for.

"Matt!"

She left her dishes and came to stand over him.

"Matt, you're goin' in business with me. I want you should git me three hundred dollars. I want to set up a eight-barrel still back o' the house, down by the branch."

Trax had crashed like a meteor into the flat-woods. It had not occurred to her that his world must follow him. That was detached from him, only a strange story that he had told. She had a sensation of dismay that any thing, any person, must intrude on her ecstasy.

She said anxiously, "I got enough to make out on, Trax. You don't need to go startin' up nothin' like that."

"All right—if you want I should put my outfit some'eres else—"

"No, no. Don't you do that. Don't you go 'way. I didn't know you was studyin' on nothin' like that—you jest go ahead an' put it clost as you like."

"Down by the branch, like I said."

He visioned the layout for her. She listened, distraught. The platform here, for the barrels of mash. There, the woodpile for the slow fire. Here again, the copper still itself. The cover was dense, utterly concealing. The location was remote.

"The idee, Matt," he was hunched forward, glowing, "is to sell your own stuff what they call retail, see? It costs you fifty, seventy-five cents a gallon to make. You sell by the five-gallon jug for seven dollars, like they're doin' now, you don't make nothin'. That's nigger pay. But what do you git for it by the drink? A quarter. A quarter a drink an' a dollar a pint. You let people know they kin git 'em a drink out here ary time to Trax Colton's, you got 'em comin' in fro two-three counties for it. You git twenty gallons ahead an' color some up, cook it a whiles underground to darken it, an' you take it to places like Jacksonville an' Miami—you got you real money."

It was as though thunder and lightning threatened over the flat-woods. The darkness of impending violence filled them. She stared at him.

"'Course, if you don' want to invest in my business with me, I got to be gittin' back when I come from."

The smoke from his cigarette drifted across her.

"No, no! It's all right!"

His glamorousness enfolded her like the April sun.

"Honey, anything you want to do's all right."

Setting up the still was a week's work. Men began to come and go. Where there had been, once in five days, the silent turpentiners, once in a while the winter hunters, there were now negroes bringing in cut wood; a local mason putting together brick and mortar; a hack carpenter building a platform with a roof; men in trucks bringing in sacks of meal and sugar, glass demijohns and oak kegs.

The storekeeper brought five hundred pounds of sugar.

"Howdy, Mis' Colton. Reckon you never figgered you'd be 'shinin'."

"No."

"But you couldn't git you no better place for it."

Her square face brightened.

"That's jest what Trax says."

That night she approached him.

"Trax, all these here men knowin' what you're doin'—reckon it's safe?"

"They got no reason to say nothin'. The only reason anybody'd turn anybody else up was if he'd done somethin' to him. Then they'd git at him that-a-way. Git his still, see? Git him tore up. That way they'd git him."

She made no further comment. Her silence made its way through the wall of his egotism.

"You don't talk as much as you did, Matt. Else I got used to it."

"I was alone so long, honey. Seemed like I had to git caught up."

But the spring warmth was no longer so loosening to the tongue. The alien life the man was bringing in chilled the exuberance that had made her voluble.

"I'm fixin' to learn you to make the whiskey, Matt."

She stared at him.

"Less help we have, knowin' how much I got an' where 'tis, better it suits me, see?"

She said finally, "I kin learn."

The work seemed strange, when all her folk had farmed and timbered. But her closest contact with Trax was over the sour, seething mash. When they walked together back of the house, down to the running branch, their bodies pushing side by side through the low palmettos, they were a unit. Except to curse her briefly when she was clumsy, he was good-natured at his work. Crouching by the fire burning under the copper drum, the slow dripping from the coils, of the distillate, the only sound except for small woods life, she felt themselves man and wife. At other times his lovely body and unlovely spirit both evaded her.

He was ready to sell his wares. He drove to the village and to neighboring towns and cities, inviting friends and acquaintances to have a drink from one of the gallon jugs under the rear seat of the borrowed car. They pronounced it good 'shine. To the favored few financially able to indulge themselves he gave a drink of the "aged" liquor. Accustomed to the water-clear, scalding rawness of fresh 'shine, they agreed gravely that no better whiskey ever came in from Cuba. He let it be known that both brands would be available at any time, day or night, at the old Terry house four miles south of the village. He made a profound impression. Most bootleggers sold stuff whose origin and maker were unknown. Most 'shiners had always made it, or drifted into it aimlessly. Trax brought a pomp and ceremony to the local business.

Men found their way out the deep-rutted road. They left their cars among the pines and stumbled through the hammock to the house. They gathered in the big room Trax had recognized as suitable for his purposes. The long trenchered table old man Terry had sliced from red bay held the china pitcher of "corn" and the jelly glasses from which they drank. Their bird-dogs and hounds padded across the piazza and lay before the fire. Trax drank with them, keying their gatherings to hilarity. He was a convivial host. Sometimes Blaine brought along his guitar, and Trax clapped his hands and beat his feet on the floor as the old man picked the strings. But he was uneasy when a quarrel developed. Then he moved, white-faced among the men, urging some one else to stop it.

At first the woman tried to meet them hospitably. When, deep in the hammock at the still, she heard the vibration of a motor, she hurried up to the house to greet the guests. She smoothed back the gray hair from her worn face and presented her middle-aged bulk in a clean apron. If there was one man alone, Trax introduced her casually, insolently.

"This is my old woman."

When a group of men came together, he ignored her. She stood in the doorway, smiling vaguely. He continued his talk as though she was not there. Sometimes one of the group, embarrassed, acknowledged her presence.

"How do, Ma'am."

For the most part they took their cue from Trax and did not see her. Once, on her withdrawal to the kitchen, a stranger had followed for a match.

"Don't you mind workin' way out here in the woods?"

But she decided that Trax was too delicate to want his wife mixing with men who came to drink. At night he sometimes invited her into the big room with conspicuous courtesy. That was when one or two women had come with the men. Her dignity established the place as one where they might safely come. She sat miserably in their midst while they made banal jokes and drank from the thick glasses. They were intruders. Their laughter was alien among the pine trees. She stayed at the still most of the time. The labor was heavy and exacting. The run must be made when the mash was ready, whether it was day or night. It was better for Trax to stay at the house to take care of the customers.

In early fall he was ready to expand. Matt was alone, scrubbing the floors between runs of whiskey. She heard a powerful car throbbing down the dirt road. It blew a horn constantly in a minor key. Men usually came into this place silently. She went to the piazza, wet brush in hand. With the autumnal drying of foliage, the road was discernible. The scent of wild vanilla filled the flat-woods. She drew in the sweetness, craning her neck to see.

A large blue sedan of expensive make swerved and rounded into the tracks other cars had made to the house. Trax was driving. He swung past the twin live oaks and into the sandy yard. He slammed the door behind him as he stepped out. He had bought the car with the remainder of Matt's three thousand and most of the summer's profits. He was ready to flash across his old haunts, a big operator from the interior.

"I kin sell that hundred gallons of aged stuff now for what it's worth."

He nodded wisely. He sauntered into the house, humming under his breath.

"Hi-diddy-um-tum—" He was vibrant with an expectancy in which she had no part.

She heard him curse because the floor was wet. The cat crossed his path. He lifted it by the tail and slid it along the slippery boards. The animal came to her on the piazza. She drew it into her lap and sat on her haunches a long time, stroking the smooth hard head.

Life was a bad dream. Trax was away a week at a time. He hired the two Lantry boys to take his place. Matt worked with them, for the boys unwatched would let the mash ferment too long. Trax returned to the flat-woods only for fresh supplies of liquor and of clean clothes. It pleased him to dress in blues that harmonized not too subtly with the blue sedan. He wore light-blue shirts and a red necktie that was a challenging fire under the dark insolent face. Matt spent hours each week washing and ironing the blue shirts. She protested his increasing absences.

"Trax, you jest ain't here at all. I hardly got the heart for makin' the runs, an' you gone."

He smiled.

"Ary time it don't suit you, I kin move my outfit to the east coast."

He laid the threat across her like a whip.

The young Lantrys too saw Trax glamorously. They talked of him to Matt as they mixed the mash, fired, and kept their vigils. This seemed all she had these day of the man: talk of him with the boys beside the still. She was frustrated, filled, not with resentment, but with despair. Yet she could not put her finger on the injustice. She flailed herself with his words, "Ary time you don't like it, I kin move."

She waited on Trax' old customers as best she could, running up the slight incline from the still-site to the house when she heard a car. Her strong body was exhausted at the end of the week. Yet when she had finished her elaborate baking on Saturday night she built up a roaring fire in the front room, hung the hot-water kettle close to it for his bath, and sat down to wait for him.

Sometimes she sat by the fire almost all night. Sometimes he did not come at all. Men learned they could get a drink at Colton's any hour of the night on Saturday. When the square dance at Trimtree's was done, they came out to the flat-woods at two or three o'clock in the morning. The woman was always awake. They stepped up on the piazza and saw her through the window. She sat brooding by the fire, the striped cat curled in her lap. Around her bony shoulders she hugged the corduroy hunting jacket Trax had worn when he came to her.

She existed for the Saturday nights when the throb of the blue sedan came close; the Sunday mornings when he slept late and arose, sulky, for a lavish breakfast and dinner. Then he was gone again, and she was waving after him down the road. She thought that her love and knowledge of him had been always nothing but this watching through the pine trees as he went away.

The village saw more of him. Occasionally he loitered there a day to show off before he headed for the coast. At times he returned in the middle of the week and picked up fifteen or twenty gallons cached at Blaine's and did not go out to the flat-woods at all. On these occasions he had invariably a girl or woman with him; cheap pretty things whose lightness brought them no more than their shoddy clothes. The storekeeper, delivering meal and sugar to Matt, lingered one day. The still needed her but she could not with courtesy dismiss him. At last he drew courage.

"Mis' Matt, dogged if I don't hate to complain on Trax to you, but folks thinks you don't know how he's a-doin' you. You're workin' like a dog, an' he ain't never home."

"I know."

"You work at 'shinin', somethin' you nor your folks never done— not that it ain't all right—An' Trax off in that big fine car spendin' the money fast as he turns it over."

"I know."

"The Klan talks some o' givin' him down the country for it."

" 'Tain't nobody's business but his an' mine."

"Mis' Matt"—he scuffled in the sand—"I promised I'd speak of it. D'you know Trax has got him women goin' 'round with him?"

"No. I didn't know that."

"Ev'ybody figgered you didn't know that." He mopped his forehead. "The day you an' Trax was married, I was fixin' to tell you 'twa'n't nothin' but your money an' place he wanted to git him set up."

"That's my business, too," she said stonily.

He dropped his eyes before the cold face and moved to his truck. She called after him defiantly.

"What else did I have he'd want anyway!"

She went into the house. She understood the quality of her betrayal. The injustice was clear. It was only this: Trax had taken what he had not wanted. If he had said, "Give me the money and for the time, the house," it would have been pleasant to give, solely because he wanted. This was the humiliation: that she had been thrown in on the deal, like an old mare traded in with a farm.

The Lantry boys called unanswered from the palmettos.

She had known. There was no need of pretense. There was no difference between today and yesterday. There was only the dissipation of a haze, as though a sheet had been lifted from a dead body, so that, instead of knowing, she saw.

The man came home late Saturday afternoon. Startled, Matt heard the purr of the motor and hurried to the house from the still. She thought the woman with him had come for liquor. She came to meet them, wiping her hands on her brown gingham apron. Trax walked ahead of his companion, carrying his own shiny patent leather bag and a smaller, shabby one. As they came into the house, she saw that it was not a woman, but a girl.

The girl was close on his heels, like a dog. She was painted crudely, as with a haphazard conception of how it should be done. Stiff blond curls were bunched under a tilted hat. A flimsy silk dress hung loosely on an immature frame. Cheap silk stockings bagged on thin legs. She rocked, rather than walked, on incredibly spiked heels. Her shoes absorbed Matt's attention. They were pumps of blue kid, the precise blue of the sedan.

"I mean, things got hot for me on the east coat." Trax was voluble. "Used that coastal highway oncet too often. First thing I knowed, down below New Smyrna, I seed a feller at a garage give the high sign, an' I'm lookin' into the end of a .45." He flushed. "I jest did get away. It'll pay me to work this territory a whiles, till they git where they don't pay me no mind over there agin."

The girl was watching Matt with solemn blue eyes. Beside the gray bulk of the older woman, she was like a small gaudy doll. Trax indicated her to Matt with his thumb.

"Elly here'll be stayin' at the house a while."

He picked up the shabby bag and started up the stairs.

"Long as you an' me is usin' the downstairs, Matt, she kin sleep upstairs in that back room got a bed in it."

She pushed past the girl and caught him by the sleeve.

"Trax! What's this gal?"

"Ain't no harm to her." He laughed comfortably. He tweaked a wisp of her gray hair.

"She's just a little gal young un," he said blandly, "'s got no place to go."

He drew the girl after him. The woman stared at the high-heeled blue slippers clicking on every step.

A warm winter rain thrummed on the roof. The light rush of water sank muffled into the moss that padded the shingles. The sharpest sound was a gurgling in the gutter over the rain-barrel. There had been no visible rising of the sun. Only the gray daylight had protracted itself, so that it was no longer dawn, but day. Matt sat close to the kitchen stove, her bulk shadowy in the dimness. Now and then she opened the door of the fire-box to push in a stick of pine, and the light of the flames flickered over her drawn face.

She could not tell how much of the night she had sat crouched by the range. She had lain long hours unsleeping, while Trax breathed regularly beside her. When the rain began, she left the bed and dressed by the fresh-kindled fire. The heat did not warm her. Her mouth was dry; yet every few minutes an uncontrollable chill shook her body. It would be easy to walk up the unused stairs, down the dusty hall to the back room with the rough pine bed in it, to open the door and look in, to see if anyone was there. Yet if she continued to sit by the fire, moving back the coffee pot when it boiled, surely Trax would come to the kitchen alone, and she would know that yesterday no woman had come home with him. Through the long days her distraught mind had been busy with imaginings. They might easily have materialized, for a moment, in a painted girl, small and very young, in blue kid slippers.

Trax was moving about. She put the frying pan on the stove, sliced bacon into it, stirred up cornmeal into a pone with soda and salt and water. Trax called someone. He came into the kitchen, warmed his hands at the stove. He poured water into the wash basin and soused his face in it. Matt set the coffee pot on the table. The girl pushed open the door a little way and came through. She came to the table uncertainly as though she expected to be ordered away. Matt did not speak.

Trax said, "How's my gal?"

The girl brought her wide eyes to him and took a few steps to his chair.

"Where your shoes, honey?"

She looked down at her stockinged feet.

"I gottta be keerful of 'em."

He laughed indulgently.

"You kin have more when them's gone. Matt, give the young un somethin' to eat."

The thought struck the woman like the warning whir of a rattler that if she looked at the girl in this moment she would be compelled to lift her in her hands and drop her like a scorpion on the hot stove. She thought, "I can't do such as that." She kept her back turned until the impulse passed and she could control her trembling. Her body was of metal and wood. It moved of itself, in jerks. A still wooden head creaked above a frame so heavy it seemed immovable. Her stomach weighed her down. Her ample breasts hurt her ribs, as though they were of lead. She thought, "I got to settle this now."

She said aloud slowly, "I'll not wait on her nor no other woman."

The girl twisted one foot over the other.

She said, "I ain't hungry."

Trax stood up. His mouth was thin. He said to Matt, "You'll wait on her, old lady, or you'll git along without my comp'ny."

She thought, "I got to settle it. I got to say it."

But she could not speak.

The girl repeated eagerly, "I ain't a bit hungry."

Trax picked up a plate from the table. He held it out to his wife.

She thought, "Anyway, cornbread and bacon's got nothing to do with it."

She dished out meat and bread. Trax held out a cup. She filled it with coffee. The man sat down complacently. The girl sat beside him and pecked at the food. Her eyes were lowered. Between mouthfuls, she twisted her fingers in her lap or leaned over to inspect her unshod feet.

Matt thought, "Reminding me."

The paint had been rubbed from the round face. The hair was yellow, like allamanda blooms. The artificial curls that had protruded from the pert hat had flattened out during the damp night, and hung in loose waves on the slim neck. She wore the blue silk dress in which she had arrived.

Trax said, "You eat up good, Elly. May be night 'fore we git back to eat agin." He turned to Matt. "Lantry boys been doin' all right?"

"They been doin' all right. Them's good boys. I heerd 'em come in a hour back. But they needs watchin' right on. They'll let the mash go too long, spite of everything, if I ain't right on top of 'em."

She hardened herself.

"You jest as good to stay home an' do the work yourself. I ain't goin' near the outfit."

"They kin make out by theirselves," he said easily.

He rose from the table, picking his teeth.

"Come on, Elly."

The girl turned her large eyes to the older woman, as though she were the logical recipient of her confession.

"I forgot to wash my hands an' face," she said.

Trax spoke curtly.

"Well, do it now, an' be quick."

He poured warm water in the basin for her and stood behind her, waiting. She washed slowly, with neat, small motions, like a cat. Trax handed her the clean end of the towel. They went upstairs together. Trax' voice was low and muffled. It dripped through the ceiling like thick syrup. Suddenly Matt heard the girl laugh.

She thought, "I figgered all that owl face didn't let on no more'n she meant it to."

In a few minutes they came down again. Trax called from the front room.

"Best to cook dinner tonight, Matt. We're like not to git back at noon."

They ran from the porch through the rain.

She walked after them. She was in time to see them step in the blue sedan. The high-heeled slippers flickered across the running-board. The car roared through the live oaks, down the tracks among the pines. Matt closed her eyes against the sight of it.

She thought, "Maybe she takened her satchel and I just didn't see it. Maybe she ain't coming back."

She forced herself to go to the upstairs bedroom. The drumming on the roof sounded close and louder. The bed was awkwardly made. The shabby handbag stood open in a hickory rocker, exposing its sparse contents. A sound startled her. The cat had followed, and was sniffing the unfamiliar garments in the chair. The woman gathered the animal in her arms.

She thought of the Lantry boys under the palmettos. They were careless when they were cold and wet. They might not put the last five hundred pounds of sugar under cover. Shivering in the drizzle, they might use muddy water from the bank of the branch, instead of going a few yards upstream when it ran deep and clear. She threw Trax's corduroy jacket about her and went down the incline behind the house to oversee the work.

She had decided not to cook anything for the evening. But when the mist lifted in late afternoon and the sun struck slantwise through the wet dark trees, she left the Lantry boys to finish and went to the house. She fried ham and baked soda biscuits and sweet potatoes. The meal was ready and waiting and she stirred up a quick ginger cake and put it in the oven.

She said aloud, desperately, "Might be he'll be back alone."

Yet when the dark gathered the bare house into its loneliness, as she had gathered the cat, and she lighted kerosene lamps in the long front room and a fire, the man and girl came together as she had known they would. Where she had felt only despair, suddenly she was able to hate. She picked up her anger like a stone and hurled it after the blue heels.

"Go eat your dinner."

She spoke to them as she would to negro field hands. Trax stared at her. He herded Elly nervously ahead of him, as though to protect her from an obscure violence. Matt watched them, standing solidly on big feet. She had not been whole. She had charred herself against the man's youth and beauty. Her hate was healthful. It waked her from a drugged sleep, and she stirred faculties hurt and long unused.

She sat by the clay fireplace in the front room while the pair ate. They spoke in whispers, shot through by the sudden laugh of the girl. It was a single high sound, like the one note of the thrush. Hearing it, Matt twisted her mouth. When the casual clatter of plates subsided, she went to the kitchen and began scraping the dishes to wash them. Trax sat warily in his place. The girl made an effort to hand Matt odds and ends from the table. The woman ignored her.

Trax said to Elly, "Le's go by the fire."

Matt cleaned up the kitchen and fed the cat. She stroked its

arching back as it chewed sideways on scraps of meat and potato.
She took off her apron, listened at the open door for sounds from
the Lantrys, bolted the door, and walked to the front room to sit
stiff and defiant by the blazing pine fire. The girl sat with thin legs
tucked under her chair. She looked from the man to the woman
and back again. Trax stretched and yawned.

He said, "Guess I'll go down back an' give the boys a hand. I
ain't any too sure they run one batch soon enough. I got to keep
up my stuff. I got high-class trade. Ain't I, Elly?" He touched her
face with his finger as he passed her.

The woman and the girl sat silently after his going. The cat
padded in and sat between them.

The girl called timidly, "Kitty!"

Matt turned savagely.

"Keep your hands off him."

The girl laced her fingers and studied the animal.

"Do he scratch?"

Matt did not answer. She loosened her gray hair and combed it
by the fire with a side-comb, plaiting it into two thin braids over
her shoulders. Inside the childish hairdressing her face was bony
and haggard. She went into the adjoining bedroom, undressed and
got into bed. She lay reared up on one elbow, straining for every
sound. The fire popped and crackled. Once the juice oozed from a
pine log faster than it could burn. It made a sizzling, like boiling
fat. A chair scraped and Elly went up to the back bedroom. Her
high heels clicked overhead. Matt thought with satisfaction that the
girl had no light. She was floundering around in the dark in the
unfamiliar house.

In a little while the front door opened and close softly. Matt
heard Trax creak cautiously up the stairs to the back room.

Trax was sleeping away the bright March morning. Matt made
no effort to be silent about her washing. She dipped noisily into
the rain barrel. When the soft water was gone she drew from the
well, rattling galvanized buckets. Elly sat on the bottom step of the
rear stoop, scuffling her bare toes in the sand. She wore the blue
silk dress. Beside her was a handful of her own garments in need
of washing, a pair of silk stockings and two or three pieces of
underwear. Matt passed front of her to go to the clothes line.

Elly said "Trax give me this dress."

The woman did not seem to hear her.

Elly continued. "Reckon it'll wash? It's spotted."

Matt did not answer. She hung flour-sacking towels on the line. The girl picked up her small pile, looked uncertainly at the tub of soapsuds, laid down the clothes. She went to the tub and began rubbing on the first garment she drew from the suds. It was one of Matt's gingham aprons. She rubbed with energy, and Matt towered over her before she noticed that the woman had left the line.

"Take your dirty hands out o' my tub."

The girl drew back, dripping suds from her thin arms. She turned her hands back and forth.

"They ain't dirty," she protested.

Matt laughed shortly. "Mighty simple, ain't you?"

An obscure doubt brushed her, like a dove that wavers to a perch and is gone again without lighting.

"Who do you figger I am?"

The girl faced her across the wash-tub. She said gravely, "The lady lives in Trax' house."

"Trax' house? Well, he lives in mine. Never heerd tell o' no sich thing as his wife, eh?"

The girl hesitated. "Trax jest said the old woman."

Matt breathed heavily. The girl took her silence and her questions for a mark of interest.

"Trax said you'd romp on me," she offered confidentially. "But you ain't." She wrapped one bare leg around the other. "I been romped on," she went on brightly. "Pa romped on me reg'lar."

"You got you folks then!"

"Yessum, but I don't know where he is. He run a blacksmith shop an' garage offen the hard road, but he closed up an' goed to Georgia with a lady. Then I lived with another lady down the road a piece. Trax sold her liquor, that's how come him to know me. She moved off, an' he takened me with him from there. Now I'm gonna live with him," she finished, adding with studied tact "— and you."

Trax came yawning to the rear stoop in time to see Matt walk toward the girl. Elly stared uncomprehending. He jumped to the sand and caught the woman's muscular arms from behind.

"Don't you touch her." He cracked his familiar whip over her.

"You hurt that gal young un an' you've seed the last o' me."

The woman shook free from him in the strength of her rage.

"You git out o' here before I hurts her an' you, too. You take your gal young un an' git."

He adjusted his mind slowly. Inconceivably, he had gone too far. Bringing the girl to the flat-woods had been dangerously brazen. It was done now. He understood that his hold on this place had become suddenly precarious. He had the car and he could move the still. Yet the layout suited his needs too exactly to be relinquished. He could not give it up. If the gray-headed woman was done with her infatuation, he was in trouble.

He said boldly, "I got no idee o' goin'. Me an' Elly'll be here right on."

She said, "I kin break ary one o' you in two with my hands."

"Not me, you cain't. Leave me tell you, ol' woman, I'm too quick for you. An' if you hurt Elly"—his dark face nodded at her—"if you crack down on her—with them big hands o' yourn—if you got any notion o' knifin' "—he paused for emphasis—"I'll git you sent to the chair, or up for life—an' I'll be here in these flat-woods—in this house—right on."

He pushed the girl ahead of him and walked into the house, lighting a cigarette. He said over his shoulder, thickly between puffs, "An' that'd suit me jest fine."

She turned blindly to the wash-tub. She soaped the blue shirts without seeing them, rubbing them up and down automatically. Her life that had run like the flat-woods road, straight and untraveled, was now a maze, doubling back on itself darkly, twisted with confusion. The man stood with his neat trap at the end of every path; the girl with her yellow hair and big eyes, at the beginning.

She thought, "I got to settle it."

Trax and Elly came and went like a pair of bright birds. The blue kid slippers, scuffed by the sand, flashed in and out of the old house. Matt watched the comings and goings heavily, standing solidly on the hand-hewn pine-board floors.

She did not go near the still. Her absence did not make the difference she had imagined. The Lantrys had the work well in hand. Trax paid their wages, and their product was satisfactory. Often she did not hear them come to their work through the pines and past the hammock. A northwest wind sometimes brought the scent of the mash to her nose. The storekeeper brought in sugar and meal by a lower trail, and she seldom saw him. Trax was selling all his liquor at a high urban price, and local patronage dwindled away. The woods were quiet day and night.

Then Trax and Elly were back again, talking of hotels and highways, of new business, the talk pierced through now and again by the girl's single-noted laughter. She eyed Matt gravely, but the woman felt that the girl, oddly, had no fear. Trax was insolent, as always, his eyes narrow and his ways wary. Matt cut down on the table. She cooked scarcely enough for the three to eat. Elly ate with her catlike slowness, taking twice as long at her meager plate as the others. Matt took to rising and clearing the table as soon as she and Trax had finished. She picked up the plates casually, as though unaware that the third one still showed half its food uneaten. Trax did not seem to notice. The girl sometimes looked hungrily after the vanishing portion. She made no protest. Once Matt found her in the kitchen between meals, eating cold cornbread. Trax backed her up in her curt order to Elly to keep out.

It enraged Matt to see Elly feed the cat. Elly saved bits from her sparse helpings and held them under the table when she thought herself unobserved. Occasionally when the girl held the animal in her lap, and Matt ignored it, Trax stroked him too, because it was Elly who held him. Matt knew they sometimes had food in Elly's room at night. She began to hear a soft padding up the stairs and on the bare floor overhead, and knew the cat went up to join them. In the morning he was smug, washing his whiskers enigmatically. His desertion was intolerable. She shut him out at night. He wailed for hours at the door, accustomed to sleeping snugly inside the house.

Suddenly Trax was not taking Elly with him any more. The village had become accustomed to the grave childish face beside him when it disappeared. Casually he left her behind with Matt in the flat-woods. He drove away one morning and did not come back that night or the next.

Matt took it for a taunt. It seemed to her that he was daring her to trap herself. Elly watched the road anxiously the first day. She accepted, hours before Matt, his solitary departure.

At their first breakfast alone together, she said hesitantly, "I had a idee Trax was fixin' to go off alone."

Matt thought, "The fool don't know enough to keep quiet about it."

After the second day, Elly devoted herself to exploring outside the house. Trax had kept her close to him, and the hammock had been only a cluster of shrubs and great trees through which they came and went. The Spanish moss was hazed with green by the early spring, and she discovered that the gray stands were alive with infinitesimal rosy blossoms. Matt saw her sitting at the far edge of the hammock, pulling the stuff apart.

The woman thought, "She better get herself out of my sight."

Elly roamed through the pines as far as the road, staring up and down its silent winding, then scampered back toward the house like an alarmed squirrel. She walked stealthily to the palmettos where the Lantrys worked the still, and watched them for hours unseen. Except when Matt stared directly at her, her round-eyed gravity lifted into a certain lightness, as though she felt newly free to move about in the sunlight. She seemed content.

On a rainy afternoon Matt, ironing in the kitchen, heard a steady snipping from the front room. She stole to the door and peered through a crack. Elly was cutting pictures from an old magazine and making an arrangement of rooms and figures of men and women and children. She was talking to herself and occasionally to them. The cat was curled in her lap, shifting lazily as she moved forward or back.

Their meals together were silent. Matt became aware at dinner one day that the pink oleanders in a jelly glass were not of her picking and placing. She had always a spray of flowers or greenery on the table. Because Elly had brought in the blooms, she snatched them from the water and stuffed them in the stove.

She allowed the girl a minimum of food. Once when she took away the plates before Elly had fairly begun, the girl reached after her desperately and said, "Matt!" Again, when Matt moved from the table, leaving a plate of biscuits behind, Elly pounced on the largest and crammed it into her mouth. She began to laugh, poking in the crumbs.

She said, "You ain't romped on me yet."

Matt decided that Trax had put Elly up to goading her. She spoke for the first time in days.

"Don't you let Trax put no notions in your head. I got no idee o' rompin' on you. That ain't what I'm fixin' to do."

For the most part, the girl was uncomplaining and strangely satisfied. The immature body, however, was becoming emaciated.

Trax was gone two weeks. He came in for an afternoon and loaded up with twenty gallon-jugs concealed under the large rear seat, and went hurriedly away. He called to the two women who stood watching on the piazza.

"Got a order."

Matt nodded grimly after him. She thought, "You got you one more chance, too, if you only knowed it." She turned to observe the girl beside her. There was apparent on the young face a faint wistfulness and no surprise. Matt thought, "She's got her orders just to set tight."

Trax came home for the following weekend. He slept most of the time and was sulky. He paid no more attention to Elly then to the older woman. At no time in the two days or nights did he go to the upstairs room. When he was about, Elly followed him a few steps. Then, as he continued to ignore her, she dropped behind and took up her own simple affairs. Matt told herself that if he left this time without the girl, she was ready. On Monday morning, after loading, he went alone to the car.

She said carelessly, "I might take a notion to go some'eres or do somethin'. When you comin' back this time?"

He laughed insolently. "Steppin' out, Matt?" He was sure of himself. He was too quick for her. Whatever futilities she was planning, it would surprise her most to return on the day he named.

"Be back Sat'day."

He drove off smiling.

Matt was nervous all week. On Saturday morning she surprised the Lantry boys by appearing at the still. They had come and gone without contact with her for some weeks.

She said, "Boys, I jest got word the Pro-hi's is comin' lookin' for Trax' outfit. Now I ain't quick as you-all, an' I want each one o' you should go down the road a good piece an' stay there all day, watchin', one to the north an' t'other to the south. I'll tend the outfit, an' if I hears a whistle I'll know what it means an' it'll give me time to smash the jugs an' git to the house."

The boys were in instant alarm.

"Must be somebody's turned Trax up," they said.

Matt said, "Mighty likely. Somebody's likely got it in for him. Trax hisself done tol' me a long ways back, if anybody had it in for a man, that was the way they'd git at him."

They nodded in agreement.

"That's about it, Mis' Matt. Git him tore up an' git at him that-a-way."

They hid several demijohns in near-by cover and hurried anxiously the two ways of the road. They reported later in the village that they heard no sound for an hour or so. Toward noon their straining ears caught the crash of an axe on metal. There was a high thin splintering of glass. The isolated crashes settled into a steady shattering of wood and iron and copper. A column of smoke began to rise from the vicinity of the still. The Lantry to the south skirted the road through the pines and joined his brother. They cut through the woods to the village and announced that the Pro-hi's had come in from the west and were tearing up Colton's outfit. The word went out to avoid the flat-woods road.

The Lantrys were waiting for Trax when he came through in late afternoon. They flagged him down. They drove with him as far as their own place, telling him what they knew.

"When we lit out we could hear 'em maulin' on the barrels an' purely see the smoke. Things is tore up an' burnt up all right."

They conjectured who, of his numerous enemies, might have betrayed him. He drove at a spring-breaking clip over the root-filled ruts of the sand road. His face was black and frightened. When he let the boys out of the car he had said nothing about the week's wages. They looked at each other.

One said, "How 'bout us gittin' ten dollars, anyway, Trax?"

"That's it. I ain't got it. I on'y got five myself. I was fixin' to turn over this lot quick."

"We hid out 'bout twenty gallons, if they ain't found it," they informed him eagerly. He listened tensely to a description of the location and was gone.

He drove into the yard and stopped the car in gear with a jerk.

No one was in sight. He ran back of the house to the palmettos. A ring of fire had blackened palms and oaks and myrtle for a hundred feet around. A smoldering pile of bricks and barrel hoops and twisted metal in the center marked the site of the still. He began a frenzied search for the hidden jugs.

Matt peered from a window in the front room. She ordered Elly upstairs.

"You stay there 'til I tell you different."

The woman hurried into the yard with a jug of kerosene and a handful of papers. The sedan was twenty-five feet from the house, but the direction of the wind was safe. She soaked the hood and seats of the car with oil and piled papers on the floor. She tied a bundle of oil-soaked paper on the end of her longest clothes prop; touched a match to it. She lowered the pole to the machine. The oil caught fire. When the blaze reached the gas tank, the explosion disintegrated an already charring mass.

Trax heard the muffled roar up the incline behind him. The demijohns were where the Lantry boys had indicated. They were broken. He left the stench of overturned mash and spilled alcohol and ran to the house. He could not for a moment comprehend that the twisting mass of metal and flame was the blue sedan.

Matt stood on the rear stoop. He looked at her in bewilderment. His stare dropped from her straggling gray hair down the length of her frame. Her apron was smudged and torn. He hands were black and raw. He came back to her implacable cold eyes. He choked.

"You done it yourself!"

He burst into spasmodic curses, then broke off, overcome by their futility. The sweat ran into his eyes. He wiped it out and gaped about him in loose-mouthed confusion. He shuffled a few feet to the stoop and sank down on the bottom step. The woman looked down at him.

"Better git goin'."

He rose, swaying.

"You ol' . . ."

His obscenities fell away from her as rain washed from the weathered shingles of the old house. She towered over him. The tall house towered over him. He was as alien as on the bright day when he had first come hunting here.

He plunged up the steps toward her, his head low between his shoulders.

"Better git back."

His outstretched fists dropped at his sides. The fingers fell open. The woman lifted the shotgun.

"Better git—"

He shook his head, unbelieving. His eyes clung to the dark cavities of the pitted steel. He moved one foot slowly to the next step.

The woman aimed carefully at the shoe, as though it were some strange reptile creeping into the house. She fired a trifle to the left, so that the pattern of the double-ought buckshot shell sprayed in a close mass into the sand. One pellet clipped through the leather, and a drop of blood sank placidly into the pine step. The man stared fascinated. His hand jerked to his mouth, like a wooden toy moved by strings. He stifled a sound, or tried to make one. The woman could not tell. He lifted a face dry with fear and backed down the steps.

It was necessary to walk widely to the side to avoid the heat of the burned car. He threw out his hands hopelessly and hesitated. The sun slanted orange and gold through the hammock. Beyond, there were already shadows among the dark pines. It would be twilight before he could be out of the flat-woods. He found voice.

"Matt," he whined, "how'll I git to town?"

The woman wiped her streaked face with a corner of her apron.

"Reckon you'll have to git there on foot, Mister—the way you come in the first place."

She turned her back and went into the house. The girl had come down the stairs and was flattened against a wall. Her face was brushed with a desperate knowledge. Matt jerked her head at the open front door.

"All right. I'm thu. You kin go on with him now."

"Matt—"

"Go on. Git."

The girl did not move. Matt pushed her headlong to the door. Elly took hold of the big arm with both hands, drawing back, and Matt struck her away. She went confusedly down the steps. Trax was leaving the hammock. He struck wildly through the pines. The

girl took a few steps after him, then turned toward the woman
watching from the doorway.

Matt called loudly, "Go on. Git."

The man had reached the road and was plunging along it to the
north. The girl ran three or four paces in his direction, then stopped
again, like a stray dog or cat that would not be driven away. She
hesitated at the edge of the hammock. The small uncertain figure
was visible between the twin oaks beyond the high porch. Matt
turned into the house and closed the door.

She was strong and whole. She was fixed, deep-rooted as the
pine trees. They leaned a little, bent by an ancient storm. Nothing
more could move them.

The car in the yard had settled into a smoking heap. The acrid
smell of burned rubber and paint filled the house. Matt closed the
north window to keep out the stench. The glass rattled in its frame.
The air was gusty and the spring night would be cold. There were
swift movements and rustlings among the oak boughs above the
roof, as though small creatures were pattering across the floor of
the wind.

Matt shivered and kindled a fire in the front room. She looked
about for the cat. The noise and disorder of the day had driven him
to distant hunting grounds and he had not yet ventured to return.
She drew close to the fire in her rocker and held her smudged hands
to the blaze.

She thought, "I've lit a bait o' fires today."

That was over and done with. There would be no more 'shining
among the palmettos; no more coming and going of folk; no more
Trax and his owl-faced girl. She was very tired. Her square frame
relaxed in its exhaustion. She leaned back her head and drowsed
deeply in her chair.

When she wakened, the fire had burned to ashes. The moon rode
high over the flat-woods, with clouds scurrying underneath. The
room was silver, then black, as the moonlight came and went. The
chill wind sucked through the pines. There was another sound; the
sobbing of a lighter breath. Suddenly Matt knew the girl was still
there.

She rose in a plunge from the rocker. She wasn't done with them yet . . . She opened the door a few inches and listened. The muffled sound was unmistakable. It was the choked gasping of a child that had cried itself breathless. It came from the edge of the hammock. Where the pines began she could distinguish a huddle on the ground that was neither stump nor bushes. She closed the door.

Trax was gone—and Elly was here.

He had flung away and left her behind. She was discarded, as Matt had been long discarded. He was through with Elly, too. For the first time the woman was able to conceive of them separately. And the one was gone, and the other was here. She groped her way stupefied to the kitchen, lighted a kerosene lamp, and made a fire in the range. She wanted a scalding pot of tea to stop her shivering. She split a cold biscuit and fried it and sat down with her plate and tea-cup. She breathed hard, and ate and drank mechanically.

"He was done with her a long ways back."

He had driven off alone in the blue sedan, not to infuriate, but because there was nothing else to do with the girl. Matt chewed her biscuit slowly. She laughed grimly.

"I give him too much credit for smartness."

A flash of anger stirred her, like a spurt of flame from an old fire, that Elly should be now at the edge of the hammock.

"Trax wa'n't man enough to take off his mess with him."

She sipped her cooling tea.

She remembered grudgingly the girl's contentment. The shadow of the man, passing away, left clear the picture of a child, pulling moss apart and cutting paper dolls. Rage at Trax possessed her.

"I'd orter hided him for takin' sich a young un along his low-down way."

In a burst of fury she conceded the girl's youth. Elly was too young . . .

"I'd orter been hided. Me an' Trax together."

Matt rose from the table and gathered up the few dishes. She stopped in the act. She looked at her hands as though their knotty strength were strange to her.

"Snatchin' off a young un's rations . . ."

She leaned heavily on the table. Emptiness filled the house.

She strode abruptly out the door and through the hammock to the pines. The moon had swung toward its setting and the rays lay long under the trees. The girl lay crouched against a broad mottled trunk.

Matt said, "You kin come on back."

The emaciated figure wavered from the ground on spindling legs. It tried to crowd close to the warmth of the woman's body. As they moved toward the house, the girl stumbled in the run-over slippers.

Matt said, "Here. Gimme them crazy shoes."

Elly stooped and took them from her bare feet. The woman put them in her apron pockets. She went ahead of the girl into the front room and bent down to kindle a fire.

Lee Yu-Hwa

The Last Rite
1964

Lee Yu-Hwa's "The Last Rite," first published in the Literary Review *in 1964 and reprinted in Martha Foley's* The Best American Short Stories: 1965, *is a story in which two women represent competing lifestyles, conflicting sets of risks, privileges, and values, and different visions of responsibility. The only story in this collection told from a man's point of view and emphasizing the symbolic nature of the two women, the strong role of community in what is usually perceived as a strictly interpersonal situation is clear. The multiple strands of community involvement pull at the young man, forcing him to face the implications and repercussions of his behavior. His relationships with his grandmother, mother, father, and sister, each of which is brought deftly and poignantly alive, are all contingent upon his submission to the pressure to conform.*

This story reinforces the vision of a powerful traditional community that offers protection from abandonment to the women who submit to its demands. "Papago Wedding" and "Chayah" both allude strongly to this exchange of personal choice and independence for protection and support, but in "The Last Rite" what has thus far been only alluded to becomes the central focus. The "new" woman, the woman who has cut herself off from familial duty and community tradition to seek self-actualization and participation in social and political change that would ultimately free all women from bound feet, is left without protection or sympathy. But this story ends with no real resolution; we do not know where or how or with whom the young man will choose to live. Any decision he makes will mean profound disappointment for at least one woman. Even he recognizes that he has too much power over the lives of the women he loves.

Like Helen Reimensnyder Martin, who couched her fiercely feminist critique of

*the oppression of women in quaint representations of a minority ethnic community,
and like Mary Austin, who criticized sexist society in the guise of telling stories
about a powerless aboriginal people, Lee Yu-Hwa wrote stories in which the oppression
of women in both eastern and western culture is sharply depicted—the dependency,
the humiliation, the painful abrogation of personality. But for western readers, she
embedded her vision in the context of an eastern culture. She emigrated from China
to the United States in 1946, after having earned a degree in foreign literature at
Southwest Associated Universities in Kunming. She was awarded an M.A. in
English Literature by the University of Pennsylvania. No more information is
available about this talented writer.*

Chou Nan-An reached home before sunset. In the first courtyard
he did not meet anyone. At the threshold of the second court his
heart beat faster. The place looked unusually empty without his
grandmother sitting in the low bamboo chair on the broad veranda.
A pungent sensation crept up his nose. As long as he could remember
she had been sitting there, rain or shine, ready to greet anyone who
walked into the court. In his childhood this was the heart of the
house. He was always sure that his grandmother would be there to
receive him, and inside the wide folds of her sleeves, he would find
cookies or fruits of the season.

He ran through the stone-paved courtyard and up the few steps
to the raised veranda. He was met by his mother who had just
come out of the room to the right of the center altar room.

"Is she . . ." he asked.

She nodded and held him for a moment to look at him; she had
not seen him in three years.

His grandmother's bedroom seemed full of silent women, her
kinfolk, there to sit with her, according to custom, taking turns at
night, until she either recovered or passed away in their loving care.
The women all looked up when he entered. He followed his mother
on tiptoe to the big built-in bed lit by an oil lamp on a nearby table.
His grandmother was resting with her eyes closed. Her brown face
was furrowed and her features sunken.

It seemed a long time before his grandmother stirred and asked
for tea. Someone quickly handed his mother a bowl of the pale
clear reddish broth of dried dates, believed to have the power of

fortifying a weakened life. His mother kneeled on the low bench in front of the bed to feed the broth to the old woman. The old woman drank the broth with her eyes closed. After a few spoonfuls she asked, "Has my son come home yet?"

"Not yet. Shio-An-Erh is here. He has come home to see you, grandma."

The old woman opened her eyes slowly. Chou's mother got up quickly and stepping back, pushed her son to the foreground. He knelt on the low bench and took his grandmother's hand.

"I am home, grandma."

"Shio-An-Erh, I did not think I would see you again. You took a long time to come home." She spoke slowly and with great effort, then she nodded agreeably and closed her eyes, her hand clasping his.

His grandmother fell asleep with his hand in hers. He patiently kept his kneeling pose so as not to disturb her sleep. He loved his grandmother more dearly than he did his parents. In his childhood his mother was always too busy with housework to play with him, and his father had always treated him in the traditional way, serving as his strict disciplinarian. His grandmother had for him all the leisure and the unrestrained affection privileged to grandparents. It was to his grandmother he had made his childish vows to love her always. The memories of these vows brought him back home to her bedside. Watching the old woman sleeping with a sweet smile on her face, he was glad that he had come home.

In her sleep his grandmother frowned, made a little frightened sound and grasped his hand hard as if she had had a bad dream. Chou patted her hand with his free hand. She opened her eyes with a far-away look and when she finally focused them on him, she smiled, "I knew you would come home, I told them so," she said, pleased and somewhat boastfully.

In the evening his father walked in, still in his street robe, and kneeled on the low bench to have a look at his grandmother who was now asleep. When his father got up, his eyes swept about the room for Chou. He nodded to Chou and went out.

Chou delayed as long as possible leaving his grandmother to go to his father as requested by that look. He had hoped that his grandmother would wake up in time to furnish an excuse for him to postpone seeing his father alone. But since his grandmother went on sleeping peacefully and his mother kept casting worried glances at him, he got up and left.

As he came down the steps of the raised veranda and drew close to his father's room, Chou became panicky. He had to check his impulse to run back to his grandmother's room, his sanctuary in childhood. He was seized by that old familiar fear that he was not going to be able to speak clearly. Words would get stuck in his throat as in the old days whenever his father shouted at him. And his conversation with his father had never failed to produce thunder.

Yet in the years he had been away he had come to see his father in a different light. His father was not, as he had thought, his tormentor, nor was his father so staunch a believer in the old system. He did not oppose the new ways and the new people for what they were. He had not really had a taste of the good old days under the rule of the emperor. Just under twenty when the revolution of 1911 broke out, he had never had the chance to take the Imperial Civil Service Examinations and be appointed to an office, the first proof of a man's ability in his times and the first reward for his years of diligent study. The overthrow of the emperor nipped his budding dream of a useful successful life. If the revolutionists had made Sun Yat-sen an emperor, things would have been fine, his father had often said. When Chou had been away from home, away from his father, he read a deeper meaning into this comment of his father's. His father did not really care that the emperor had been overthrown or that the revolution had taken place. All he wanted was that there should be another emperor to hold the world together which he was born to and educated for. This personal disappointment made him hostile to the new world and the new people of whom Chou was one. It was a very tragic thing that happened to his father; the revolution had reduced him from a young man with as big a future as he could make it to a man who spent his life taking care of the family land. "A housekeeper," his father often called himself. When he understood this, Chou was sorry for his father and forgave him for the unfair treatment he had suffered at his hand.

During the last two days on the boat trip home Chou often thought that with his new understanding of his father he would have known how to handle him. In a way his father was like a disturbed youth who had not yet out-grown his young manhood's disappointment. Chou even went further towards this dream of reconciliation with his father. He had imagined many dialogues to convert his father, keyed to the various philosophical views of his father's that were familiar to him. Now in the grips of his fear to meet his father alone, he hoped only to summon enough courage to lift up the door drape and step over the threshold, let alone engage in conversation.

His father was in the study, actually the bookkeeping room where he went over the domestic accounts with the servants and kept no books worth reading. He had removed his street robe, rolled the sleeves of his white silk undergarment above the elbows, and was washing his face and hands in a porcelain basin. He dried his face with a plain cotton cloth. His eyes were bloodshot and his square jaw jutted out under the two strokes of a black mustache. He studied his son attentively.

Dinner was set in the center of a long table, at one end of which were a blue cloth-bound ledger, abacus, brushes and an inkstone. His father sat at the table and rolled down his sleeves. At a slight motion of his hand, Chou hurried forward to pour tea, holding the cup respectfully in both hands and at chest-level while his father took his time fastening the top button of his under-jacket and gave his collar a few pulls to make it stand upright. When he took the cup his head bent a trifle to acknowledge the courtesy his son had shown him.

"Sit down," his father said as he picked up his chopsticks.

In the silent room the clinking of chinaware was exaggeratedly and uncomfortably loud. Chou sat straight on the edge of his chair. He wanted to lean back but could not move. His body seemed to be better disciplined than his mind; in the presence of his father, it behaved independently from his will, in compliance with his childhood training. He remained sitting respectfully on the edge of his chair.

His father did not seem to enjoy his dinner. He ate absentmindedly, absorbed in his own thoughts. Occasionally his eyes would rest on his son, but gave no indication of recognition. When he finished his dinner, Chou, again according to custom, got up and poured him fresh tea. His father's intent stare made him tremble and spill some tea in the saucer.

"What did they teach you in the last three years?" his father asked, sipping his tea.

"English, chemistry, physics . . ." Before he could finish recounting the curriculum, his father waved for him to stop. He was not impressed by the titles of these strange foreign studies.

"I mean what have you learned? What knowledge is taught in the modern school?"

"It is complicated to explain . . ." The frown on his father's face cut Chou short. He paused and thought for a second. "In the modern school knowledge is much broader. The students are taught a general understanding of the cultures of various peoples and a fundamental knowledge of science—studies made on the natural aspects of the universe. And then the student proceeds to specialize in a branch of study chosen according to his interests and ability."

"Complicated and broader! Hern!" His father sneered. "What can be more complicated than to live the life of a man? Incidentally, in case they did not tell you this at school, let me tell you that the old-fashioned Chinese education teaches one to be a man."

Chou did not retort; again he had to face up to the impossibility of discussing anything with his father.

"We were taught our duties, duties to the emperor and duties to our parents. And we live by them." His father waited and then impatiently shouted. "What do you have to say for yourself?"

"Things are changing . . ." Chou faltered.

"What is changing and who does the changing? The same things go on: spring planting, fall harvest, rent collecting, paying taxes, feeding the family and going to the post office to send you money. Nothing is changing here."

Chou withdrew to greater depths of silence.

"You have been gone three years and you come home without having learned a thing. If good money was wasted to buy you common sense, I will teach you myself. The first duty you owe to me and to the old woman who is lying there dying, waiting for you, is to get yourself married. I do not want to remind you of the agony and humiliation you have inflicted upon your fiancée and her family because you do not understand—you never had any understanding."

"I cannot . . ." Chou's voice failed him in the middle of the sentence.

"I know. You never could do a good thing." His father snorted. "But you do not have to trouble yourself. I have taken care of everything, and I have checked the calendar, too. The day after tomorrow is a fair day and I only hope your grandmother can last that long to see you married." His father dismissed him with a wave of his hand.

Next morning after breakfast his sister came to see him. She filled in the details of the wedding arrangements. The family had been waiting for him to come home after the alarming telegram about their grandmother's illness had been sent to him. They had prepared everything, since it was also the grandmother's wish for him to get married on the first propitious day after his arrival. There would be no celebration or wedding party. These would follow either when his grandmother got well or on the hundredth day after her funeral. The east wing chambers were decorated as a bridal suite. From his room he could see that the windows were done up in red paper.

"Why are you so excited?" he said.

"I shall have someone to talk to and to sew with. She is so very nice, she really is."

"What do you know about her? You hardly ever had a chance to see her." Chou was surprised, since according to tradition his fiancée should not have come in contact with any member of his family until the wedding.

"But I do know her well," his sister said. "Since last year we have been going to the same school."

"School! What for?"

"What does anyone go to school for?" Her voice came quick and angry.

He ignored her anger, since they both knew his fiancée's purpose in obtaining an education was to raise his estimation of her.

"She wants me to give you this." His sister pointed to the package which she had put on his desk when she came in.

Shooting a glance at the tissue-wrapped package he said, "I cannot marry her. Doesn't anyone understand that is why I have not come home in three years?"

"What should she do?"

"It is not my concern."

"She is your fiancée."

"You, too! Have you forgotten what we used to talk about before I went away?"

"I remember. But I have grown up and understand things better. She is your fiancée, you have responsibilities towards her."

"Responsibilities and duties! That is all I have been hearing. And false responsibilities and duties at that! Of course, I have a great sense of responsibility and duty, but only to myself, as an individual, and to a better future for mankind. My utmost responsibility and duty are to destroy your type of responsibility and duty."

"But why destroy her?"

"She must fight her own way out!"

"How?"

"First and foremost by freeing herself from this feudalistic culture, rejecting the teachings and patterns of living formed and arranged for her before she was born and then by firmly insisting on her individual rights."

"Do not make speeches! You are not on a platform," his sister said. "Just tell me how is she going to accomplish all this? She cannot set foot outside her house without her parents' permission."

"They have done a lot of harm to you. You have learned to yield and to compromise," Chou said regretfully. "I will take you with me this time when I leave. I shall introduce you to new friends who will help you to consolidate your thinking."

For reply his sister looked at her bound feet. "Their feet are not like mine."

An awkward moment lapsed as Chou was reminded of this overlooked impediment to his sister's emancipation.

"Mind is more important than physical appearance. You most not let this small hindrance prevent you from living a full life."

"Without this small hindrance your fiancée would stand more of a chance to please you."

"Your mind is poisoned. I do not wish to marry her because she is not the type of woman I would choose." His voice was raised to the pitch of impatience and temper, characteristic of student debates. "I do not care for women who consider uppermost the task of pleasing their husbands."

"But you can teach her new ways and new ideas. She is just as bright and willing to learn as I am."

"It is not a question of my willingness to help her. I would like to help her if at the same time I can preserve my independence, my freedom and my integrity."

"I used to think new ways and people with new ideas were better. But now I am grateful that my fiancée does not mind my bound feet and wants to marry me." She burst into tears and ran out of the room.

His talk with his sister was not what he had expected. He had counted on her as a mediator between him and his parents. And if that were to fail, he had taken it for granted that she would help him run away.

His father had taken, as expected, the precaution of posting a servant near him. On the pretext of being waited upon, he found that he was not left alone. While he was in his room the servant stayed in the room next to his, and when he walked about the house, he was followed.

A servant brought him a silk robe and said that his father wished him to wear it. He removed his student's cotton suit. He came out to the courtyard, went up the broad veranda and lingered a moment near his grandmother's chair, his early refuge. Thousands of times he had run here to enlist her power against unpleasant orders from his parents. He touched the worn arm of the low chair and wished that once more his grandmother would exercise that authority on his behalf.

He sat down in her chair, the big square courtyard bare before his eyes. He saw every open and shut window and door and anyone who came in or went out of the gate. He realized that this was how the feeble old woman had participated in the activities of her household and knew so much about them.

His eyes dwelt upon the suite of three rooms at the upper end of the east chambers. How many hours, he asked himself, had his grandmother spent looking the the lattice windows and hoped to see them papered red.

His mother came out to the veranda and took the low roomy cushioned chair of the grandmother which he vacated for the stool that used to be his mother's.

"Grandmother is taking a nap. You have done her good. The doctor said this morning that her pulse is stronger."

"Good! Then we do not have to rush into this thing."

"It will be tomorrow. Your grandmother and father agreed," his mother said gravely. "It is not rushing. Your fiancée's getting to be an old maid. Eighteen years old and still she stays at home and braids her hair. Besides, there is your sister. You are holding up her wedding, too. Her fiancée's family is anxious to have a daughter-in-law."

"If I had known this, I would not have come home. No one cares about what happened to me."

His mother looked at him curiously and warily.

"No one wants to listen to me. I cannot marry this girl because I am already married. Now, do you understand?"

"Married," His mother repeated dubiously and then corrected him, "you mean you have taken a woman."

"I said I am married, married to a girl who goes to the same college with me."

"Ah, a modern girl," his mother said. She looked thoughtful. He waited impatiently for the serious nature of his marriage to penetrate her mind. "Do not tell your father," she said finally, "til this is over." She jutted her chin towards the red-papered lattice windows.

He walked angrily away from his mother. He had been away too long and had forgotten the paradoxical aspects of their morality. Laxity and indulgence loopholed a rigid code of behavior. His mother's attitude represented that of his family. To divulge his marriage to them would not matter in the least so far as their preparations to celebrate his wedding were concerned. A marriage which was not arranged by the family was not a marriage. And a girl, despite her upbringing and the prestige of her family, was not respectable if she entered into marriage unauthorized and unrecognized by the families of both sides. The most his wife could hope for was to come and beg humbly for recognition as his second wife.

His talk with his mother ended all hope of understanding from his family. Were he to tell his father of his marital status, his father would ignore him and send him tomorrow anyhow, on schedule, in a green sedan to bring home his childhood betrothed.

He had not written his family earlier of his marriage because he had thought it was the only way to avoid a break in relations—his father would instantly have cabled back cutting off his allowance and threatening to disown him. But as he now realized, it was a dimly felt distrust of his family that had prevented him from announcing the marriage. The repercussions of this great offense and disobedience, he must have subconsciously felt, would be more than disinheritance. His marriage could not alter the fact, in his

parents' eyes, that he, their son, was meant to fit in their scheme
of things and should be brought around to marry the girl they had
engaged him to in his childhood. And his father was capable and
unscrupulous. He had not been able to score an easy victory over
him.

In the evening Chou had dinner with his cousins. One of them
brought along a jug of wine. The excuse for their merry-making
was that their grandmother rejoiced in it, too. After dinner, they
all crowded into the grandmother's room. The old woman looked
over the Chou descendants and signaled Chou to come forward. He
knelt on the low bench, but his grandmother gestured for him to
sit on the edge of her bed.

"They say I have spoiled you, but I know you will make up for
everything. I will hang on—" she pointed in mid-air as if her life
were being dispersed there, "till tomorrow".

"Do not talk like that! You will live for many, many years yet."
Tears rushed down Chou's cheeks.

"Not many years but . . ." The old woman paused to gather
strength and smiled sweetly at her last wish. "The last banquet and
all the friends and relative to celebrate it."

Chou nodded; he had lost his voice.

He was sent to sleep in his own room and did not stay up to care
for the sick woman. The lingering effects of the dinner wine made
him sleep soundly.

In the morning when he woke up he noticed the package on the
desk. He picked it up and opened it. It was an embroided writing
brush-holder, a pet souvenir women gave to men. Inside the brush-
holder he found a letter from his fiancée. She acknowledged her
awareness of his reluctance to marry her, begged for tolerance and
thanked him for being merciful to allow her to assume his name.
"I know only," she wrote, "of the traditional way of living. I shall
be obedient to you as I am obedient to my parents. And I shall not
question the propriety of anything you do since I cannot question
what I do not understand."

He put the letter aside and concluded that she was a cunning
woman. She pleaded for his sympathy and affection and at the same
time hinted that he was free; she would not hold him to the
conventional responsibilities of a husband.

There was much activity in the suite with the red-papered lattice windows. The door was open and the windows propped up. The servants kept going in and out.

After his visit to his grandmother he was sent to bathe and dress in formal gowns. At the propitious hour he was carried in a green sedan to his bride's house and came home followed by her red sedan. They held a simple ceremony without music. Afterwards, when they went to the grandmother's room, the sick old woman was propped up on pillows to receive them. Chou's parents stood by the bed and behind them stood the uncles, aunts and cousins. The crowded room was hushed; only the sound of the dangling pearls of the bride's headdress and the rustling of her stiff brocade were heard when they kowtowed to the grandmother.

During dinner he drank rounds of drinks with his cousins. Tottering, he was helped into the bridal chamber. He sat down in a red-lacquered armchair by a long red-lacquered table on which two thick red columnar candles were burning. The candles were to last out the night. So was the oil lamp under the bed. They were symbols of their long life together. Placed around the oil lamp were five kinds of nuts, symbolic of their prosperity. A red silk quilt was spread on the bed. His bride, still in her wedding gown, sat on the edge of the bed, her head bowed a little. A servant brought in strong tea, good for sobering up, and fastened the door on the outside. Chou drank two cups of tea.

"Go to sleep," he said to the girl who sat so still amidst the blazing red of the room. This was the only thing they could not force him to do, he said to himself. Yung-Chu, his wife by choice, might understand, he persuaded himself, if he held out at the last step and proved that he gave in to his family only on superficial grounds. He fulfilled his obligation to them as their son to take this woman into their house and be their daughter-in-law. She was as much his wife as he was their son, by circumstances and not by affection or choice.

Besides there was no other way for him to leave home and to go back to the city except through this compromise. But compromise was one word that Yung-Chu was afraid of. One compromise led to another, she had often warned him. She, too, was a student from a distant county who had come to the city to study. Like many young people around her, she lived as though she had no family and no awareness of the society around her. She cared for her approval of herself and for the approval of those who shared similar rebellious thoughts with her. When he first knew her, he was awed and, in turn, admired her for her advanced views and her resolution and courage to act upon them. When she found herself responding to his love, she came to live with him. There was no fuss and no bother about the significance of their union in relation to society. She did not tell him whether she had written her family about her marriage nor did she inquire about what he had done concerning his. The Chinese family, to her, was the remnant of a bankrupt society and the last restraint to young Chinese attempting to find a new life for themselves. When he showed her the telegram about his grandmother's illness, she merely looked at him, offended, and said in a challenging tone, "You must deal with it yourself. It is your own affair."

Chou understood and approved his wife's attitude but at the same time he could not pretend that he was not hurt by it nor could he pretend that it was easy to live with a woman who constantly imposed upon themselves such unprecedented views. With her he had had some of the grandest moments of his life. Their visions of life conveyed him to a state in which he believed that life as it ought to be was within their reach, and they and their friends, undamaged and unspoiled by society, were the ones to live this good life, although in reality his life with Yung-Chu was very painful. When they were not talking about ideas, they seemed to be lost. They did not know how to do the least little thing without getting into a serious argument with each other. She refused to be addressed as Mrs. Chou, using only her own name, Lu Yung-Chu, if she had to assume a family name, and as a result involved themselves in needless and endless explanations to the conventional. She did the cooking and cleaning one week and he did it the next. This judicious distribution of housework afforded a good source of friction and Yung-Chu fought vigorous and valiant battles against the opposite sex in her own home. But all in all, she was the woman he loved and valued and he had admitted that his conventional male prerogatives were much at fault for the difficulties in his life with a woman like Yung-Chu. There was no doubt in his mind that she was the woman he wanted to go back to and the life with her was what he had chosen through his own free will.

Turning his chair away from the woman dressed in red who sat on the bed spread with red silk, he cushioned his head with his folded arms on the table and calculated the earliest possible date when he could leave. His grandmother was expected to die within a few days—the family had prepared for his wedding in the first and second main courts while in the third court preparations for the funeral went on steadily. In that case he had no choice but to wait till she died. But if the doctor gave a contrary prediction then he would leave as soon as he could persuade his parents of his urgent desire to go back to school. He expected them to be lenient since he had compromised in marrying this woman, even though his father had hinted that he needed someone to help him manage the family estate and that his son had had enough education. Chou took this as another outburst of his father's hostility towards the new world; without the emperor there was no career worthwhile for a man to work at.

The sooner he could get back to the city, the better chance Chou had to explain to Yung-Chu what had happened. It would not be an easy task. He did not see how he could manage to convey to her his intricate relationship with his family, no more than he could explain to his family how he and Yung-Chu had been thinking and living. In some ways Yung-Chu was just as dogmatic as his father. She would judge him harshly and call his sympathy and love for his family cowardice. If she should condemn him as a coward and a renegade to their ideas, she would leave him. She and the friends they both had were, so he often felt even when he was with them, like the mules in a mill; they wore blinders in order to pursue without distraction their singleminded purpose of finding a new pattern of living for China. They would have wanted him to ignore, to destroy and to deny his feelings for everybody in this house where an old woman lay dying and a young girl waited to be made into a woman. But he did have feelings for them all, even for this girl whom he had just turned his back on. He was responsible for her, as his sister had said. If he did not go to take her home in the red sedan today he would have abandoned her to the sad life of an old maid. She would never be able to marry again and would be disgraced all her life through no fault of her own.

He turned around and saw that his bride had not moved. She sat in exactly the same pose, almost a part of the red decorations of the room, as though she were going to sit there guarding the edge of the bed throughout the night.

The red candles flickered and he had an impulse to blow them out. But this would have given alarm if someone were watching his windows.

"Go to sleep," he said.

The girl in red did not move.

Fine obedience! Chou was getting angry at her. It was not only his name she wanted, she was waiting for him to lift her headdress, to exercise his right as her husband.

"I said go to sleep!"

She trembled but made no move. The pearl curtain of her jeweled headdress was shaking. He went to her and parted the strings of pearls hanging down from her headdress. She was weeping quietly. Her eyes were downcast and tears were streaming down her powdered and rouged cheeks. She looked exceedingly beautiful in the candle light.

He let fall the strings of pearls and walked away from her. He knew that she was worrying about the next morning's questioning by her mother-in-law of the evidence of premarital chastity. He went back to her and took off her jeweled headdress. She had not raised her eyes but her tears had stopped, her lips were parted slightly and the rouge on her cheeks had deepened in color. His hand touched her black silky hair, which, for the first time in her life, was combed back and knotted into a chignon, and he felt for the essential gold pin that held the chignon in place. When he pulled the gold pin her hair fell loose and hung down her back, scattering the rest of the ornamental jeweled pins on the embroidered red silk quilt.

Louise Meriwether

A Happening in Barbados
1968

Like Alice Dunbar Nelson (1875–1935) and Ann Petry (b. 1911), Louise Meriwether turned to writing children's literature about historically important black Americans after she had given evidence of major talent as a writer of adult fiction. Her 1970 novel, Daddy Was a Number Runner, *tells the story of a young girl growing up in the later 1930s. Living in Harlem, she experiences and witnesses poverty, fear, and various forms of abuse, from that practiced by the white-run welfare system on the spirit of black women to that practiced on women by men whose sexuality has become a tool for punishment.*

Her next three books were The Freedom Ship of Robert Smalls *(1971),* The Heart Man: The Story of Daniel Hale Williams *(1972), and* Don't Ride the Bus on Monday: The Rosa Parks Story *(1973), all juveniles. This literary versatility is reminiscent of that of such nineteenth-century writing women as Elizabeth Stuart Phelps, Mary E. Wilkins Freeman, and Sarah Orne Jewett, all of whom wrote for children as well as adults. But, to editor Mary Helen Washington, in* Black Eyed Susans: Classic Stories by and about Black Women *(1975), Meriwether explained:*

> After publication of my first novel . . . I turned my attention
> to black history for the kindergarten set, recognizing that the
> deliberate omission of Blacks from American history has
> been damaging to the children of both races. It reinforces in
> one a feeling of inferiority and in the other a myth of
> superiority.

Paule Marshall, who reviewed Daddy Was a Number Runner *for the New*

York Times, *commented on Meriwether's vision of the individual as part of a community, simultaneously its victim and its hope. She wrote,*

> The truly talented black writer gives the larger dimension to
> our experience. . . . Meriwether . . . reaches deeply into the
> lives of her characters to say something about the way black
> people relate to each other—the customs, traditions and
> manners that bind us together and sustain our underground
> life. It is her expression of this tribal or communal quality of
> black life, its group solidarity and sharing, that lends such
> strength and humanity to the novel.

This sensitivity to the connections within communities is equally clear in "A Happening in Barbados," first published in the Antioch Review *in 1968. Like Paule Marshall in "Reena" and Ann Petry in* Miss Muriel and Other Stories, *Meriwether writes about the professionally educated, competent, middle-class heterosexual black woman who is living her life without a man. Goal-oriented, she has worked hard and without much pleasure in order to pull herself out of the poverty and danger of Harlem's slums. But the time for that delayed gratification has arrived, and is passing quickly, with few rewards. She is part of a sharing, caring network of other women with strong connections to their pasts, both personal and communal as black Americans.*

The histories that impinge on the characters in this story are not those of the people involved. The various histories are of relationships among white women, black women, and black men. The three characters in the triangle have only brief connections with each other. There is no real potential for permanence in their relationships. Since they are separated even further by class, age, and national culture, the abstract dynamics are not obscured by individual personalities or histories or possibilities. The sexual and racial dynamics are clear.

Meriwether is one of the first writers to examine the black woman/white woman relationship, portraying a black woman moving from a response based on historical racial issues to one based on shared womanhood: "Suddenly Glenda was just another woman, vulnerable and lonely, like me. . . . I had forgotten my own misery long enough to inflict it on another woman."

Louise Meriwether was born in Haverstraw, New York, and reared in Harlem, the only daughter among five children. She earned a B.A. at New York University, worked as a legal secretary, a reporter for the Los Angeles Sentinal, *a black weekly, returned to school for an M.S. at the University of California at Los Angeles, worked as a story analyst at Universal Studios, became an active member of CORE (Congress on Racial Equality) in Los Angeles, a staff memer of the Watts (California) Writers' Workshop, and then moved back to New York in 1970. Currently she teaches writing at Sarah Lawrence College in Bronxville, New York, and is at work on a Civil War novel.*

The best way to pick up a Barbadian man, I hoped, was to walk alone down the beach with my tall, brown frame squeezed into a skintight bathing suit. Since my hotel was near the beach, and Dorothy and Alison, my two traveling companions, had gone shopping, I managed this quite well. I had not taken more than a few steps on the glittering, white sand before two black men were on either side of me vying for attention.

I chose the tall, slim-hipped one over the squat, muscle-bound man who was also grinning at me. But apparently they were friends, because Edwin had no sooner settled me under his umbrella than the squat one showed up with a beach chair and two other boys in tow.

Edwin made the introductions. His temporary rival was Gregory, and the other two were Alphonse and Dimitri.

Gregory was ugly. He had thick, rubbery lips, a scarcity of teeth, and a broad nose splattered like a pyramid across his face. He was all massive shoulders and bulging biceps. No doubt he had a certain animal magnetism, but personally I preferred a lean man like Edwin, who was well built but slender, his whole body fitting together like a symphony. Alphonse and Dimitri were clean-cut and pleasant looking.

They were all too young—twenty to twenty-five at the most— and Gregory seemed the oldest. I inwardly mourned their youth and settled down to make the most of my catch.

The crystal-blue sky rivaled the royal blue of the Caribbean for beauty, and our black bodies on the white sand added to the munificence of colors. We ran into the sea like squealing children when the sudden raindrops came, then shivered on the sand under a makeshift tent of umbrellas and damp towels waiting for the sun to reappear while nourishing ourselves with straight Barbados rum.

As with most of the West Indians I had already met on my whirlwind tour of Trinidad and Jamaica, who welcomed American Negroes with open arms, my new friends loved their island home, but work was scarce and they yearned to go to America. They were hungry for news of how Negroes were faring in the States.

Edwin's arm rested casually on my knee in a proprietary manner, and I smiled at him. His thin, serious face was smooth, too young for a razor, and when he smiled back, he looked even younger. He told me he was a waiter at the Hilton, saving his money to make it to the States. I had already learned not to be snobbish with the island's help. Yesterday's waiter may be tomorrow's prime minister.

Dimitri, very black with an infectious grin, was also a waiter, and lanky Alphonse was a tile setter.

Gregory's occupation was apparently women, for that's all he talked about. He was able to launch this subject when a bony white woman—more peeling red than white, really looking like a gaunt cadaver in a loose-fitting bathing suit—came out of the sea and walked up to us. She smiled archly at Gregory.

"Are you going to take me to the Pigeon Club tonight, sugar?"

"No, mon," he said pleasantly, with a toothless grin. "I'm taking a younger pigeon."

The woman turned a deeper red, if that was possible, and, mumbling something incoherent, walked away.

"That one is always after me to take her some place," Gregory said. "She's rich, and she pays the bills but, mon, I don't want an old hag nobody else wants. I like to take my women away from white men and watch them squirm."

"Come down, mon," Dimitri said, grinning. "She look like she's starving for what you got to spare."

We all laughed. The boys exchanged stories about their experiences with predatory white women who came to the islands looking for some black action. But, one and all, they declared they liked dark-skinned meat the best, and I felt like a black queen of the Nile when Gregory winked at me and said, "The blacker the berry, mon, the sweeter the juice."

They had all been pursued and had chased some white tail, too, no doubt, but while the others took it all in good humor, it soon became apparent that Gregory's exploits were exercises in vengeance.

Gregory was saying: "I told that bastard, 'You in my country now, mon, and I'll kick your ass all the way back to Texas. The girl agreed to dance with me, and she don't need your permission.' That white man's face turned purple, but he sat back down, and I dance with his girl. Mon, they hate to see me rubbing bellies with their women because they know once she rub bellies with me she wanna rub something else, too." He laughed, and we all joined in. Serves the white men right, I thought. Let's see how they liked licking *that* end of the stick for a change.

"Mon, you gonna get killed yet," Edwin said, moving closer to me on the towel we shared. "You're crazy. You don't care whose woman you mess with. But it's not gonna be a white man who kill you but some bad Bajan."

Gregory led in the laughter, then held us spellbound for the next hour with intimate details of his affair with Glenda, a young white girl spending the summer with her father on their yacht. Whatever he had, Glenda wanted desperately, or so Gregory told it.

Yeah, I thought to myself, like LSD, a black lover is the thing this year. I had seen a white girls in the Village and at off-Broadway theaters clutching their black man tightly while I, manless, looked on with bitterness. I then vowed I would find me an ofay in self-defense, but I could never bring myself to condone the wholesale rape of my slave ancestors by letting a white man touch me.

We finished the rum, and the three boys stood up to leave, making arrangements to get together later with us and my two girl friends and go clubbing.

Edwin and I were left alone. He stretched out his muscled leg and touched my toes with his. I smiled at him and let our thighs come together. Why did he have to be so damned young? Then our lips met, his warm and demanding, and I thought, what the hell, maybe I will. I was thirty-nine—good-bye, sweet bird of youth—an angry divorcee, uptight and drinking too much, trying to disown the years which had brought only loneliness and pain. I had clawed my way up from the slums of Harlem via night school and was now a law clerk on Wall Street. But the fight upward had taken its toll. My husband, who couldn't claw as well as I, got lost somewhere in that concrete jungle. The last I saw of him, he was peering under every skirt around, searching for his lost manhood.

I had always felt contempt for women who found their kicks by robbing the cradle. Now here I was on a Barbados beach with an amorous child young enough to be my son. Two sayings flitted unbidden across my mind. "Judge not, that ye be not judged" and "The thing which I feared is come upon me." I thought, ain't it the god-damned truth?

Edwin kissed me again, pressing the length of his body against mine.

"I've got to go," I gasped. "My friends have probably returned and are looking for me. About ten tonight?"

He nodded; I smiled at him and ran all the way to my hotel.

At exactly ten o'clock, the telephone in our room announced we had company downstairs.

"Hot damn," Alison said, putting on her eyebrows in front of the mirror. "We're not going to be stood up."

"Island men," I said loftily, "are dependable, not like the bums you're used to in America."

Alison, freckled and willowy, had been married three times and was looking for her fourth. Her motto was, if at first you don't succeed, find another mother. She was a real estate broker in Los Angeles, and we had been childhood friends in Harlem.

"What I can't stand," Dorothy said from the bathroom, "are those creeps who come to your apartment, drink up your liquor, then dirty up your sheets. You don't even get a dinner out of the deal."

She came out of the bathroom in her slip. Petite and delicate with a pixie grin, at thirty-five Dorothy looked more like one of the high school girls she taught then their teacher. She had never been married. Years before, while she was holding onto her virginity with a miser's grip, her fiancé messed up and knocked up one of her friends.

Since then, all of Dorothy's affairs had been with married men, displaying perhaps a subconscious vendetta against all wives.

By ten-twenty we were downstairs and I was introducing the girls to our four escorts, who eyed us with unconcealed admiration. We were looking good in our Saks Fifth Avenue finery. They were looking good, too, in soft shirts and loose slacks, all except Gregory, whose bulging muscles confined in clothing made him seem more gargantuan.

We took a cab and a few minutes later were squeezing behind a table in a small, smoky room called the Pigeon Club. A Trinidad steel band was blasting out the walls, and a tiny dance area was jammed with wiggling bottoms and shuffling feet. The white tourists trying to do the hip-shaking calypso were having a ball and looking awkward.

I got up to dance with Edwin. He had a natural grace and was easy to follow. Our bodies found the rhythm and became one with it while our eyes locked in silent ancient combat, his pleading, mine teasing.

We returned to our seats and to tall glasses of rum and cola tonic. The party had begun.

I danced every dance with Edwin, his clasp becoming gradually tighter until my face was smothered in his shoulder, my arms locked around his neck. He was adorable. Very good for my ego. The other boys took turns dancing with my friends, but soon preferences were set—Alison with Alphonse and Dorothy with Dimitri. With good humor, Gregory ordered another round and didn't seem to mind being odd man out, but he wasn't alone for long.

During the floor show, featuring the inevitable limbo dancers, a pretty white girl, about twenty-two, with straight, red hair hanging down to her shoulders, appeared at Gregory's elbow. From his wink at me and self-satisfied grin, I knew this was Glenda from the yacht.

"Hello," she said to Gregory. "Can I join you, or do you have a date?"

Well, I thought, that's the direct approach.

"What are you doing here?" Gregory asked.

"Looking for you."

Gregory slid over on the bench, next to the wall, and Glenda sat down as he introduced her to the rest of us. Somehow, her presence spoiled my mood. We had been happy being black, and I resented this intrusion from the white world. But Glenda was happy. She had found the man she'd set out to find and a swing party to boot. She beamed a dazzling smile around the table.

Alphonse led Alison onto the dance floor, and Edwin and I followed. The steel band was playing a wild calypso, and I could feel my hair rising with the heat as I joined in the wildness.

When we returned to the table, Glenda applauded us, then turned to Gregory. "Why don't you teach me to dance like that?"

He answered with his toothless grin and a leer, implying he had better things to teach her.

White women were always snatching our men, I thought, and now they want to dance like us.

I turned my attention back to Edwin and met his full stare.

I teased him with a smile, refusing to commit myself. He had a lusty, healthy appetite, which was natural, I supposed, for a twenty-one-year-old lad. Lord, but why did he have to be that young? I stood up to go to the ladies' room.

"Wait for me," Glenda cried, trailing behind me.

The single toilet stall was occupied, and Glenda leaned against the wall waiting for it while I flipped open my compact and powdered my grimy face.

"You married?" she asked.

"Divorced."

"When I get married, I want to stay hooked forever."

"That's the way I planned it, too," I said dryly.

"What I mean," she rushed on, "is that I've gotta find a cat who wants to groove only with me."

Oh Lord, I thought, don't try to sound like us, too. Use your own, sterile language.

"I really dug this guy I was engaged to," Glenda continued, "but he couldn't function without a harem. I could have stood that, maybe, but when he didn't mind if I made it with some other guy, too, I knew I didn't want that kind of life."

I looked at her in the mirror as I applied my lipstick. She had been hurt, and badly. She shook right down to her naked soul. So she was dropping down a social notch, according to her scale of values, and trying to repair her damaged ego with a black brother.

"You gonna make it with Edwin?" she asked, as if we were college chums comparing date.

"I'm not a one-night stand." My tone was frigid. That's another thing I can't stand about white people. Too familiar because we're colored.

"I dig Gregory," she said, pushing her hair out of her eyes. "He's kind of rough, but who wouldn't be, the kind of life he's led."

"And what kind of life is that?" I asked.

"Didn't you know? His mother was a whore in an exclusive brothel for white men only. That was before when the British owned the island."

"I take it you like rough men?" I asked.

"There's usually something gentle and lost underneath," she replied.

A white woman came out of the toilet and Glenda went in. Jesus, I thought, Gregory gentle? The woman walked to the basin, flung some water in the general direction of her hands, and left.

"Poor Daddy is having a fit," Glenda volunteered from the john, "but there's not much he can do about it. He's afraid I'll leave him again, and he gets lonely without me, so he just tags along and tries to keep me out of trouble."

"And he pays the bills?"

She answered with a laugh. "Why not? He's loaded."

Why not, I thought with bitterness. You white women have always managed to have your cake and eat it, too. The toilet flushed with a roar like Niagara Falls. I opened the door and went back to our table. Let Glenda find her way back alone.

Edwin pulled my chair out and brushed his lips across the nape of my neck as I sat down. He still had not danced with anyone else, and his apparent desire was flattering. For a moment, I considered it. That's what I really needed, wasn't it? To walk down the moonlit beach wrapped in his arms, making it to some pad to be made? It would be a delightful story to tell at bridge sessions. But I shook my head at him, and this time my smile was more sad than teasing.

Glenda came back and crawled over Gregory's legs to the seat beside him. The bastard. He made no pretense of being a gentleman. Suddenly, I didn't know which of them I disliked the most. Gregory winked at me. I don't know where he got the impression I was his conspirator, but I got up to dance with him.

"That Glenda," he grinned, "she's the one I was on the boat with last night. I banged her plenty, in the room right next to her father. We could hear him coughing to let us know he was awake, but he didn't come in."

He laughed like a naughty schoolboy, and I joined in. He was a nerveless bastard all right, and it served Glenda right that we were laughing at her. Who asked her to crash our party, anyway? That's when I got the idea to take Gregory away from her.

"You gonna bang her again tonight?" I asked, a new, teasing quality in my voice. "Or are you gonna find something better to do?" To help him get the message I rubbed bellies with him.

He couldn't believe this sudden turn of events. I could almost see him thinking. With one stroke he could slap Glenda down a peg and repay Edwin for beating his time with me on the beach that morning.

"You wanna come with me?" he asked, making sure of his quarry.

"What you got to offer?" I peered at him throught half-closed lids.

"Big Bamboo," he sang, the title of a popular calypso. We both laughed.

I felt a heady excitement of impending danger as Gregory pulled me back to the table. The men paid the bill, and suddenly we were standing outside the club in the bright moonlight. Gregory deliberately uncurled Glenda's arm from his and took a step toward me. Looking at Edwin and nodding in my direction, he said, "She's coming with me. Any objections?"

Edwin inhaled a mouthful of smoke. His face was inscrutable. "You want to go with him?" he asked me quietly.

I avoided his eyes and nodded. "Yes."

He flipped the cigarette with contempt at my feet and lit another one. "Help yourself to the garbage," he said, and leaned back against the building, one leg braced behind him. The others suddenly stilled their chatter, sensing trouble.

I was holding Gregory's arm now, and I felt his muscle tense. "No," I said as he moved toward Edwin. "You've got what you want. Forget it."

Glenda was ungracious in defeat. "What about me?" she screamed. She stared from one black face to another, her glance lingering on Edwin. But he wasn't about to come to her aid and take Gregory's leavings.

"You can go home in a cab," Gregory said, pushing her ahead of him and pulling me behind him to a taxi waiting at the curb.

Glenda broke from his grasp. "You bastard. Who in the hell do you think you are, King Solomon? You can't dump me like this." She raised her hands as if to strike Gregory on the chest, but he caught them before they landed.

"Careful, white girl," he said. His voice was low but ominous. She froze.

"But why," she whimpered, all hurt child now. "You liked me last night. I know you did. Why are you treating me like this?"

"I didn't bring you here"—his voice was pleasant again—"so don't be trailing me all over town. When I want you, I'll come to that damn boat and get you. Now get in that cab before I throw you in. I'll see you tomorrow night. Maybe."

"You go to hell." She eluded him and turned on me, asking with incredible innocence, "What did I ever do to you?" Then she was running past toward the beach, her sobs drifting back to haunt me like a forlorn melody.

What did she ever done to me? And what had I just done? In

order to degrade her for the crime of being white, I had sunk to the gutter. Suddenly Glenda was just another woman, vulnerable and lonely, like me.

We were sick, sick, sick. All fucked up. I had thought only Gregory was hung up in his love-hate black-white syndrome, decades of suppressed hatred having sickened his soul. But I was tainted, too. I had forgotten my own misery long enough to inflict it on another woman who was only trying to ease her loneliness by making it with a soul brother. Was I jealous because she was able to function as a woman when I couldn't, because she realized that a man is a man, color be damned, while I was crucified on my own, anti-white-man cross?

What if she were going black trying to repent for some ancient Nordic sin? How else could she atone except with the gift of herself? And if some black brother wanted to help a chick off her lily-white pedestal, he was entitled to that freedom, and it was none of my damned business anyway.

"Let's go, baby," Gregory said, tucking my arm under his.

The black bastard. I didn't even like the ugly ape. I backed away from him. "Leave me alone," I screamed. "Goddamit, just leave me alone!"

For a moment, we were all frozen into an absurd fresco —Alison, Dorothy, and the two boys looking at me in shocked disbelief, Edwin hiding behind a nonchalant smokescreen, Gregory off balance and confused, reaching out toward me.

I moved first, toward Edwin, but I had slammed the door behind me. He laughed, a mirthless sound in the stillness. He knew. I had forsaken him, but at least not for Gregory.

Then I was running down the beach looking for Glenda, hot tears of shame burning my face. How could I have been such a bitch? But the white beach, shimmering in the moonlight, was empty. And once again, I was alone.

James Tiptree, Jr.

The Girl
Who Was Plugged In
1973

The Science Fiction Writers of America annually vote to determine who among them shall be honored by their colleagues with the Nebula Award for the best work in a variety of genres. James Tiptree, Jr. (b. 1915) was awarded the Nebula for best short story in 1973, for "Love is the Plan, the Plan is Death"; for best novella, 1976; for "Houston, Houston, Do You Read?"; and for the best novelette in 1977, "The Screwfly Solution," written under the pseudonym Racoona Sheldon.

Science fiction fans, who also vote on annual literary prizes, awarded the 1974 Hugo for the best novella to "The Girl Who Was Plugged In." It was originally published in New Dimensions III, *edited by Robert Silverberg, 1973, and is reprinted in Tiptree's collection* Warm Worlds and Otherwise, *1975.*

In addition to Warm Worlds, *Tiptree has published three more volumes of short stories:* Ten Thousand Light-Years from Home *(1973),* Star-Songs of an Old Primate *(1978), and* Out of the Everywhere and Other Extraordinary Visions *(1981), and one novel,* Up the Walls of the World *(1978).*

Tiptree's biography includes an exotic childhood (as the only one of ten siblings to survive beyond birth) spent largely in Africa and India on exploratory expeditions with extraordinarily talented, accomplished, and achievement-oriented parents; an early career as a graphic artist and painter; a stint in the U.S. Air Force during World War II as a photo-intelligence officer; involvement in the creation of the Central Intelligence Agency; a midlife career change leading to the successful pursuit of a Ph.D. in experimental psychology; and a brief teaching career. Tiptree has written that the early exposure to "dozens of cultures and sub-cultures whose values,

*taboos, imperatives, religions, languages, and mores conflicted with each other"
resulted in "profound alienation from any nominal peers, and an enduring cultural
relativism."*

*Among Tiptree's exotic experiences as a youngster was that of being given "one of
the most expensive debutante parties ever seen, in the middle of the Depression." Like
the nineteenth-century writers, Ellis, Acton, and Currer Bell, George Eliot, and
George Sand, James Tiptree, Jr. is a woman. Tiptree, whose real name is Alice
Sheldon, explains her choice of a male nom de plume on the grounds that "it seemed
like a good camouflage. I had the feeling that a man would slip by less observed.
. . . Men have so pre-empted the area of human experience that when you write
about universal motives, you are assumed to be writing like a man." The male name
gives the writer the privilege of assuming that her perspective is normative. That
which makes the work distinctive is not gender, but other, chosen and personal,
matters.*

*One of the aspects of Tiptree's distinctiveness is the authorial assumption that the
reader is leisured, educated, and literate. She assumes that her readers are her peers.
Her stories are filled with details and innuendos reflecting wide experience and
erudition. When a woman writer is presumptuous about her audience in this way,
she is often criticized.*

*"The Girl Who Was Plugged In" might be read as a metaphor for the heterosexual
romantic tragedy. Both females and males in our culture are conditioned to want to
love and be loved by a "real" man or a "real" woman. But no one conforms to the
dimensions, often contradictory, of the sex roles: we must all learn. The heterosexual
romantic tragedy is that women and men are disappointed in love because they
neither find the "real" thing to love nor find their authentic selves loved once both
are revealed as failing to be the "real" things. From a woman's perspective, the
woman's tragedy is greater than the man's, perhaps because the world allows men
such comforting consolations as money, power, freedom, and wider opportunity.*

*Most women perceive their failure to correspond to the idea of the feminine (which
is what a "real" woman is) as evidence of personal inadequacy, as an exposure of
their failure to be "normal," and as cause for shame, embarrassment, and apology.
Women frequently go to self-crippling, self-denying, self-distorting lengths to force
themselves into the feminine mold, inevitably an expensive procedure.They are, in
effect, involved in a struggle to "cure" themselves of personhood.*

*However, the segmented being who emerges from this struggle often finds itself in
intramural competition for the fulfillment of basic human needs, for the love of
another. In "The Girl Who Was Plugged In," Philadelphia Burke represents the
authentic female—a person with no value to the patriarchy. Her unadorned self,
regardless of her internal yearnings for "the good life," is a threat to the system. A
system that operates on the consuming behavior of people conditioned to feel
dissatisfaction with their own unadorned selves and unenhanced lives does, however,
have a use for Philadelphia's self when it has been transformed into another woman,*

into an inauthentic, feminine self, an expensive, consuming creation.

Delphi's obedience, usefulness, and her delight in serving the system that has arranged for this transfiguration is no guarantee of happiness, however, for her creators do not love her. They are as utterly unconcerned with the internal life of Delphi as they have been with the needs and feelings and thoughts of her "operator," Philadelphia Burke.

The culturally imposed dissociation between the female person and the "real" woman, that is, the feminine image represented by the merchandising artifact, resembles the dissociation between female people and the images of "real" women represented in the pornographic artifacts described in Alice Walker's story, "Coming Apart." When female people who have been used in the creation of feminine artifacts— and female people who have not been so used, or who have been differently used—do not embrace each other and unite in their refusal to be reduced to functionaries, they will continue in the relationship of Other Women to each other, and the end can only be tragic, as it is in this story.

Listen, Zombie. Believe me. What I could tell you—you with your silly hands leaking sweat on your growth-stocks portfolio. One-ten lousy hacks of AT&T on twenty-percent margin and you think you're Evel Knievel. AT&T? You doubleknit dummy, how I'd love to show you something.

Look, dead daddy, I'd say. See for instance that rotten girl?

In the crowd over there, that one gaping at her gods. One rotten girl in the city of the future (That's what I said.) Watch.

She's jammed among bodies, craning and peering with her soul yearning out of her eyeballs. Love! OO-ooh, love them! Her gods are coming out of a store called Body East. Three youngbloods, larking along loverly. Dressed like simple street-people but . . . smashing. See their great eyes swivel above their nose-filters, their hands lift shyly, their inhumanly tender lips melt? The crowd moans. Love! This whole boiling megacity, this whole fun future world loves its gods.

You don't believe gods, dad? Wait. Whatever turns you on, there's a god in the future for you, custom-made. Listen to this mob. "I touched his foot! Ow-oow, I TOUCHED Him!"

Even the people in the GTX tower up there love the gods—in their own way and for their own reasons.

The funky girl on the street, she just loves. Grooving on their beautiful lives, their mysterioso problems. No one ever told her about mortals who love a god and end up as a tree or a sighing sound. In a million years it'd never occur to her that her gods might love her back.

She's squashed against the wall now as the godlings come by. They move in a clear space. A holocam bobs above but its shadow never falls on them. The store display screens are magically clear of bodies as the gods glance in and a beggar underfoot is suddenly alone. They give him a token. "Aaaaah!" goes the crowd.

Now one of them flashes some wild new kind of timer and they all trot to catch a shuttle, just like people. The shuttle stops for them—more magic. The crowd sighs, closing back. The gods are gone.

(In the room far from—but not unconnected to—the GTX tower a molecular flipflop closes too, and three account tapes spin.)

Our girl is still stuck by the wall while guards and holocam equipment pull away. The adoration's fading from her face. That's good, because now you can see she's the ugly of the world. A tall monument to pituitary dystrophy. No surgeon would touch her. When she smiles, her jaw—it's half purple—almost bites her left eye out. She's also quite young, but who could care?

The crowd is pushing her along now, treating you to glimpses of her jumbled torso, her mismatched legs. At the corner she strains to send one last fond spasm after the godlings' shuttle. Then her face reverts to its usual expression of dim pain and she lurches onto the moving walkway, stumbling into people. The walkway junctions with another. She crosses, trips and collides with the casualty rail. Finally she comes out into a little place called a park. The sportshow is working, a basketball game in 3-di is going on right overhead. But all she does is squeeze onto a bench and huddle there while a ghostly free-throw goes by her ear.

After that nothing at all happens except a few furtive hand-mouth gestures which don't even interest her bench-mates.

But you're curious about the city? So ordinary after all, in the FUTURE?

Ah, there's plenty to swing with her—and it's not all that *far* in the future, dad. But pass up the sci-fi stuff for now, like for instance the holovision technology that's put TV and radio in museums. Or the world-wide carrier field bouncing down from satellites, controlling communication and transport systems all over the globe. That was a spin-off from asteroid mining, pass it by. We're watching that girl.

"I'll give you just one goodie. Maybe you noticed on the sportshow or on the streets? No commercials. No ads.

That's right. NO ADS. An eyeballer for you.

Look around. Not a billboard, sign, slogan, jingle, sky-write, blurb, sublimflash, in this whole fun world. Brand names? Only in those ticky little peep-screens on the stores and you could hardly call that advertising. How does that finger you?

Think about it. That girl is still sitting there.

She's parked right under the base of the GTX tower as a matter of fact. Look way up and you can see the sparkles from the bubble on top, up there among the domes of godland. Inside that bubble is a boardroom. Neat bronze shield on the door: Global Transmissions Corporation—not that that means anything.

I happen to know there are six people in that room. Five of them technically male, and the sixth isn't easily thought of as a mother. They are absolutely unremarkable. Those faces were seen once at their nuptials and will show again in their obituaries and impress nobody either time. If you're looking for the secret Big Blue Meanies of the world, forget it. I know. Zen, do I know! Flesh? Power? Glory? you'd horrify them.

What they do like up there is to have things orderly, especially their communications. You could say they've dedicated their lives to that, to freeing the world from garble. Their nightmares are about hemorrhages of information; channels screwed up, plans misimplemented, garble creeping in. Their gigantic wealth only worries them, it keeps opening new vistas of disorder. Luxury? They wear what their tailors put on them, eat what their cooks serve them. See that old boy there—his name is Isham—he's sipping water and frowning as he listens to a databall. The water was prescribed by his medistaff. It tastes awful. The databall also contains a disquieting message about his son Paul.

But it's time to go back down, far below to our girl. Look!

She's toppled over sprawling on the ground.

A tepid commotion ensues among the bystanders. The consensus is she's dead, which she disproves by bubbling a little. And presently she's taken away by one of the superb ambulances of the future, which are a real improvement over ours when one happens to be around.

At the local bellevue the usual things are done by the usual team of clowns aided by a saintly moppusher. Our girl revives enough to answer the questionnaire without which you can't die, even in the future. Finally she's cast up, a pumped-out hulk on a cot in the long, dim ward.

Again nothing happens for a while except that her eyes leak a little from the understandable disappointment of finding herself still alive.

But somewhere one GTX computer has been tickling another, and toward midnight something does happen. First comes an attendant who pulls screens around her. Then a man in a business doublet comes daintily down the ward. He motions the attendant to strip off the sheet and go.

The groggy girl-brute heaves up, big hands clutching at bodyparts you'd pay not to see.

"Burke? P. Burke, is that your name?"

"Y-yes." Croak. "Are you . . . policeman?"

"No. They'll be along shortly, I expect. Public suicide's a felony."

" . . . I'm sorry."

He has a 'corder in his hand. "No family, right?"

"No."

"You're seventeen. One year city college. What did you study?"

"La—languages."

"H'm. Say something."

Unintelligible rasp.

He studies her. Seen close, he's not so elegant. Errand-boy type.

"Why did you try to kill yourself?"

She stares at him with dead-rat dignity, hauling up the gray sheet. Give him a point, he doesn't ask twice.

"Tell me, did you see Breath this afternoon?"

Dead as she nearly is, that ghastly love-look wells up. Breath is the three young gods, a loser's cult. Give the man another point, he interprets her expression.

"How would you like to meet them?"

The girl's eyes bug out grotesquely.

"I have a job for someone like you. It's hard work. If you did well you'd be meeting Breath and stars like that all the time."

Is he insane? She's deciding she really did die.

"But it means you never see anybody you know again. Never, *ever*. You will be legally dead. Even the police won't know. Do you want to try?"

It all has to be repeated while her great jaw slowly sets. *Show me the fire I walk through*. Finally P. Burke's prints are in his 'corder, the man holding up the big rancid girl-body without a sign of distaste. It makes you wonder what else he does.

And then—THE MAGIC. Sudden silent trot of litterbearers trucking P. Burke into something quite different from a bellevue stretcher, the oiled slide into the daddy of all luxury ambulances—real flowers in that holder!—and the long jarless rush to nowhere. No-where is warm and gleaming and kind with nurses. (Where did you hear that money can't buy genuine kindness?) And clean clouds folding P. Burke into bewildered sleep.

. . . Sleep which merges into feedings and washings and more sleeps, into drowsy moments of afternoon where midnight should be, and gentle businesslike voices and friendly (but very few) faces, and endless painless hyposprays and peculiar numbnesses. And later comes the steadying rhythm of days and nights, and a quickening which P. Burke doesn't identify as health, but only knows that the fungus place in her armpit is gone. And then she's up and following those few new faces with growing trust, first tottering, then walking strongly, all better now, clumping down the short hall to the tests, tests, tests, and the other things.

And here is our girl, looking—

If possible, worse than before. (You thought this was Cinderella transistorized?)

The disimprovement in her looks comes from the electrode jacks peeping out of her sparse hair, and there are other meldings of flesh and metal. On the other hand, that collar and spinal plate are really an asset; you won't miss seeing that neck.

P. Burke is ready for training in her new job.

The training takes place in her suite and is exactly what you'd call a charm course. How to walk, sit, eat, speak, blow her nose, how to stumble, to urinate, to hiccup—DELICIOUSLY. How to make each nose-blow or shrug delightfully, subtly different from any spooled before. As the man said, it's hard work.

But P. Burke proves apt. Somewhere in that horrible body is a gazelle, a houri who would have been buried forever without this crazy chance. See the ugly duckling go!

Only it isn't precisely P. Burke who's stepping, laughing, shaking out her shining hair. How could it be? P. Burke is doing all right, but she's doing it through something. The something is to all appearances a live girl. (You were warned, this is the FUTURE.)

When they first open the big cryocase and show her the new body she says just one word. Staring, gulping, "How?"

Simple, really. Watch P. Burke in her sack and scuffs stump down the hall beside Joe, the man who supervises the technical part of her training. Joe doesn't mind P. Burke's looks, he hasn't noticed them. To Joe, system matrices are beautiful.

They go into a dim room containing a huge cabinet like a one-man sauna and a console for Joe. The room has a glass wall that's all dark now. And just for your information, the whole shebang is five hundred feet underground near what used to be Carbondale, Pa.

Joe opens the sauna-cabinet like a big clamshell standing on end with a lot of funny business inside. Our girl shucks her shift and walks into it bare, totally unembarrassed. *Eager.* She settles in face-forward, butting jacks into sockets. Joe closes it carefully onto her humpback. Clunk. She can't see in there or hear or move. She hates this minute. But how she loves what comes next!

Joe's at his console and the lights on the other side of the glass wall come up. A room is on the other side, all fluff and kicky bits, a girly bedroom. In the bed is a small mound of silk with a rope of yellow hair hanging out.

The sheet stirs and gets whammed back flat.

Sitting up in the bed is the darlingest girl child you've EVER seen. She quivers—porno for angels. She sticks both her little arms straight up, flips her hair, looks around full of sleepy pazazz. Then she can't resist rubbing her hands down over her minibreasts and belly. Because, you see, it's the godawful P. Burke who is sitting there hugging her perfect girl-body looking at you out of delighted eyes.

Then the kitten hops out of bed and crashes flat on the floor.

From the sauna in the dim room comes a strangled noise. P.

Burke, trying to rub her wired-up elbow, is suddenly smothered in *two* bodies, electrodes jerking in her flesh. Joe juggles imputs, crooning into his mike. The flurry passes; it's all right.

In the lighted room the elf gets up, casts a cute glare at the glass wall and goes into a transparent cubicle. A bathroom, what else? She's a live girl, and live girls have to go to the bathroom after a night's sleep even if their brains are in a sauna cabinet in the next room. And P. Burke isn't in that cabinet, she's in the bathroom. Perfectly simple, if you have the glue for that closed training circuit that's letting her run her neural system by remote control.

Now let's get one thing clear. P. Burke does not *feel* her brain is in the sauna room, she feels she's in that sweet little body. When you wash your hands, do you feel the water is running on your brain? Of course not. You feel the water on your hand, although the "feeling" is actually a potential-pattern flickering over the electrochemical jelly between your ears. And it's delivered there via the long circuits from your hands. Just so, P. Burke's brain in the cabinet feels the water on her hands in the bathroom. The fact that the signals have jumped across space on the way in makes no difference at all. If you want the jargon, it's known as eccentric projection or sensory reference and you've done it all your life. Clear?

Time to leave the honey-pot to her toilet training—she's made a booboo with the toothbrush, because P. Burke can't get used to what she sees in the mirror—

But wait, you say. Where did that girl-body come from?

P. Burke asks that too, dragging out the words.

"They grow 'em," Joe tells her. He couldn't care less about the flesh department. "PDs. Placental decanters. Modified embryos, see? Fit the control implants in later. Without a Remote Operator it's just a vegetable. Look at the feet—no callus at all." (He knows because they told him.)

"Oh . . . oh she's incredible . . .' "

"Yeah, a neat job. Want to try walking-talking mode today? You're coming on fast."

And she is. Joe's reports and the reports from the nurse and the doctor and style man go to a bushy man upstairs who is some kind of medical cybertech but mostly a project administrator. His reports in turn go—to the GTX boardroom? Certainly not, did you think this is a *big* thing? His reports just go up. The point is, they're green, very green. P. Burke promises well.

So the bushy man—Doctor Tesla—has procedures to initiate. The little kitten's dossier in the Central Data Bank, for instance. Purely routine. And the phase-in schedule which will put her on the scene. This is simple: a small exposure in an off-network holoshow.

Next he has to line out the event which will fund and target her. That takes budget meetings, clearances, coordinations. The Burke project begins to recruit and grow. And there's the messy business of the name, which always gives Doctor Tesla an acute pain in the bush.

The name comes out weird, when it's suddenly discovered that Burke's "P." stands for "Philadelphia." Philadelphia? The astrologer grooves on it. Joe thinks it would help identification. The semantics girl references *brotherly love*, *Liberty-Bell*, *main-line*, *low terato-genesis*, blah-blah. Nicknames Philly? Pala? Pooty? Delphi? Is it good, bad? Finally "Delphi" is gingerly declared goodo. ("Burke" is replaced by something nobody remembers.)

Coming along now. We're at the official checkout down in the underground suite, which is as far as the training circuits reach. The bushy Doctor Tesla is there, braced by two budgetary types and a quiet fatherly man whom he handles like hot plasma.

Joe swings the door wide and she steps shyly in.

Their little Delphi, fifteen and flawless.

Tesla introduces her around. She's child-solemn, a beautiful baby to whom something so wonderful has happened you can feel the tingles. She doesn't smile, she . . . brims. That brimming joy is all that shows of P. Burke, the forgotten hulk in the sauna next door. But P. Burke doesn't know she's alive—it's Delphi who lives, every warm inch of her.

One of the budget types lets go a libidinous snuffle and freezes. The fatherly man, whose name is Mr. Cantle, clears his throat.

"Well, young lady, are you ready to go to work?"

"Yes, sir," gravely from the elf.

"We'll see. Has anybody told you what you're going to do for us?"

"No, sir." Joe and Tesla exhale quietly.

"Good." He eyes her, probing for the blind brain in the room next door.

"Do you know what *advertising* is?

He's talking dirty, hitting to shock. Delphi's eyes widen and her little chin goes up. Joe is in ecstacy at the complex expression P. Burke is getting through. Mr. Cantle waits.

"It's, well, it's when they used to tell people to buy things." She swallows. "It's not allowed."

"That's right." Mr. Cantle leans back, grave. "Advertising as it used to be is against the law. *A display other than the legitimate use of the product, intended to promote its sale.* In former times every manufacturer was free to tout his wares any way, place or time he could afford. All the media and most of the landscape was taken up with extravagant competing displays. The thing became uneconomic. The public rebelled. Since the so-called Huckster Act sellers have been restrained to, I quote, "displays in or on the product itself, visible during its legitimate use or in on-premise sales." Mr. Cantle leans forward. "Now tell me, Delphi, why do people buy one product rather than another?"

"Well . . ." Enchanting puzzlement from Delphi. "They, um, they see them and like them, or they hear about them from somebody?" (Touch of P. Burke there: she didn't say, from a friend.)

"Partly. Why did *you* buy your particular body-lift?"

"I never had a body-lift, sir."

Mr. Cantle frowns; what gutters do they drag for these Remotes?

"Well, what brand of water do you drink?"

"Just what was in the faucet, sir," says Delphi humbly. "I—I did try to boil it—"

"Good God." He scowls: Tesla stiffens. "Well, what did you boil it in? A cooker?"

The shining yellow head nods.

"What *brand* of cooker did you buy?"

"I didn't buy it, sir," says frightened P. Burke through Delphi's lips. "But—I know the best kind! Ananga has a Burnbabi. I saw the name when she—"

"Exactly!" Cantle's fatherly beam comes back strong; the Burnbabi account is a strong one, too. "You saw Ananga using one so you thought it must be good, eh? And it is good or a great human being like Ananga wouldn't be using it. Absolutely right. And now,

Delphi, you know what you're going to be doing for us. You're going to show some products. Doesn't sound very hard, does it?"

"Oh, no, sir . . ." Baffled child's stare; Joe gloats.

"And you must never, *never* tell anyone what you're doing." Cantle's eyes bore for the brain behind this seductive child.

"You're wondering why we ask you to do this, naturally. There's a very serious reason. All those products people use, foods and healthaids and cookers and cleaners and clothes and cars—they're all made by *people*. Somebody put in years of hard work designing and making them. A man comes up with a fine new idea for a better product. He has to get a factory and machinery, and hire workmen. Now. What happens if people have no way of hearing about his product? Word-of-mouth is far too slow and unreliable. Nobody might ever stumble onto his new product or find out how good it was, right? And then he and all the people who worked for him— they'd go bankrupt, right? So Delphi, there has to be *someway* that large numbers of people can get a look at a good new product, right? How? By letting people see you using it. You're giving that man a chance."

Delphi's little head is nodding in happy relief.

"Yes, sir, I do see now—but sir, it seems so sensible, why don't they let you—"

Cantle smiles sadly.

"It's an overreaction, my dear. History goes by swings. People overreact and pass harsh unrealistic laws which attempt to stamp out an essential social process. When this happens, the people who understand have to carry on as best they can until the pendulum swings back. He sighs. "The Huckster Laws are bad, inhuman laws, Delphi, despite their good intent. If they were strictly observed they would wreak havoc. Our economy, our society would be cruelly destroyed. We'd be back in caves!" His inner fire is showing; if the Huckster Laws were strictly enforced he'd be back punching a databank.

"It's our duty, Delphi. Our solemn social duty. We are not breaking the law. You will be using the product. But people wouldn't understand, if they knew. They would become upset just as you did. So you must be very, very careful not to mention any of this to anybody."

(And somebody will be very, very carefully monitoring Delphi's speech circuits.)

"Now we're all straight, aren't we? Little Delphi here"—He is speaking to the invisible creature next door—"Little Delphi is going to live a wonderful, exciting life. She's going to be a girl people watch. And she's going to be using fine products people will be glad to know about and helping the good people who make them. Yours will be a genuine social contribution." He keys up his pitch: the creature in there must be older.

Delphi digests this with ravishing gravity.

"But sir, how do I—?"

"Don't worry about a thing. You'll have people behind you whose job it is to select the most worthy products for you to use. Your job is just to do as they say. They'll show you what outfits to wear to parties, what suncars and viewers to buy and so on. That's all you have to do."

Parties—clothes—suncars! Delphi's pink mouth opens. In P.Burke's starved seventeen-year-old head the ethics of product sponsorship float far away.

Now tell me in your own words what your job is, Delphi."

"Yes sir. I—I'm to go to parties and buy things and use them as they tell me, to help the people who work in factories."

"And what did I say was so important?"

"Oh—I shouldn't let anybody know, about the things."

"Right." Mr. Cantle has another paragraph he uses when the subject shows, well, immaturity. But he can sense only eagerness here. Good. He doesn't really enjoy the other speech.

"It's a lucky girl who can have all the fun she wants while doing good for others, isn't it?" He beams around. There's a prompt shuffling of chairs. Clearly this one is go.

Joe leads her out, grinning. The poor fool thinks they're admiring her coordination.

It's out into the world for Delphi now, and at this point the up-channels get used. On the administrative side account schedules are opened, subprojects activated. On the technical side the reserved bandwidth is cleared. (That carrier field, remember?) A new name is waiting for Delphi, a name she'll never hear. It's a long string of binaries which have been quietly cycling in a GTX tank ever since a certain Beautiful Person didn't wake up.

The name winks out of cycle, dances from pulses into modulations of modulations, whizzes through phasing, and shoots into a giga-band beam racing up to synchronous satellite poised over Guatemala.

From there the beam pours twenty thousand miles back to earth again, forming an all-pervasive field of structured energics supplying tuned demand-points all over the Can-Am quadrant.

With that field, if you have the right credit rating you can sit at a GTX console and operate a tuned ore-extractor in Brazil. Or—if you have some simple credentials like being able to walk on water— you could shoot a spool into the network holocam shows running day and night in every home and dorm and rec. site. *Or* you could create a continentwide traffic jam. Is it any wonder GTX guards those inputs like a sacred trust?

Delphi's "name" appears as a tiny analyzable nonredundancy in the flux, and she'd be very proud if she knew about it. It would strike P. Burke as magic; P. Burke never even understood robotcars. But Delphi is in no sense a robot. Call her a waldo if you must. The fact is she's just a girl, a real-live girl with her brain in an unusual place. A simple real-time on-line system with plenty of bit-rate—even as you and you.

The point of all this hardware, which isn't very much hardware in this society, is so Delphi can walk out of that underground suite, a mobile demand-point draining an omnipresent fieldform. And she does—eighty-nine pounds of tender girl flesh and blood with a few metallic components, stepping out into the sunlight to be taken to her new life. A girl with everything going for her including a meditech escort. Walking lovely, stopping to widen her eyes at the big antennae system overhead.

The mere fact that something called P. Burke is left behind down underground has no bearing at all. P. Burke is totally unselfaware and happy as a clam in its shell. (Her bed has been moved into the waldo cabinet room now.) And P. Burke isn't in the cabinet: P. Burke is climbing out of an air-van in a fabulous Colorado beef preserve and her name is Delphi. Delphi is looking at live Charlais steers and live cottonwoods and aspens gold against the blue smog and stepping over live grass to be welcomed by the reserve super's wife.

The super's wife is looking forward to a visit from Delphi and her friends and by a happy coincidence there's a holocam outfit here doing a piece for the nature nuts.

You could write the script yourself now, while Delphi learns a few rules about structural interferences and how to handle the tiny time lag which results from the new forty-thousand-mile parenthesis in her nervous system. That's right—the people with the leased holocam rig naturally find the gold aspen shadows look a lot better on Delphi's flank than they do on a steer. And Delphi's face improves the mountains too, when you can see them. But the nature freaks aren't quite as joyful as you'd expect.

"See you in Barcelona, kitten," the head man says sourly as they pack up.

"Barcelona?" echoes Delphi with that charming little subliminal lag. She sees where his hand is and steps back.

"Cool, it's not her fault," another man says wearily. He knocks back his grizzled hair. "Maybe they'll leave in some of the gut."

Delphi watches them go off to load the spools on the GTX transport for processing. Her hand roves over the breast the man had touched. Back under Carbondale, P. Burke has discovered something about her Delphi-body.

About the difference between Delphi and her own grim carcass.

She's always known Delphi has almost no sense of taste or smell. They explained about that: Only so much bandwidth. You don't have to taste a suncar, do you? And the slight overall dimness of Delphi's sense of touch—she's familiar with that, too. Fabrics that would prickle P. Burke's own hide feel like a cool plastic film to Delphi.

But the blank spots. It took her a while to notice them. Delphi doesn't have much privacy; investments of her size don't. So she's slow about discovering there's certain definite places where her beastly P. Burke body *feels* things that Delphi's dainty flesh does not. H'mm! Channel space again, she thinks—and forgets it in the pure bliss of being Delphi.

You ask how a girl could forget a thing like that? Look. P. Burke is about as far as you can get from the concept *girl*. She's a female, yes—but for her, sex is a four-letter word spelled P-A-I-N. She isn't quite a virgin. You don't want the details; she'd been about twelve and the freak-lovers were bombed blind. When they came down they threw her out with a small hole in her anatomy and a mortal one elsewhere. She dragged off to buy her first and last shot and she can still hear the clerk's incredulous guffaws.

Do you see why Delphi grins, stretching her delicious little numb body in the sun she faintly feels? Beams, saying. "Please, I'm ready now."

Ready for what? For Barcelona like the sour man said, where his nature-thing is now making it strong in the amateur section of the Festival. A winner! Like he also said, a lot of strip-mines and dead fish have been scrubbed but who cares with Delphi's darling face so visible?

So it's time for Delphi's face and her other delectabilities to show on Barcelona's Playa Nueva. Which means switching her channel to the EurAf synchsat.

They ship her at night so the nanosecond transfer isn't even noticed by that insignificant part of Delphi that lives five hundred feet under Carbondale, so excited the nurse has to make sure she eats. The circuit switches while Delphi "sleeps," that is, while P. Burke is out of the waldo cabinet. The next time she plugs in to open Delphi's eyes it's no different—do you notice which relay boards your phone calls go through?

And now for the event that turns the sugarcube from Colorado into the PRINCESS.

Literally true, he's a prince, or rather an Infante of an old Spanish line that got shined up in the Neomonarchy. He's also eighty-one, with a passion for birds—the kind you see in zoos. Now it suddenly turns out that he isn't poor at all. Quite the reverse: his old sister laughs in their tax lawyer's face and starts restoring the family hacienda while the Infante totters out to court Delphi. And little Delphi begins to live the life of the gods.

What do gods do? Well, everything beautiful. But (remember Mr. Cantle?) the main point is Things. Ever see a god empty-handed? You can't be a god without at least a magic girdle or an eight-legged horse. But in the old days some stone tablets or winged sandals or a chariot drawn by virgins would do a god for life. No more! Gods make it on novelty now. By Delphi's time the hunt for new god-gear is turning the earth and seas inside-out and sending frantic fingers to the stars. And what gods have, mortals desire.

So Delphi starts on a Euromarket shopping spree squired by her old Infante, thereby doing her bit to stave off social collapse.

Social what? Didn't you get it, when Mr. Cantle talked about a world where advertising is banned and fifteen billion consumers are glued to their holocam shows? One capricious self-powered god can wreck you.

Take the nose-filter massacre. Years, the industry sweated years to achieve an almost invisible enzymatic filter. So one day a couple of pop-gods show up wearing nose-filters like *big purple bats*. By the end of the week the world market is screaming for purple bats. Then it switched to bird-heads and skulls, but by the time the industry retooled the crazies had dropped bird-heads and gone to injection globes. Blood!

Multiply that by a million consumer industries and you can see why it's economic to have a few controllable gods. Especially with the beautiful hunk of space R&D the Peace Department laid out for and which the taxpayers are only too glad to have taken off their hands by an outfit like GTX which everybody knows is almost a public trust.

And so you—or rather, GTX—find a creature like P. Burke and give her Delphi. And Delphi helps keep things *orderly*, she does what you tell her to. Why? That's right, Mr. Cantle never finished his speech.

But here come the tests of Delphi's button-nose twinkling in the torrent of news and entertainment. And she's noticed. The feedback shows a flock of viewers turning up the amps when this country baby gets tangled in her new colloidal body-jewels. She registers at a couple of major scenes, too, and when the Infante gives her a suncar, little Delphi trying out suncars is a tiger. There's a solid response in high-credit country. Mr. Cantle is humming his happy tune as he cancels a Benelux subnet option to guest her on a nude cook-show called Wok Venus.

And now for the superposh old-world wedding! The hacienda has Moorish baths and six-foot silver candelabras and real black horses and the Spanish Vatican blesses them. The final event is a grand gaucho ball with the old prince and his little Infanta on a bowered balcony. She's a spectacular doll of silver lace, wildly launching toy doves at her new friends whirling by below.

The Infante beams, twitches his old nose to the scent of her sweet excitement. His doctor has been very helpful. Surely now, after he has been so patient with the suncars and all the nonsense—

The child looks up at him, saying something incomprehensible about "Breath." He makes out that she's complaining about the three singers she had begged for.

"They've changed!" she marvels. "Haven't they changed? They're so dreary. I'm so happy now!"

And Delphi falls fainting against a gothic vargueno.

Her American duenna rushes up, calls help. Delphi's eyes are
open, but Delphi isn't there. The duenna pokes among Delphi's
hair, slaps her. The old prince grimaces. He has no idea what she
is beyond an excellent solution to his tax problems, but he had been
a falconer in his youth. There comes to his mind the small pinioned
birds which were flung up to stimulate the hawks. He pockets the
veined claw to which he had promised certain indulgences and
departs to design his new aviary.

And Delphi also departs with her retinue to the Infante's newly
discovered yacht. The trouble isn't serious. It's only that five
thousand miles away and five hundred feet down P. Burke has been
doing it too well.

They've always known she has terrific aptitude. Joe says he never
saw a Remote take over so fast. No disorientations, no rejections.
The psychomed talks about self-alienation. She's going into Delphi
like a salmon to the sea.

She isn't eating or sleeping, they can't keep her out of the body-
cabinet to get her blood moving, there are necroses under her grisly
sit-down. Crisis!

So Delphi gets a long "sleep" on the yacht and P. Burke gets it
pounded through her perforated head that she's endangering Delphi.
(Nurse Fleming thinks of that, thus alienating the psychomed.)

They rig a pool down there (Nurse Fleming again) and chase P.
Burke back and forth. And she loves it. So naturally when they let
her plug in again Delphi loves it too. Every noon beside the yacht's
hydrofoils darling Delphi clips along in the blue sea they've warned
her not to drink. And every night around the shoulder of the world
an ill-shaped thing in a dark burrow beats its way across a sterile
pool.

So presently the yacht stands up on its foils and carries Delphi
to the program Mr. Cantle has waiting. It's long-range; she's
scheduled for at least two decades' product life. Phase One calls for
her to connect with a flock of young ultra-riches who are romping
loose between Brioni and Djakarta where a competitor named PEV
could pick them off.

A routine luxgear op, see; no politics, no policy angles, and the
main budget items are the title and the yacht which was idle anyway.
The storyline is that Delphi goes to accept some rare birds for her
prince—who cares? The *point* is that the Haiti area is no longer

radioactive and look!—the gods are there. And so are several new Carib West Happy Isles which can afford GTX rates, in fact two of them are GTX subsids.

But you don't want to get the idea that all these newsworthy people are wired-up robbies, for pity's sake. You don't need many if they're placed right. Delphi asks Joe about that when he comes down to Baranquilla to check her over. (P. Burke's own mouth hasn't said much for a while.)

"Are there many like me?"

"Nobody's like you, buttons. Look, are you still getting Van Allen warble?"

"I mean, like Davy. Is he a Remote?"

(Davy is the lad who is helping her collect the birds. A sincere redhead who needs a little more exposure.)

"Davy? He's one of Matt's boys, some psychojob. They haven't any channel."

"What about the real ones? Djuma van O, or Ali, or Jim Ten?"

"Djuma was born with a pile of GTX basic where her brain should be, she's nothing but a pain. Jimsy does what his astrologer tells him. Look, peanut, where do you get the idea you aren't real? You're the reallest. Aren't you having joy?"

"Oh, Joe!" Flinging her little arms around him and his analyzer grids. Oh, *me gust mucho, muchissimo!'*

"Hey, hey." He pets her yellow head, folding the analyzer.

Three thousand miles north and five hundred feet down a forgotten hulk in a body-waldo glows.

And is she having joy. To waken out of the nightmare of being P. Burke and find herself a peri, a star-girl? On a yacht in paradise with no more to do than adorn herself and play with toys and attend revels and greet her friends—her, P. Burke, having friends!—and turn the right way for the holocams? Joy!

And it shows. One look at Delphi and the viewers know: DREAMS CAN COME TRUE.

Look at her riding pillion on Davy's sea-bike, carrying an apoplectic macaw in a silver hoop. Oh, Morton, let's go there this winter! Or learning the Japanese chinchona from that Kobe group, in a dress that looks like a blowtorch rising from one knee, and which should sell big in Texas. Morton, is that real fire? Happy, happy little girl!

And Davy. He's her pet and her baby and she loves to help him fix his red-gold hair. (P. Burke marveling, running Delphi's fingers through the curls.) Of course Davy is one of Matt's boys—not impotent exactly, but very *very* low drive. (Nobody knows exactly what Matt does with his bitty budget but the boys are useful and one or two have made names.) He's perfect for Delphi; in fact the psychomed lets her take him to bed, two kittens in a basket. Davy doesn't mind the fact that Delphi "sleeps" like the dead. That's when P. Burke is out of the body-waldo up at Carbondale, attending to her own depressing needs.

A funny thing about that. Most of her sleepy-time Delphi's just a gently ticking lush little vegetable waiting for P. Burke to get back on the controls. But now and again Delphi all by herself smiles a bit or stirs in her "sleep." Once she breathed a sound: "Yes."

Under Carbondale P. Burke knows nothing. She's asleep too, dreaming of Delphi, what else? But if the bushy Dr. Tesla had heard that single syllable his bush would have turned snow-white. Because Delphi is TURNED OFF. He doesn't. Davy is too dim to notice and Delphi's staff boss, Hopkins, wasn't monitoring.

And they've all got something else to think about now, because the cold-fire dress sells half a million copies, and not only in Texas. The GTX computers already know it. When they correlate a minor demand for macaws in Alaska the problem comes to human attention: Delphi is something special.

It's a problem, see, because Delphi is targeted on a limited consumer bracket. Now it turns out she has mass-pop potential— those macaws in *Fairbanks*, man!—it's like trying to shoot mice with an ABM. A whole new ball game. Dr. Tesla and the fatherly Mr. Cantle start going around in headquarters circles and buddy-lunching together when they can get away from a seventh-level weasel boy who scares them both.

In the end it's decided to ship Delphi down to the GTX holocam enclave in Chile to try a spot on one of the mainstream shows. (Never mind why an Infanta takes up acting.) The holocam complex occupies a couple of mountains where an observatory once used the clear air. Holocam total-environment shells are very expensive and electronically superstable. Inside them actors can move freely without going off-register and the whole scene or any selected part will show up in the viewer's home in complete 3-di, so real you can look up their noses and much denser than you get from mobile rigs.

You can blow a tit ten feet tall when there's no molecular skiffle around.

The enclave looks—well, take everything you know about Hollywood-Burbank and throw it away. What Delphi sees coming down is a neat giant mushroom-farm, domes of all sizes up to monsters for the big games and stuff. It's orderly. The idea that art thrives on creative flamboyance has long been torpedoed by proof that what art needs is computers. Because this showbiz has something TV and Hollywood never had —*automated inbuilt viewer feedback*. Samples, ratings, critics, polls? Forget it. With that carrier field you can get real-time response-sensor readouts from every receiver in the world, served up at your console. That started as a thingie to give the public more influence on content.

Yes.

Try it, man. You're at the console. Slice to the sex-age-educ-econ-ethno-cetera audience of your choice and start. You can't miss. Where the feedback warms up, give 'em more of that. Warm—warmer—*hot!* You've hit it—the secret itch under those hides, the dream in those hearts. You don't need to know its name. With your hand controlling all the input and your eye reading all the response you can make them a god . . . and somebody'll do the same for you.

But Delphi just sees rainbows, when she gets through the degaussing ports and the field relay and takes her first look at the insides of those shells. The next thing she sees is a team of shapers and technicians descending on her, and millisecond timers everywhere. The tropical leisure is finished. She's in gigabuck mainstream now, at the funnel maw of the unceasing hose that's pumping the sight and sound and flesh and blood and sobs and laughs and dreams of *reality* into the world's happy head. Little Delphi is going plonk into a zillion homes in prime time and nothing is left to chance. Work!

And again Delphi proves apt. Of course it's really P. Burke down under Carbondale who's doing it, but who remembers that carcass? Certainly not P. Burke, she hasn't spoken through her own mouth for months. Delphi doesn't even recall dreaming of her when she wakes up.

As for the show itself, don't bother. It's gone on so long no living soul could unscramble the plotline. Delphi's trial spot has something to do with a widow and her dead husband's brother's amnesia.

The flap comes after Delphi's spots begin to flash out along the world-hose and the feedback appears. You've guessed it, of course. Sensational! As you'd say, they IDENTIFY.

The report actually says something like InskinEmp with a string of percentages meaning that Delphi not only has it for anybody with a Y-chromosome, but also for women and everything in between. It's the sweet supernatural jackpot, the million-to-one.

Remember your Harlow? A sexpot, sure. But why did bitter hausfraus in Gary and Memphis know that the vanilla-ice-cream goddess with the white hair and crazy eyebrows was *their baby girl*? And write loving letters to Jean warning her that their husbands weren't good enough for her? Why? The GTX analysts don't know either, but they know what to do with it when it happens.

(Back in his bird sanctuary the old Infante spots it without benefit of computers and gazes thoughtfully at his bride in widow's weeds. It might, he feels, be well to accelerate the completion of his studies.)

The excitement reaches down to the burrow under Carbondale where P. Burke gets two medical exams in a week and a chronically inflamed electrode is replaced. Nurse Fleming also gets an assistant who doesn't do much nursing but is very interested in access doors and identity tabs.

And in Chile, little Delphi is promoted to a new home up among the stars' residential spreads and a private jitney to carry her to work. For Hopkins there's a new computer terminal and a full-time schedule man. What is the schedule crowded with?

Things.

And here begins the trouble. You probably saw that coming too.

"What does she think she is, a goddam *consumer rep?*" Mr. Cantle's fatherly face in Carbondale contorts.

"The girl's upset," Miss Fleming says stubbornly. "She *believes* that, what you told her about helping people and good new products."

"They are good products," Mr. Cantle snaps automatically, but his anger is under control. He hasn't got where he is by irrelevant reactions.

"She says the plastic gave her a rash and the glo-pills made her dizzy."

"Good god, she shouldn't swallow them," Doctor Tesla puts in agitatedly.

"You told her she'd use them," persists Miss Fleming.

Mr. Cantle is busy figuring how to ease this problem to the weasel-faced young man. What, was it a goose that lays golden eggs?

Whatever he says to level Seven, down in Chile the offending products vanish. And a symbol goes into Delphi's tank matrix, one that means roughly *Balance unit resistance against PR index*. This means that Delphi's complaints will be endured as long as her Pop Response stays above a certain level. (What happens when it sinks need not concern us.) And to compensate, the price of her exposure-time rises again. She's a regular on the show now and response is still climbing.

See her under the sizzling lasers, in a holocam shell set up as a walkway accident. (The show is guesting an acupuncture school shill.)

"I don't think this new body-lift is safe," Delphi's saying. "It's made a funny blue spot on me—look, Mr. Vere."

She wiggles to show where the mini-grav pak that imparts a delicious sense of weightlessness is attached.

"So don't leave it *on*, Dee. With your meat—watch that deck-spot, it's starting to synch."

"But if I don't wear it it isn't honest. They should insulate it more or something don't you see?"

The show's beloved old father, who is the casualty, gives a senile snigger.

"I'll tell them," Mr. Vere mutters. "Look now, as you step back bend like this so it just shows, see? And hold two beats."

Obediently Delphi turns, and through the dazzle her eyes connect with a pair of strange dark ones. She squints. A quite young man is lounging alone by the port, apparently waiting to use the chamber.

Delphi's used by now to young men looking at her with many peculiar expressions, but she isn't used to what she gets here. A jolt of something somber and knowing. *Secrets.*

"Eyes! Eyes, Dee!"

She moves through the routine, stealing peeks at the stranger. He stares back. He knows something.

When they let her go she comes shyly to him.

"Living wild, kitten." Cool voice, hot underneath.

"What do you mean?"

"Dumping on the product. You trying to get dead?"

"But it isn't right," she tells him. "They don't know, but I do, I've been wearing it."

His cool is jolted.

"You're out of your head."

"Oh, they'll see I'm right when they check it," she explains. "They're just so busy. When I tell them—"

He is staring down at little flower-face. His mouth opens, closes. "What are you doing in this sewer anyway? Who are you?"

Bewilderedly she says, "I'm Delphi."

"Holy Zen."

"What's wrong? Who are you, please?"

Her people are moving her out now, nodding at him.

"Sorry we ran over, Mister Uhunh," the script girl says.

He mutters something but it's lost as her convoy bustles her toward the flower-decked jitney.

(Hear the click of an invisible ignition-train being armed?)

"Who was he?" Delphi asks her hairman.

The hairman is bending up and down from his knees as he works.

"Paul. Isham. Three," he says and puts a comb in his mouth.

"Who's that? I can't see."

He mumbles around the comb, meaning "Are you jiving?" Because she has to be, in the middle of the GTX enclave.

Next day there's a darkly smoldering face under a turban-towel when Delphi and the show's paraplegic go to use the carbonated pool.

She looks.

He looks.

And the next day, too.

(Hear the automatic sequencer cutting in? The system couples, the fuels begin to travel.)

Poor old Isham senior. You have to feel sorry for a man who values order: when he begets young, genetic information is still transmitted in the old ape way. One minute it's a happy midget with a rubber duck—look around and here's this huge healthy stranger, opaquely emotional, running with God knows who.

Questions are heard where there's nothing to question, and eruptions claiming to be moral outrage. When this is called to Papa's attention— it may take time, in that boardroom—Papa does what he can, but without immortality-juice the problem is worrisome.

And young Paul Isham is a bear. He's bright and articulate and tender-souled and incessantly active and he and his friends are choking with appallment at the world their fathers made. And it hasn't taken Paul long to discover that *his* father's house has many mansions and even the GTX computers can't relate everything to everything else. He noses out a decaying project which adds up to something like, Sponsoring Marginal Creativity (the free-lance team that "discovered" Delphi was one such grantee). And from there it turns out that an agile lad named Isham can get his hands on a viable packet of GTX holocam facilities.

So here he is with his little band, way down the mushroom-farm mountain, busily spooling a show which has no relation to Delphi's. It's built on bizarre techniques and unsettling distortions pregnant with social protest. An *underground* expression to you.

All this isn't unknown to his father, of course, but so far it has done nothing more than deepen Isham senior's apprehensive frown.

Until Paul connects with Delphi.

And by the time Papa learns this, those invisible hypergolics have exploded, the energy-shells are rushing out. For Paul, you see, is the genuine article. He's serious. He dreams. He even reads—for example, *Green Mansions*—and he wept fiercely when those fiends burned Rima alive.

When he hears that some new GTX pussy is making it big he sneers and forgets it. He's busy. He never connects the name with this little girl making her idiotic, doomed protest in the holocam chamber. This strangely simple little girl.

And she comes and looks up at him and he sees Rima, lost Rima the enchanted bird girl, and his unwired human heart goes twang.

And Rima turns out to be Delphi.

Do you need a map? The angry puzzlement. The rejection of the dissonance Rima-hustling-for-GTX-My-Father. Garbage, cannot be. The loitering around the pool to confirm the swindle . . . dark eyes hitting on blue wonder, jerky words exchanged in a peculiar stillness . . . the dreadful reorganization of the image into Rima-Delphi *in my Father's tentacles*—

You don't need a map.

Nor for Delphi either, the girl who loved her gods. She's seen their divine flesh close now, heard their unamplified voices call her name. She's played their god-games, worn their garland. She's even become a goddess herself, though she doesn't believe it. She's not disenchanted, don't think that. She's still full of love. It's just that some crazy kind of *hope* hasn't—

Really you can skip all this, when the loving little girl on the yellow-brick road meets a Man. A real human male burning with angry compassion and grandly concerned with human justice, who reaches for her with real male arms and—boom! She loves him back with all her heart.

A happy trip, see?

Except.

Except that its really P. Burke five thousand miles away who loves Paul. P. Burke the monster, down in a dungeon, smelling of electrode-paste. A caricature of a woman burning, melting, obsessed with true love. Trying over twenty-double-thousand miles of hard vacuum to reach her beloved through girl-flesh numbed by an invisible film. Feeling his arms around the body he thinks is hers, fighting through shadows to give herself to him. Trying to taste and smell him through beautiful dead nostrils, to love him back with a body that goes dead in the heart of the fire.

Perhaps you get P. Burke's state of mind?

She has phases. The trying, first. And the shame. The SHAME. *I am not what thou lovest.* And the fiercer trying. And the realization that there is no, no way, none. Never. *Never* . . . A bit delayed, isn't it, her understanding that the bargain she made was forever? P. Burke should have noticed those stories about mortals who end up as grasshoppers.

You see the outcome—the funneling of all this agony into one dumb protoplasmic drive to fuse with Delphi. To leave, to close out the beast she is chained to. *To become Delphi.*

Of course it's impossible.

However her torments have an effect on Paul. Delphi-as-Rima is a potent enough love object, and liberating Delphi's mind requires hours of deeply satisfying instruction in the rottenness of it all. Add in Delphi's body worshipping his flesh, burning in the fire of P. Burke's savage heart—do you wonder Paul is involved?

That's not all.

By now they're spending every spare moment together and some that aren't so spare.

"Mister Isham, would you mind staying out of this sports sequence? The script calls for Davy here."

(Davy's still around, the exposure did him good.)

"What the difference?" Paul yawns. "It's just an ad. I'm not blocking that thing."

Shocked silence at his two-letter word. The script girl swallows bravely.

"I'm sorry, sir, our directive is to do the *social sequence* exactly as scripted. We're having to respool the segments we did last week, Mister Hopkins is very angry with me."

"Who the hell is Hopkins? Where is he?"

"Oh, please, Paul. *Please.*

Paul unwraps himself, saunters back. The holocam crew nervously check their angles. The GTX boardroom has a foible about having things *pointed* at them and theirs. Cold shivers, when the image of an Isham nearly went onto the world beam beside that Dialadinner.

Worse yet, Paul has no respect for the sacred schedules which are now a full-time job for ferret boy up at headquarters. Paul keeps forgetting to bring her back on time and poor Hopkins can't cope.

So pretty soon the boardroom data-ball has an urgent personal action-tab for Mr. Isham senior. They do it the gentle way, at first.

"I can't today, Paul."

"Why not?"

"They say I have to, it's *very* important."

He strokes the faint gold down on her narrow back. Under Carbondale, Pa. a blind mole-woman shivers.

"Important. Their importance. Making more gold. Can't you see? To them you're just a thing to get scratch with. A *huckster*. Are you going to let them screw you, Dee? Are you?"

"Oh, Paul—"

He doesn't know it but he's seeing a weirdie; Remotes aren't hooked up to flow tears.

"Just say no, Dee. No. Integrity. You have to."

"But they say, it's my job—"

"You won't believe I can take care of you, Dee, baby, baby, you're letting them rip us. You have to choose. Tell them, no."

"Paul . . . I w-will . . ."

And she does. Brave little Delphi (insane P. Burke). Saying "No, please, I promised, Paul."

They try some more, still gently.

"Paul, Mr. Hopkins told me the reason they don't want us to be together so much. It's because of who you are, your father."

She thinks his father is like Mr. Cantle, maybe.

"Oh great. Hopkins. I'll fix him. Listen, I can't think about Hopkins now. Ken came back today, he found out something."

They are lying on the high Andes meadow watching his friends dive their singing kites.

"Would you believe, on the coast the police have *electrodes in their heads?*"

She stiffens in his arms.

"Yeah, weird. I thought they only used PP on criminals and the army. Don't you see, Dee—something has to be going on. Some movement. Maybe somebody's organizing. How can we find out." He pounds the ground behind her: "We should make *contact*! If we could only find out."

"The, the news?" she asks distractedly.

"The news." He laughs. "There's nothing in the news except what they want people to know. Half the country could burn up and nobody would know it if they didn't want. Dee, can't you take what I'm explaining to you? They've got the whole world programmed! Total control of communication. They've got everybody's minds wired in to think what they show them and want what they give them and they give them what they're programmed to want— you can't break in or out of it, you can't get *hold* of it anywhere. I don't think they even have a plan except to keep things going round and round—and God knows what's happening to the people or the earth or the other planets, maybe. One great big vortex of lies and garbage pouring round and round getting bigger and bigger and nothing can ever change. If people don't wake up soon we're through!"

He pounds her stomach softly.

"You have to break out, Dee."

"I'll try, Paul, I will—"

"You're mine. They can't have you."

And he goes to see Hopkins, who is indeed cowed.

But that night up under Carbondale the fatherly Mr. Cantle goes to see P. Burke.

P. Burke? On a cot in a utility robe like a dead camel in a tent, she cannot at first comprehend that he is telling *her* to break it off with Paul. P. Burke has never seen Paul. *Delphi* sees Paul. The fact is, P. Burke can no longer clearly recall that she exists apart from Delphi.

Mr. Cantle can scarcely believe it either but he tries.

He points out the futility, the potential embarrassment for Paul. That gets a dim stare from the bulk on the bed. Then he goes into her duty to GTX, her job, isn't she grateful for the opportunity, etcetera. He's very persuasive.

The cobwebby mouth of P. Burke opens and croaks.

"No."

Nothing more seems to be forthcoming.

Mr. Cantle isn't dense, he knows an immovable obstacle when he bumps one. He also knows an irresistible force: GTX. The simple solution is to lock the waldo-cabinet until Paul gets tired of waiting for Delphi to wake up. But the cost, the schedules! And there's something odd here . . . he eyes the corporate asset hulking on the bed and his hunch-sense prickles.

You see, Remotes don't love. They don't have real sex, the circuit designed that out from the start. So it's been assumed that it's *Paul* who is diverting himself or something with a pretty little body in Chile. P. Burke can only be doing what comes natural to any ambitious gutter-meat. It hasn't occurred to anyone that they're dealing with the real hairy thing whose shadow is blasting out of every holoshow on earth.

Love?

Mr. Cantle frowns. The idea is grotesque. But his instinct for the fuzzy line is strong; he will recommend flexibility.

And so, in Chile:

"Darling, I don't have to work tonight! And Friday too—isn't that right, Mr. Hopkins?"

"Oh, great. When does she come up for parole?"

"Mr. Isham, please be reasonable. Our schedule—surely your own production people must be needing you?"

This happens to be true. Paul goes away. Hopkins stares after him wondering distastefully why an Isham wants to ball a waldo.

(How sound are those boardroom belly-fears—garble creeps, creeps in!) It never occurs to Hopkins that an Isham might not know what Delphi is.

Especially with Davy crying because Paul has kicked him out of Delphi's bed.

Delphi's bed is under a real window.

"Stars," Paul says sleepily. He rolls over, pulling Delphi on top. "Are you aware that this is one of the last places on earth where people can see the stars? Tibet, too maybe."

"Paul . . ."

"Go to sleep. I want to see you sleep."

"Paul, I . . . I sleep so *hard*, I mean, it's a joke how hard I am to wake up. Do you mind?"

"Yes."

But finally, fearfully, she must let go. So that five thousand miles north a crazy spent creature can crawl out to gulp concentrates and fall on her cot. But not for long. It's pink dawn when Delphi's eyes open to find Paul's arms around her, his voice saying rude, tender things. He's been kept awake. The nerveless little statue that was her Delphi-body nuzzled him in the night.

Insane hope rises, is fed a couple of nights later when he tells her she called his name in her sleep.

And that day Paul's arms keep her from work and Hopkins' wails go up to headquarters where the sharp-faced lad is working his sharp tailbone off packing Delphi's program. Mr. Cantle defuses that one. But next week it happens again, to a major client. And ferret-face has connections on the technical side.

Now you can see that when you have a field of complexly heterodyned energy modulations tuned to a demand-point like Delphi there are many problems of standwaves and lashback and skiffle of all sorts which are normally balanced out with ease by the technology of the future. By the same token they can be delicately unbalanced too, in ways that feed back into the waldo operator with striking results.

"Darling—what the hell! What's wrong! DELPHI!"

Helpless shrieks, writhings. Then the Rima-bird is lying wet and limp in his arms, her eyes enormous.

"I . . . I wasn't supposed to . . . " she gasps faintly, "They told me not to . . . "

"Oh my god—*Delphi*."

And his hard fingers are digging in her thick yellow hair. Electronically knowledgeable fingers. They freeze.

"You're a *doll*! You're one of those PP implants. They control you. I should have known. Oh God, I should have known."

"No, Paul," she's sobbing "No, no, no—"

"Damn them. Damn them, what they've done—you're not *you*—"

He's shaking her, crouching over her in the bed and jerking her back and forth, glaring at the pitiful beauty.

"No!" she pleads (it's not true, that dark bad dream back there). "I'm Delphi!"

"My father. Filth, pigs—damn them, damn them, damn them."

"No, No," she babbles. "They were good to me—"

P. Burke underground mouthing, "They were good to me— AAH-AAAAH!"

Another agony skewers her. Up north the sharp young man wants to make sure this so-tiny interference works. Paul can scarcely hang onto her, she's crying too. "I'll kill them."

His Delphi, a wired-up slave! Spikes in her brain, electronic shackles in his bird's heart. Remember when those savages burned Rima alive?

"I'll *kill* the man that's doing this to you."

He's still saying it afterward but she doesn't hear. She's sure he hates her now, all she wants is to die. When she finally understands that the fierceness is tenderness she thinks it's a miracle. *He knows— and he still loves!*

How can she guess that he's got it a little bit wrong?

You can't blame Paul. Give him credit that he's even heard about pleasure-pain implants and snoops, which by their nature aren't mentioned much by those who know them most intimately. That's what he thinks is being used on Delphi, something to *control* her. And to listen—he burns at the unknown ears in their bed.

Of waldo-bodies and objects like P. Burke he has heard nothing.

So it never crosses his mind as he looks down at his violated bird, sick with fury and love, that he isn't holding *all* of her. Do you need to be told the mad resolve jelling in him now?

To free Delphi.

How? Well, he is, after all, Paul Isham III. And he even has an idea where the GTX neurolab is. In Carbondale.

But first things have to be done for Delphi, and for his own stomach. So he gives her back to Hopkins and departs in a restrained and discreet way. And the Chile staff is grateful and do not understand that his teeth don't normally show so much.

And a week passes in which Delphi is a very good, docile little ghost. They let her have the load of wild-flowers Paul sends and the bland loving notes. (He's playing it coony.) And up in headquarters weasel boy feels that *his* destiny has clicked a notch onward and floats the word up that he's handy with little problems.

And no one knows what P. Burke thinks in any way whatever, except that Miss Fleming catches her flushing her food down the can and next night she faints in the pool. They haul her out and stick her with IVs. Miss Fleming frets, she's seen expressions like that before. But she wasn't around when crazies who called themselves Followers of the Fish looked through flames to life everlasting. P. Burke is seeing Heaven on the far side of death, too. Heaven is spelled P-a-u-l, but the idea's the same. *I will die and be born again in Delphi.*

Garbage, electronically speaking. No way.

Another week and Paul's madness has become a plan. (Remember, he does have friends.) He smolders, watching his love paraded by her masters. He turns out a scorching sequence for his own show. And finally, politely, he requests from Hopkins a morsel of his bird's free time, which duly arrives.

"I thought you didn't *want* me any more," she's repeating as they wing over mountain flanks in Paul's suncar. "Now you *know*—"

"Look at me!"

His hand covers her mouth and he's showing her a lettered card. DON'T TALK THEY CAN HEAR EVERYTHING WE SAY. I'M TAKING YOU AWAY NOW.

She kisses his hand. He nods urgently, flipping the card.

DON'T BE AFRAID. I CAN STOP THE PAIN IF THEY TRY TO HURT YOU.

With his free hand he shakes out a silvery scrambler-mesh on a power pack. She is dumbfounded.

THIS WILL CUT THE SIGNALS AND PROTECT YOU DARLING.

She's staring at him, her head going vaguely from side to side. No.

"Yes!" He grins triumphantly. "Yes!"

For a moment she wonders. That powered mesh will cut off the field, all right. It will also cut off Delphi. But he is *Paul*. Paul is kissing her, she can only seek him hungrily as he sweeps the suncar through a pass.

Ahead is an old jet ramp with a shiny bullet waiting to go. (Paul also has credits and a Name.) The little GTX patrol courier is built for nothing but speed. Paul and Delphi wedge in behind the pilot's extra fuel tank and there's no more talking when the torches start to scream.

They're screaming high over Quito before Hopkins starts to worry. He wastes another hour tracking the beeper on Paul's suncar. The suncar is sailing a pattern out to sea. By the time they're sure it's empty and Hopkins gets on the hot flue to headquarters the fugitives are a sourceless howl above Carib West.

Up at headquarters weasel boy gets the squeal. His first impulse is to repeat his previous play but then his brain snaps to. This one is too hot. Because, see, although in the long run they can make P. Burke do anything at all except maybe *live*, instant emergencies can be tricky. And—Paul Isham III.

"Can't you order her back?"

They're all in the GTX tower monitor station, Mr. Cantle and ferret-face and Joe and a very neat man who is Mr. Isham senior's personal eyes and ears.

"No sir," Joe says doggedly. "We can read channels, particularly speech, but we can't interpolate organized pattern. It takes the waldo op to send one-to-one—"

"What are they saying?"

"Nothing at the moment, sir." The console jockey's eyes are closed. "I believe they are, ah, embracing."

"They're not answering," a traffic monitor says. "Still heading zero zero three zero—due north, sir."

"You're certain Kennedy is alerted not to fire on them?" the neat man asks anxiously.

"Yes, sir."

"Can't you just turn her off?" The sharp-faced lad is angry. "Pull that pig out of the controls!"

"If you cut the transmission cold you'll kill the Remote," Joe explains for the third time. "Withdrawal has to be phased right, you have to fade over to the Remote's own autonomics. Heart, breathing, cerebellum would go blooey. If you pull Burke out you'll probably finish her too. It's a fantastic cybersystem, you don't want to do that."

"The investment." Mr. Cantle shudders.

Weasel boy puts his hand on the console jock's shoulder, it's the contact who arranged the No-no effect for him.

"We can at least give them a warning signal, sir." He licks his lips, gives the neat man his sweet ferret smile. "We know that does no damage."

Joe frowns, Mr. Cantle sighs. The neat man is murmuring into his wrist. He looks up. "I am authorized," he says reverently, "I am authorized to ah, direct a signal. If this is the only course. But minimal, minimal."

Sharp-face squeezes his man's shoulder.

In the silver bullet shrieking over Charleston Paul feels Delphi arch in his arms. He reaches for the mesh, hot for action. She thrashes, pushing at his hands, her eyes roll. She's afraid of that mesh despite the agony. (And she's right.) Frantically Paul fights her in the cramped space, gets it over her head. As he turns the power up she burrows free under his arm and the spasm fades.

"They're calling you again, Mister Isham!" the pilot yells.

"Don't answer. Darling, keep this over your head damn it how can I—"

An AX90 barrels over their nose, there's a flash.

"Mr. Isham! Those are Air Force jets!"

"Forget it," Paul shouts back. "They won't fire. Darling, don't be afraid."

Another AX90 rocks them.

"Would you mind pointing your pistol at my head where they can see it, sir?" the pilot howls.

Paul does so. The AX90s take up escort formation around them. The pilot goes back to figuring how he can collect from GTX too, and after Goldsboro AB the escort peels away.

"Holding the same course," Traffic is reporting to the group around the monitor. "Apparently they've taken on enough fuel to bring them to towerport here."

"In that case it's just a question of waiting for them to dock." Mr. Cantle's fatherly manner revives a bit.

"Why can't they cut off that damn freak's life-support," the sharp young man fumes. "It's ridiculous."

"They're working on it." Cantle assures him.

What they're doing, down under Carbondale, is arguing.

Miss Fleming's watchdog has summoned the bushy man to the waldo room.

"Miss Fleming, you will obey orders."

"You'll kill her if you try that, sir. I can't believe you meant it, that's why I didn't. We've already fed her enough sedative to affect heart action; if you cut any more oxygen she'll die in there."

The bushy man grimaces. "Get Doctor Quine here fast."

They wait, staring at the cabinet in which a drugged, ugly madwoman fights for consciousness, fights to hold Delphi's eyes open.

High over Richmond the silver pod starts a turn. Delphi is sagged into Paul's arm, her eyes swim up to him.

"Starting down now, baby. It'll be over soon, all you have to do is stay alive, Dee."

". . . Stay alive. . . ."

The traffic monitor has caught them. "Sir! They've turned off for Carbondale—Control has contact—"

"Let's go."

But the headquarters posse is too late to intercept the courier wailing into Carbondale. And Paul's friends have come through again. The fugitives are out through the freight dock and into the neurolab admin port before the guard gets organized. At the elevator Paul's face plus his handgun get them in.

"I want Doctor—What's his name, Dee? Dee!"

" . . . Tesla . . ." She's reeling on her feet.

"Doctor Tesla. Take me down to Tesla, fast."

Intercoms are squalling around them as they whoosh down, Paul's pistol in the guard's back. When the door slides open the bushy man is there.

"I'm Tesla."

"I'm Paul Isham. *Isham*. You're going to take your flaming implants out of this girl—now. Move!"

"What?"

"You heard me. Where's your operating room? Go!"

"But—"

"Move! Do I have to burn somebody?"

Paul waves the weapon at Dr. Quine, who has just appeared.

"No, no," says Tesla hurriedly "But I can't, you know. It's impossible, there'll be nothing left."

"You screaming well can, right now. You mess up and I'll kill you," says Paul murderously. "Where is it, there? And wipe the feke that's on her circuits now."

He's backing them down the hall, Delphi heavy on his arm.

"Is this the place, baby? Where they did it to you?"

"Yes," she whispers, blinking at a door. "Yes . . ."

Because it is, see. Behind that door is the very suite where she was born.

Paul herds them through it into a gleaming hall. An inner door opens and a nurse and a gray man rush out. And freeze.

Paul sees there's something special about that inner door. He crowds them past it and pushes it open and looks in.

Inside is a big mean-looking cabinet with its front door panels ajar.

And inside that cabinet is a poisoned carcass to whom something wonderful, unspeakable, is happening. Inside is P. Burke the real living woman who knows that HE is here, coming closer—Paul whom she had fought to reach through forty thousand miles of ice—PAUL is here!—is yanking at the waldo doors—

The doors tear open and a monster rises up.

"Paul darling!" croaks the voice of love and the arms of love reach for him.

And he responds.

Wouldn't you, if a gaunt she-golem flab-naked and spouting wires and blood came at you clawing with metal studded paws—

"Get away!" He knocks wires.

It doesn't much matter which wires, P. Burke has so to speak her nervous system hanging out. Imagine somebody jerking a handful of your medulla—

She crashes onto the floor at his feet, flopping and roaring "PAUL-PAUL-PAUL" in rictus.

It's doubtful he recognizes his name or sees her life coming out of her eyes at him. And at the last it doesn't go to him. The eyes find Delphi, fainting by the doorway, and die.

Now of course Delphi is dead, too.

There's a total silence as Paul steps away from the thing by his foot.

"You killed her," Tesla says. "That was her."

"Your control." Paul is furious, the thought of that monster fastened into little Delphi's brain nauseates him. He sees her crumpling and holds out his arms. Not knowing she is dead.

And Delphi comes to him.

One foot before the other not moving very well—but moving. Her darling face turns up. Paul is distracted by the terrible quiet, and when he looks down he sees only her tender little neck.

"Now you get the implants out," he warns them. Nobody moves.

"But, but she's dead," Miss Fleming whispers wildly.

Paul feels Delphi's life under his hand, they're talking about their monster. He aims his pistol at the gray man.

"You. If we aren't in your surgery when I count three I'm burning off this man's leg."

"Mr. Isham," Tesla says desperately, "you have just killed the person who animated the body you call Delphi. Delphi herself is dead. If you release your arm you'll see what I say is true."

The tone gets through. Slowly Paul opens his arm, looks down. "Delphi?"

She totters, sways, stays upright. Her face comes slowly up.

"Paul . . ." Tiny voice.

"Your crotty tricks." Paul snarls at them. "Move!"

"Look at her eyes," Dr. Quine croaks.

They look. One of Delphi's pupils fills the iris, her lips writhe weirdly.

"Shock." Paul grabs her to him. "*Fix* her!" He yells at them, aiming at Tesla.

"For God's sake . . . bring it in the lab." Tesla quavers.

"Goodbye-bye," says Delphi clearly. They lurch down the hall, Paul carrying her, and meet a wave of people.

Headquarters has arrived.

Joe takes one look and dives for the waldo room, running into Paul's gun.

"Oh no, you don't."

Everybody is yelling. The little thing in his arm stirs, says plaintively, "I'm Delphi."

And all through the ensuing jabber and ranting she hangs on, keeping it up, the ghost of P. Burke or whatever whispering crazily "Paul . . . Paul . . . Please, I'm Delphi . . . Paul?"

"I'm here, darling, I'm here." He's holding her in the nursing bed. Tesla talks, talks, talks unheard.

"Paul . . . don't sleep . . . " The ghost-voice whispers. Paul is in agony, he will not accept, WILL NOT believe.

Tesla runs down.

And then near midnight Delphi says roughly, "Ag-ag-ag—" and slips onto the floor, making a rough noise like a seal.

Paul screams. There's more of the *ag-ag* business and more gruesome convulsive disintegrations, until by two in the morning Delphi is nothing but a warm little bundle of vegetative functions hitched to some expensive hardware—the same that sustained her before her life began. Joe has finally persuaded Paul to let him at the waldo-cabinet. Paul stays by her long enough to see her face change in a dreadfully alien and coldly convincing way, and then he stumbles out bleakly through the group in Tesla's office.

Behind him Joe is working wet-faced, sweating to reintegrate the fantastic complex of circulation, respiration, endocrines, midbrain homeostases, the patterned flux that was a human being—it's like saving an orchestra abandoned in midair. Joe is also crying a little; he alone had truly loved P. Burke. P. Burke, now a dead pile on a table, was the greatest cybersystem he has ever known and he never forgets her.

The end, really.

You're curious?

Sure, Delphi lives again. Next year she's back on the yacht getting sympathy for her tragic breakdown. But there's a different chick in Chile, because while Delphi's new operator is competent, you don't get two P. Burke's in a row—for which GTX is duly grateful.

The real belly-bomb of course is Paul. He was *young*, see. Fighting abstract wrong. Now life has clawed into him and he goes through gut rage and grief and grows in human wisdom and resolve. So much so that you won't be surprised, some time later, to find him— where?

In the GTX boardroom, dummy. Using the advantage of his birth to radicalize the system. You'd call it "boring from within."

That's how he put it, and his friends couldn't agree more. It gives them a warm, confident feeling to know that Paul is up there. Sometimes one of them who's still around runs into him and gets a big hello.

And the sharp-faced lad?

Oh, he matures too. He learns fast, believe it. For instance, he's the first to learn that an obsure GTX research unit is actually getting something with their loopy temporal anomalizer project. True, he doesn't have a physics background, and he's bugged quite a few people. But he doesn't really learn about that until the day he stands where somebody points him during a test run—

—and wakes up lying on a newspaper headlined NIXON UN-VEILS PHASE TWO.

Lucky he's a fast learner.

Believe it, Zombie. When I say growth I mean *growth*. Capital appreciation. You can stop sweating. There's a great future there.

Alice Walker

Coming Apart
1980

Originally published in Ms. *in February 1980 under the title "When Women Confront Porn at Home," this story was included in the volume* Take Back the Night: Feminist Papers on Pornography *(1980) edited by Laura Lederer and Lunn K. Campbell and, under the title "Coming Apart," a title with multiple layers of meaning, puns intended, in Alice Walker's second volume of short stories,* You Can't Keep a Good Woman Down *(1981). Walker received both the Pulitzer Prize and the American Book Award for her third novel,* The Color Purple *(1982).*

Alice Walker (b. 1944), the youngest of eight children of poor sharecroppers in rural Georgia, has become one of the most critically acclaimed and generally loved writers in the United States. Walker was not only the baby of her family and cherished by her mother and other strong women in the community for her brains and her spirit, but she was "cute." She was favored, privileged, praised—until, at the age of eight, she was blinded in one eye in an accident. She lost her self-confidence and that special favor in her world until the appearance of the blinded eye was normalized once again, in adolescence. Not until her late twenties did she overcome her estrangement from, and ambivalence about, her own appearance. That understanding and acceptance of shame and anger and inner vision, that appreciation of the impact of the perception of deformity, whether it be caused by color or sex or physical disability, illuminates all that she writes.

An extraordinarily versatile writer, she has published three volumes of poetry, Once *(1968),* Revolutionary Petunias and Other Poems *(1973), and* Goodnight, Willie Lee, I'll See You in the Morning *(1979); two other novels,* The Third Life of Grange Copeland *(1970) and* Meridian *(1976); an earlier volume of short stories*, In Love and Trouble: Stories of Black Women *(1973); a recent collection of essays*, In Search of Our Mothers' Gardens *(1983); and a children's biography*, Langston Hughes: American Poet *(1973)*. She also edited I Love Myself When I'm Laughing . . . and Then Again When I Am Looking Mean and Impressive: A Zora Neale Hurston Reader *(1979)*.

Alice Walker keeps a picture of herself at the age of six on her desk—"dauntless eyes, springy hair, optimistic satin bow—and I look at it often; I realize I am always trying to keep faith with the child I was." Her sense of history and commitment to keeping faith with the past includes herself, those she has identified as her people, black people, black women most particularly, and those individuals she has taken as mentors, in particular Zora Neale Hurston (1901–1960), the novelist and folklorist, in whose work she found inspiration and sustenance.

In her own work, Walker depicts the struggle of black women to survive in the face of the double oppression of racism and sexism, poverty, a history of disempowerment, of physical, mental, and spiritual abuse. She depicts not only the triumphs in the struggle, but the cost and the defeats. She knows her subject matter not only from her personal experience and the stories she grew up on, but also from her participation in the civil rights movement. She is a feminist with an international perspective who understands that "women's freedom is an idea whose time (has) come . . . an idea sweeping the world."

Perhaps no other story in this collection makes more explicit the use of the other woman by the husband (with the support and encouragement of the patriarchy and its institutions) to hurt and belittle the wife. The husband's power and freedom to hurt her in this way, this flaunting of her culturally prescribed replaceable object-nature, doesn't even require the presence of a real other woman. A doll will do. A picture will do. Even pictures of pieces, parts, portions of female anatomy.

This story offers the most optimistic vision of a redeemed heterosexual future, but is explicit about the pain and struggle both for women and for men if that future is to be realized, a future of honesty, of honor, of being able to look into each other's eyes while making love.

"Coming Apart" was written in response to an invitation to write an introduction to a chapter on Third World Women in a book on pornography. The author says that, while she believes that it works as a story, it was not written as one originally. Its form reflects a kinship with early nineteenth-century stories written when the genre was new and still showed traces of the literary sources from which it was fashioned.

A middle-aged husband comes home after a long day at the office. His wife greets him at the door with the news that dinner is ready.

He is grateful. First, however, he must use the bathroom. In the bathroom, sitting on the commode, he opens up the *Jiveboy* magazine he has brought home in his briefcase. There are a couple of jivemate poses that particularly arouse him. He studies the young women— blond, perhaps (the national craze), with elastic waists and inviting eyes—and strokes his penis. At the same time, his bowels stir with the desire to defecate. He is in the bathroom a luxurious ten minutes. He emerges spent, relaxed—hungry for dinner.

His wife, using the bathroom later, comes upon the slightly damp magazine. She picks it up with mixed emotions. She is a brownskin woman with black hair and eyes. She looks at the white blondes and brunettes. Will he be thinking of them, she wonders, when he is making love to me?

"Why do you need these?" she asks.

"They mean nothing," he says.

"But they hurt me somehow," she says.

"You are being a.) silly, b.) a prude, and c.) ridiculous," he says. "You know I love you."

She cannot say to him: But they are not me, those women. She cannot say she is jealous of pictures on a page. That she feels invisible. Rejected. Overlooked. She says instead, to herself: He is right. I will grow up. Adjust. Swim with the tide.

He thinks he understands her, what she has been trying to say. It is *Jiveboy*, he thinks. The white women.

Next day he brings home *Jivers*, a black magazine, filled with bronze and honey-colored women. He is in the bathroom another luxurious ten minutes.

She stands, holding the magazine: on the cover are the legs and shoes of a well-dressed black man, carrying a briefcase and a rolled *Wall Street Journal* in one hand. At his feet—she turns the magazine cover around and around to figure out how exactly the pose is accomplished—there is a woman, a brownskin woman like herself, twisted and contorted in such a way that her head is not even visible. Only her glistening body—her back and derriere-so that she looks like a human turd at the man's feet.

He is on a business trip to New York. He has brought his wife along. He is eagerly sharing 42nd Street with her. "Look!" he says.

"How *free* everything is. A far cry from Bolton!" (The small town they are from.) He is elated to see the blonde, spaced-out hookers, with their black pimps, trooping down the street. Elated at the shortness of the black hookers' dresses, their long hair, inevitably false and blond. She walks somehow behind him, so that he will encounter these wonders first. He does not notice until he turns a corner that she has stopped in front of a window that has caught her eye. While she is standing alone, looking, two separate pimps ask her what stable she is in or if in fact she is in one. Or simply "You workin'?"

He struts back and takes her elbow. Looks hard for the compliment implied in these questions, then shares it with his wife: "*You* know you're foxy!"

She is immovable. Her face suffering and wondering. "But look," she says, pointing. Four large plastic dolls—one a skinny Farrah Fawcett (or so the doll looks to her) posed for anal inspection; one, an oriental, with her eyes, strangely, closed, but her mouth, a pouting red suction cup, open; an enormous eskimo woman, with fur around her neck and ankles, and vagina; and a black woman dressed entirely in a leopard skin, complete with tail. The dolls are all life-size, and the efficiency of their rubber genitals is explained in detail on a card visible through the plate glass.

For her this is the stuff of nightmares—possibly because all the dolls are smiling. She will see them for the rest of her life. For him the sight is also shocking, but arouses a prurient curiosity. He will return, another time, alone. Meanwhile, he must prevent her from seeing such things, he resolves, whisking her briskly off the street.

Later, in their hotel room, she watches TV as two black women sing their latest hits: the first woman, dressed in a gold dress (because her song is now "solid gold!") is nonetheless wearing a chain around her ankle—the wife imagines she sees a chain—because the woman is singing: "Free me from my freedom, chain me to a tree!"

"What do you think of that?" she asks her husband.

"She's a fool," says he.

But when the second woman sings: "Ready, aim, fire, my name is desire," with guns and rockets going off all around her, he thinks the line "Shoot me with your love!" explains everything.

She is despondent.

She looks in a mirror at her plump brown and black body, crinkly hair and black eyes and decides, foolishly, that she is not beautiful. And that she is not hip, either. Among her other problems is the fact that she does not like the word "nigger" used by anyone at all, and is afraid of marijuana. These restraints, she feels, make her old, too much like her own mother, who loves sex (she has lately learned) but is highly religious and, for example, thinks cardplaying wicked and alcohol deadly. Her husband would not consider her mother sexy, she thinks. Since she herself is aging, this thought frightens her. But, surprisingly, while watching herself become her mother in the mirror, she discovers that *she* considers her mother—who carefully braids her average-length, average-grade, graying hair every night before going to bed; the braids her father still manages to fray during the night—*very* sexy.

At once she feels restored.
Resolves to fight.

"You're the only black woman in the world that worries about any of this stuff," he tells her, unaware of her resolve, and moody at her months of silent studiousness.

She says, "Here, Colored Person, read this essay by Audre Lorde."

He hedges. She insists.

He comes to the line about Lorde "moving into sunlight against the body of a woman I love," and bridles. "Wait a minute," he says, "what kind of a name is 'Audre' for a man? They must have meant 'An*dré*.' "

"It *is* the name of a woman," she says. "Read the rest of that page."

"No dyke can tell me anything," he says, flinging down the pages.

She has been calmly waiting for this. She brings in the *Jiveboy* and *Jivers*. In both, there are women eating women they don't even know. She takes up the essay and reads:

> *This brings me to the last consideration of the erotic. To share the power of each other's feelings is different from using another's feelings as we would use Kleenex. And when we look the other way from our experience, erotic or otherwise, we use rather*

> *than share the feelings of those others who participate in the*
> *experience with us. And use without consent of the used is abuse.*

He looks at her with resentment, because she is reading this passage
over again, silently, absorbedly, to herself, holding the pictures of
the phony lesbians (a favorite, though unexamined, turn-on) absentmindedly on her lap. He realizes he can never have her again
sexually the way he has had her since the second year of marriage,
as though her body belonged to someone else. He sees, down the
road, the dissolution of the marriage, a constant search for more
perfect bodies, or dumber wives. He feels oppressed by her incipient
struggle, and feels somehow as if her struggle to change the pleasure
he has enjoyed is a violation of his rights.

Now she is busy pasting Audre Lorde's words on the cabinet
over the kitchen sink.

When they make love she tries to look him in the eye, but he
refuses to return her gaze.

For the first time he acknowledges the awareness that the pleasure
of coming without her is bitter and lonely. He thinks of eating
stolen candy alone, behind the barn. And yet, he thinks greedily,
it is better than nothing, which he considers her struggle's benefit
to him.

The next day, she is reading another essay when he comes home
from work. It is called "A Quiet Subversion" and is by Luisah
Teish. "Another dyke?" he asks.

"Another one of your sisters," she replies, and begins to read,
even before he's had dinner:

> *During the "Black Power Movement" much cultural education*
> *was focused on the black physique. One of the accomplishments*
> *of that period was the popularization of African hairstyles and*
> *the Natural. Along with this new hair-do came a new self-*
> *image and way of relating. Then the movie industry put out*
> *"Superfly," and the Lord Jesus Look, the Konked head, and an*
> *accompanying attitude, ran rampant in the black community.*
> *Films like "Shaft" and "Lady Sings the Blues" portray black*
> *"heroes" as cocaine-snorting, fast-life fools. In these movies a*
> *black woman is always caught in a web of violence . . .*

> *A popular Berkeley theatre featured a porno movie titled "Slaves of Love." Its advertisement portrayed two black women, naked, in chains, and a white man standing over them with a whip! How such* racist *pornographic material escaped the eye of black activists presents a problem . . .*

Typically, he doesn't even hear the statement about the women. "What does the bitch know about the Black Power Movement?" he fumes. He is angry at his wife for knowing him so long and so well. She knows, for instance, that because of the Black Power Movement (and really because of the Civil Rights Movement before it), and not because he was at all active in it, he holds the bourgeois job he has. She remembers when his own hair was afroed. Now it is loosely curled. It occurs to him that, because she knows him as he was, he cannot make love to her as she is. Cannot, in fact, *love* her as she is. There is a way in which, in some firmly repressed corner of his mind, he considers his wife to be *still* black, whereas he feels himself to have moved to some other plane.

(This insight, a glimmer of which occurs to him, frightens him so much that he will resist it for several years. Should he accept it at once, however unsettling, it would help him understand the illogic of his acceptance of pornography used against black women: that he has detached himself from his own blackness in attempting to identify black women only by their sex.)

The wife has never considered herself a feminist—though she is, of course, a "womanist."* A womanist is a feminist, only more common. (The author of this piece is a womanist.) So she is surprised when her husband attacks her as a "women's libber," a "white women's lackey," a "pawn" in the hands of Gloria Steinem, an incipient bra-burner! What possible connection could there be, he wants to know, between her and white women—those overprivi-ledged hags now (he's recently read in *Newsweek*) marching and preaching their puritanical horseshit up and down Times Square!

(He remembers only the freedom he felt there, not her long standing before the window of the plastic doll shop.) And if she is going to

* "Womanist" approximates "black feminist."

make a lot of new connections with dykes and whites, where will that leave him, the black man, the most brutalized and oppressed human being on the face of the earth? (*Is it because he can now ogle white women in freedom and she has no similar outlet of expression that he thinks of her as still black and himself as something else?* This thought underlines what he is actually saying, and his wife is unaware of it.) Didn't she know it is over these very same white bodies he has been lynched in the past, and is lynched still, by the police and the U.S. prison system, dozens of times a year *even now!*?

The wife has cunningly saved Tracey A. Gardner's essay for just this moment. Because Tracey A. Gardner has thought about it *all*, not just presently but historically, and she is clear about all the abuse being done to herself as a black person, and as a woman, and she is bold and she is cold—she is furious. The wife, given more to depression and self-abnegation than to fury, basks in the fire of Gardner's high-spirited anger.

She begins to read:

> *Because from my point of view, racism is everywhere, including in the women's movement, and the only time I really need to say anything about it is when I* do not *see it . . . and the first time that happens, I will tell you about it.*

The husband, surprised, thinks this very funny, not to say pertinent. He slaps his knee and sits up. He is dying to make some sort of positive dyke comment, but nothing comes to mind.

> *American slavery relied on the denial of the humanity of Black folks, and the undermining of our sense of nationhood and family, on the stripping away of the Black man's role as protector and provider, and on the structuring of Black women into the American system of white male domination . . .*

"In other words," she says, "white men think they have to be on top. Other men have been known to savor life from other positions."

> *The end of the Civil War brought the end of a certain "form" of slavery for Black folks. It also brought the end of any "job*

> *security" and the loss of the protection of their white enslaver.*
> *Blacks were now free game, and the terrorization and humil-*
> *iation of Black people, especially black men, began anew. Now*
> *the Black man could have his family and prove his worth, but*
> *he had no way to support or protect them, or himself. . . .*

As she reads, he feels ashamed and senses his wife's wounded
embarrassment, for him and for herself. For their history together.
But doggedly, she continues to read:

> *After the Civil War, popular justice, which meant there usually*
> *was no trial and no proof needed, began its reign in the form*
> *of the castration, burning at the stakes, beheading, and lynching*
> *of Black men. As many as 5,000 white people would turn out*
> *to witness these events, as though going to a celebration.* [She
> pauses, sighs: *beheading?*] *Over 2,000 Black men were lynched*
> *in a 10 year period from 1889-99. There were also a number*
> *of Black women lynched.* [She reads this sentence quickly
> and forgets it.] *Over 50% of the lynched Black males were*
> *charged with rape or attempted rape.*

He cannot imagine a woman being lynched. He has never even
considered the possibility. Perhaps this is why the image of a black
woman chained and bruised excites rather than horrifies him? It is
the fact that the lynching of her body has never stopped that forces
the wife, for the time being, to blot out the historical record. She
is not prepared to connect her own husband with the continuation
of that past.

She reads:

> *If a Black man had sex with a consenting white woman, it*
> *was rape.* [Why am I always reading about, thinking
> about, worrying about, my man having sex with white
> women? she thinks, despairingly, underneath the read-
> ing.] *If he insulted a white woman by looking at her, it was*
> *attempted rape.*

"Yes," he says softly, as if in support of her dogged reading, "I've read Ida
B.—what's her last name?"

"By their lynchings, the white man was showing that he hated
the Black man carnally, biologically; he hated his color, his
features, his genitals. Thus he attacked the Black man's body,
and like lover gone mad, maimed his flesh, violated him in the
most intimate, pornographic fashion . . ."

I believe that this obscene, inhuman treatment of Black men
by white men, has a direct correlation to white men's increasingly
obscene and inhuman treatment of women, particularly white
women, in pornography and real life. White women, working
towards their own strenth and identity, their own sexuality,
have in a sense become uppity niggers. As the Black man
threatens the white man's masculinity and power, so now do
women.

"That girl's onto something," says the husband, but thinks, for the
first time in his life, that when he is not thinking of fucking white
women—fantasizing over *Jiveboy* or clucking at them on the street—
he is very often thinking of ways to humiliate them. Then he thinks
that, given his history as a black man in America, it is not surprising
that he has himself confused fucking them *with* humiliating them.
But what does that say about how he sees himself? This thought
smothers his inward applause for Gardner, and instead he casts a
bewildered, disconcerted look at his wife. He knows that to make
love to his wife as she really is, as who she really is—indeed, to
make love to any other human being as they really are—will require
a soul-rending look into himself, and the thought of this virtually
straightens his hair.

His wife continues:

Some Black men, full of the white man's perspective and values,
see the white woman or Blond Goddess as part of the American
winning image. Sometimes when he is with the Black woman,
he is ashamed of how she has been treated and how he has been
powerless, and that they have always had to work together and
*protect each other. [*Yes, she thinks, we were always all
we had, until now. He thinks: We are all we have still,
only now we can live without permitting ourselves to
know this.*] Frantz Fanon said about white women, "By*
loving me she proves that I am worthy of white love. I am

loved like a white man. I am a white man. I marry the culture,
white beauty, white whiteness. When my restless hands caress
those white breasts, they grasp white civilization and dignity
and make them mine." [She cannot believe he meant to
write "white dignity."]

She pauses, looks at her husband: "So how does a black woman
feel when her black man leaves *Playboy* on the coffee table?"

For the first time he understands fully a line his wife read the day
before: "The pornography industry's exploitation of the black
woman's body is *qualitatively* different from that of the white
woman," because she is holding the cover of *Jivers* out to him and
asking: "What does this woman look like?"

What he has refused to see—because to see it would reveal yet
another area in which he is unable to protect or defend black
women—is that where white women are depicted in pornography
as "objects," black women are depicted as animals. Where white
women are depicted at least as human bodies if not beings, black
women are depicted as shit.

He begins to feel sick. For he realizes that he has bought some if
not all of the advertisements about women, black and white. And
further, inevitably, he has bought the advertisements about himself.
In pornography the black man is portrayed as being capable of
fucking anything . . . even a piece of shit. He is defined solely by
the size, readiness and unselectivity of his cock.

Still, he does not know how to make love without the fantasies fed
to him by movies and magazines. Those movies and magazines
(whose characters' pursuits are irrelevant or antithetical to his
concerns) that have insinuated themselves between him and his
wife, so that the totality of her body, her entire corporeal reality is
alien to him. Even to clutch her in lust is automatically to shut his
eyes. Shut his eyes, and . . . he chuckles bitterly . . . dream of
England.

For years he has been fucking himself.

At first, reading Lorde together, they reject celibacy. Then they
discover they need time apart to clear their heads, to search out

damage, to heal. In any case, she is unable to fake response; he is unwilling for her to do so. She goes away for a while. Left alone, he soon falls hungrily on the magazines he had thrown out. Strokes himself raw over the beautiful women, spread like so much melon (he begins to see how stereotypes transmute) before him. But he cannot refuse what he knows—or what he knows his wife knows, walking along a beach in some black country where all the women are bleached and straightened and the men never look at themselves; and are ugly, in any case, in their imitation of white men.

Long before she returns he is reading her books and thinking of her—and of her struggles alone and his fear of sharing them—and when she returns, it is sixty percent *her* body that he moves against in the sun, her own black skin affirmed in the brightness of his eyes.

Jane Rule

A Perfectly Nice Man
1981

Among the many fictional worlds Jane Rule has created in her five novels and two volumes of short stories is the one reflected in "A Perfectly Nice Man." It is a world in which women take relationships with women seriously in the way that women in heterosexual literature have always been portrayed as taking men seriously. That means the world looks "different" from the world portrayed in heterosexual literature, in terms of who is in the background and who is in the foreground. Yet the world feels familiar emotionally because most of the relational dynamics are the same. Heterosexual women who ever, as girls, had serious friendships with other girls before they "got interested in boys," have been involved in relationships that, in the fiction of Jane Rule, are recognized and validated. The relationships she portrays between and among women run the gamut from tragic to lighthearted, from politically conscious to ideologically naive.

Once her women characters have acknowledged that they can have primary relationships with women as well as with men, those relationships often become competitive. Once men cease to have a monopoly on a woman's sexual, romantic, and affiliational impulses, once they cease to represent the "only game in town," they become competitors with women for the affection of other women. And since so many men are, whether by cultural conditioning or hormonal predestination, incapable of emotional parity with women because they lack depth of feeling, imagination, nurturant skills, and grounding in relational ethics as women understand them— they may lose the bid for primacy in the emotional lives of women.

He's a "perfectly nice man"—that is, perfectly nice considering that he is, after all, a man. *And, "a perfectly nice man"—but no longer even potentially interesting because not emotionally trustworthy or emotionally rich enough to sustain a worthwhile relationship. Oh, he's a "perfectly nice man"—if you're willing to settle for just that.*

No malice, but some amusement. And a tender, sympathetic but definitely not nostalgic memory of the years when that's all the women knew to want. How foolish and pathetic to have been so vulnerable, to have cared so much about having or losing so trivial a thing as a "perfectly nice man."

Jane rule was born in Plainfield, New Jersey in 1931. She has a B.A. from Mills College and has worked variously as a typist, a teacher of handicapped children, a change girl in a gambling house, and a store clerk, mostly, she writes, as background material for her writing. She lives on an island off the coast of British Columbia, Canada. Her novels are Desert of the Heart *(1964), which is being made into a film,* This Is Not for You *(1970),* Against the Season *(1971),* The Young in One Another's Arms *(1977), and* Contract with the World *(1980). She has published a volume of literary criticism,* Lesbian Images *(1975) and two collections of short fiction,* Theme for Diverse Instruments *(1975) and* Outlander *(1981) from which "A Pefectly Nice Man" is reprinted. The Canadian novelist Margaret Laurence has written about her work: "Jane Rule explores with delicate precision the interpersonal and sexual relationships between men and women, men and men, women and women. She takes as her difficult theme the many meanings and manifestations of love and friendship, their hazards, their sometimes grace, and she realizes this theme splendidly."*

"I'm sorry I'm late, darling," Virginia said, having to pick up and embrace three-year-old Clarissa before she could kiss Katherine hello. "My last patient needed not only a new crown but some stitches for a broken heart. Why do people persist in marriage?"

"Your coat's cold," Clarissa observed soberly.

"So's my nose," Virginia said, burying it in the child's neck. "It's past your bath time and your story time, and I've probably ruined dinner."

"No," Katherine said. "We're not eating until seven-thirty. We're having a guest."

"Who?"

"Daddy's new friend," Clarissa said. "And I get to stay up until she comes."

"Really?"

"She said she needed to talk to us," Katherine explained. "She sounded all right on the phone. Well, a little nervous but not at all hostile. I thought, perhaps we owe her that much?"

"Or him?" Virginia wondered.

"Oh, if him, I suppose I should have said no," Katherine decided. "People who don't even want to marry him think this is odd enough."

"Odd about him?"

"Even he thinks it's odd about him," Katherine said.

"Men have an exaggerated sense of responsibility in the most peculiar directions," Virginia said. "We can tell her he's a perfectly nice man, can't we?" She was now addressing the child.

"Daddy said I didn't know who was my mommie," Clarissa said.

"Oh?"

"I have two mommies. Will Elizabeth be my mommie, too?"

"She just might," Virginia said. "What a lucky kid that would make you."

"Would she come to live with us then?" Clarissa asked.

"Sounds to me as if she wants to live with Daddy," Virginia said.

"So did you, at first," Clarissa observed.

Both women laughed.

"Your bath!" Virginia ordered and carried the child up the stairs while Katherine returned to the kitchen to attend to dinner.

Clarissa was on the couch in her pajamas, working a pop-up book of *Alice in Wonderland* with Virginia, when the doorbell rang.

"I'll get that," Katherine called from the kitchen.

Elizabeth, in a fur-collared coat, stood in the doorway, offering freesias.

"Did he tell you to bring them?" Katherine asked, smiling.

"He said we all three liked them," Elizabeth answered. "But don't most women?"

"I'm Katherine," Katherine said, "wife number one."

"And I'm Virginia, wife number two," Virginia said, standing in the hall.

"And I'm Elizabeth, as yet unnumbered," Elizabeth said. "And you're Clarissa."

Clarissa nodded, using one of Virginia's legs as a prop for leaning against or perhaps hiding behind.

Elizabeth was dressed, as the other two women were in a very well cut trousers and an expensive blouse, modestly provocative.

And she was about their age, thirty. The three did not so much look alike as share a type, all about the same height, five feet seven inches or so (he said he was six feet tall but was, in fact, five feet ten and a half), slightly but well proportioned, with silky, well cut hair and intelligent faces. They were all competent, assured women who intimidated only unconsciously.

Virginia poured three drinks and a small glass of milk for Clarissa, who was allowed to pass the nuts and have one or two before Katherine took her off to bed.

"She looks like her father," Elizabeth observed.

"Yes, she has his lovely eyes," Virginia agreed.

"He doesn't know I'm here." Elizabeth confessed. "Oh, I intend to tell him. I just didn't want it to be a question, you see?"

"He did think it a mistake that Katherine and I ever met. We didn't, of course, until after I'd married him. I didn't know he was married until quite a while after he and I met."

"He was a patient of yours?" Elizabeth asked.

"Yes"

"He's been quite open with me about both of you from the beginning, but we met in therapy, of course, and that does make such a difference."

"Does it?" Virginia asked. "I've never been in therapy."

"Haven't you?" Elizabeth asked, surprised. "I would have thought both of you might have considered it."

"He and I?"

"No, you and Katherine."

"We felt very uncomplicated about it," Virginia said, "once it happened. It was such an obvious solution."

"For him?"

"Well, no, not for him, of course. Therapy was a thing for him to consider."

Katherine came back into the room. "Well, now we can be grownups."

"She looks like her father," Elizabeth observed again.

"She has his lovely eyes," it was Katherine's turn to reply.

"I don't suppose a meeting like this could have happened before the women's movement," Elizabeth said.

"Probably not," Katherine agreed. "I'm not sure Virginia and I could have happened before the women's movement. We might not have known what to do."

"He tries not to be antagonistic about feminism," Elizabeth said.

"Oh, he's always been quite good about the politics. He didn't resent my career," Virginia offered.

"He was quite proud of marrying a dentist," Katherine said. "I think he used to think I wasn't liberated enough."

"He doesn't think that now," Elizabeth said.

"I suppose not," Katherine agreed.

"The hardest thing for him has been facing . . . the sexual implications. He has felt . . . unmanned."

"He's put it more strongly than that in the past," Virginia said.

"Men's sexuality is so much more fragile than ours." Elizabeth said.

"Shall we have dinner?" Katherine suggested.

"He said you were a very good cook." Elizabeth said to Katherine.

"Most of this dinner is Virginia's. I got it out of the freezer," Katherine explained. "I've gone back to school, and I don't have that much time."

"I cook in binges," Virginia said, pouring the wine.

"At first he said he thought the whole thing was some kind of crazy revenge," Elizabeth said.

"At first there might have been that element in it," Virginia admitted. "Katherine was six months' pregnant when he left her, and she felt horribly deserted. I didn't know he was going to be a father until after Clarissa was born. Then I felt I'd betrayed her, too, though I hadn't known anything about it.

"He said he should have told you," Elizabeth said, "but he was very much in love and was afraid of losing you. He said there was never any question of his not supporting Katherine and Clarissa."

"No, I make perfectly good money," Virginia said. "There's no question of his supporting them now, if that's a problem. He doesn't."

"He says he'd rather he did," Elizabeth said.

"He sees Clarissa whenever he likes," Katherine explained. "He's very good with her. One of the reasons I wanted a baby was knowing he'd be a good sort of father."

"Did you have any reservations about marrying him?" Elizabeth asked Virginia.

"At the time? Only that I so very much wanted to," Virginia said. "There aren't that many marrying men around for women dentists, unless they're sponges, of course. It's flattering when someone is so afraid of losing you he's willing to do something legal about it. It oughtn't to be, but it is."

"But you had other reservations later," Elizabeth said.

"Certainly, his wife and his child."

"Why did he leave you, Katherine?"

"Because he was afraid of losing her. I suppose he thought he'd have what he needed of me anyway, since I was having his child."

"Were you still in love with him?" Elizabeth asked.

"I must have been," Katherine said, "or I couldn't have been quite so unhappy, so desperate. I was desperate."

"He's not difficult to be in love with, after all," Virginia said. "He's a very attractive man."

"He asked me if I was a lesbian," Elizabeth said. "I told him I certainly didn't think so. After all, I was in love with him. He said so had two other women been, in love enough to marry him, but they were both lesbians. And maybe he only attracted lesbians even if they didn't know it themselves. He even suggested I should maybe try making love with another woman before I made up my mind."

There was a pause which neither Katherine nor Virginia attempted to break.

"Did either of you know . . . before?"

Katherine and Virginia looked at each other. Then they said, "No."

"He's even afraid he may turn women into lesbians," Elizabeth said.

Both Virginia and Katherine laughed, but not unkindly.

"Is that possible?" Elizabeth asked.

"Is that one of *your* reservations?" Katherine asked.

"It seemed crazy," Elizabeth said, "but . . ."

Again the two hostesses waited.

"I know this probably sounds very unliberated and old-fashioned and maybe even prejudiced, but I don't think I could stand being a lesbian, finding out I'm a lesbian; and if there's something in him that makes a woman . . . How can either of you stand to be together instead of with him?"

"But you don't know you're a lesbian until you fall in love," Katherine said, "and then it's quite natural to want to be together with the person you love."

"What's happening to me is so peculiar. The more sure I am I'm in love with him, the more obsessively I read everything I can about what it is to be a lesbian. It's almost as if I *had* fallen in love with a woman, and that's absurd."

"I don't really think there's anything peculiar about him," Katherine said.

"One is just so naturally drawn, so able to identify with another woman," Virginia said. "When I finally met Katherine, what he wanted and needed just seemed too ridiculous."

"But it was you he wanted," Elizabeth protested.

"At Katherine's and Clarissa's expense, and what was I, after all, but just another woman."

"A liberated woman," Katherine said.

"Not then, I wasn't," Virginia said.

"I didn't feel naturally drawn to either of you." Elizabeth protested. "I wasn't even curious at first. But he's so obsessed with you still, so afraid of being betrayed again, and I thought, I've got to help him somehow, reassure him, understand enough to let him know, as you say, that there's nothing peculiar about him . . . or me."

"I'm sure there isn't," Katherine said reassuringly and reached out to take Elizabeth's hand.

Virginia got up to clear the table.

"Mom!" came the imperious and sleepy voice of Clarissa.

"I'll go," Virginia said.

"But I don't think you mean what I want you to mean," Elizabeth said.

"Perhaps not," Katherine admitted.

"He said he never should have left you. It was absolutely wrong; and if he ever did marry again, it would be because he wanted to make that commitment, but what if his next wife found out she didn't want him, the way Virginia did?"

"I guess anyone takes that risk," Katherine said.

"Do you think I should marry him?" Elizabeth asked.

Katherine kept Elizabeth's hand, and her eyes met Elizabeth's beseeching, but she didn't answer.

"You *do* think there's something wrong with him."

"No, I honestly don't. He's a perfectly nice man. It's just that I sometimes think that isn't good enough, not now when there are other options."

"What other options?"

"You have a job, don't you?"

"I teach at the university, as he does."

"Then you can support yourself."

"That's not always as glamorous as it sounds."

"Neither is marriage," Katherine said.

"Is this?" Elizabeth asked, looking around her, just as Virginia came back into the room.

"It's not nearly as hard as some people try to make it sound."

"Clarissa wanted to know if her new mother was still here."

"Oh my," Elizabeth said.

"Before you came, she wanted to know, if you married her father, would you be another mother and move in here."

Elizabeth laughed and then said, "Oh, God, that's just what he wants to know!"

They took their coffee back into the living room.

"It must be marvelous to be a dentist. At least during the day you can keep people from telling you all their troubles," Elizabeth said.

"That's not as easy as it looks," Virginia said.

"He says you're the best dentist he ever went to. He hates his dentist now."

"I used to be so glad he wasn't like so many men who fell in love with their students," Katherine said.

"Maybe he'd be better off," Elizabeth said in mock gloom. "He says he isn't threatened by my having published more than he has. He had two wives and a baby while I was simply getting on with it; but does he mean it? Does he really know?"

"We're all reading new lines, aren't we?" Virginia asked.

"But if finally none of us marries them, what will they do?" Elizabeth asked.

"I can hardly imagine that," Katherine said.

"You can't imagine what they'll do?"

"No, women saying 'no,' all of them. We can simply consider ourselves, for instance," Katherine said.

"Briefly anyway," Virginia said. "Did you come partly to see if you were at all like us?"

"I suppose so," Elizabeth said.

"Are you?"

"Well, I'm not surprised by you . . . and very surprised not to be."

"Are you sorry to have married him? " Virginia asked Katherine.

"I could hardly be. There's Clarissa, after all, and you. Are you?" she asked in return.

"Not now," Virginia said, "having been able to repair the damage."

"And everyone knows," Elizabeth said, "that you did have the choice."

"Yes," Virginia agreed, "there's that."

"But I felt I didn't have any choice," Katherine said. "That part of it humiliated me."

"Elizabeth is making a distinction," Virginia said, "between what everyone knows and what each of us knows. I shared your private humiliation, of course. All women must."

"Why?" Elizabeth demanded.

"Not to believe sufficiently in one's own value," Virginia explained.

"But he doesn't even quite believe he's a man."

"I never doubted I was a woman," Katherine said.

"That's smug," Elizabeth said, "because you have a child."

"So does he," Katherine replied.

"But he was too immature to deal with it; he says so himself. Don't you feel at all sorry for him?"

"Yes," said Katherine.

"Of course," Virginia agreed.

"He's been terribly hurt. He's been damaged," Elizabeth said.

"Does that make him more or less attractive, do you think?" Virginia asked.

"Well, damn it, less, of course," Elizabeth shouted. "And whose fault is that?"

Neither of the other two women answered.

"He's not just second, he's third-hand goods," Elizabeth said.

"Are women going to begin to care about men's virginity?" Katherine asked. "How extraordinary!"

"Why did you go into therapy?" Virginia asked.

"I hardly remember," Elizabeth said. "I've been so caught up with his problems since the beginning. The very first night of group, he said I somehow reminded him of his wives . . ."

"Perhaps that is why you went," Katherine suggested.

"You think I'd be crazy to marry him, don't you?" Elizabeth demanded.

"Why should we?" Virginia asked. "We both did."

"That's not a reassuring point," Elizabeth said.

"You find us unsatisfactory." Katherine said, in apology.

"Exactly not," Elizabeth said sadly. "I want someone to advise me . . . to make a mistake. Why should you?"

"Why indeed?" Virginia asked.

They embraced warmly before Elizabeth left.

"Perhaps I might come again?" she asked at the door.

"Of course," Katherine said.

After the door closed, Katherine and Virginia embraced.

"He'd be so much happier, for a while anyway, if he married again," Katherine said.

"Of course he would," Virginia agreed, with some sympathy for him in her voice. "But we couldn't encourage a perfectly nice woman like Elizabeth . . ."

"That's the problem, isn't it?" Katherine said. "That's just it."

"She'll marry him anyway," Virginia predicted, "briefly."

"And have a child?" Katherine asked.

"And fall in love with his next wife," Virginia went on.

"There really isn't anything peculiar about him," Katherine said.

"I'm sorry he doesn't like his dentist."

"He should never have married you."

"No, he shouldn't" Virginia agreed. "Then at least I could still be taking care of his teeth." Barring that, they went up together to look in on his richly mothered child sleeping soundly, before they went to their own welcoming bed.

We gratefully acknowledge permission to reprint the following material:

Mary Austin, "Papago Wedding." First published in *American Mercury*, 1925. Reprinted in her collection *One Smoke Stories*, Houghton, 1925.

Alice Brown, "Natalie Blayne." First published in *Harper's Magazine*, 1902.

Lydia Maria Child, "The Quadroons." From *The Liberty Bell*, 1842.

Mary E. Wilkins Freeman, "A Moral Exigency." First published in *Harper's Bazaar*, 1884. Reprinted in her collection *A Humble Romance and Other Stories*, Harper & Brothers, 1887.

Charlotte Perkins Gilman, "Turned." First published in *The Forerunner*, 1911.

Ellen Glasgow, "The Difference." From *Harper's Magazine*, 1923.

Helen Hunt Jackson, "How One Woman Kept Her Husband." From *Scribner's Monthly Magazine*, 1872.

A. R. Leach, "A Captain Out of Etruria." From *Harper Prize Short Stories*, 1925.

Helen Reimensnyder Martin, "A Poet Though Married." First published in *Hampton's Magazine*, 1911. Reprinted in her collection *Yoked with a Lamb and Other Stories*, 1930; reprinted by Books for Libraries Press. Used by permission of The Ayer Company.

Louise Meriwether, "A Happening in Barbados." From *The Antioch Review*, 1968. Reprinted by permission of the author.

Elizabeth Stuart Phelps, "No News." First published in *Atlantic Monthly*, 1868. Reprinted in her collection *Men, Women, and Ghosts*, Houghton, 1869.

Marjorie Kinnan Rawlings, "Gal Young Un." First published in *Harper's Magazine*, 1932. Reprinted in *When the Whippoorwill*. Copyright © 1940 Marjorie Kinnan Rawlings; copyright renewed 1968 Norton Baskin. Reprinted with permission of Charles Scribner's Sons.

Jane Rule, "A Perfectly Nice Man." From *Outlander*, The Naiad Press, 1981. Reprinted by permission of the author. Copyright © 1981 by Jane Rule.

Harriet Prescott Spofford, "Her Story." From *Lippincott's Magazine*, 1872.

James Tiptree, Jr., "The Girl Who Was Plugged In." First published in

The Magazine of Fantasy and Science Fiction, 1973. Reprinted in her collection *Warm Worlds and Otherwise*, Ballantine Books, 1975. Used by permission of the author.

Alice Walker, "Coming Apart." Copyright © 1980 by Alice Walker. Reprinted from her volume *You Can't Keep a Good Woman Down* by permission of Harcourt Brace Jovanovich, Inc.

Martha Wolfenstein, "Chayah." From *A Renegade and Other Tales*, Jewish Publication Society of America, 1905.

Lee Yu-Hwa, "The Last Rite." Reprinted from *The Literary Review* 7, no. 4, Summer 1964. Published by Fairleigh Dickinson University.

FEMINIST CLASSICS
FROM THE FEMINIST PRESS

Antoinette Brown Blackwell: A Biography, by Elizabeth Cazden. $16.95
cloth, $9.95 paper.

Between Mothers and Daughters: Stories Across a Generation. Edited by Susan
Koppelman. $8.95 paper.

Brown Girl, Brownstones, a novel by Paule Marshall. Afterword by Mary
Helen Washington, $7.95 paper.

Call Home the Heart, a novel of the thirties, by Fielding Burke.
Introduction by Alice Kessler-Harris and Paul Lauter and afterwords
by Sylvia J. Cook and Anna W. Shannon. $8.95 paper.

Cassandra, by Florence Nightingale. Introduction by Myra Stark.
Epilogue by Cynthia Macdonald. $3.50 paper.

The Convert, a novel by Elizabeth Robins. Introduction by Jane Marcus.
$6.95 paper.

Daughter of Earth, a novel by Agnes Smedley. Afterword by Paul Lauter.
$6.95 paper.

The Female Spectator, edited by Mary R. Mahl and Helen Koon. $8.95
paper.

Guardian Angel and Other Stories, by Margery Latimer. Afterwords by
Louis Kampf, Meridel Le Sueur, and Nancy Loughridge. $8.95
paper.

*I Love Myself When I Am Laughing . . . And then Again When I Am Looking
Mean and Impressive*, by Zora Neal Hurston. Edited by Alice Walker
with an introduction by Mary Helen Washington, $9.95 paper.

Käthe Kollwitz: Woman and Artist, by Martha Kearns. $7.95 paper.

Life in the Iron Mills, by Rebecca Harding Davis. Biographical
interpretation by Tillie Olsen. $4.95 paper.

The Living Is Easy, a novel by Dorothy West. Afterword by Adelaide M.
Cromwell. $7.95 paper.

The Maimie Papers. Edited by Ruth Rosen and Sue Davidson.
Introduction by Ruth Rosen. $11.95 paper.

The Other Woman: Stories of Two Women and a Man. Edited by Susan
Koppelman. $8.95 paper.

Portraits of Chinese Women in Revolution, by Agnes Smedley. Edited with an introduction by Jan MacKinnon and Steve MacKinnon and an afterword by Florence Howe. $5.95 paper.

Reena and Other Stories, selected short stories by Paule Marshall. $8.95 paper.

Ripening: Selected Work, 1927–1980, by Meridel Le Sueur. Edited with an introduction by Elaine Hedges. $8.95 paper.

The Silent Partner, a novel by Elizabeth Stuart Phelps. Afterword by Mari Jo Buhle and Florence Howe. $6.95 paper.

These Modern Women: Autobiographical Essays from the Twenties. Edited with an introduction by Elaine Showalter. $4.95 paper.

The Unpossessed, a novel of the thirties, by Tess Slesinger. Introduction by Alice Kessler-Harris and Paul Lauter and afterword by Janet Sharistanian. $8.95 paper.

Weeds, a novel by Edith Summers Kelley. Afterword by Charlotte Goodman. $7.95 paper.

The Woman and the Myth: Margaret Fuller's Life and Writings, by Bell Gale Chevigny. $8.95 paper.

The Yellow Wallpaper, by Charlotte Perkins Gilman. Afterword by Elaine Hedges. $2.95 paper.

OTHER TITLES
FROM THE FEMINIST PRESS

The Sex-Role Cycle: Socialization from Infancy to Old Age, by Nancy Romer. $6.95 paper.

Witches, Midwives, and Nurses: A History of Women Healers, by Barbara Ehrenreich and Deirdre English. $3.95 paper.

With These Hands: Women Working on the Land. Edited with an introduction by Joan M. Jensen. $17.95 cloth, $8.95 paper.

Woman's "True" Profession: Voices from the History of Teaching. Edited with an introduction by Nancy Hoffman. $17.95 cloth, $8.95 paper.

Women Have Always Worked: A Historical Overview, by Alice Kessler-Harris. $14.95 cloth, $6.95 paper.

Women Working: An Anthology of Stories and Poems. Edited and with an introduction by Nancy Hoffman and Florence Howe. $7.95 paper.

Women's Studies in Italy, by Laura Balbo and Yasmine Ergas. A Women's Studies International Monograph. $5.95 paper.

For free catalog, write to: The Feminist Press, Box 334, Old Westbury, NY 11568. Send individual book orders to The Feminist Press, P.O. Box 1654, Hagerstown, MD 21741. Include $1.50 postage and handling for one book and 50¢ for each additional book. To order using MasterCard or Visa, call: (800) 638-3030.